Novels by
JULIE E. CZERNEDA
available from DAW Books:

The Clan Chronicles

Stratification:
REAP THE WILD WIND
RIDERS OF THE STORM
RIFT IN THE SKY

Trade Pact Universe
A THOUSAND WORDS FOR STRANGER
TIES OF POWER
TO TRADE THE STARS

****

Species Imperative
SURVIVAL
MIGRATION
REGENERATION

****

Web Shifters
BEHOLDER'S EYE
CHANGING VISION
HIDDEN IN SIGHT

****

IN THE COMPANY OF OTHERS

RIFT IN THE SKY

A Novel of the Clan Chronicles

Julie E. Czerneda

DAW BOOKS, INC.

DONALD A. WOLLHEIM, FOUNDER

375 Hudson Street, New York, NY 10014

ELIZABETH R. WOLLHEIM

SHEILA E. GILBERT

PUBLISHERS

http://www.dawbooks.com

First Paperback Printing, July 2010

1 2 3 4 5 6 7 8 9 10

To Luis Royo

There are moments in life you remember with such clarity, merely closing your eyes brings them rushing back. The moment I laid eyes on Luis Royo's art for the first time is like that for me.

I'm sitting in a small room at the back of our house, the only spot with sun at three on a wintry afternoon. It's not the cold draft down my neck that makes me shiver as I gaze at the envelope in my hand. My editor's forewarned me. This is the cover art for my first novel.

Forewarned. The cover can't be changed. I can make minor changes to the final draft of *A Thousand Words for Stranger* to suit, if I wish.

Roger stands beside me. Our kids are in school. I take a deep breath. "All I want," I assure him, "is not to have a bimbo in a zipped-open spacesuit." I'm brave. No, not really, but I intend to be professional.

My hands shake as I rip the tab. Inside the envelope is a single piece of paper. I grasp a corner carefully, close my eyes, and pull out the print. Then I look.

I see.

Tears well up so quickly the image blurs. I hand the print to Roger, grab for tissues, look again.

It's a masterpiece. There'd been a lilt in Sheila's voice, and now I know why. Suit my story? It's better than any dream. To think, an artist of such surpassing skill has seen *this* in my words.

I love writing, but that was the moment I first understood the joy of being read. To have another mind be inspired by my words. To have another mind and hands produce something so wonderful from them. I remain in awe.

Thank you, Luis, for that moment and for every one since. As I begin each new story I look forward more than I can say to seeing your vision of it. Each time I do, I happily admit, there are tears of joy.

Usted toca mi corazón.
Usted siempre.

Acknowledgments

Lucky thirteen! It's a popular number in our family, being my Poppa's birthday. Even better, he now lives close by, so my breaks while writing this book included our frequent Timmies' Runs. Our thanks to all who've sent stamps and encouragement this past year. As Poppa would say, you're the best. (And Yum!)

Among those who helped us the most this year are the wonderful folks at DAW. I appreciate all you did (and suffered!) to publish this book in a timely fashion, and make it beautiful too, I might add. Sheila, I will never forget your phone call during the second period of the Leafs/Canucks game. You'd finished *Rift,* and wanted to reassure me immediately it was not only done, but very well done. What a relief that was!

Several individuals supplied names for characters, many contributing substantial sums to charity for the privilege. I hope you like what I've done to "you." My thanks to Karen Witthun Gould (congratulations!), Cindy Raskin, Howard Slapcoff, Kelly Scoffield, Karina Sumner-Smith, Jana Paniccia, Kristen Britain, Gene Maynard, and last, but not least, the real Lawren Louli! (Who looks great in that hat.)

My thanks to Jennifer Czerneda for being my alpha reader for this book. Couldn't have managed without you. Merci, Jihane Billacois, for your thoughtful comments. Thank you, Mike Gillis, official first reader. Glad you enjoyed it! Thanks to my BF and fellow writer, Janet Chase, for coming through as always.

In 2008, I had to cancel most of my public appearances, and I apologize to any who were inconvenienced. 2009 should see me all over the world, so hopefully we'll catch up. I must thank the marvelous concom of Ad Astra 08 and staff of Bakka-Phoenix for more stunning book launches. And Necronomicon 08? You rock. Hugs to Heather (and family), Rick, Ann, and Cap'n Kendall! Our thanks to Janny Wurts and Don Maitz for giving us a very special break from it all when we most needed it.

Rift is in many ways about the power of family. May it be a gift, from ours to all of you.

Cersi

Prelude

MOTHERS SCREAMED.

Tikitik listened for the sound, harkened to it, drew pleasure from it. None other could be mistaken for the wondrous moment of birth.

When the screams died, echoes fleeing through the dark mists of the Lay Swamp, Tikitik would press their necks against the trunk of the great, fertile rastis and strain to be first to hear the soft sizzle and pop of its tissues bursting within, proof of life unleashed.

That the rastis die too was only fitting.

When the newborn Tikitik exhausted their food supply, they would drum the empty husk of the rastis with feet and hands, begging for release. Others listened, too. Outside, creepers tapped their antennae, searching for weakness in the wood, a way into the bounty. Inside, somgelt erupted, lacy white tendrils racing down the ruined vessels of the rastis to seek the defenseless flesh. Only the strongest—and loudest—young would be freed in time.

All Tikitik understood the Balance. That which lived must be consumed by that which would live.

And that which would live must be strong.

Chapter 1

OLD, THESE MOUNTAINS. Their gray eroded fingers stretched out and down, as if greedy for the lush land far below. Between plunged valleys, graveled and scarred and barren. Winter storms scoured what life was left after the M'hir Wind roared through and cracked stone.

Spring meltwater gifted the valleys with gentler sounds. The burble of streams. The rustle of breezes through thin stems and leaves. For hardy plants emerged from the ground with the return of warmth and moisture.

Quickly followed by the rattle as rock-that-wasn't found any plant that dared grow too far from a stream and crushed it into tasty goo.

Old, these mountains.

And life here dared many things.

"Of course they made a game of it."

"It's not safe!" Aryl Sarc's hands flattened possessively over the faint swell at her waist. "What if—" She stopped, chagrined. "I sound like Husni."

Enris sud Sarc chuckled. "Never." The two shared a smile as much inside as out. Chosen, Aryl thought happily, could do that. "Trust the young ones," he suggested. "They're already better at it than we are."

"It" being the Om'ray's newest Talent, the ability to use Power to move from place to place through the black tumultuous storm that was the inner M'hir, to travel within one heartbeat and the next anywhere the mind remembered. The Human, Marcus Bowman, had given them his word: teleportation, something no other beings could, according to his cautious search through *databanks,* do.

Though why Humans had a name for what they believed impossible, Aryl couldn't imagine.

She rocked back on her heels, comfortable on the slope. Enris gave her a look and kept his grip on a protruding beam. He tried, but the former Tuana would never be at ease perched on a roof. Especially one that creaked under his bulk.

To one born in the canopy, this roof was as boringly safe as the flat motionless ground, but it did provide a better view. "There's Yao." Aryl pointed at the small shadow beside the Meeting Hall. "Gone again," she said as the shadow vanished.

"Ziba's catching up." The second, larger child appeared out of nothing in the same spot, then scampered to the Meeting Hall roof in a blur of yellow and blue. Once there, she waved a cheerful greeting to Aryl and Enris . . . "There she goes." Enris chuckled. "Taen said they call it 'port and seek. Each tries to arrive first to surprise the other." A shriek and crash of pots erupted from the small building the Sona used for preparing food. "Like that."

Aryl winced. Husni Teerac was not fond of surprises; their eldest Om'ray wasn't fond of this new Talent either, calling it frivolous. "They'll be doing dishes for the next fist."

"If they don't hide."

She didn't worry on that score. Not yet. Aryl could, if she lowered her shields the slightest amount, feel where any of her people were at the moment. Taen and her daughter, Ziba, would soon lose their tight bond, but not yet. Yao . . .

"Yao will be fine."

She pretended to frown at him. "Don't pry." Chosen were Joined, mind-to-mind, Power-to-Power. They weren't, thankfully, one and the same mind or Power.

Where would be the fun in that?

His laugh rumbled the roof boards. "I didn't need to. Your face scrunches adorably when you worry about our youngest. You'll do it over Sweetpie, too, I'm sure." A surge of *caring* under the words, directed both at Aryl and the tiny form within.

"Must you call her a dessert?" she protested absently. Not yet aware, the life inside her. Not yet of a size to affect her movement or balance. Yet, she grumbled to herself. Seru Parth, Sona's Birth Watcher, was sure the birth would come at summer's end, with the M'hir Wind. Others were due sooner.

Much sooner.

"Speaking of dessert—" A relieved creak of boards as Enris disappeared from the roof, only to reappear on the road below.

Bad enough the children do it. Aryl added a *warning* snap. *We don't know who might be watching!* The Strangers had brought a wealth of technology designed to satisfy their endless curiosity. While the Om'ray of Sona weren't their goal, Enris knew better than to risk exposing what they could do. They all did.

Why should they have all the fun? She could see, *feel,* his impish grin. *Look up, Aryl. There's nothing in the sky but sky.* An image filled her mind: a shady grove of nekis, complete with a nest of soft vegetation and stolen pillows. *'Port and seek with me, my little Yena. No one will miss us.*

Hush. But wistfully. *Go find your dessert.*

The truth was, everyone would miss them. A moment on the roof was all the time anyone could spare while the plantings were so young and fragile.

Aryl rose to her feet, took a long stride to the edge, and jumped lightly to the ground. All around her Sona bustled, guided by dreams left by the dead and scraps of knowledge held by the living. This was spring, an urgent season in the mountain valleys. No more snow, no more ice storms, though truenights remained bitter. The wind lifted dust into wispy towers. Green promised growth only where water touched.

Water that trickled in a narrow ribbon within what had been a vast river. Nothing like the flood they must have to overflow and fill the gravel ditches of Sona's unique fields. The Oud promised it would come.

At least, she thought they had. Never easy, deciphering the others who shared Cersi. The Oud mangled the few words they used. The Tikitik were accomplished speakers, but what they said was rarely, in her experience, what they meant. As for the Strangers?

Only one spoke to Om'ray, and to his credit Marcus Bowman did his earnest best to speak properly. Which was fine, until he became excited and threw in words of his own—that disturbing notion, a language not of Cersi.

For now, starting each firstlight, they carried water to what sprouted in the fields nestled between their homes, homes rebuilt from the destruction the Oud had caused here, generations past. Until new Om'ray arrived, Sona had been dead and forgotten.

While Tuana's death was fresh in every mind.

For how long?

Aryl stepped along a walkway of boards, once part of a wall. No one remembered who had lived here before. Why should they? It was the way of Om'ray that only the living and those directly known to the living were *real*.

Because only those could they *feel*.

Humans weren't *real* to Om'ray senses. They lacked this sense of one another. They existed alone, apart, solitary. She'd seen it—had to believe.

Like Yao Gethen. The child had been born unable to

feel other Om'ray, though they could all *feel* her. She was normal otherwise. Bright, affectionate, brimming with Power and Talent. Her disability seemed not to trouble her, however much it appalled her father, the Adept Hoyon d'sud Gethen.

Though Yao could get lost. Other Om'ray knew their location within the world; wasn't Cersi defined by their innermost sense of one another? Enris might tease, but he'd be among the first to chase after the child if she wandered too far from Sona.

Her lips were dry. They'd rested on the rooftop too long. She'd best check on the small field separating their home from its neighbor. All of Sona was laid out this way, tiny fields surrounded by low stone walls, those walls linking one building to the next. Protection for the crops, they guessed, though from what no one knew. Shelter from the wind, that for sure. There was always wind here. Not like the M'hir, but lips chapped and what didn't receive water daily withered before their eyes.

This field, like the others, wasn't much yet. They'd chipped holes in the hardened soil and planted seeds from Sona's marvelous storage chambers. Green, blue, and yellow had sprouted in a confusion of shapes and sizes. Some were sprigs of life too tender to trust, apt to drown in the tiny puddles of their water ration. Others writhed up where no seed had been buried, growing sideways to flop over on themselves, ever reaching as if determined to choke out the rest.

Aryl watched where she put her feet. The Oud—perhaps hunting Om'ray—had left the fields intact, destroying buildings and roadways instead; years of neglect and drought had encouraged some plantings to take over. Sona's abandoned vines, for one, had spent their last growth wrapping around any upright scrap of wood and were a particular nuisance even dead. Their Grona lamented the lack of neat rows, but the Tuana insisted on planting seeds only in soil free of withered remains.

She and the other Yena, used to plants that looked after themselves, thought both ideas peculiar, but kept that opinion to themselves.

The Tuana were partly right. Given water, specks of pale red had appeared at each vine tip and some of the withered stalks showed yellow at their bases.

Rebirth or rot? Aryl wasn't convinced, so she watered daily. What did grow would most likely prove to be weeds, to be removed. A future problem. The dreams from the Cloisters hadn't shown what to nurture and what to discard. She knew the names of seeds and how to plant them, not the food they'd produce. For now, they could only let everything grow and wait to see what water inspired.

Though that, she decided, eyeing a thick purple leaf girdled in thorns, had to be a weed. How many seasons had she helped hack and pull free the plants growing in riotous abandon on Yena's bridges and rooftops? Those had had thorns, too. And prickles. Not to forget the ones with stinging spines.

This one might sting, too. She squatted to examine the purple growth, fingers pressed to the dry ground. Ground. Grit. Dust. Sometimes mud. The still-unfamiliar feel of it distracted her. Solid—or was it? The Oud promised not to be below. Marcus had given her a device that would warn her if they trespassed.

Tuana had had no such warning. Hundreds of Om'ray had died; an uncounted, unmourned number of Oud. The deaths had reshaped the world. The few survivors, those Adepts and Lost and aged in Tuana's Cloisters, hardly made a difference. Aryl closed her eyes and *reached* with her inner sense. Cersi no longer expanded to Tuana and beyond, but instead stopped short at Pana, bulging to where the sun rose behind populous Amna.

"It's not right," Aryl muttered. Enris had rescued his young brother Worin and Yuhas and his Chosen Caynen S'udlaat from the disaster. The Oud had inadvertently saved more, bringing fifteen Tuana they'd found in their tunnels to Sona. The Tikitik claimed all who remained, taking Tuana for their own in some bizarre trade with the Oud.

Tuana, now Tikitik.

What was it like, to stand on the platforms of Tuana's Cloisters and watch the Tikitik flood the ground, plant their wilderness of rastis and nekis? Did the swarms already climb during truenight, to eat anything alive and exposed to their jaws?

Enris and his people had never dealt with danger like that. He'd told her their greatest risk, other than the whim of Oud, was of accidents around harvesting machinery.

"Not right." Aryl took her knife and stabbed at the roots of the purple thorn plant.

"For all you know, that's our one and only rokly. Leave it be."

"Rokly grows on some kind of vine." Knife poised for another strike, Aryl scowled up at Naryn S'udlaat. "I think it's a weed."

Her friend laughed. "Because it has thorns? Many fruiting plants protect themselves. You Yena think everything's a threat."

Everything was, if it could be. But Aryl shrugged peacefully, conceding the point. Yena skills weren't of use in this—only their strength. She wished, not for the first time, for Costa. There'd be one Yena the ground dwellers couldn't mock. Only her brother had stuck clippings into jars and tried to grow plants on purpose. "We're all Sona now," she countered. "We'll learn what we must."

Naryn gestured apology, though her blue eyes continued to sparkle. "True, though some of us learn faster than others. I'm glad I found you."

Aryl studied the other as she rose to her feet. Naryn's Clan had been Tuana, but she'd been exiled before the Oud brought her here. Like Yao, she was different. Her willful red hair might be tamed by a net much like

Aryl's—though Aryl's was of ancient metal, a treasure cleaned and repaired for her by Enris—but it hadn't been the result of a true Choice and Joining. Her abdomen thickened with new life, too—larger, since her time would be early summer—but the baby within had no father.

And its birth would kill both mother and child.

You have bigger worries. The sending was tinged with *impatience.* Naryn hid any fear for her future behind shields stronger than any Om'ray Aryl had known. She refused sympathy, using her strength and training to help the rest of Sona. She also refused friendship other than Aryl's, though she had an understanding of sorts with Haxel Vendan, their First Scout. The two, powerful in their own ways, shared a contempt for those they considered fools. Aloud, "We have a problem."

Especially fools who caused problems. Aryl sighed, wiping her knife blade on her leggings. The purple plant looked smug; weed, she warned it silently. "For once, tell me it isn't Oran."

Her former heart-kin's Chosen was almost as Powerful as Naryn. Better schooled, having made full Adept as part of Grona Clan. Not a day passed when Oran didn't find some way to remind them of their great good fortune in having her decide to make her home at Sona.

Naryn raised a shapely eyebrow in mock surprise. "How did you know?"

If there was anyone Aryl herself would exile, it was Oran di Caraat.

If there was anyone they couldn't afford to lose, it was their only Healer.

"What did she do?"

"Came out of the Cloisters this morning, bold as you like. Ezgi was there to see."

"Is that all?" Relieved, Aryl slipped her knife into its sheath on her belt, then dusted her hands. "She's welcome to it." She couldn't help the bitter note to her voice.

The Cloisters made the perfect destination for those practicing their new skill. Easy to *remember,* while safe from surprises and watching eyes of any kind.

So far, it was good for nothing else. No one but Aryl could unlock its doors. She had an Adept's Power; Naryn had taught her the trick. In the end, it had taken the child growing within her, the touch of one who belonged to Sona. She'd hoped that meant Seru could as well, being pregnant, but her cousin's attempt had failed, leaving her miserable and Oran contemptuous.

Inside? Empty halls and silence. They'd all explored, heard nothing but their own voices and footsteps, turned doors to vacant rooms. Either Sona's Adepts had abandoned their haven to die with their kin, or their bodies lay together in some hidden place. Unlike the mounds, no treasures of food or supplies beckoned. No water flowed from its outlets. The lights shone, as if someone had forgotten to turn them off.

There were secrets. Some doors couldn't be opened. Some levels couldn't be reached.

Secrets that could wait, all had agreed, until the vital spring seeding was complete.

All but two, she recalled with a grimace. Their pair of Grona Adepts had envisioned moving right in, eager to live apart from the rest and do whatever Adepts did alone.

Not, Haxel ordered in no uncertain terms, while Sona needed every hand to dig dirt and carry water. The Cloisters wasn't going to feed them.

Naryn tilted her head just so. Impatience, by any measure.

What had she missed? "He saw her 'come out,' " Aryl repeated, then blinked. "She can unlock the doors?"

"With no trouble at all."

"Then Oran's finally pregnant." Aryl wasn't sure how she felt about that, though it was, she realized with a wince, the right timing. The Adept and Bern had, to his obvious relief, finally consummated their Joining.

Though she detested the notion, it was apparently her doing. She and Bern had been heart-kin, a connection that encouraged a certain resonance, Myris had explained, with dimples, when Aryl and Enris had so robustly consummated their own.

Enris, wisely, had refrained from any comment whatsoever.

"Seru's problem." Naryn dismissed the subject of Oran's pregnancy with a callous shrug.

Aryl felt a rush of sympathy for her cousin. Well aware of the Adept's opinion of her, Seru kept her distance. Now they'd be forced into one another's company, for the sake of the unborn.

Pregnancy, however, didn't explain why Oran would bother with locks. If anything, she 'ported more frivolously than the children. "Why the doors?"

Naryn's smile was unpleasant. "Her friend can't get in otherwise."

"Hoyon." Who had yet to 'port.

Like any Talent, there were those who took to it like breathing, those who struggled, and those who possessed no ability at all. The Adept could send objects into the M'hir, just not himself. His Chosen, Oswa, though less powerful, had needed only to share Aryl's memory of how it was done.

How much of Hoyon's "couldn't" was fear? Not the first time she'd wondered that. For something this new, Adept training was of no use. There'd been no way to predict who of Sona would be capable or how the Talent would manifest beyond oneself. Touch mattered. Only Aryl could 'port another Om'ray through the M'hir without touching that individual, but she couldn't do the same for an object unless she held it in her hands. Enris and Fon could send anything they saw into the M'hir, but not reliably bring it out again.

As for 'porting itself, Power made a difference: the weaker couldn't travel as far as those stronger, though no one knew why. Aryl suspected a deeper instinct kept

Om'ray from staying too long with the M'hir. That *darkness* was utterly strange. Terrifying, consuming, alluring. It took Power to stay sane amid its chaos, to forge a connection to another mind. All the while, time crawled, measured itself in that outpouring of strength, became finite. Overstay, and risk losing oneself.

She and Enris had yet to find limits to their range. Seru and a few of the others, including Haxel, could 'port no farther than the mounds. The rest practiced 'porting to and from the Cloisters' Council Chamber, safe from watchers, when not working the fields. Or played 'port and seek to torment their elders.

Hoyon should be strong enough.

Fear, then. She and Enris had been driven into the M'hir by desperate need. Maybe they should find Hoyon his own crisis. At the thought, the free ends of Aryl's hair lashed against her back.

The two Grona, busy inside the abandoned Cloisters. "What are they doing?" she puzzled aloud. "The place is empty."

Its surroundings weren't. The Oud gnawed at the nearby cliff with their machines, day through truenight according to scouts. The Stranger camp stood between that busyness and the grove around the Cloisters. It was no place for Om'ray to be careless.

"Someone should find out."

Meaning her. Aryl glared. "Why me?"

Her friend merely smiled gently. *You're the one they fear.*

Games. Fine for children, Aryl fumed to herself as she drew on her second-best tunic, then yanked free the Speaker's Pendant to lie on top. Her hair shivered itself free of dust, then fought her attempt to bind it again. The stuff was every bit a nuisance. If she could, she'd shave it off.

The notion sent it writhing into her eyes.

Let me. Enris was behind her, as abruptly as the sun coming from behind a cloud. Aryl closed her eyes, feeling her hair ripple and wind itself through his fingers, cling to his wrists. Highly unfair, that it obeyed his touch and not hers.

Unfair ... and delicious. Her bones wanted to melt. More often than not, this was where her hair escaped the net entirely, along with all responsible thought. Not this time. *I have to deal with them.*

"I know." Aloud, to hide his opinion. Which, she thought with some asperity, told her anyway.

"I can't leave it to Haxel," she said, turning to face him. "Last time ..."

His lips quirked. "What's wrong with a turn at the watch fire?"

Aryl didn't bother mentioning their restless sleep that particular truenight. Had anyone trusted the inexperienced Adepts to stay awake? "If there's another confrontation, you know what'll happen. Haxel will insist they go back to Grona. Cetto and Morla would agree in a heartbeat. The rest—?" They hadn't had an issue divide them. She'd prefer to keep it that way. Sona's numbers were too few, their cohesiveness as a Clan still fragile. "Having our own Healer is a comfort," she finished lamely.

"We wouldn't need a Healer if Marcus—"

"No."

Aryl recognized the glint in his eye: one of her Chosen's usually admirable qualities, that stubborn streak. "—if Marcus taught me to use his technology," Enris went on as if she hadn't objected. "You've seen it. Worin's leg might never have been smashed. The Strangers' healing machine is as good or better than anything Oran can do. Marcus would teach me." *If you asked.*

Oh, she understood that desire. The wonders in Marcus Bowman's camp by the waterfall tempted her as well. But the Human had agreed to let her and her alone decide how much contact he should have with other Om'ray. For good reason. Aryl pressed two fingers gently over her Chosen's lips. *We can't rely on their devices. They won't be on Cersi forever. We must depend on ourselves.*

Enris caught her fingers, kissed them, held them in his. "And we will. The Strangers' machine gives us time to find another Healer. Aryl. You must see it. Those Adepts have to go. Why wait for the next time they cause trouble? Sona won't be whole as long as Oran and Hoyon fight you for leadership."

"I'm not fight—" His smile stopped her protest; Aryl settled for glowering. "We can't send them to Grona," she said instead. "Oswa and Yao belong here, with us."

"And Bern?"

Anything but a simple question. Enris was the most easygoing and charming Om'ray imaginable, willing and able to find the best in others, to inspire it. That he'd come to so thoroughly dislike Bern sud Caraat, her former heart-kin, had nothing to do with jealousy. Chosen, Joined for life, could have no doubt of each other. But *distrust* rumbled beneath the words.

And *contempt.*

Aryl leaned her forehead against Enris' chest. "He was my friend."

"Who smiles and whispers, and spreads doubt about everything you say or do, while Oran plays the noble Healer."

He supports his Chosen. You do the same.

Not so. His big arms drew her close. *I love my Chosen to distraction, but when you're wrong*—Aryl felt his deep laugh—*I'm the first to tell you.*

And you're so perfect . . .

A rush of *heat.* "How right you are," he murmured into her hair, which squirmed joyfully against its net. His hands began exploring.

Insufferable Tuana. "I'll see you later," Aryl told him, then concentrated and *pushed . . .*

Aroused, the M'hir's heaving *darkness* was wilder than usual. No surprise, Aryl thought wryly in the brief instant before she emerged.

So was she.

Sona's Cloisters didn't rise on a stalk, like Yena's, but rather sat on the ground like a discarded flower. Oud had thrown dirt against its windows and filled in the lowermost platform. They'd sought a way inside . . . curious about what none of their kind had seen.

Marcus Bowman was curious, too, but knew better than to attempt such trespass. He might hope for an invitation, but even if she could bring herself to consider it, her Human friend was no longer alone.

For the Oud had made a discovery in their cliff, drawing what Haxel and Aryl glumly considered too much attention to Sona's remote valley. First had come the rest of Marcus' new Triad, for the Strangers worked in threes, each with a specific task. In his words: Analyst, Scantech, and Recorder. Aryl had seen them from a distance. Not Human, unless they came in a wider range of body shapes than she'd appreciated; he'd explained once that each Triad had to have different species.

Only a few, those who were or looked Human, stayed past truenight; in that, Marcus managed to keep some order in his camp, or the prohibition against non-Humans too close to Cersi's own races continued. A third building had gone up. More aircars came and went, even in storms, as if what had been found here mattered more than personal safety.

Not, Aryl thought with a sigh, that she'd noticed much concern for that in Marcus Bowman either. The Human made Ziba seem cautious, not to mention he could be distracted by a biter.

She delayed the inevitable.

Aryl brushed imaginary dust from her tunic. She'd

'ported inside the Council Chamber. Windows stretched to the high ceiling, their lower two thirds obscured by gravel and dust thanks to the Oud. The floor, which should gleam, was dull. No dust, as if the inside of the Cloisters cleaned itself, but no feet or cloth had burnished its surface for long years.

Eighty-three years, according to Marcus, had passed since Sona's destruction by the Oud. That was his skill: to follow trails through the past as a hunter would prey by the bend of a frond or an impression on bark. What Marcus and his fellows sought lay so long ago that—if she believed him—lakes and mountains had swallowed the remains of those who'd once lived on this and other worlds.

The Hoveny Concentrix, he called them. A vast civilization blending thousands of different kinds of beings that had failed long before the current blend of races, the First, laid claim to this part of space. Most recent of all, his kind, *Humanity*, with their far-flung Commonwealth. At this edge, a Trade Pact had formed with the First. Layer upon layer of civilizations, stretched through time as much as distance.

Enris found the concept fascinating.

Aryl found it troubling, if she thought of it at all.

Though it was hard not to think of the past, here, standing where unknown Om'ray had stood. Her sleep was no longer visited by their memories, the dreams a Cloisters sent to inform Choosers and Adepts at need. On the journey here, Seru had dreamed the death of Sona's Om'ray, a warning to keep away. When they'd refused to take heed and settled in the ruined village, new dreams had shown them where to find food, as well as images of how the Sona had lived.

This had been a prosperous, advanced Clan. Every Sona, not just Adepts, could read and write. They'd lived in peace with their Tikitik neighbors, trading certain crops for wood for their homes, for the knowledge of how to make a difficult land fruitful. Numerous, too.

Cetto estimated Sona's village could have housed over a thousand Om'ray, and there had been a second settlement, outside the Cloisters, devoted to the aged and infirm.

No Clan boasted such numbers now. Pana came closest, at over seven hundred.

The dreams had ended—as if they should somehow have learned all that was necessary. But they hadn't, Aryl thought, gnawing her lower lip in frustration. Was the purple plant a weed? Would summer here be hot and dry, or turn cold too soon? How did they preserve any food that grew? They didn't know how the mounds worked, or if their once-opened doors could be resealed.

All of Sona had died when the Oud moved in to reshape their valley. Aryl's darker imaginings suggested a second disaster, because the Tikitik and Oud lived in Balance, trading Om'ray Clans like baskets of fruit. No one knew of another lost Clan, which meant nothing. None had known of Sona either. When she'd led the exiles here, the Oud had claimed them. It hadn't been long before the Tikitik had demanded and received that terrible compensation: the Oud reshaped Tuana, leaving only its Cloisters, and those sheltered within, unharmed.

Only the Cloisters.

Like Sona.

Aryl stilled, the way she would if she'd heard a strange sound in the canopy and waited to see if it was something with a taste for Om'ray flesh.

Last spring, she'd known the world was defined by Om'ray.

An illusion. Om'ray did not travel beyond their sense of one another and inhabited just this small corner of Cersi. Cersi herself was but a single small world; the stars overhead shone on more than she could count in a lifetime.

Last spring, she'd known a Cloisters was where Adepts

practiced their Talents, safe from observation by Tikitik or Oud, aloof from the rest. A Cloisters was where Adepts added to a Clan's record of names and Joinings, and where the aged and the Lost could live out their days in peace.

Was that illusion, too? Did Clans have Cloisters for no other reason than Om'ray were frail things and some must survive each change in their neighbors, Tikitik or Oud?

"Why?" Aryl asked. "What use are we to them? Why is there an Agreement at all?" The words rebounded from pale yellow walls and closed doors, hung at the ceiling as if searching for answers. Died into silence.

A silence broken by distant footsteps.

Abandoning questions about the past, Aryl sped in pursuit. Oran, at a guess. She favored the lighter footwear they'd found among Sona's supplies. Hoyon preferred his Grona boots.

She knew her way. Like Speaker's Pendants, every Cloisters followed the same design; she'd been in this part of Yena's. As Aryl ran for the closest door to the corridor outside, she kept her shields tight, though she doubted either Adept would welcome contact with her mind. They'd tried to force the secret of 'porting from her once. Tried. That day, she'd discovered her mind could be a weapon as deadly as a longknife.

Naryn hadn't been wrong about the fear between them, only in who felt it most.

A knife was clean, honest. What she could do—Aryl shuddered inwardly—what she could do if rage gripped her, if she lost all decent control, was an abomination. To rip apart *who* someone was and toss the terrified fragments of their aware mind into the M'hir . . .

She'd never do it again. She'd never let another Om'ray learn how.

A promise she couldn't expect Oran and Hoyon to believe.

The corridor was lit by glows lining the junction of

wall to ceiling, glows with no power cells to replace, as ordinary lights had. The floor, smooth and resilient underfoot, was of no material known to Om'ray. Every so often, the plain walls were broken by closed doors of metal, clear unbreakable windows, or by small metal frames surrounding disks and squares of unknown purpose.

Advanced technology.

A thought impossible before she'd met Marcus and seen the devices and buildings of the Strangers.

Om'ray had built this and forgotten.

Another impossible concept. Until the Human had told her of other worlds and how cultures changed over vast lengths of time. Of how the Hoveny Concentrix had covered more worlds, with technology superior to the Trade Pact's, only to collapse to ruins long before the Cloisters existed.

He'd gladly bring his devices inside this one, if she gave him the chance. He'd pore over every part, babbling his Comspeak to himself, making *vids* and records and drawing Human conclusions about Om'ray that would change them even more.

Some risks she wouldn't take.

Aryl turned the corner and stopped in her tracks.

Empty corridor stretched ahead.

Oran must have 'ported away. Coward. Aryl lowered her shields the merest amount and *reached*.

"I don't believe it," she whispered aloud.

Not one, not two, but seven Om'ray—below, on another level. Furious, she *reached* to learn who else shirked their responsibilities.

Oran. Hoyon. Oran's brother and shadow, Kran Caraat, as yet unChosen. Bern. No surprise.

Two former Tuana: Deran Edut, another unChosen, and Menasel Lorimar, cousin of the twisted Mauro, dead by Haxel's ever-pragmatic knife.

Gijs sud Vendan, who should keep better company.

Oran had a gift for finding weakness.

Poor Gijs. She sighed to herself. When he wasn't careful, anyone nearby could *taste* his fear, but only those of Yena understood. His Chosen, Juo, would give birth to their daughter any day and in the canopy, Gijs had been sure of himself and his ability to keep his family safe. On Sona's dirt? It didn't matter how well he could climb or hunt. Against the Oud's unstoppable force, what use were Yena skills to repel the swarm? No surprise Gijs turned to Power instead, driving himself to learn whatever Talents he could, from anyone with something to teach him.

From Oran.

Whom Juo detested. The resulting schism between Chosen was a discord racing along her nerves, if Aryl let down her shields when the two were together.

No doubt the shirkers were aware of her presence. If Bern hadn't sensed her, Menasel had the same Talent, to *know* identity.

The level above was reached by a corridor that gradually wound upward. How to reach the one below? Aryl chewed her lower lip. The Adepts knew more of the inner workings of the Cloisters than they'd revealed. Not a comforting thought.

Knowledge Sona needed. Maybe they'd been wrong not to let the Adepts have their haven here.

They'd made one anyway.

Haxel would— Aryl shrugged. What Haxel would or wouldn't do counted as much as a biter's opinion unless she found the way to the next level. She went to the nearest door and turned it open, finding the empty room she'd expected. On to the next. And the next. A set of chairs. A lonely table. No purpose remained here, only remnants.

They were entertained by her search. Smug. She didn't need to *feel* their emotions to know. An adult game, this, a test of her worth against their secret.

A game she couldn't win, Aryl realized abruptly. Fail to find the way down and she'd lose any respect they had left for her. Find the way, confront them, and they'd cling tighter to one another. Neither helped Sona.

There was another way.

She took the corridor that led up, following it to where the Cloisters walls became layers of white petals, neither metal nor wood. No windows here, but at the very top, where the petals met, an irregular slice of cloud and sky could be seen. The light here was warmer than the corridors and rooms, the air fresher.

Whatever the purpose of this uppermost level, there was seating. Long benches curved in rows along one side, facing a span of empty floor.

Aryl sat on the nearest, poked a rebellious strand of hair, and settled her mind. Anger had to go. Resentment with it. Fear of failure, pointless. She focused on the life within, its faint yet growing warmth. She thought about the future she wanted for this child, one of peace and security, the one she wanted for all Om'ray—friends or not—and built it in her imagination.

This new Talent, to 'port from place to place. The next time the Tikitik and Oud traded lands, mightn't it prevent the cost in Om'ray lives? Speakers from each race could inform the others. There could be negotiation, an evacuation planned that didn't violate the rules of Passage.

As for Passage itself, no more would young un-Chosen face a difficult, deadly journey alone. They'd already learned a shared memory was enough for a 'port. Locates for other Clans could be shared, mind-to-mind, through the M'hir. Those able would simply 'port to a waiting Chooser. If that match wasn't suitable, they could as easily return home.

A perfect future. Once the Strangers finished groping at the past and left Cersi forever, Aryl reminded herself. Before that, they must be careful, secretive. Oh, she believed the Human's warning not to reveal themselves as anything but simple villagers. "*Remnants*," he'd called the Om'ray, of no interest to the Trade Pact. She earnestly hoped to stay that way. Nothing good came of the interest of others.

"What do you want?"

The future trembled on her lips, gone as Aryl stiffened, looking up at the angry Om'ray who'd appeared before her. In Grona fashion, Oran's hair was free beneath a token cap. Its golden locks writhed with temper. She wore the white embroidered robe of her office as Adept, in clear defiance.

Or as defense, Aryl thought, forcing herself to stay calm. Oran had courage, whatever their disagreements. "We need to talk."

Oran tightened her shields until she almost disappeared from Aryl's inner sense. "I've nothing to say to you."

There were dark circles beneath Oran's eyes; her mouth was pinched with exhaustion. Why?

Aryl gestured to the bench between them. "Sit with me, Adept di Caraat." A peace offering, to grant the other her title for the first time in their stormy acquaintance. "Tell me what you hope to accomplish here. Perhaps I can help."

The derisive snort was pure Oran, but the other did sit, her body sagging with relief despite her attempt at composure, hair abruptly still. Something had drained her Power to the point of risk, Aryl concluded, holding in her own alarm. What?

Though exhausted, Oran was all pricklish pride and disdain. "What we will accomplish, Speaker Sarc," she stated, "despite no support from our own Clan, is to restore our Cloisters to its full and proper function."

Glows lit every corner. Doors unlocked and turned. The air stayed a comfortable temperature—for Yena in light coats. Aryl doubted the Adept referred to anything so comprehensible. "And you do that by living here ..."

"No. By dreaming here."

" 'Dreaming?' " Aryl sat straighter. "You mean you've been learning about this place? How to tell the weeds, what to do to help the food grow ... the seasons?"

"You think so small. A Cloisters contains the knowledge of all its Adepts. I could continue my training as a Healer. Learn to protect myself from fools like you."

Aryl accepted the rebuke. None of them had realized how dangerous it would be for Oran to try to heal Myris Sarc, whose head injury had damaged her mind as well. That she'd stepped in and completed the task hadn't helped endear her to Oran. But what mattered was the future. The knowledge of Sona's Adepts could help achieve it.

Shadow lapped across the floor, grayed Oran's robe, dulled her hair. A cloud passing.

"Have you dreamed?" Aryl asked, guessing the answer.

Oran's lips pressed together.

Which meant no. She resisted the urge to shake the other. The Grona Adepts' hoarding of secrets made everyone's life more difficult, including their own. Her hair slithered restlessly over one shoulder. She mollified her tone—the hair being another matter—and allowed *sincerity* and *concern* past her shields. "How can the rest of us help?"

"The others can't." Oran smoothed the robe over her knees, traced a curl of embroidery in the fabric, her gaze intent on those actions. "You might," she said after a long moment.

Aryl carefully tightened her shields, particularly those which—sometimes—kept her dear and ever-vigilant Chosen from sensing her reactions. Amazing, the self-control their Joining had taught her. Among other things.

She coughed and focused. "How?"

Oran turned her hand. Its calluses were hardened now, no longer red and swollen. She'd learned their value. "Come with me."

Courage indeed. Without hesitation, Aryl touched her fingertips to the other's palm.

The chamber disappeared . . .
. . . to be replaced by chaos.

Aryl blinked and stood. Oran remained seated, head down, face in her hands. She'd used the last of her strength in the 'port.

A 'port into a stinger nest, Aryl decided. One just prodded with a stick. Her. Angry voices crossed from every side. *Suspicion* and *fear* rilled from mind to mind. "Fool! Why did you bring her here?" "She found us!" "Can't trust her! Send her away!" "Oran, did she hurt you?"

The last, from Bern as he dropped to his knees before his Chosen while giving her a scathing look, was more than enough. Aryl sent a *snap* of irritation. Deran cried out. The rest fell silent and stared at her.

In the respite, doubtless brief, Aryl surveyed the strange room. What was this place? As large as the Council Chamber. An entire Clan could fit in here. The construction matched the rest of the Cloisters, plain yellow walls and resilient floor, but the windowless walls were broken by narrow doors, five evenly spaced along each long side, two on each shorter one. The lighting came not from ceiling strips but from panels behind knee-high platforms.

The platforms. Oran and she had 'ported to sit on one; there were more. Far more. Oval in shape, they lined the walls, each topped with a soft pad of some brown material she'd never seen before. Beds, Aryl decided. For the Adepts? She'd believed her mother had had her own room, sparse but comfortable. Had she been wrong?

Yena had thirteen Adepts. There were beds here for many times that number.

The two closest bore additional blankets, familiar ones. They'd come from the storage mound. As had, Aryl frowned, the incongruous pile of dishes, pots, and—yes, that was one of the oil heaters used for cooking—on the floor. The bulging sacks leaning against the wall doubtless contained food as well as extra clothing. The Tuanas' doing, she guessed. No Yena would take from his own.

Yet two were part of it. Gijs had the grace to flush a dark red. Bern, preoccupied with his weary Chosen, paid no attention. Fools. She restrained her temper. "How can I help?"

Hoyon sank down on the bed behind him. His hands trembled. "You can't."

"You don't belong here." This from Menasel.

Aryl smiled her mother's smile. "Neither do you. They—" with a nod to exhausted Adepts, "—I can understand. Why are you here? Or you, Gijs. Kran. Deran. Bern. Someone else does your share of the work right now."

Deran scowled fiercely. "I'm no digger in dirt."

"What do you plan to eat next winter?" Aryl found herself honestly curious. The Tuanas of Sona shared a past and future, but remained distinct: Naryn and the Runners, who worked as hard as any Yena, and Deran and his once-privileged kin, who had the oddest notion they should be entitled to not work at all. The two groups spared no words or kindness for one another.

Oran lifted her head, golden hair flooding over her shoulders. "Peace, Aryl. They work here, for us. We must concentrate on our task; we are helpless while dreaming. Without any Lost—" A shrug.

As if it was a detriment, not to have mind-shattered Chosen to serve her. And she never would, Aryl hoped fiercely, though what she could do against a fact of Om'ray life was beyond her imagining. The death of one of a Joined pair meant the loss of the other's sense of self, if not another death. The only exception had been her own mother, Taisal. "You brought me here, Adept," she stated grimly, regretting that decision. Though now she could return to this sanctum of theirs at whim; from the unsettled feel of their Power, the others realized it too.

Hoyon scowled. "Why, Oran?"

Oran gestured a perfunctory apology. "You need more than I can give you."

That was it? Oran wanted her to restore Hoyon's strength with her own. Aryl's hand wanted to find the hilt of her longknife. Not helpful. She rested her fingers on her belt. "Strength for what?"

"The Cloisters must accept him—" Oran flinched and fell silent, but her eyes were hot.

Aryl had felt it, too. A *crack* of Power, stinging even to those not its target. Oran wasn't the leader of this pair, as she'd believed. Hoyon d'sud Gethen was.

Leader of nothing else. *Don't think to challenge me,* she sent to the Grona Adept. She'd kept it private, but his defiant glare at her didn't fool anyone. *Fear* spilled past his shields, thick and cloying. The others exchanged troubled looks.

Aryl felt unclean.

"Explain yourselves," she pressed. "Now."

"He's tried and failed." Bern was clearly pleased to have Hoyon put in his place. "A gift of strength won't help. The Cloisters doesn't want him."

Would none of them make sense? "The Cloisters is a building."

"It's much more." Oran gestured at the room. "This is the Dream Chamber. Here, we can learn whatever we need. Once the Cloisters accepts Hoyon as its Keeper."

"You talk of what's forbidden to non-Adepts!" Hoyon subsided at Aryl's lifted brow, though he looked as if he'd bitten into a rotten fruit.

" 'Keeper?' " she repeated. "What's that?"

"Not what. Who." As if goaded by Hoyon's warning, Oran spoke quickly. "The Keeper is the one Adept given the ability to open the dream records for the rest. But Sona's hasn't listened to Hoyon."

Adept babble. Aryl decided to leave the question of how a building could listen alone, though she did approve this one's taste. "Will it listen to you?"

A reasonable question. Hoyon jerked as if she'd hit him.

From the joyous lift of Oran's hair, this wasn't the first time she'd considered stepping into Hoyon's place. However, she schooled her face and bowed very properly toward the other Adept. "I would not presume. Hoyon d'sud Gethen is my senior. My teacher."

A poor time for Oran di Caraat to exhibit humility, false or real. Aryl was conscious of their audience: the pair of Tuana, Kran and Bern, Gijs. Nothing that happened with such witnesses would be secret for long.

Which worked both ways.

She smiled. "I'll ask Naryn, then. She's had Adept training—"

"No!" from Hoyon.

"She can't," from Oran, whose lips twisted. "Even if she were a full Adept, there's what grows inside her. The Cloisters won't accept a pregnant candidate." She rose to her feet, shaking off Bern's solicitous hand. "I will make the attempt, with Hoyon's permission."

"But you're pregnant," Aryl protested.

"I'm hardly so careless."

"You were seen opening the lock—"

Before Oran could reply, Menasel spoke up. "We all can," the Tuana Chosen boasted. "They added our names to the records—"

"Only yours?" Aryl cut in.

In the ensuing silence, she looked at each of them in turn. Gijs lowered his eyes. "Only yours," she repeated, sure now. Poor Juo.

Games and secrets. They destroyed bridges. They left Om'ray stranded and alone. They risked everything. Sona had forty-six Om'ray. Barely enough to plant and tend a crop. There would soon be babies needing care. The eldest among them could fail in the coming winter.

The river had yet to flood.

The blood pounding in her ears was louder than their breathing. A presence filled her mind—Enris, alerted, not yet alarmed. Aryl sent a pulse of *reassurance* she most assuredly didn't feel, then tightened her shields.

She looked at the Grona Adepts. "Every name. By truenight."

Oran's hair flailed, but she didn't argue.

"Everyone to see this place and understand what you would do here."

Hoyon opened his mouth, then closed it.

"And if you succeed—anyone who wishes dreams with you."

That was too much. "Only Adepts dream to order!" Hoyon shouted.

"Then," Aryl told him calmly, "when you correct the records, make everyone an Adept."

She concentrated and *pushed* herself through the M'hir before they could react.

Chapter 2

"ENRIS D'SUD SARC." Enris stretched out his long legs, put his hands behind his head, and grinned. "Has a nice ring to it, don't you think?"

What she thought, Aryl told herself grimly, she'd keep to herself. She concentrated on sharpening her knife. There'd been almost no reaction to her news about Oran and Hoyon, and the Cloisters. That didn't mean there wouldn't be. Sona's Om'ray tended to consider before they spoke. Meanwhile, Deran and Menasel, along with Bern and Kran, carried water. Gijs escaped that duty to finish his new home's roof under the baleful eye of his Chosen. Oran and Hoyon remained at the Cloisters to prepare.

Whatever that meant.

Seru, bent over her sewing, glanced through a restless curl of black hair. "Seru di Parth." Her nose wrinkled. "Doesn't make me an Adept."

That deep chuckle. "What I want to know is when we get our robes. There'd best be one my size."

Aryl put down her knife and tossed an empty mug at his head. It disappeared mid arc.

" 'A waste of good dishes!' " The Tuana's excellent imitation of Husni's frequent complaint to those practicing their Talent made her lips quirk.

"You could have caught it," she pointed out. To

Seru, "The Cloisters answers to names it knows. Don't ask me how. But only those with the 'di' of Adepts are allowed into certain areas. Only they are free to learn through dreams." She had no more desire than Seru to be an Adept and none to live within the Cloisters, but to learn? Her breath quickened. To be able to read and write ... to discover the past of this place ... "We could become so much wiser," Aryl said earnestly. "All of us."

"Not all." Morla entered the Meeting Hall, shook dust from her jerkin, then took a seat at the table with them. She gestured gratitude as Enris poured her a mug of water. Her still willful white hair was tamed by a tight net. That hair and those wide-set gray eyes were Sarc traits; her diminutive size and clever hands? Pure Kessa'at. She'd been an outspoken Councillor of Yena, leader of her family, before the betrayal. At Sona, she plied her first trade again, woodworker, and rarely offered her opinion on anything else. Until now.

"Why not?" Aryl asked.

"There's a reason Adepts are selected for their Power, why they are tested. The teaching dreams are risky. Few Om'ray have the strength to endure them."

"According to the Adepts themselves. Convenient." She gestured apology for her harsh tone—the elderly Om'ray didn't deserve it. "We've dreamed. Seru and I. We were fine."

A shiver of *dread*. No doubt of the source. Seru had been sent dreams of Sona's death, full of screams and pain. A warning not to approach.

"They were useful dreams," Aryl insisted. "We'll be careful, of course, but—"

WE?? Enris' sending made her wince. *You mean to try this?*

Don't you?

Shields slammed between them. Outwardly, her Chosen appeared preoccupied with the packs hung from the rafters. Perhaps, she grumbled to herself, he searched for the mug he'd *pushed*. Given his Power, it was probably in Grona, if it left the M'hir at all.

So much they didn't know.

"The ceremony will be a tenth after truenight," Aryl said aloud. The dark wasn't yet a friend, but it would hide the disappearance of Sona from any non-Om'ray observers. They'd 'port to the Council Chamber, the stronger taking the weaker. There, Oran and Hoyon would add their names to the records.

For Husni, their keeper of tradition, had insisted there be a proper ceremony. In Yena, there would be flowers and dresel cake once a baby received its name, or a Chosen arrival was granted his new one. Tuana and Grona— no surprise—believed in feasts. Tai sud Licor, from Amna, spoke wistfully of boiled swimmers and dancing.

"About that." Morla leaned forward on her elbows, eyes somber. Both wrists were wrapped with colorful cloth—a habit she'd kept after the broken one healed. Many of Sona's new Om'ray had taken to the harmless fashion, that warmed arms and left hands bare. The Yena had adopted Tuana-style boots. The Tuana and Grona Chosen liked Yena hairnets, except for Oran. So quickly, they became different from other Clans. "Being together, not working for once. We could ring a bell for Mauro."

Every Cloisters contained deep-throated bells; by tradition, one was rung for each death. Aryl glanced at Enris. He pursed his lips and gave that small head-shake the Human used for "no." Their habit now. As for Seru . . .

Her cousin hunched over her work, applying needle and thread with unusual force, considering she sewed baby clothes.

Mauro Lorimar had come to Sona with his fellow Tuana, bringing with him a dreadful, un-Om'ray joy in the pain of others. At home, he'd led a group against Enris, beating him severely. Here, he'd tried to Join Seru, dragging her mind into his madness.

He'd deserved his fate, Aryl thought grimly. As did Seru, happily Joined to Ezgi, once of Serona.

Morla waited, the image of patience. She hadn't, Aryl realized abruptly, come to suggest this on her own. "Haxel sent you." The First Scout's quick knife had saved Aryl, trapped in the M'hir by Mauro's attempt to Join with her instead. No Om'ray was known to have killed another before, though to be fair, Mauro had hardly seemed one of them by the end. She shuddered inwardly. "She shouldn't regret what she did."

"That one?" Morla's face wrinkled. "Haxel's only regret is that she didn't move faster."

Enris dropped his feet to the wooden floor. "Rorn," he declared.

Haxel's Chosen? "Why?"

"Haven't you noticed? He's her conscience."

"It might help Menasel." They all looked at Seru, who blushed. "Mauro was her cousin," she went on, determined, if hesitant. "It might help—everyone. We've done nothing to mark the passing of Tuana."

Aryl was jolted by *grief.* Enris gestured apology as he tightened his shields, his eyes hooded. She laid her fingers on his arm. *We are one,* she sent gently. *Never fear to share your pain.*

"How can we ring bells for Tuana?" Morla asked. "We don't know—I'm sorry, Enris—but we don't know how many died there, or who." She gestured apology, but went on, "Surely the survivors have rung their own bells."

"This isn't about their grief, but ours," Seru insisted, her voice growing firm. Whether pregnancy or a blissful Choice, something had brought out the strength Aryl had known lay in her cousin. "You can *reach* that far, Aryl. You can tell us who lives. Then we'll know who to mourn."

No one had asked this of her. Not even Enris, who looked at her with sudden *hope.*

An Om'ray who left his Clan was as if dead to that

Clan. It had always been so. UnChosen took Passage to find Choice and a new home, or die in the attempt. The family and friends they had in the past never spoke of them again. It was the way of the world.

A way her Talent could change forever. Aryl swallowed. *Is this what you want?*

Not for myself. His eyes fixed on hers. *I have my new life. But for Worin's sake. For the others. They didn't choose to leave their families. They should know what became of them.*

Aryl's fingers strayed to the metal bracelet she wore, turned it on her wrist, explored the smooth ripples that mirrored a mountain stream. It was of Tuana; Enris had made it there before he'd left. Before they'd met. "Stay with me," she said out loud, then closed her eyes.

She relaxed, let herself be attracted to the glow of other Om'ray, moved past Sona's cluster of life to touch Grona's, moved farther and ignored all between, until . . .

Tuana.

Having *reached* the *here-I-am,* she relaxed further to allow each glow to become *who-I-am* . . . names filled her mind . . . more than names. Identities, full and rich and connected one to the other. No Om'ray existed alone, whole or Lost. Their bonds were threads of light through the darkness.

Too few.

Enris. *With* her. She shared her awareness of Tuana's Om'ray; in return, she couldn't escape his *despair* and *anguish.* She took his pain into herself, soothed it, helped him past it. *Showed* him.

There. *Mendolar.* A connection that stretched, however tenuous, to him and back. Other names. Serona. S'udlaat. Edut. Licor. Annk. Other connections. Faint, too faint. But real.

If she let herself, she could trace them between every living Om'ray, see the world's shape as it truly was, know her place in it.

With an effort, Aryl shrank her awareness to her own body and opened her eyes.

"Dama Mendolar," Enris said wonderingly. "I should have known. My grandmother," he clarified for the rest of them. "It's not the first reshaping she's survived."

"Could you—?" Aryl found herself unable to say it.

Enris seemed to fill the room as he rose to his feet. Only his uncle, Galen sud Serona, rivaled him in size. "I have the names of the living. I'll tell the rest." Then he paused to gaze down at Seru. "But there aren't enough bells for the dead."

In the end, Sona's bells were silent. Instead, when everyone had gathered within the Cloisters' Council Chamber, dressed in their finest—or at least cleanest—clothes, the Tuana stepped upon the raised dais. Murmurs and sendings stopped. The dark of truenight pressed above the gray dirt piled outside the windows. It reflected the glowstrip that banded the ceiling, so rivers of light appeared beyond the Tuana, meeting at some unimaginable distance.

Enris stood in the midst of his new Clan, at the center of his old, the focus of all eyes. He was magnificent, Aryl thought, holding in a rush of *pride* that had no place here and now. Straight-shouldered, serious, with a lift to his head that gathered attention and kept it. Nothing of uncertainty or youth. Everything of strength.

"This truenight, we will give our names to Sona. So doing, in the way of our people, we become Sona and leave our past Clans behind." His deep voice carried through the room. Through their bones. "Yet we need not."

Naryn stepped forward. Though freed, her glorious red hair cloaked her shoulders in calm, obedient waves. In her hands was a stack of the metal plates Adepts used for their records. Enris gestured. "Here are the names of those who died in the reshaping of Tuana. We who remember them as the living ask that they be given to Sona with ours. We ask that they not be forgotten with our deaths, but remain here to touch the future. Forever real."

To keep the past. A concept he'd learned from the Human.

The others hadn't expected this. Aryl lowered her shields and tasted their *puzzlement*. They weren't unwilling; they simply didn't understand. How could the past stay *real*?

Something was rising in the M'hir. Could the others feel it? Aryl wondered. Surely they must.

Then . . . like a flood . . . memories burst into her mind. Vivid, crisp.

. . . *A roadway. Buildings of wood and colored metal and a kind of block that wasn't stone. Strong, sturdy, elegant shapes. A Meeting Hall with stairlike benches that rose to the ceiling.*

Faces. Voices. Om'ray she'd never met or known. *Hands busy at work. Metal melting and flowing into shapes. Fields that stretched to the horizon. Immense machines, blades slicing through stalks.*

Voices. Faces.

The smell of baking. Something sweet and fragrant. Her mouth watered.

Laughter, ease. A life so different from that of Yena she felt unmade. *Stars overhead. Glows in a tunnel. Ramps and twists and beams of heavy wood.*

Everywhere, life. People. Connected and whole. They had names . . .

Names she could hear because all around her they were being spoken aloud, as if in greeting. Her mouth was moving, too.

The memories faded . . . the echoes died.

The Om'ray of Sona stared at one another, then at Enris.

There was a sheen of sweat on his face. The *sharing*

had come with effort. Beko Serona wept silently beside him. Stryn Licor's daughters supported their mother. The Tuana were shaken, if triumphant.

Naryn started, then smiled as the metal plates lifted from her hands, rose into the air over their heads, then came to the outstretched hands of Fon Kessa'at. The un-Chosen hugged them to his chest, as if relieved by his own control. His friend, Cader Sarc, squeezed his shoulder, looking askance at Veca and Tilip, Fon's parents. They merely smiled at him. So, Aryl thought with approval, the younger generation understood.

"We'll enter them into the record," Oran said quietly. *Aryl.*

Ah, yes. The original reason for the clothes and clean hair, for the rokly cakes cooling on the tables of rough wood they'd had to bring with them, for the tables themselves. She took her place on the dais, the Tuana quietly stepping aside. When Enris would have gone with them, she captured his hand in hers but didn't look at him.

"This truenight," Aryl told her people, consciously following the pattern he'd set, "we give our names to Sona." Smiles. A sense of *relaxation*. This, they'd expected. "Each and every one of you will be shown how to open the Cloisters' doors."

Not expected. She hadn't prepared the rest for this.

A few exchanged looks. Husni's mouth hung open. Haxel spoke. "Only Adepts open a Cloisters. We're not Adepts."

"You don't need to be." Hoyon's face was impassive, but Oswa flinched. Aryl paused to frown at him. "Secrets," she said pointedly, "have no value here. We are too few, too far from any other safety. Sona's Cloisters must open for anyone. The outer doors are a simple trick of Power, easily done by anyone whose name is recorded here."

Or by an unknown bearing a child conceived in Sona, if she had Power enough to impress the Cloisters; a less-than-tactful speculation of Oran's Aryl preferred not to mention.

"The inner doors and levels open in the same way, but only to those bearing the 'di.' " She paused. "So all of us will."

Enris had preened, however insincerely. Seru had been dismayed. Haxel frowned thoughtfully. "A change."

The words were profound. The Agreement that kept the peace between the races of Cersi forbade change. Yet nothing stayed the same. Not and survived. An unseen ripple of *dread* passed through them all. Could they *taste* it?

Aryl squeezed her Chosen's hand, then released it, taking her Speaker's Pendant in the same still-warm palm. "A change," she agreed, her voice ringing. "For the better. For our future." She could see it all, clear and certain. Could they? "We claim a new closeness with one another. We claim the same rights and responsibilities as each other. We refuse to let Power divide us! We are all Sona."

"Sona!" Eyes gleamed. Shouts echoed throughout the hall. "Sona!"

Words slipped into her mind, heavy with conviction. *Now who's the fool?*

When Aryl looked for Naryn, she'd vanished into the jubilant crowd.

"A full fist and we're still finding new rooms." Haxel perched on a step, taking a cup with an absent gesture of gratitude. The morning was crisp and they kept a pot of sombay—a gift from Marcus—warm by the watch fire. She squinted at Aryl through whorls of steam. "Empty ones."

"Oran—"

The First Scout's grin whitened the scar that ran from eye to jaw. "Ah. Our illustrious Keeper. Dreamed anything of use yet?"

Aryl grimaced. According to Hoyon, his niece—

the relationship abruptly worth announcing at every opportunity—had indeed been accepted by Sona's Cloisters. For what good it did. "No. They tell me it's normal for a new Keeper to have trouble sorting the dreams, to learn fine control—"

"Empty rooms and an empty head." Haxel snorted. "We should let your Human help search." A sly look. "I'd like to see what he'd find."

Not the first time the First Scout had made such a suggestion. She should have realized nothing would keep those too-keen eyes from studying Marcus Bowman and his camp. Aryl stiffened, prepared to argue.

With a warmer smile, Haxel raised her cup. "Don't worry. I know better than to trouble peaceful neighbors. "Speaking of which," all innocence, "when's your next meeting with the Oud?"

Nothing innocent at all. So far, the most successful outcome of Aryl's negotiation with the Oud had been their absence. She'd insisted they refrain from tunneling beneath Sona itself, and remove their existing tunnel entrance on the far side of the river. There hadn't been a Visitation since, which was fine with Sona's Speaker. "I did tell them to stay away," she pointed out.

"Helping me sleep through truenight." Unlikely. Haxel brought up a booted foot and rested her arm on one knee. Her gray hair was always quiet, as if cowed by her will. A secret she'd like to learn, Aryl thought as hers tested its net. But the long-ago Sona crafted well. A larger version, Enris averred with his usual tact, would hold a Tikitik esask. A shame it left the fall down her back free to express itself. "There are always," the First Scout mused, "Oud around the Stranger camp."

Visit Marcus? Aryl did her best to look serious, but doubted she fooled the other Om'ray. Between her duties as Speaker and work in the fields—and his frequent visitors—there'd been too few chances to see her Human friend. For he was that, a friend.

Sure enough, Haxel drained her cup and showed it to her, empty. "Just don't forget to ask about the river."

Sona's road to the waterfall showed little signs of use. Haxel and her scouts patrolled the valley, but stayed to the shadowed walls. She had four, now: their Looker, Weth Teerac—di Teerac, Aryl corrected to herself—and Aryl's uncle Ael d'sud Sarc were of Yena, along with two Tuana Runners: the di Licor sisters, Josel and Netta. The Runners, according to Haxel, showed rare aptitude for the work. Enris, amused, thought it more likely the way their remarkable dappled skin matched the local rock. No others could be spared, not yet. Their patrols were also hunting expeditions. Being Yena, Haxel deemed it prudent to keep the valley clear of large predators and free of ambush. The hook-claw that buried itself in loose dirt was easily found, if less easily killed. The rock hunters?

They showed prudence of their own, and were now scarce on the valley floor. Scarce wasn't the same as absent. Aryl watched the shadows for movement.

"I've an idea." Enris slipped his arm around her waist as they walked. "Why don't you relax and enjoy all this?"

Aryl blinked up at him. "Enjoy what?"

His free arm waved expansively, as if it were necessary to include the entire world in the gesture. "This. Time."

Time. "We should have 'ported," she said, wondering again how she'd lost that argument. "Walking leaves us less time with Marcus."

His hand tugged at her belt. "While I enjoy his company, too, I think you're confused, my dear Chosen. Walking means—" he nuzzled her ear, "—we have more time together."

We're always together.

"But rarely alone."

Aryl slowed her pace. They hadn't brought packs, only longknives and flasks of water at their belts, a small bag with a gift for Marcus. She eyed the rough rock and dusty paving stones dubiously. "Can't you wait?"

Enris roared with laughter and swept her up despite her protest. Holding her over his head, big hands easily spanning her waist, he brought her down for a quick kiss, then put her lightly—and now breathless—back on her feet. "Conversation, my wild little Yena. Though," a *flash* of *heat,* "I'd be a most happy mattress."

" 'Conversation.' " Not about Marcus and his healing machine. She hated to disappoint Enris, but this she couldn't— "You already know what I think—"

"About visiting other Clans?" He took a longer stride, then turned to walk backward, facing her. Fine on a flat stretch. "No, I don't."

"Visiting . . . why?" Enris had visited more Clans than any other Om'ray, having been to Yena, Grona, and distant Vyna. Two of the three had almost cost him his life. "We aren't ready to find others who could learn to 'port." Mealtimes, around the communal fire, the notion regularly spun itself around, only to waft away like smoke. How could they contain the secret if it spread? What if such Om'ray came to Sona, who couldn't feed more, not yet? Worst of all, what if they offended the Oud or Tikitik before they could negotiate a change— that word—to the Agreement? "It's too dangerous."

"Of course it is." He almost tripped on a tilted stone and hopped instead. She restrained herself. Far be it from her to dissuade him from being lighter-of-foot. "But we could trade."

Aryl stopped. Trade was a Tuana concept; she forced aside her Yena aversion for his sake. "Trade what?"

"We'd have to open the rest of the mounds, assess what we could spare. Coats. Baskets. We could hunt for more metalwork."

They did, she admitted reluctantly, have an overabundance of coats. "And what would we trade for?"

"Food. Tai said Amna catches more swimmers than they can eat—other Clans may have extra. New boots from Grona before next winter. Tools. My father—I've heard Rayna does fine metalwork. If we had such tools—and the Oud would build a furnace—I could work metal again. Yuhas is willing to learn the skill. Improve our blades. Replacements! Think of it, Aryl."

He'd omitted Vyna because its Om'ray rejected contact with any others. He'd omitted Yena because . . .

Because, Aryl thought sadly, her former Clan had nothing left.

She started walking again. He fell in beside her. "Well?"

They crossed one of the arched bridges. Echoes fooled the senses; the insignificant trickle of water allowed them by the Oud sounded like distant rain. She licked dry lips. "It's too great a risk. Tikitik trade. Oud do. Clans never have. We'd be ignoring the Agreement. It wouldn't be safe."

Oh, he'd been thinking, behind those perfect shields. His face lit up as if she'd already agreed to . . . what? "We start too small for the Oud or Tikitik to notice. I'd go to Amna with Tai. He remembers where. A coat for a basket of fish, from someone he trusts. That's all. Gradually work up to more."

The Tikitik, splashing through the darkness on their beasts, ready to trade, insistent on amounts and compensation. The Oud, with their compulsive lists of everything, not only what they themselves needed. "There may be nothing too small to notice."

"You may be right. But—Aryl, it's best we do something and soon."

"Why?"

"Because—" his voice roughened, "—not all of us are Yena. It wasn't unheard of for a Tuana to try and take what wasn't hers. Nor a Grona. With this Talent you've given us, nothing is beyond reach."

Enris was serious. The hairs rose at the back of her neck. He thought Om'ray capable of this.

"Ask Naryn, if you don't believe me. You saw the children. Today it's a game. Tomorrow? We need an outlet for the adults who won't be playing. They'll take risks. They'll push the limits of their Power. Without Passage as a challenge?" Enris lifted both hands. "Trade with a hint of danger. It might be enough for some."

Cetto d'sud Teerac had feared it, so long ago. His words welled up in memory and Aryl *shared* them. *"To be able to have a thing in your hands, without climbing for it? How long before it becomes the ability to take a thing, without right to it?"*

"A wise Om'ray."

Aryl shook her head. "I see a better future."

I know. Enris touched her cheek, sent a rush of *affection.* "Just keep in mind some of us who don't always look where we're going."

He spoke to her Yena-self, well aware what she'd take from it.

That some would fall.

The stone of pavement and bridge, the jagged arch and plunge of bare rock, gave way at the head of Sona's valley to ruin and riotous growth. The Oud had done this, Aryl thought. They'd heaved corpses and buildings and gardens into a mound to dam the mighty river; dug a pit into the depths to divert its source, the sky-touching waterfall beyond; and refused to share more than a trifle. Even now, she didn't know why.

A curiosity she'd leave to others.

"Our waterfall." Enris nodded to where a single metal pipe cracked the paving of the roadway at the base of the mound, aimed down the valley. By chance or Oud design, the gush of water coming from it splashed on a tilt of rock that directed it to the side, where it disappeared into the chasm of the river's original course.

Though the water came out with force, Enris could touch the top of the pipe with an upraised hand. Their share. Compared to the abundance that roared down the cliff and sent spray into the clouds? As well call a sigh the M'hir. "They can't mean this to be all we get," Aryl said, as much to herself as her Chosen. "Their Speaker agreed we'd have more than the Oud."

"More than. Less than. Past that, who knows what they mean?" But he didn't move immediately, instead shading his eyes and staring at the mound. She felt the *distance* between them she'd learned was her Chosen lost in thought.

"What is it?"

"Nothing." Enris looked self-conscious. "A notion." With that highly unsatisfactory response, he began to climb the slope, boots crunching bone. Impossible not to step on remains, though Aryl tried to move lightly over the loose material. The rock hunters, able scavengers elsewhere, refused to risk any chance of water.

From the top, they followed the trail the scouts had made. Like the new Sona, it blended their habits. The Yena had thrown a swaying bridge over the froth-filled abyss, anchored to the largest of the stalks leaning inward; the Tuana continued it with a wide flat swath cut through the grove, avoiding as much of the Oud-bared space before the Cloisters as possible before swinging to meet the ramp over the Cloister wall. Aryl ran along the bridge, enjoying the spray hitting her face. Enris, to his credit, no longer clung to the hand ropes. He did, however, give an exaggerated sigh of relief once on solid ground.

Aryl grinned. "You know it can hold all of Sona plus Veca's cart, fully loaded."

"But one of me? That's the question."

He had no complaint as they took the path through the nekis. Yellow-throated flowers littered the ground, like a carpet of sunshine. Leaves and stalks glistened with spray. Droplets shook free in miniature rainstorms, complete with bows of color in the air.

Lovely.

She shuddered. Leaves shouldn't be perfect. Flowers shouldn't fall without making fruit. There should be other plants here: vines and thorns and—weeds. More sounds than footsteps and the drumming of the waterfall. "I miss biters."

Enris chomped noisily and gave her a hopeful look.

She shoved him with her shoulder. "You know what I mean."

"Tell me what's wrong with keeping one's skin intact and blood where it belongs."

"And there should be flitters." The clear-winged ones, with bright blue bodies. They hovered over the flowers, like blooms themselves. Others sang or danced in the air. In the canopy, senses were flooded with movement, color, sound. Smell. This grove, she decided with disgust, was as barren as Oran.

"Cader saw a wastryl on the cliff last fist."

The black-and-white gliders soared over the valley, never more than two. Haxel believed they searched for carrion wherever the rock hunters were less. Only during the M'hir Wind did they gather in numbers and head for the canopy. "Dresel thieves," she snorted.

Dresel. Her mouth watered. Something in the Sona diet satisfied her body's need for it; nothing replaced Yena longing for the taste. Maybe this M'hir, she'd go to Yena, help with the Harvest in return for . . . aghast at the turn of her thoughts, Aryl rushed to hide the idea from her Chosen.

Too late. "Craving dresel?" To her relief Enris laughed. "Feel free to get it for yourself," he assured her, an arm around her shoulders. "You won't catch me waving a hook with nothing below but swamp."

When they reached the opening, they fell silent. Enris let Aryl go first; he stayed close. Their practiced caution was likely unnecessary, she knew. Nonetheless, she surveyed the edge of the grove, checked the dirt around the Cloisters for new disturbance, and glanced at the sky before taking the step that exposed her to non-Om'ray watchers.

"We could surprise our Adepts. See how they're coming."

Aryl eyed the Cloisters. "Hardly a surprise." The Om'ray hadn't wasted strength to dig the lower portion free of the Oud's dirt, so no one could look out the windows and watch their approach. Even so, she restrained a childish impulse to make a face. "The instant Oran has any success, be sure everyone will know."

"Some feel it should be you."

Be trapped in the Dream Chamber with Hoyon, his entire being sour with envy? "I'd rather," she told him testily, "dig waste pits."

Satisfaction. "That's what I said."

The path to the Stranger's camp was hidden. A *screen* blocked it, covered by a *projection* of another dense portion of the grove, nekis stalks too close together for easy passage. In truth, all one had to do was approach the screen from one side, and it became nothing more than a white sheet strung across a path every bit as wide and open as the Tuana's.

Simple and effective. She approved. The last thing Sona needed was for a curious Om'ray—and they had their share, starting with Enris' brother Worin—to roam where curiosity ran around on more legs than two. Or had none at all. One of Marcus' new Triad was unable to move on land and floated above the ground in a tiny version of an aircar. Why such an unsuitable creature would come here puzzled her, although she hoped for a better look at it.

But first . . . she stopped and turned to face Enris. "If we see an Oud, let me do the talking."

He raised a dark eyebrow. "You're the Speaker."

Which meant she was the only Sona permitted by the Agreement to talk to non-Om'ray, and then only to her counterpart. She'd learned neither Oud nor Tikitik cared overmuch for the rules. And her Chosen, for all his matter-of-fact demeanor and charm, was incapable of not caring about Oud.

Already the M'hir between them sizzled with pent rage.

Enris.

Don't worry about me. His remarkable shields strengthened until all she could sense was the warmth of their bond. "You remember not to use Power. Some of these Oud could be Torments."

The Tuana name for Oud with Power. There was no evidence the beings used their Power to any purpose, but it did affect Om'ray. To use their abilities near such Oud produced pain and disorientation, increasing with greater Power. Aryl, having felt the effect for herself, agreed completely. "Once was enough, thank you."

The path opened on another clearing in the nekis grove, this one smooth and circular. At its far side stood three long buildings of the plain white material the Strangers favored, a white usually disguised behind more illusion.

Not that it would matter at the moment, considering the crowd of beings in the clearing itself. That was the worst of non-Om'ray, Aryl thought with disgust. You couldn't *feel* them before you found them.

They'd been found, too. Marcus hurried toward them, pushing by an Oud with Human carelessness, his smile wide beneath the dark eye coverings he insisted on using during the day. He wore Stranger pants and a shirt with his name in Stranger lettering. Both looked new.

Why?

"Welcome! Welcome!" She could barely hear his shout above the grind of Oud machine treads into the stony ground. There were four vehicles, each pulling a pair of flat-topped carriers loaded with crates. In typical Oud-fashion, the slumped drivers appeared not to care about collision, imminent or occurring, or risk to their cargo. Aryl and Enris stayed near the grove and let the Human risk his life to join them.

The building to the left was where Marcus stayed and worked. The other two, one new this spring, she'd been told were for storage. The door of the middle one gaped open for the first time. Inside, over the brown-cloaked humps of Oud, she could make out tables covered in objects. Two figures, disappointingly Human-shaped, stood to one side, busy sorting.

As for the Oud, whenever one stopped its vehicle near the open door, other Oud grabbed the crates from the carriers and tossed them onto a growing, haphazard pile. Maybe the Humans were sorting what didn't break under this treatment.

What Aryl didn't see was the Oud Speaker. Or rather, an Oud with a pendant. The beings were too alike otherwise: massive quivering lumps beneath brown, tentlike cloaks. One end was covered by a dust-covered, transparent dome and non-Oud treated that as a "head." To an Oud, this didn't always matter. They could move backward as readily as forward.

After one last swerve to avoid an Oud machine, Marcus joined them, coughing at the dust. "Welcome," he said again. His lean body, tousled brown hair, and green-brown eyes, edges crinkled by his cheerful smile, might be those of an Om'ray Chosen of middle age; the not-*real* of him to her *inner* sense was proof he was anything but. Aryl shrugged inwardly, and the customary confusion passed.

His hands reached for theirs; Humans touched, Aryl had learned, when Om'ray would not. She and Enris allowed it. In fact, such were their feelings for this one Human, they reached out as well.

Greeting done, Aryl waved at the activity behind Marcus. "Should we come back another time?"

Marcus shook his head vehemently. "This is good time. Best. Very best. Glad you are here." He slapped Enris on the shoulder. "Hungry?"

The Tuana slapped him back, careful not to rock the slighter being off his feet. "Starving."

She'd look for the Oud Speaker later, Aryl decided.

"Sorry for the mess." Objects flew in every direction as the Human burrowed to what should be a table. "Don't spend much time in here. Oops! Thanks." As Enris intercepted the flight of what looked fragile and gently deposited it on a crate. "Mustn't break another *densitometer* this early in the day. It is early, isn't it?" He looked uncertain. "Breakfast?"

"Lunch," Enris supplied willingly, despite knowing full well the Human ate reheated rations from small boxes. He'd eat anything, Aryl thought fondly. She wouldn't. She offered the small packet of baked turrif she'd obtained from Rorn: sweet, crispy, and his latest triumph using Sona's stores. Best of all, the ingredients were ones that wouldn't make the Human, in his words, turn green and die.

Marcus Bowman, Triad First, Analyst, Human, took it with a glad expression that needed no translation. "You've picked a very good time," he assured them again, hunting a clear space to put the treat. "No one needs me. Vogt and Tsessas are *cataloging*."

Fewer of his words were unfamiliar. It wasn't that she'd learned them, Aryl decided as she helped toss clothing from the benchlike chairs that sprouted from the floor. Marcus spoke less about his work each visit, preferring to ask about Sona, about their fields, about her.

Well, not her exactly.

"May I?" There he was again, bioscanner held hopefully to his chest. It had been on the table. "See baby?"

Aryl sighed and sat down, arms wide. "Humans." Her fond, if exasperated, use of the name always made Marcus smile.

Enris leaned forward, eyes intent. Noticing, Marcus

offered him the 'scanner. "You see?" Now there was an Om'ray smile to dazzle the sun.

They conspired against her. Aryl grumbled to herself, but didn't object as first Enris, then Marcus, waved the device over her abdomen and made various approving noises.

Until Marcus frowned distractedly at the 'scanner, and played with its lighted buttons.

Enris frowned, too. "I thought it said Sweetpie was healthy."

"Yes. Oh, yes. Very healthy. Perfect."

"And not a dessert," Aryl muttered.

The Human ducked his head to look at her in that sidelong way he had when he wanted to ask an awkward question. "How much longer?"

"Until she's born?" Aryl shrugged. "Up to her." Mother and unborn were tightly bound. When physically mature, the baby must relax her grip on that link for birth to take place. Not all had the courage or will, leaving it to a Birth Watcher to convince the unformed mind that freedom did not mean loss. Theirs was Seru.

"Human mothers, nine *monthgestation.*" He smiled at her frown. "Sorry. Three seasons, Cersi." A lift of the bioscanner. "This says your baby grows quicker than Human. How long for Om'ray?"

Three seasons? That, she didn't envy his Chosen. "This summer. Why?"

"Oh." He looked unhappy. "I wanted to be here."

Both Om'ray stared at the Human. "You're leaving," Enris said at last.

He couldn't leave, Aryl assured herself, swallowing hard. Her belief in other worlds was a fragile thing. Easier to believe in Marcus slipping into the abyss of the M'hir than taking flight beyond the sky. "I thought the Oud had found your Hoveny ruins. Didn't they?"

"They did," the Human said in such a bleak tone Enris came to sit beside Aryl, sought her hand. "So I must go home. *Stonerim III*. Present *preliminarydata* to *fundingcommittee*. Orders. No one else qualified."

No one else could be trusted. That's what he meant.

She hadn't guarded the thought. Aryl sensed *agreement* from Enris. This Human knew about the Om'ray, what they could do. He knew and cared.

Would anyone else?

She gave him back his question. "How much longer?"

"Soon." His hand floated toward the sky. "*Starship* coming. Special, for me. Cersi to be *priority* site." There was a wry twist to his mouth. She understood. If he hadn't met her, if they hadn't become friends, he'd be celebrating. "A fist, less, then I go. Don't worry. We'll close site, *temporary shutdown,* pack all this. I won't allow work here while I'm *offworld*. No one will disturb you."

"You'll come back." She didn't let it be a question. Beside her, Enris nodded in Human fashion.

"*Bet* on it! Yes," to their uncertain looks. "They can't keep me away. But I don't know how long all this will take." A shake of his head. "My people like to talk."

She'd noticed. To distract them all, Aryl reached for the turrif and broke it into equal pieces. "Then we must celebrate, Marcus." At his blank look, "You'll be with your family again." He'd shown her the images he carried: his Chosen, Kelly, their son Howard and the baby Karina, his sister, Cindy. To be so far from them—she'd had trouble imagining it. Better to think of their joy. "They must be glad—"

"I'll be back as soon as I can," he interrupted gruffly. "Here. I have something for you." Marcus tugged a white crate from one of the upper shelflike beds and dropped it on the table, Enris rescuing his piece of turrif just in time. "You should take this. Keep it safe." The Human broke some kind of sealing material with his thumb. "The Oud have sense of how old things are. These are not old enough—not Hoveny artifacts—so they discard them. Not worth show me." He lost words when excited. "They right. Not Hoveny. But I find. I know what they must be. The *tracecontaminants* confirm it. These—" he bowed at them and threw open the lid, "—are yours."

Enris understood first. "Om'ray devices?!"

"We can't be sure," Aryl cautioned, wary of the *eagerness* bubbling through their link. Before she'd met him, an Oud had brought something to Enris and his father, curious about its function. Enris had discovered that the small cylinder, torn from a larger device, had technology he could affect with his Power. It contained voices, talking in a language he hadn't understood. At the time, it made little sense. Having met the Strangers and learned something of Cersi's past, he'd become convinced Om'ray had once possessed devices to do much that the Strangers could now. "Wait."

But Enris leaned to look in the crate.

Disgust!

He flung himself back, knocking a precariously balanced stack and scattering the Human's belongings to the floor. As Aryl and Marcus stared, Enris collected himself. "Where did you find them?" he demanded in a strained voice.

The Human, anxious, looked at Aryl then Enris. "What wrong? What do wrong?"

"Nothing. You've done nothing. It's—" Enris ran his fingers through his unruly black hair, then gestured apology. "Where?"

Aryl, puzzled, reached for the crate.

Her Chosen barred her way with his arm. "Don't get close."

Annoyed, Aryl tried to see past him.

NO!

"What wrong?" Marcus repeated. He put his hands into the crate and lifted them full of clear wafers, like smooth chips of ice. "These harmless," he insisted. "No *energysignature.*"

"They aren't harmless to the unborn."

"Enris?"

He looked right at her, and Aryl's heart pounded at the foreboding in his eyes.

"The Vyna call these the Glorious Dead." His mouth twisted. "You wanted to know what happened to Sona's Adepts? They're here. Right here. Waiting for their chance to live again."

Interlude

ONCE SURE ARYL WOULD stay back, Enris controlled himself. No need to snatch up the crate, run to the waterfall, and toss its repugnant contents into the Oud's pit. Not yet. Explaining himself to his Chosen—presently regarding him with that hint of challenge—and their friend—who appeared miserable—had to come first.

"I watched a Vyna Chosen press one of these over her unborn child," he told them, doing his best to sound calm. "They claimed it held the personality of a long-dead Adept, complete with all the knowledge and Power from the past. That the Adept would be reborn in that child."

Something he said made Marcus relax. "*Datadisk*," the Human offered, holding one of the wafers between his fingers. It caught the light from the glows; colors slid over the white walls as he moved it back and forth. "Need a *reader*. A device to take information from this, so anyone can see. Harmless."

"Om'ray technology." Enris tapped his own head. "What if the reader is inside? I told you about the device the Oud brought us, that I could touch with my Power. This could be the same."

Aryl frowned. Usually he liked it when she needed to be convinced. Nothing kept him sharper than her quick mind. Not this time. "You must believe me," he told her. "These are dangerous."

"Did you sense it? The Adept replacing the baby?"

He'd done his utmost *not* to sense anything or anyone in that Council Chamber. Between the Vyna and whatever leered through the window of their sunken Cloisters, he'd known his only protection had been his shields. "No. But they believed it. So do I."

"Say I believe it, too."

Aryl made a choked noise as she turned to stare at the Human. "You?"

Marcus almost smiled. "Teleportation?" Point made, he dropped the offending wafer into the crate and sat, waving them to do the same. "Why would they do this?"

Enris hesitated.

"These Om'ray, the Vyna," the Human continued, taking time to choose his words. "All you've told me about them is they want to be left alone. That no other Om'ray should go there. If this is true, why would Vyna want a baby to have self of Sona Adept?"

An excellent question. One that should have occurred to him, not a Human. "I don't know," he admitted, chagrined.

Aryl scowled. On learning about Vyna's treatment of him, she'd wanted to confront their perverse Council to express her opinion; he hoped in words. "I can guess," she ventured grimly. "Adepts have more in common with each other than with anyone else. Secrets. Power. Training. Maybe Vyna's Council values those where they don't value Om'ray lives."

Marcus closed the lid. "What do with these?"

Aryl sat back, her hands folded, leaving the decision to him. The pit or . . . ? Enris stared at the crate. Secrets. Power. Training. Did he really know what the Vyna had done or tried to do? Nothing about them made sense.

What if the wafers were what Marcus first assumed: a record left by Sona, waiting only for the right device to read them?

Was he dismissing the Om'ray technology he'd sought so long?

"The Oud find these with bones, Om'ray bones, in a cave behind the waterfall." Marcus took his piece of turrif, turning it over and over in his hands as if deciding where to bite. "People tried to hide there, to protect what mattered to them. Your people. The Oud threw these away."

Will you? That was the question behind the gentle voice.

"They can't be near Aryl, near anyone who's pregnant," Enris heard himself say. "We can't take that risk."

The Human nodded vigorously, eyes bright. "Safe here, if you want." He wrinkled his nose. "Soon too safe. Extra *security.*" At their puzzled looks, he spread his hands. "Danger, people die. Doesn't matter. No *budget* for *repulsionfields.* No protection, us, from Tikitik or Oud. Problems our fault. My fault." This, low and troubled. He looked up. "If First confirms intact Hoveny find here, with possibility of *activeinstallation,* this small place will suddenly become more important than thousands of other Triad, other Hoveny sites. Understand? Go from lowest potential to *highriskvalue.* Suddenly we rate *orbitalscanners* and *dedicatedpatrolruns.* Protect things, not people. Always our way."

"Not yours," Aryl said firmly. "You care."

Marcus patted her hand, another familiarity they allowed the Human. Husni would be horrified.

They unloaded crates into the storage building.

Marcus was taking samples with him to another place, a place with decision makers who cared about things.

Enris realized he'd broken his turrif crisp into crumbs. "Say you were to trade these old things, these Hoveny artifacts, to someone," he said lightly. "What could you get in return?"

Despite his easy tone, the question brought the Human half out of his seat. "No! I not trade! Never!"

Not what he'd asked. He sensed Aryl's *confusion*. His dear Yena struggled with the concept of a mutually beneficial trade between two Om'ray. In her view, an object's only worth was if someone needed it, and whomever needed it most should have it. Fine in the canopy, where everyone's life depended on the whole.

He'd come from a different Clan and understood immediately. The Human had been offered something for the artifacts and refused. These old things, however useless to Om'ray, had value to the Strangers. Value worth protecting.

Value that was dangerous.

Clang!

"Don't worry," Marcus said quickly, as if relieved by the interruption. "Oud outside. It's how they call me to the door."

CLANG!

"I'm coming!" The Human grumbled something in his own language as he got up and went to the door. He didn't open it, consulting a small screen to one side. "Their Speaker," he announced.

"Good." Aryl rose to join him, her grace making poor Marcus look clumsier than usual. Doubtless, she did the same to him, Enris thought. It didn't matter. All that mattered was that this superb Om'ray had Chosen him.

He would keep her safe.

He didn't look at the crate of Glorious Dead.

"You go," Enris said, stretching as if lazy. "Marcus and I will finish the turrif." *Be careful.*

A flash of *warmth*; a trace of *relief* he pretended not to notice. Her mind grew focused on the task ahead. *All I can do is try.*

CLANG!

Aryl opened the door. "Stop that," she ordered impatiently. "I'm here!"

"Goodgoodgood . . ."

The door closed behind her.

Marcus hesitated, his hand on the control, and looked at Enris. "You sure it's all right to leave her with them? Alone?"

How could he be?

But one thing Enris did know. "We'd be a distraction."

Marcus nodded listless agreement. He waved the turrif. "All for you, Enris. I'm not hungry."

Enris pursed his lips, ignoring the food. He wanted to trust the Human. To an extent he did, though how much of that was Aryl's belief in Marcus, how much his own?

The Human couldn't read Om'ray emotion. He was disturbingly good at reading Om'ray faces. Whatever he saw on Enris' brought Marcus slowly from the door, to stand within reach. "There is no trade," he stated. "Not by me. Not of my work. Not of this." He moved his hand to draw a connection between them. A smile that didn't light his eyes. "But you were right to ask. What we've collected . . . the samples—" a nod at the door, "—I'll take with me. I could trade one item and *retire*—stop working. I could live in comfort for the rest of my life, travel wherever I want, not worry." He sat on the edge of his bed, hands on his knees. "There are people who would *pay*—trade—anything for verified Hoveny artifacts."

While he had no idea what "anything" might mean to the Strangers and their vast Trade Pact, he wouldn't say no to a bioscanner and Marcus' healing technology.

It hadn't been offered. Nothing would be, Enris realized abruptly. "But not with the Oud. Or us."

"No." The Human blew out a breath, then ducked his head to look up at Enris. "Not my idea, Enris. Not a Human one. Before we came, before the Commonwealth reach this far, this space *governed* by species already here. The First. They made rules for those searching for what remained of the Hoveny Concentrix. The search must be by Triads. Triads must be of different species. Discoveries must be shared. Include Humans. Good rules." He grimaced. "One not good rule. On worlds with *vestigial populations*, with people who no longer remember the Hoveny existed, or maybe later *colonists* who never *overlapped*—lived together—any discoveries belong to the Triads. These," he pointed to the crate of wafers, "are yours. The Cloisters are yours. The artifacts are not."

"Do the Oud understand this? That you'll take what they've found?"

"Think so. Hope so. Maybe." Marcus looked older, weary. "Oud don't want the artifacts. They want to know what they are for."

"What is?" the Oud had asked him. Enris would never forget that day. "Why?"

Another sidelong look, something of a smile. "Oud are makers. They want ideas, more and more ideas. What could be made? What would it do? How to make it—they work that out themselves. Busy. Always busy. Like you, that way."

He bristled. "They are not," Enris said through clenched teeth, "like me."

"Not like you," Marcus agreed, too quickly. "Because some Oud want something else. They want to know why they are here." His toe tapped the floor.

"Here. At Sona?"

An appraising look. A second tap. "On Cersi."

It was as if the floor tilted, or the light changed color. Aryl had warned him how mere words could make the Human suddenly strange and terrifying. That if they weren't careful what they asked, Marcus could change their world the same way. He hadn't understood.

Until now.

Enris found himself short of breath. "The Oud," he said finally, firmly, "have always been here. Like the Tiki-tik. Like us."

Marcus considered him silently for a moment, then made the gesture of apology he'd learned. "My mistake."

There was nothing on his face but kindness.

Without touching him, without *reaching* for the Human's feelings—certain to cause Marcus pain—Enris couldn't be sure.

He didn't need to be. After Marcus Bowman was willing to believe what he'd told him of the Vyna and the Glorious Dead, he, Enris di Sarc, had refused to make a similar leap.

Failing a challenge as real and as important as any he'd faced.

And the Human pitied him.

He pushed the crate on the table closer to Marcus. "Best these stay here. For now." And stood.

Marcus rose too. "Enris—"

"Don't—" he began and stopped, ashamed, unsure why.

"I must. Listen to me. I should be more careful what I say. What I ask. I know better. Did Aryl tell you, she ran from me? Almost died because of my foolish words? Because I forget you are not Human."

Enris clapped Marcus on one shoulder, in Human-fashion. "A mistake we'd never make, my friend."

I'm done. Finished your snack?

"Aryl," Marcus announced. At Enris' startled look, "Your face says so."

Perceptive in the oddest ways. "Aryl," he confirmed, then took both of the Human's shoulders in a gentle grip. "Listen to me, Marcus. Don't be more careful. Tell us what we should know." He shook his head ruefully. "But maybe not so much at once."

"I understand." But as Enris turned to leave, Marcus held his wrist, palm against bare skin. An invitation. Lowering his shields just enough, the Om'ray sensed *goodwill* and *determination*. "Something you must do. Before I leave Cersi. Wait. Wait." Muttering to himself, the Human rushed away to dig through the disorganized mass of objects on a counter. It was a wonder, Enris thought with amusement, any of the devices continued to work.

"Wait! Must take these. Should have done before." More muttering.

Enris?

Our Human's being his confusing self.

He's not the only one. But she didn't *feel* concerned.

Marcus emerged triumphant, clutching what looked like a pair of pink eggs attached by a metal thread. "Here!" He pressed the eggs over his eyes, the thread behind his head, then pulled the device off and thrust it at Enris. "*Sleepteach.* You learn *Comspeak.* Both? Maybe no," he appeared to be arguing with himself. "Not Aryl. Wait for baby. You. You can learn now." When Enris didn't take them, unsure, the Human shook the little eggs, making them click together. "Everyone in the Trade Pact uses same words. Use this, you will understand anyone. Everyone." A fleeting frown. "If it works for Om'ray. Should. Won't harm."

Enris? A tinge of worry. She was picking up his doubt. *What's going on?*

It's complicated.

Say no. To whatever it is.

He couldn't do that. Not if he grasped what Marcus offered. "Will I still understand real words—Om'ray words?"

"Yes yes yes. Sleepteach adds information to the memory, not take any away. You won't notice any change. But if you hear Comspeak words," Marcus nodded vigorously, "you will hear what they mean. You will be able to answer, using those words. With my *innerworldaccent,*" he added confusingly. "Sorry. Don't know how to *reprogram.* You'll sound like someone from Stonerim III. That's not a bad thing. Proper *vowels.*"

Enris found he had taken the device. It was warm from Marcus' hands. There were no controls or markings. He made to put it on his head.

"Not yet. Lie down, ready for sleep. Put over eyes, then say these words: *activate . . . standard . . . teach . . . mode.* You say them."

" 'Activate standard teach mode.' " The little eggs went from pink to white.

"To stop, take it off, or say *end . . . session.*"

" 'End session.' " Pink again. Enris wanted to try the words again, to see the colors change, but didn't. The Human was used to such effects. He didn't want to seem like a child caught up by novelty.

He could do it later anyway.

"Thank you, Marcus."

Enris? Calm, but this time with the faintest touch of *confusion*. So much for the water. If Aryl couldn't convince the Oud, no one could. Shaking his head to himself, he headed for the door.

"Come again to visit." The Human sounded almost wistful. "Before I go."

Enris glanced over his shoulder. "We'll try, Marcus. Hard to spare anyone right now, with water so . . ." he let his voice trail away, eyes searching the room, jammed with devices and technology and crates. And dirty clothes. "You know our problem. You watch us, don't you? From above."

The Human's cheeks turned pink. "*Surveillancemandatory.* Not my choice."

"We understand. But—" An idea took hold. An idea worthy of Aryl di Sarc, if it worked. "Can you see us outside in truenight?"

Marcus hesitated, then shrugged. "Yes."

Enris smiled broadly. "I need a favor, my friend. A favor that could let us visit you as often as you want until you go."

Marcus Bowman raised one eyebrow. "What?"

"Make sure no one watches Sona this truenight. Can you do it? No vids, no recordings. No eyes. Of any kind," Enris added hastily, thinking of the Strangers who looked nothing like Human or Om'ray. "Just for this truenight. That's all."

"That's all. Interrupt surveillance. Leave a hole in the record." A corner of Marcus' lips twitched upward. "You don't ask what's easy, do you?"

"We didn't ask you to watch us," Enris countered.

"Good point." The Human nodded to himself. "All

right. I can give you privacy for one night. But don't wander through the site after dark. The security fields and autodefense will still be on. Those need a pair of *idents* to be deactivated and I don't want to explain that to Vogt or Tsessas."

"No need. Privacy for Sona, until dawn. Thank you."

"Do I want to know why?"

"If it works, you'll find out tomorrow." Enris smiled warmly. "You're a good friend, Marcus. A good friend."

The Human's fond yet skeptical expression at this reminded him of Jorg. His father had had the same look whenever Enris tried to blame Kiric for the latest abuse of the family kitchen. Their mother, Ridersel, would hide a smile. They'd known him so well.

They were dead now. Because of the Oud.

"Enris?"

"Nothing." He restored his smile. "Time to see what's happening outside. Good-bye and thank you, Marcus."

First, Enris pushed his wonderful new idea as far down in his consciousness as he could. After all, if it worked, he wanted his Chosen surprised.

If it didn't, the fewer who knew the better.

Chapter 3

TO SPEAK INTELLIGIBLE WORDS, an Oud had to rear and expose its limbs. There were many, most with hooks or claws, but a clustered few worked together—somehow—to produce sound.

Making sense of those words, Aryl thought impatiently, was the hard part. The Oud Speaker, it turned out, believed the Om'ray had received exactly what they'd been promised.

"No, we haven't," she told it again. "The Oud still get more. You haven't sent enough to Sona. You promised we'd get most of the river!"

"Did! YESYESYESYES!" It reared higher, rocking back and forth to emphasize its point. Having descended from its vehicle—she assumed to knock on the Human's door—the rocking made it sink slightly into the ground. Rather, mud. Wherever Oud treads hadn't torn up the dirt, small plants sprouted, a single leaf curled just so. Nekis, most likely. The waterfall's spray reached this far with the right breeze. Water was everything, Aryl thought with longing. She even missed the rains that drove Yena under roofs for days. "Sona enough."

"No." She tried to think of a more mature response. "No. Not enough!"

"Sent share. Sent enough. YESYESYES. Oud good. Sona waste."

" 'Waste ...!' " Aryl bit her lip, holding back a satisfying but likely useless retort. The accusation made no sense. How could they be more careful with the trickle that arrived at Sona? They took turns filling buckets for the plants and spared little for themselves. She couldn't remember her last proper bath. If the rest of her Clan hadn't been suffering, too, she'd have leaped into the Human's marvelous fresher device. With Enris.

A tendril of hair tickled her ear, expressing its opinion.

Aryl poked it into the net. "We don't waste a drop," she told the Oud. "We must have more than you send us!"

It reared and fell silent. A few lower limbs fidgeted. Throughout the clearing, other Oud stopped moving, as if she'd said something remarkable. Well, not all. One vehicle ran into the carts towed by another, both drivers unconcerned by the collision. But otherwise, she felt their attention. Eyes or not.

What had she said?

" 'More than,' " the Speaker said at last. "Why?"

"To grow food." Oud lived with Tuana, who'd been farmers. The Grona, also neighbors to Oud, planted fields. The concept couldn't be new to this one, Aryl thought, exasperated.

"Not fill courseways."

Courseways. That was what the Tikitik called the shallow stone-lined ditches that crossed the valley floor. The only value they had, so far as Sona's Om'ray could tell, was to deter rock hunters, who avoided them.

Because in the past they had filled with water.

Water the Oud clearly didn't want them to have. Was this why it had gone back on its promise, that Sona would have the greater share? Had it realized—or been told by other Oud—what might happen?

What the connection might be—if there was one—she had no idea. Aryl drew herself up and lifted her pendant. "As Speaker for Sona, I promise we won't fill the courseways if you return more water to the river."

"Not fill if not water more than." The creature managed to sound smug.

The not-*real* were different, not stupid. She usually didn't forget, having Marcus as an example.

She winced inwardly. So much for her negotiation skills. "We'll starve!" An exaggeration, given the stores at Sona, but the Oud might not be aware of those. "I thought you wanted us here."

"Food enough. Water enough. Sona waste." The cluster of limbs it used for speech folded into a tight knot.

No mistaking the end of a conversation.

I'm done, she sent to her Chosen, keeping her disappointment to herself. They could share the details on the walk home. A slow walk, she decided, in no hurry to explain her failure to Haxel. *Finished your snack?*

But before she could turn back to the Human's shelter, the Oud Speaker lowered itself and approached her, slowly. Almost in reach, it hurriedly backed away, a flurry of small stones and mud hitting her legs. Before Aryl could protest, it did the same again: a slow approach, then hasty retreat, but not the full distance. This continued until it came to rest where she could have stretched out her hand to touch it—not that she would. She watched it rear, slowly, as if to assure her of its good intentions.

No, she realized suddenly. Despite its swollen bulk shading her from the sun, it was wary of her.

This was different.

The new Humans, or Human-shaped Strangers, gave up any pretense of ignoring what was happening and leaned in the doorway of the storage building to watch.

Enris?

Our Human's being his confusing self.

He's not the only one. She trusted Enris to deal with Marcus—or was it the other way around? Sometimes, Aryl thought distractedly, she wasn't sure which of them she could trust to be sensible.

From this proximity, she had a too-good view of the Speaker's underside. The flesh was glossy and pale, flushed in places with blue. The black limbs, hard and jointed like a biter's, were in rows. Most were folded, like rows of neatly aligned utensils, though a few jutted at odd angles as if forgotten. Or broken. This close, it smelled of dust and the oil they used on their vehicles.

And decay.

Whirr/clicks settled to the ground around it—and her. She eyed them uneasily. The small black things were too like biters to be trusted, though none had shown an interest in Om'ray flesh. Yet. They clung outside tunnel entrances until an Oud came out, followed that particular Oud in an annoyingly noisy cloud, and would wait like this, occasionally milling around, unless another Oud moved nearby. Then they'd desert the first in a flurry of whirrs and clicks. Not that any of the other Oud in the clearing were moving.

She was stuck with them.

Worry that wasn't hers.

Enris?

It's complicated.

And he was fascinated. That couldn't be good. Aryl glared at the Oud, as if it were to blame for her Chosen's curiosity and the Human's unlimited ability to provoke it. *Say no. To whatever it is.*

He immediately tightened his shields, letting her feel only a vague *reassurance.*

As if that helped.

Then she forgot all about Enris and the dangerous allure of Human technology as the Oud Speaker brought together two limbs and made a sound that was no sound at all.

Because she *heard* it in the M'hir.

It rang along her nerves and through her mind, like a distant bell. Once only. Larger than the world, smaller than a breath. Undeniable.

Aryl wasn't sure what startled her more: that this

Oud could make a *sound* in the M'hir, or that it did so as if expecting her to *hear* it.

Good thing her Chosen was distracted.

"Oud tunnel. Under. Safe is. Goodgood," the Oud Speaker said next, word-making limbs working quickly, hunched as if to keep those words private or in a bizarre—and unsuccessful—attempt to whisper. "Sona Om'ray tunnel. All ways. Safe is. Secret. GoodgoodgoodGOOD."

The Oud Speaker had been present for one 'port: when she'd been forced to save herself and Marcus from being buried alive during the Oud attack on the Tikitik. When the Oud had said nothing on the matter, she'd assumed they'd been too busy committing murder to notice how she and the Human survived.

If they had proper eyes . . . but who knew what they could or couldn't sense?

Who knew what they thought?

"Good we talk. GoodgoodgoodGOOD!" The Oud Speaker swayed toward her as if about to topple. Aryl flinched but stood her ground. "Careful. CareCareCare." Again the unheard *bell*. "Tikitik. Count. Follow. Measure."

Not attention she wanted. "Tikitik here?" She tried not to look obvious as she searched the encircling edge of the grove for their lean shapes. The creatures were adept at skulking, their skin able to match their surroundings, but Haxel's scouts knew what to look for— surely trespassers would have been noticed.

"Nonononono. Balance. Agreement."

Something she'd find comforting if she didn't know exactly what "Balance" meant to both Oud and Tikitik. Bad enough this Oud appeared able to comprehend their movement through the M'hir. At least it didn't seem upset. Aryl was quite sure the reaction of the Tikitik would not be as calm. "How—?" She stopped.

Even the question felt dangerous.

The folded limbs opened along one side, moving with blinding speed in sequence to convey something from the lowermost part of its body. Aryl frowned. Oud had pouches of some kind down there. She'd yet to have a gift from one that didn't come with trouble attached. "I don't want—" She closed her mouth.

A Speaker's Pendant came to rest, dangled from an upper limb. It was attached to a scrap of filthy fabric patterned black and white in the fashion of its former bearer, the Tikitik Speaker killed before her eyes by the Oud. The gruesome relic wasn't offered to her. Instead the Oud shook it vigorously. "Count." Another shake. "Follow." Again. "Measure." Then it passed the pendant to the opposite row of limbs. Each set went into opposing motion; when they stopped, the pendant had been replaced by something else.

A token.

What did it mean? Tuana's Oud Speaker had given Enris his first; another Oud had taken it. Could this be the same one? Not that they were rare. A token was given to each Om'ray unChosen who took Passage, granting the right to trespass through the lands of Tikitik and Oud. The Yena exiles had had tokens when they arrived at Grona; only Enris had kept his, intending all along to seek Vyna. He'd brought it back with him, along with a handful collected from one of Vyna's traps, to prove no unChosen should go there again.

Enris? she sent, this time sharing her *confusion.*

"Count. Follow. Measure."

All of Cersi's races had the pendants. Only Om'ray wore tokens. If she assumed she understood the Oud— which was like stepping on an untried frond over the Lay—then it was claiming the Tikitik somehow used both pendant and token to keep track of . . . what?

Count. That was easy. One Speaker per Clan, one Speaker per neighbor. Eight Om'ray Clans, seven with neighbors, meant no less than fifteen pendants. Tokens?

Every Clan knew how many it sent out, how many arrived. Easy to believe the Tikitik, being inclined to spy on others, kept track of such movements between Clans.

Follow. A Tikitik had followed Enris to Vyna; it had found him afterward. So it could be done. But how could a token help?

As for "measure." That made even less sense. Tokens and pendants were metal ornaments, not devices like the geoscanner presently riding her hip in a hidden pocket. And what would Tikitik measure if they could?

Profoundly annoyed, Aryl shook her head. "You're making no sense at all."

"YESYESYES." As if the Oud were made desperate by her inability to understand. "Tikitik do. All life. Tikitik count. All life. Tikitik follow. All life. Tikitik measure. All."

Biters, too? The silliness of it restored her confidence. The creature might be confused—and confusing—but she made the gesture of gratitude. It was trying, in its way, to convey a warning. "That should keep them too busy to be trouble," she suggested.

"Trouble. Tikitik trouble. Tikitik other. Not Makers! Notnotnot!! Not First. Not Only. Tikitik Least Is!" The words made no sense, but the Oud flung itself backward in a paroxysm of emotion, limbs writhing. Somehow its cloak remained attached to its back. Whirr/clicks threw themselves into the air and hovered, like a cloud of interested bystanders.

Aryl, having jumped in the other direction, gazed worriedly at the creature.

"I'm going to guess this means no more water." Her Chosen came to stand beside her. If amused by the spectacle of the Oud Speaker flat on its back, Enris kept it to himself.

"It claims we have enough now, that we're wasting it." Aryl let him sense some of her *frustration*. "I don't see how."

They'd kept their voices quiet, though the sound

didn't appear to bother the Oud Speaker. However the creature, finished whatever display it required, rolled back to its feet and reared, stones and dirt sliding off its cloak, whirr/clicks settling to the ground. "Waste," it agreed, as if the other matter—of Om'ray "tunnels" and Tikitik and care—had been forgotten.

Then it made the *sound* again, to prove her wrong.

"What was—" Enris gripped her arm, stared at the Oud. "Is it a Torment?"

"No Power I. Speaker." The Oud lowered itself slightly. A conciliatory posture, Aryl decided. Hoped. "Balance good. Peace good. Om'ray, Oud. Best is. Us. Best is. Tikitik. NononoNO. Water more than?"

It couldn't mean what she feared, could it? Their two races, somehow working against the third . . . *Enris?*

And you worry we'll *break the Agreement?*

He was right. The mug would shatter on the floor. The world would end. Taisal had warned there'd be no safety for Om'ray if the Oud and Tikitik weren't at peace. None for the life inside her.

"Sona abides by the Agreement," Aryl said calmly, though inside she trembled. Rage or terror? They felt the same. They were the same. "You will abide by the Agreement, you will keep the peace of Cersi, or I will tell the Strangers to leave, now. You will never know about your past."

The Oud sank lower and lower until it was flat against the ground.

She took a shaky breath. "Good."

Good guess. Enris loosened his grip on her arm, turned it into a brief caress. *Best we don't have to test that.*

He was right, of course. Now that Hoveny artifacts had been found, not even Marcus could stop his people from coming. *He could stop them cooperating with the Oud. Say they were dangerous. He'd do it for us.*

And it wouldn't be a lie.

"I—"

Every Oud in the clearing suddenly reared and turned to face in the direction of Sona. The Speaker rocked back and forth, uttering that *sound,* over and over. The M'hir surged closer, pulled at her conscious mind.

"Stop—" she pleaded. The *sound* ended; the Oud continued to sway back and forth. "Why did you do that?"

"Sona Om'ray less than."

Enris stiffened. "Who!?"

She *reached,* uncaring about Torments or the M'hir. *Reached* and was trapped by waves of *PAIN* and *NEED* and . . .

ARYL! Enris had her, held her body and mind. *Stay with me. Stay. Don't follow . . . don't follow . . .*

Eyes shut, she buried her face into his chest and closed her mind until all she could feel was her place in the world and his presence, until she no longer heard the echo of *DESPAIR* through the M'hir.

Until she knew it was over.

Everything became too quiet.

"Someone's gone into the M'hir. Gone in and not— not come out." She'd never heard his voice break before. "Who?"

The quiet trapped the name, protected her for a heartbeat, let her breathe. Once. Again.

Then, she knew.

Ael d'sud Sarc.

Her uncle, with his bright eyes and clever wit. Fostered with Haxel's family. Connected to everyone . . .

Aryl clung to Enris with all her strength; his arms were like bands of metal, keeping her safe, keeping them together. They had to be; there was no other Choice. She didn't care if Oud or Human watched or wondered. They were not-*real*. They could never understand, never experience the full implication of being Joined, one mind forever linked to another.

Only Om'ray knew their fate, should their Chosen die.

Ael was gone.

And Myris, his Chosen, was Lost.

The First Scout burst into the Meeting Hall. "What happened?" The scar was drawn stark and white against her reddened skin. Aryl wouldn't have been surprised to see a knife in her hand.

For what good it would do.

The others looked up, weary with grief, unsettled by Haxel's barely contained *fury*. No one spoke. Morla looked to Aryl.

"There's no way to know," Aryl said gently. Beside her, on a bench covered with blankets, lay her aunt. Her hair hung limp as a child's. Her eyes were closed. She might have been alive.

She was not.

Her mind had followed Ael's. According to Oran, assigned the task of making sure, not enough had been left to keep her body breathing.

Aryl wasn't sorry to be grateful.

Three long strides brought Haxel looming over her. "There must be. Ael doesn't—didn't—he was strong. Capable. We have to know what happened!"

Such *pain*. Aryl felt it, shared it, as she did from all around. It bound them together, Sona to Sona, as nothing else could have done. She wasn't Myris, to ease another's suffering, to turn grief into acceptance. But she understood Haxel's desperation. Beyond the grief of losing her foster brother, training and instinct made the First Scout need to identify the threat, find a way to counter or avoid it.

"We can't," Aryl said, lifting her gaze to Haxel's. "I named the Dark the M'hir because it's like that wind. It can tear the best climber from a branch, snap the strongest rastis, without warning. When we ride it, we take that risk."

"You think Ael was careless." Clear threat.

"How?" From Enris, leaning against the wall nearby. His arms were folded, his face in shadow. "The M'hir is new to all of us. We can only explore it by trying. We've learned a shared memory is enough for a 'port. But can I 'port to another Om'ray? Can I follow a trail through the M'hir? Someone has to try first. Some ideas will work. Some won't."

"And some will kill."

"And some will kill."

"No. No more 'firsts.' " Haxel looked at them all in turn, her face as grim and set as Aryl had ever seen. "Do you understand me? There's only us. We were barely keeping up with watering before losing these—these two. If we lose anyone else, we could all die."

Galen rose to his feet, equally grim. "I agree we should use caution. But make no mistake, Haxel, this ability we have will save more lives than it risks. Let the Oud reshape the ground. Sona will 'port to safety. Let our crops fail. We'll 'port to another Clan and trade for food. This is the most important Talent ever discovered by Om'ray and we must never fear to use it."

Agreement. Emphatic from some. Aryl hoped Haxel missed the faint *glee* coming from their unChosen. Though to be callous, those were best suited to trying "firsts."

UnChosen died alone.

"Doubt causes falls." Her voice sharpened. "So does carelessness. I suggest we leave the risks to our daring unChosen—" so she had sensed them. Haxel's eyes flicked to the body. "Why is this still here?"

She was right to ask. Om'ray only *felt* the presence of the living. The body on the bench was no longer Om'ray, but simply a problem.

"There's no swamp." Husni clenched her gnarled hands in distress. "There's no proper water below." Her Chosen, Cetto d'sud Teerac, tried to soothe her, but she'd have none of it. "We have traditions for good reason," she snapped. "The husk must be removed from the village."

"We could bury it in the ground," Oswa offered carefully. "It's the Grona way."

From too few voices to too many. "No!" "Don't disturb the Oud!" "It's dangerous!" The objections came from Tuana and Yena both.

Oswa sank back and hugged Yao. Aryl caught her eye and gestured gratitude. It wasn't the Grona's fault others had had worse experiences with the Oud.

Before anyone suggested feeding what remained of Myris to the rock hunters, which would entail carrying the sad husk a day's journey across the exposed valley, she sent a quick plea. *Enris.*

And what was left of Myris di Sarc disappeared. The blanket sighed to the bench and lay empty.

It was done.

In the following hush, Juo di Vendan's ragged gasp drew everyone's attention.

"The baby!" Gijs shouted, leaping to his feet to hover anxiously over his Chosen who, for her part, looked more embarrassed by the attention than in distress.

Seru was already on the move. The room began to hum and sizzle with words spoken and not, everyone's attention shifting from death to life.

It was their way.

Aryl pressed her hand to the blanket beside her. Still warm. She and Enris had run into the nekis grove, out of sight—that much sense—before 'porting here. Her legs were coated in flecks of drying mud from the Oud. She could, if she wasn't careful, *hear* the dreadful sound it had made in the M'hir. How could the creature know of Ael's loss before they did?

Despite that warning, they hadn't been in time. The breath had fled Myris' lips with her Chosen's name; she'd fallen into Rorn's arms, already gone. It had been that quick. It often was.

What was she to do without Myris and Ael?

Comfort waiting; *strength* if she needed it. No words.

They should never have been exiled. Aryl felt a tear trace her cheek, curl along her jaw. Her mother had claimed Yena's Adepts dreamed who should go, choosing those who could survive together. Myris and Ael had no new Talents, no unusual strength or Power. Only compassion and courage.

Is Yena safer?

"No." The room seethed with emotion. Easier to form words aloud. "No, it's not."

Her mother had sent them. Because of a dream.

Adepts dreamed to a purpose. A purpose set by their Cloisters' Keeper.

"I'll be back."

ARYL . . . his protest vanished with her surroundings.

The M'hir taunted, sang of death and insanity, tried to confuse. These were her reactions to the roiling *darkness*, not the truth. Not that the truth belonged here. Nothing *real* did. Aryl concentrated on *where* she should be . . .

. . . and was.

The Meeting Hall had been humid with breath, warmed with bodies and cookstoves, fragrant with the remains of the morning meal. Crowded with the living and the dead.

This was no place as peaceful or safe. Overhead, green metal had been woven into a mesh tight enough to keep out the rain. She stood on metal slats, raised the height of a grown rastis above the black water of the Lay. To either side, the mesh widened to allow the hot, heavy air of the canopy to caress her, thick with the scent of flower, fruit, and rot. There was no sky, no ground, no rock. Only that which struggled to live, and that which failed and died.

Home. This would always be home.

Mother.

Driven through the M'hir, the summons couldn't be overheard or ignored. How long Taisal di Sarc would let her daughter wait on Yena's bridge—that was a question.

Biters arrived first. The mountain spring encouraged bare arms and hands during the heat of day, bare legs made it easier when filling buckets. Aryl gritted her teeth, accepting the bites as deserved. Not that Enris would let her forget it. Despite the distance between them, their link was as strong as ever. He kept his shields in place. Let her have this.

Aryl scratched the rising welts on her forearm. Maybe they wouldn't all swell.

Yena's Cloisters rose on its own massive stalk. The bridge met the paired doors to its lowermost platform, the level buried at Sona by the Oud. Aryl faced them, not seeing the lovely colors coaxed from the metal, or their size.

If she lowered her shields and *reached,* she'd know who was on the other side. The solitary presence at her back would be the scout assigned to the bridge platform. He wouldn't have *sensed* her arrival, so close to the rest of Yena. Few Om'ray had her ability to sense exact numbers within the glow of their kind.

That glow was potent, alluring. Almost two hundred, mere steps away. It made Sona's few more precious.

Mother.

Here.

The doors turned open, spilling light, creating new shadows. A slender figure in a hooded brown robe stepped through. Another pulled the doors closed again.

The locks reset.

She had their secret. These would open to her knowledge, to her name in the records of this Cloisters—unless they'd stripped it.

Not that she'd be welcome.

The figure stopped and threw back her hood, revealing a netted mass of black hair and a pale face as closed as the doors. Taisal di Sarc. For the first time, Aryl could see the resemblance between sisters. The wide-set eyes, the high forehead, the graceful line of throat were the same. The differences had always mattered more. Myris would have been incapable of this intimidating glare. Her Power would never have *tested* Aryl's shields like this.

"Mother."

"Come to explain yourself?"

"Explain myself?" Hard to frown with dignity while biters feasted on her ears, but Aryl did her best. "It's your turn for that. I know Yena's Cloisters has a Keeper; someone who controls the dreams of your Adepts. Why dream to exile us? Don't tell me it was to protect Yena from the Tikitik. There had to be an Om'ray purpose. Why?"

The very essence of dignity, Taisal lifted an eyebrow. "While I, Daughter, want to know why Yena's Adepts now dream of Sona."

Her heart thudded in her chest; could her mother hear it?

Oran.

It had to be. She'd succeeded after all, but told no one. Instead of controlling Sona's Cloisters to dream of what might help her own Clan, somehow she was reaching out to others. But why? Aryl swallowed bile. "What do you dream?"

Distaste. "Walking on dirt. Cold. Darkness. Oud." Taisal's shields tightened until she seemed to disappear. "And what you can do. All of you."

Not the time to admit "all" was an exaggeration. Not the time to vent her fury at Oran di Caraat or try to comprehend what the Adept might have hoped to accomplish.

"It wasn't our doing. But—"

Her mother *knew*. Everything.

Relief made Aryl shake. She found words spilling out, urgent, important. "It means safety for everyone. Once every Om'ray can 'port, unChosen won't have to risk Passage. We can travel wherever we want as easily as breathing. Share with each other. Once the other races accept it—"

"They won't. They can't."

"The Oud have—"

"Some Oud—" *disgust,* "—Sona's Oud. You're a Speaker, Aryl. You of all Sona should realize just because the not-*real* look alike doesn't make them the same. And what of the Tikitik? What of the Strangers? Will they let Om'ray become independent? Let us ascend to a power of our own? Shatter the Agreement?" Every word calm, measured. Aryl could hardly breathe. "Even if they do, for reasons of their own—" Taisal paused. Her hand grasped air and threw it aside. "Om'ray won't."

"Sona—"

"One Clan. What of the rest? What of those Om'ray who can't do this—this 'porting? What of those who will not? Who rightly fear the Dark. Would you force them? Is that why you've made us dream?"

"I didn't—" To Aryl's dismay, her voice came out sullen, like a child's. She did her best to modify it. "It doesn't have to be that way. Those who can't—others can do it for them. Those who won't—" she didn't finish.

Taisal did it for her. "—will if they must? Do you hear yourself? You would split our kind in two. Not Yena." The words echoed along the bridge. "We will protect ourselves. Sian spent much of his life searching for ways to protect Om'ray from the *Dark*. Now he works to help us resist the urge to step into it, awake or asleep. We will keep even those who might be tempted safe from your—" her lips twisted, "—M'hir."

Sian d'sud Vendan. Her mother's heart-kin, before they'd Chosen otherwise. He'd come to the Sarc home regardless, stay till firstlight with Taisal debating this or that obscure detail about the Power and its use. She should have listened, Aryl thought desperately. Here was expertise, where she least expected it. Someone to guide their exploration of the M'hir. "We could use his help," she began, unconsciously fingering her Speaker's Pendant.

"To stop this?" Taisal stepped closer, her eyes alight. "Is that what you're saying—is that the reason for the dreams? That Sona calls out for help, before it's too late? Or is it already too late?" She lifted her hand to trace the curve of Aryl's cheek in the air, then let it fall to her side. The relief in her face became something else. *Dread.* "Who?"

"Ael."

Myris . . . ? They'd worked together to save her once; Taisal had helped pull her sister's mind from the M'hir . . .

GRIEF howled through it now. It tore at them both—or did they feed it, mind-to-mind, for an endless moment, until it united them . . . the *who-I-am* of mother and daughter blurred together . . .

An echo. Enris, carefully distant. Carefully present.

Aryl *reached* for their link, used it and his strength to pull away from her mother. But not completely. She looked at Taisal, blinked tears to see her more clearly, and finally saw the truth.

Taisal di Sarc, who'd held to life and sanity when her Chosen died, hadn't escaped the M'hir at all. She existed *there*. Only a constant outpouring of Power kept her here, too, and whole. It wove a net of connections that held Taisal's mind together, connections on a level Aryl had never sensed before. She doubted her mother even knew. But they were there, binding Taisal to Aryl, Taisal to every Yena. More tenuous, still strong, Taisal to the exiles.

Immense Power, so much that the small fragment free of the struggle was enough to make Taisal an Adept. But if she weakened, if she gave up, she would be Lost.

And along came her daughter, romping through the M'hir like a child swinging on vines, playing with death. Causing it. A son, now a sister. Ripping Yena apart. Now, risking it again.

Was there any way she hadn't failed her mother?

"Forgive me."

Hush, child.

Sian knew, Aryl realized suddenly. He must. His study of the M'hir was no idle curiosity; he wanted to help Taisal. Were all Yena's Adepts involved? Had her daughter's exile been forced on Taisal for her own protection?

Was it her fault, as she'd believed?

They held no shields against one another; thoughts mingled. Aryl was surrounded by *compassion* and a hint of *irony.* "It's not about us, Daughter," Taisal said gently. "Other than Sian, it never was. It's about saving the Chosen. Don't you see? The rest think if they understand me, they'll be able to prevent others from being Lost. Myris—" a flare of *heartrending sorrow,* "— might have saved herself, if she'd been able to break her Joining to Ael in time."

NEVER!!! Throwing up her shields, Aryl clung to Enris with all her strength, rejected any thought of life without their bond. Without him.

Here, he sent, confused and alarmed. *I'll always be here.*

Taisal's smile was the saddest thing Aryl had ever seen. "Which is what I've told them—so very many times. They're fools. Who would want to be as I am?"

Aryl took a shuddering breath, then another, easier one. The instinct to protect their Joining had her heart hammering in her chest, but she fought to overcome it. This was her mother. The words weren't a threat. The idea—her breath caught, but she forced herself to continue—was important. To make a second Choice: follow a Chosen to his or her fate, or decide to survive. The loss it would spare a Clan . . .

Could she?

Her hands pressed over the life within her. For that life, Aryl realized with an inner shock, she might. She gestured a profound apology. "I'll stop the dreams. Whatever happens to Sona, Yena shouldn't be forced to face the same decisions—or risks."

Taisal's eyes glittered. "Do that, Speaker, and we will share whatever we know to help you protect yourselves."

"Why were we exiled?" Aryl said softly. "Will you share that?"

A shadow seemed to cross Taisal's face. "We don't know," she admitted at last. "A Keeper doesn't control the dreaming, Aryl. Only makes it possible. Tikva could say only that the dreams came from the Cloisters itself. Ours . . . were terrible. Yena ended. The Cloisters, empty. You and the exiles survived, we could see that, but we had no way to know which was cause, which effect. We were being warned, that was all. Was it something to do with the Agreement? Perhaps. About the Dark—the M'hir? That's what I believe. Still believe. You must stay out of it." *Fear.* "If not for yourself, then for her." Her hands reached, as if to gather Aryl close.

Safer to 'port back to Sona than risk climbing the canopy. Safer to stay distant, than risk the touch of an Adept. Aryl kept those hard thoughts private. This caring between them, this honesty, was an untried rope. *I'll be careful, Mother,* she sent instead, and concentrated.

Yena disappeared . . .

. . . and she was gathered close by someone else, who seemed determined to prevent her taking a full breath.

Which was fine by her.

Oran.

Aryl had shared her memory of Taisal with Enris as he'd cradled her in his lap. Now, she felt the rumble of his voice through his chest. "That, we do together."

She stiffened. "I made her Keeper."

He laughed gently. "Oh, I'm sure she'd have found her way around Hoyon somehow. But it's not our Adept who troubles me, Sweetling. It's what she can do. Dreaming between Clans? Either it's a new Talent, or the Adepts of Cersi have more in common than their attitude."

Not a comforting thought. Aryl sighed. "Let me deal with one problem at a time. Sona's—"

"Aryl. Are you in there?" Seru's voice.

"That'll teach you," Enris whispered in her ear.

Aryl squirmed with sudden guilt. *We should be hauling water.*

We will. His fingers found a ticklish spot and she stifled her giggle against his warm skin. *That's better.*

Better than the grief and melancholy that had overwhelmed her when she'd returned. There still, but deeper, freeing her thoughts. *What about the M'hir?* she sent.

"Enris—I saw you come in here." An impatient creak as Seru pushed at their closed door.

The M'hir is a tool like any other, he replied. *We'll learn to use it safely. We must. It's too important to abandon. You know that.*

"Is Aryl with you? I need her." Another, firmer creak.

She let him feel her *doubt.* As she rose from his lap her hair lingered on his shoulder, drew soft whorls along his neck. Their eyes met. Out loud, she said, "I'm coming, Seru." Beneath,

What I know is our ignorance. What's important is our children never suffer because of what we do.

Seru took her arm the moment Aryl stepped outside, waves of *worry* and *consternation* pouring through the physical contact. "Over here," she said urgently, not apologizing for the familiarity. In fact, she used her grip

to tug Aryl away from the building, in the direction that led . . . well, Aryl thought, puzzled, it led nowhere. They didn't travel down the valley anymore.

"What's wrong?"

Seru let go, but kept walking at a brisk pace. "A little farther." She took Aryl to where the paving stones of the road lay heaved and tossed—where the Oud had set up barriers to trap any Sona trying to flee—then stopped to sit on one of the larger stones. Her hair squirmed under its net. "It's about the baby. She's coming too soon."

This, on top of Taisal's warning, brought Aryl to sit beside her cousin. "Mine?" she asked anxiously.

"No." Green eyes widened. "Why would you think so?"

Never rush Seru, especially when she was agitated, as now. "Forgive me, Cousin," Aryl said, fighting for patience. "What did you come to tell me? And why here?"

"Here is where I can't *hear* the baby."

"Which baby?" She'd been gone less than a tenth. Aryl vaguely remembered Juo's gasp in the meeting hall, but birthing couldn't be that fast. Could it? "Juo's?"

"Of course, Juo's. The baby's impatient. It's the wrong time."

"Are you sure?"

Seru shrugged. "It doesn't matter what I believe— when I tried to convince her to relax and wait, that's when I discovered something." She drew up her knees and looked miserable. "The baby won't listen to me!"

"Are you doing it right?" Whatever "it" was. Aryl had to admit she knew almost nothing about Seru's special Talent. Oh, everyone knew Om'ray births often required a Birth Watcher to convince the baby to relinquish its tight hold on its mother. Otherwise—there was no otherwise. The baby had to be willing to be born. Or, apparently, not to be born. "It's your first time—"

This drew a withering look. "I've helped my mother since I was four, Aryl di Sarc. You know that. This is . . . Juo's baby is different."

"Different?" Did being pregnant herself explain why the word twisted inside her? "Is she all right?"

"Healthy, yes. But the baby—Aryl, she's only aware of her mother. She can't sense other Om'ray. She can't believe me. What do I say to such a child? How do I tell her she won't be all alone when she leaves her mother, when she always will be?"

Another one?

Aryl shivered, though the slanting sun was warm on her skin. "We need Oswa," she told Seru.

Oswa di Gethen, who'd given birth to a daughter with the same affliction.

Yao.

By dint of hard work—and a plentiful supply of weathered wood and rock—Sona could boast that each pair of Chosen, and their children, if any, had a home of their own. The Yena unChosen—Cader, Fon, and Kayd di Uruus—shared one building and had invited Worin Mendolar to join them, much to the young Tuana's joy. Oran's brother, Kran, stayed with Deran di Edut of Tuana, when not with his sister. The di Licor sisters would have happily moved away from their parents also, but when they were not scouting with Haxel, their mother kept them close. Not Choosers yet—but soon.

Myris would have known, Aryl sighed to herself. Beko di Serona would be first, already prone to such wild swings of mood that Husni suggested she move to the other side of the valley until Chosen. Instead, she lived with Menasel and her Chosen Kor d'sud Lorimar.

Only Naryn lived alone. She had kin. Her cousin Caynen di S'udlaat was Joined to Yuhas, once of Yena. But the invitation to live together hadn't been offered. Aryl wasn't sure if it was Yuhas, who was Enris' closest friend at Sona, or Caynen, with her own reasons.

The homes were small by Grona standards, adequate

by Yena. Aryl didn't know what the Tuana thought, though Enris muttered about improvements—usually after he bumped his head on the lowest end of their roof. As "improvements" required materials they didn't have at Sona, she tended to ignore him. Every home had the essentials: a door, walls, and roof. Some had a window opening; all had a hearth for a fire and a hole in the roof for its smoke. Floors were dirt or uneven paving stones. Better floors could wait until they had food growing between their homes.

Gijs and Juo had built a bed platform and roughed a table and bench. For the baby, Haxel, being Juo's closest relative at Sona, had given the Chosen her cloak. The cunning fabric, tightly woven from wing thread, was both light and waterproof. It made a fine hammock.

A touch of home in a place not yet one, Aryl thought, determinedly looking away. Four of them stood shoulder -to-shoulder by Juo's bedside: she and Seru, Naryn and Lymin di Annk. All pregnant and offering support.

All worried this might happen to them next. That, they didn't say.

Here. The door opened, cooler air swirling around their ankles. Oswa and Gijs. She looked ready to bolt the other way; he looked desperate.

Juo's eyes were half-shut, her face beaded with sweat. Her hair, freed of its net, lashed futilely at the mattress. She was conscious. And afraid. Her fingers crawled toward her Chosen; he went to his knees and caught her hand in his.

After a quick glance at Juo, Oswa looked to Aryl. "I don't know what you expect me to do." Her hands twisted in the folds of her jerkin. "I'm no Watcher."

"You survived Yao's birth," Naryn said coolly. Her shields were in place; only a trickle of *compassion* came through. And an unsettling *curiosity.* "Tell us how."

"How?" Under its Grona cap, Oswa's hair fretted.

"Was there anything the Birth Watcher did?" Seru asked eagerly. "Anything you remember could help."

"She left us to die."

Terror. That, from Lymin. She was furthest along. Seru had predicted she'd give birth with or before Juo.

Juo's eyelids snapped open. "Seru—?" She grunted with pain, half sitting up. "What's happening?"

Dread. That from Seru, her shields almost nonexistent under the wash of emotions. "It's time."

"We're here," Aryl said promptly, taking her hand. *Courage, Cousin,* she sent privately. *Tell us what to do.*

Seru's fingers tightened fiercely, then released. "Juo, listen to me. Your baby intends to be born. Now. Gijs, help her stand. Remove her clothes. The rest of you, be ready."

Lymin and Naryn each took a clean square of cloth. Aryl took one as well. They crouched.

Juo stood, legs spread, her distended abdomen rippling with powerful contractions. She threw back her head, teeth clenched in a rictus of effort. Her hair lifted like a cloud. Gijs and Seru stood behind. Her Chosen gripped her shoulders. Seru ran her fingers down Juo's sides, doing her utmost to calm the baby.

With a rush of clear fluid, the birth sac slipped from between Juo's legs. Lymin caught it with a low cry of triumph and wrapped it in her cloth. She carried it to the hammock and laid it gently within.

Seru left Juo to Gijs and Naryn, who each took an arm. Aryl stood by the hammock, looking down with wonder.

The squirming sac was as black as truenight, flecked with starlike patches of pale, torn skin. It steamed in the cooler air.

"Her turn," Seru said, moving to the other side. This was the moment. The birth sac could only be opened from within, the first independent act of all Om'ray. Fail to take that risk, and the baby would suffocate and die.

Seru's fingers hovered above the sac, then touched gently. The sac went rigid. *Little one.* The *joyful* sending was the most powerful Aryl had felt from her cousin. *Come out and join our world.*

Nothing happened. Seru frowned and tried again. More squirming, this time wild and desperate. The hammock swung; Aryl steadied it.

"Call her, Juo," Oswa whispered urgently. "She wants to find you. She knows your voice, your mind."

"Do it," Seru ordered. Juo staggered forward, leaning on Gijs and Naryn. Her breaths were ragged and too shallow. She shivered uncontrollably, despite the blanket they'd thrown around her. It wasn't the effort of birth. Aryl's eyes met her cousin's somber ones. Juo was reflecting the baby's state. If the mother went unconscious . . . only the mother would wake again.

Seru guided Juo's hand to the sac, pressed them gently together. Juo looked up, tears in her eyes. "She's too afraid. She's not listening to me." The squirming slowed. *Despair!* "We're losing her!"

"No, we won't. Gijs, take her." Seru placed her hand on Aryl's. *Show me how you reached Yao.* A command.

Aryl sought the M'hir, feeling Seru's mind with hers. Instead of the heave and tear of a storm, the *darkness* was a smothering pressure. About to pull back, to protect her cousin, Aryl suddenly realized it was the other way around—that somehow, Seru's confidence, her serene belief in herself, extended into the *other*. That she was doing *this.*

There. Aryl spotted the glow of another mind in that darkness. *Like Yao.* It floated easily, as if it belonged and the M'hir was as natural a resting place as a bed.

Or a womb.

Little one, Seru's summons rippled outward. *Come with us. Come to your mother. The wider world is safe. Bright. Fun! We all want you in it.*

The glow pulsed with each word, began to rush toward them. Continuing to call, Seru drew herself from the M'hir. Aryl followed, opening her eyes in time to see the sac split open down its middle.

A tiny foot pushed through; a chubby fist unfurled like a flower.

HUNGER!

"Thank you, Aryl. Thank you."

Aryl hugged her cousin. "Sona has the finest Birth Watcher of any Clan." Seru's answering laugh held a sob of relief.

Breathing easily now, Juo scooped her baby from the sac, and brought her to a full breast.

JOY! MOREMOREMORE!

Wincing, Aryl took an involuntary step back and strengthened her shields. Babies. Gijs couldn't grin any wider without cracking his jaw. For everyone's sake, he and Juo would have to shield their daughter's emotions until she matured. But for now, she allowed him his pride in her obvious Power.

So long as she didn't have to be too close to it.

Happiness and relief spilled outward, *warmth* reflecting back from the rest of Sona. Their first birth. And, from the gusto with which the baby nursed, a determined one.

Seru, who'd started cleaning away the fragments of the sac, paused to smile. She glanced up at Lymin. "Someone else is eager to arrive."

"Mine? I'm not ready yet. Suen's not. You must mean—" with a cheery laugh, the very pregnant Tuana turned to look behind herself, a hand out in a sweeping wave.

At Naryn.

The silence was as thick as smoke. Before Lymin could gesture apology, before anyone could offer reassurance, Naryn was gone.

She left a trace. Like a distant bell, tolling for the dead. *Grief.*

Sona's Birth Watcher went back to tidying the new baby's bed. "Trust me, Lymin, it will be before firstnight. Let Oswa take you home. Tell Suen he will have to try hard to be as helpful as Gijs and that I'll come as soon as

I'm finished here." Aryl noticed the others took comfort from Seru's assured and confident tone, the *calm antici-pation* she felt. Her cousin had indeed come a long way.

"Don't worry, Lymin," Seru went on. "This is why we attend each other's birthings. To see there is nothing to fear."

Except for Naryn.

Their eyes met. Aryl wasn't surprised to see tears glistening in Seru's.

There were some in her own.

Chapter 4

HAXEL WAITED OUTSIDE the door. "Another like Yao. What's going on?"

A question the First Scout knew full well she couldn't answer. "Maybe nothing is." Aryl motioned toward the river, and the pair started to walk.

"Maybe it's this place." Haxel stomped on a paving stone. "These mountains. Where nothing grows. It's not natural for Om'ray."

"Oswa told me Yao was the first such born to Grona." Whose Om'ray lived quite well in the mountains, but Aryl didn't add the obvious.

"Well, I don't like it. Om'ray who don't know their place in the world. What will become of them? Can they even become Choosers?"

Surely another question Haxel couldn't expect her to answer.

Yuhas and Galen crossed their path, bringing water to the fields. Each held a thick wood splinter across his shoulders, a jar of water suspended from either end. The wheeled cart Veca and Morla had built required a ramp, something the Sona could spare neither time nor effort to build. Both Chosen were shirtless and sweating, but smiled a greeting. Other Om'ray were climbing up from the river, still others going down.

They couldn't water full-grown plants this way, not and expect an abundant crop.

"No more water from our neighbors. Am I right?"

Trust the First Scout. Had her meeting with the Oud been only this morning? Aryl decided it felt like days ago. Since? Ael and Myris were gone. She'd seen her mother. Watched Juo's baby enter the world.

Odd, how some days were filled with change while others passed without note, as if never lived at all. Aryl pushed her *grief* aside. "The Oud claimed we have enough water for our needs. That we waste what we have."

"Waste it?" Haxel snorted. "I'd like to pour it down one of their tunnels and then see what they say about water."

"We have a more urgent problem. Oran's been sending dreams about us—about traveling through the M'hir—to other Adepts."

The First Scout stopped in her tracks. A hand clamped on her wrist. *How do you know?*

Aryl, forced to stop too, tried not to notice the startled looks from those close by. It was the height of rudeness among Om'ray, to turn a public conversation private. But Haxel wasn't wrong.

Taisal told me. She accused us of trying to interfere with Yena. Don't worry. I'll talk to Oran first. With Enris, she finished dutifully, though his presence in her mind was thankfully preoccupied. *We don't know how she's doing it yet.*

You went there. To Yena. An undercurrent of *longing.* For an instant, Aryl thought Haxel, who hadn't the Power for such a long 'port, would demand she take her to the canopy. But the other Om'ray only tightened her grip, until her fingers dug into bone. *Because of Myris. That was foolish.*

Because I wanted to know why she was picked for exile—why we all were. Taisal said they didn't know why. That they dreamed of Yena's ending and our leaving it. Until Oran. Now they dream of us and fear the M'hir.

Haxel let go, her shields tight. Her eyes were stunned, as if she hadn't understood the sending, then abruptly sharpened, as if she did, more than Aryl knew. But all she said was, "There's no one to cook at the Cloisters. Oran will be back for supper." A squint at the sun. "Two tenths till firstnight." The First Scout glanced back to Aryl, the jagged scar drawn white. "Let her enjoy the meal," mild. Almost serene. "It will be her last at Sona."

Naryn did not want company. From the roadway, Aryl could feel the *warning/preoccupied/don'twantyou* blend of emotions her friend let through her shields. Reluctantly, she turned back.

A short while later, she found herself waiting by what the Sona optimistically called the New River. "River," Enris had informed her, was not the right word for something she could leap across. Or that Ziba could wade without getting wet above her knees. But the Yena had no other word for traveling water, the Grona didn't care, and those Tuana with an opinion—other than Enris—thought if it was supposed to be a river, it should be called one.

Whether it was or not.

What that said about how Tuana—or Grona—dealt with their world, Aryl wasn't sure.

She dug the toe of her sandal into the gray pebbles, finding a layer of finer stuff beneath. Bigger rocks, some larger than an Om'ray, lay scattered around as if forgotten. The largest, fractured and showing the marks of tools, were the remnants of the bridge that once connected Sona's road to the head of the valley and its Cloisters. The many smaller, rounded stones were what the river—when it had flowed with all its force—carried down from the mountains. So Marcus said.

The Human's real Talent, Aryl decided, was to make anything strange.

New River was little more than a stream. That word she knew. When they'd first come here, climbing the mountain ridges, they'd crossed innumerable such: most no wider than her foot. The one of any size had been stolen by the Oud as well.

Why? A question to make Marcus, knower of too much, shake his head in frustration. She grinned to herself.

The water at her feet babbled and bubbled, frothed white and felt cold. They'd dug into its narrow bed to make a deeper spot for filling jars and laid flat stones alongside. Not even hardy Grona boots took daily soaking well. To complicate things, New River was prone to change its course, abandoning both flat stones and deep spots without warning.

Ezgi d'sud Parth rose with a sloshing jar and grinned at her. "Sure you want full ones?"

Aryl flexed her hands on the stick across her shoulders. "I'll spill less than you."

Laughing, he slipped the neck of the jar within its noose. The match to it was on Aryl's other side. She braced herself, then straightened in a smooth motion.

Balanced, the weight wasn't a problem. The nature of the load was where a Yena had the advantage. On the flat, she took uneven steps, just as she would to cross a rope bridge, preventing any swing of the jars from growing beyond her control. Going up the crumbling riverbank was straightforward. She simply placed her feet with care and . . .

. . . stone shifted.

Without thinking, Aryl jumped to the side. Unfortunately, what would save her from a breaking branch was worse than useless where everywhere she stepped began to slip and slide apart.

She was *not* going to drop a jar. Or spill a drop.

With a growl, she bent forward and ran up the slope at full speed, pebbles flying, feet sinking with each drive of her legs. Almost at the top . . . faces peered down at her. *Disbelief.* Someone bent to offer a hand and was quickly pulled out of her way by someone wiser. Her legs burned, but she didn't slow down. One . . . more . . . thrust . . . down . . . a . . . push . . . up . . . there.

Aryl stepped calmly up and onto the flat edge, smiled at the Om'ray now very busy going down the slope with their empty jars—all but one—and began to walk to-ward the field, her jars full.

"I'd take those, but you're enjoying them too much." Enris fell in step. "You realize you almost ran over my uncle."

"What was he doing in my way?"

"Probably wondering how a such tiny Yena could carry more than his nephew. Uphill."

"Then," she grunted, shifting the stick, "he should take up climbing."

What was it like?

Sweat stung her eyes. *The birth?* Aryl gave him the memories. "Quicker than I thought," she added. "You'd best be nearby." Avoiding the topic of Yao and the new babies, she continued cheerfully, "Now Lymin and Juo can help water the fields. They aren't so tiny," this with a sly look.

"My uncle will be relieved. However," a bubble of *distraction,* "no one may have to soon."

"You've an idea."

"I've an idea."

One he had no intention of sharing. "Fine." Aryl lifted the stick and its jars over her head. "So you can't say you didn't take your turn."

When Enris cooperated by stepping close to lower his head for the load, she planted a quick kiss on his forehead and stared into his deep brown eyes. "Haxel is sending Oran home. If the rest of Grona leave, that's four less to carry water. We may have to try your trading."

His hands met hers on the stick, took the weight. "Good thing I only have brilliant ideas, isn't it?" He grinned.

Insufferable Tuana.

For the first time in this too-long day, Aryl began to feel hope.

Forty-two Om'ray crowded into Sona's Meeting Hall. Two sets of new parents, and their babies, were absent. Good thing, thought Aryl, feeling a tinge of *HUNGER* that wasn't hers. Lymin's newborn was as loud as Juo's.

And he was, according to Seru, as detached from other Om'ray as Yao. Oswa would be in demand.

Despite the babies' appetites, Aryl had none of her own. Not for the thick stew Rorn had prepared for them, nor for what had to be done.

Despite open windows and door, the air was rank with sweat. They were all weary but, from most, *satisfaction*. They could see the results of their labor in new growth. Only this afternoon, Ziba had declared a nondescript green thread to be her beloved rokly, a favorite dried and preserved. None of them had tasted it fresh.

The births dispelled the pall of *grief,* or at least pushed it aside. They'd mourn Myris and Ael tomorrow, with the ringing of the Cloisters' bell. Then, the new babies would be given names from those in the Cloisters' list—Sona names. Seru would preside. For now, she sat with Husni and Morla, accepting congratulations, and looking every bit as proud as any parent. Ezgi stood behind her, hands on her shoulders.

They should be proud, Aryl told herself. Children were Sona's future.

Children who would never meet Myris or Ael, only hear about them. A cautionary story told by their elders: The M'hir is dangerous. It killed Ael d'sud Sarc and his Chosen. Because he did this—we think. Whatever he did, don't you do it.

She snorted to herself. As if stories ever prevented a fall. She'd share her own memories, good ones, when the children were older. As for what killed Ael? They might never know. Or it could happen during the very next attempt to 'port . . .

Beside her, Enris lowered his bowl. *Trouble.*

Bern d'sud Caraat was easing his way through the others, pale eyes on her, stopping to exchange courtesies with his grandparents, Cetto and Husni, continuing on.

Until he stood in front of Aryl and gave the slightest Grona bow. "Heart-kin."

Affront surged from Enris. Bern flinched and those near enough to feel it glanced around uneasily. But the Tuana smiled and got to his feet, brandishing his bowl. "Need more stew. Take my seat, if you like."

The courtesy—and desertion—was because he believed Oran and her Chosen would soon be gone. Exasperated, Aryl did her best not to frown as Bern sat beside her and kept her shields tightly in place. "You shouldn't call me that," she said in a low voice. "What do you want?"

"Your help."

A light touch on her hip made her drop her gaze to the bench. His hand was there, between where no one else could see. It turned palm up. An invitation.

There'd been a time she'd have accepted without thought. A time when their private sendings held mystery and thrill, when they'd spent hours in each other's minds. He'd waited for her, she knew. Hoped their bond would make her ready for him.

They'd both Chosen otherwise.

Aryl looked at Bern, about to refuse, but he spoke first, a whisper. "Send us away."

"Why?"

"Oran can't stay here. Find a reason. Now!"

All of which would make more sense, Aryl thought with some disgust, if the Om'ray in question wasn't sitting beside her brother, eating with a healthy appetite, and, if not smiling, then certainly looking as if she would, given the chance.

She'd regret this.

Aryl touched her fingertips to his palm.

She'd guarded herself against an intrusion of emotion, any attempt at old intimacies. For Bern's sake as much as her own. Enris might be across the room by the cook pot—in no way was he inattentive or beyond reach.

But Bern's mind was as finely controlled as she'd ever felt it. Only words came through their contact. *Let me show you.*

A memory. He wanted to give her a memory. *Of what?*

What it does.

It?

As if her curiosity was permission, Aryl began to *see* what Bern had seen, earlier this day. She didn't resist.

Though his emotions were muted, safe, she shared his *grief* over Myris and Ael, felt his urgent *need* to be with his own Chosen. She saw the Dream Chamber, was in it with him. He'd 'ported directly there—something, Aryl recalled, Oran and Hoyon had been adamant no one should do while the Adept dreamed. That it could be dangerous.

That Bern ignored the warning didn't surprise her.

What he'd seen, what she now *saw*, did.

. . . Oran, alone in the chamber. Everything as it had been: the platforms with brown pads, the light behind each, the closed doors.

Except for the platform on which Oran lay. It rose high above the rest on a stalk, halfway to the ceiling. From the ceiling hung long threads of metal, close and densely packed, reaching to almost touch her. Almost. The threads echoed her form, moving like a Chosen's hair in waves that reflected light.

An echo, because Oran wasn't still. Straps of the same metal held her at shoulder and ankle as she struggled violently. Her eyes closed tight, her mouth open in a soundless scream, and, all the while, the threads followed her movements, lowering as she sagged, rising up as she strained.

Perspective changed. Bern climbing the stalk to reach his Chosen. The threads curling away as if he was fire, disappearing into the ceiling with no mark or opening to show where they'd been. Before he could touch her, the straps slipping away, too, vanishing within the platform, the platform itself plunging down to rest beside the others so quickly only a Yena would have landed safely at its side.

All as it had been.

Oran's eyes, opening. Her face, at first slack, then forming an impatient frown. "You! No wonder I can't dream. You can't be here. Go." A hand up when he started to protest, to demand an explanation. "Go!—"

Frustration. Fear . . .

The memory ended there.

I tried to show her—she can't see the memory. Tried to tell her—she doesn't believe me. She remembers lying down and falling asleep, nothing more. Something's wrong in there, Aryl.

Skin crawling, she couldn't disagree. *What did you sense from her while she lay there?*

The M'hir was too close. Too . . . he hesitated *. . . interested. Oran was a presence, nothing more. Helpless. This wasn't her doing.*

Aryl lifted her fingers from his palm, blew out a long slow breath. "Did she tell you what she wanted to dream?" Quietly, though their nearest neighbors gave them what distance they could. Which would last until Ziba or Yao started their post-supper chase along the benches.

Bern put his hands together on his lap. Made them fists. "About birthing."

Not what she'd expected. "Why?"

A grudging nod to where Seru sat in a place of honor.

"Adept and Keeper *and* Birth Watcher." Aryl lifted an eyebrow. "I suppose next she'll want to be Speaker. All at the same time, of course."

The corner of his mouth twitched. "You have to admire her ambition."

No, she didn't. In any way. But Aryl could understand it. The Grona Adept didn't trust anyone else to be competent; perhaps she couldn't. It made her dangerous, if only to herself.

Whatever was happening in the Dream Chamber, whatever was sending dreams to Yena's Adepts or other Clans? It didn't appear to be Oran's doing. Not consciously.

What that said about the Cloisters left her cold.

"Leave this with me, Bern," Aryl decided, rising to her feet.

"You'll send us away?"

Aryl glanced at Oran, who was staring at them. With a frown. "It's been a difficult day for all of us," she said gently, looking down at Bern. "Let's leave it for the morning." *Keep her away from the Cloisters,* she sent, only to him.

He pressed his lips together and gestured gratitude. *Thank you,* she added. *For trusting me with this.*

The startled warmth in his eyes was almost familiar. Now to convince Haxel to wait.

Cold stew. After Bern left, Aryl poked the lumps around and around with her spoon; they left trails through the thickening liquid. She should eat. On their journey here, she'd urged Myris to take bites of the dry tasteless Grona bread. When Myris lay injured, she'd been proud of her ability to coax mouthfuls of soup between her lips. Why couldn't she do the same for herself?

Sorrow takes the shape we give it.

A shape she could see. The Meeting Hall usually emptied before truenight. Tired Om'ray, seeking their beds, the company of their Chosen. A habit considered sensible by the Yena; the seemingly endless darkness and star-pierced sky remained unsettling to many. Tonight, though crowded and too warm, no one had left. Instinct, to stay close. To their inner sense, Sona was smaller, less important. The loss of Myris and Ael was more than of two people. It diminished Cersi itself.

For now. Already, the effect faded, like a bite whose itch only returned when touched. She had, Aryl grumbled to herself as she rubbed her forearms, too many of those. The sorrow would remain. She was glad of it. Though for how long? Too few Om'ray were left who'd heard Ael's quick laugh. Who'd seen Myris smile.

Enris bumped her shoulder with his. "Eat."

From profound to annoying. Restless as a whirr/click chasing an Oud. When the Tuana was unhappy, he was like Haxel, who had to *do* something, anything. Preferably loud or violent. At least the First Scout was being productive; though no one came close to the end of the long table where she sat, rewrapping the hilt of her favorite longknife. Something in the wistful way she gazed at the blade for long intervals, as if making a promise. She'd agreed to a delay.

Tomorrow was going to be … interesting. Another bump. "Leave me be," Aryl said, this time pushing back. Was a moment's peace too much to ask? "Check on your brother."

"Worin." As if the name was new to him. Enris straightened, peered at the nearest window. "It's true-night. You're right." He planted a kiss on the top of her head. "I'd better make sure he gets home safely."

Her turn to blink. Tuana were ridiculously confident in the dark. "What are you up to?"

Enris surged to his feet. "I'll let you know."

Aryl watched him leave. He collected Worin with an affectionate touch. Their departure was a signal to other unChosen, likely unsure when to leave the midst of such grim adults. First the Yena threesome, Fon, Cader, and Kayd. Then Kran and Deran, too carefully ignoring Beko. Netta and Josel, the dappled sisters.

Naryn went out the door next, wrapped in the long-coat she'd made, alone and without looking at anyone else. Seru, watching her, sighed and said something softly to Husni, who shrugged.

If only Oran had succeeded—maybe Sona's Cloisters held a dream about saving a Joined mother and child. Could they let her try again?

What had happened to Oran, left alone?

Aryl was distracted by a flash of yellow and red between the brown of dusty leggings. Wristbands. Yao, too young for sorrow—or to sit for long—wormed through the interesting maze of legs and bodies. No one laughed. Hands dropped to her shiny head to share affection.

Catching sight of Aryl, Yao came to her.

"I didn't eat my stew either," she announced with a grin, climbing on the bench beside Aryl. "It was too hot." Her little nose wrinkled. "And Rorn put in the white things. I don't like the white things."

Aryl poked one of the offending "things" with her spoon. The preserved meat—from whatever it had been—wasn't her favorite either. It had a pungent smell.

Mustn't encourage a child to waste food.

"Mine's too cold," she admitted. As Chaun walked by, she passed him her bowl and spoon with a gesture of apology, then lifted an arm in invitation.

Yao snuggled close, then looked up at Aryl. "My mother says Myris isn't coming back. Or Ael. Because they went into the M'hir." A not-so-childish frown creased her small forehead. "They should come back. They make everyone sad. I wouldn't do that." Likely a promise enacted by an anxious Oswa, given how Yao loved to play 'port and seek.

"They can't come back. They—" Aryl made herself say it, "—they are no longer *real.*" How could Yao understand what she couldn't sense?

"Yes, they are. I can feel them." Another frown. "No. Not Myris. Ael. He's thin. And he doesn't make sense."

Astonished, Aryl could only stare.

"I'm not playing a game," Yao insisted.

"I believe you," Aryl said quickly. The child might not sense other Om'ray as they could sense her, but she had ability in the M'hir. "Can you show me? Show me Ael?"

Small fingers wrapped around her thumb and squeezed. "We can't stay with him," the child warned solemnly.

... As quickly as that, they were *there*. Aryl tightened her sense of self, checked on Yao only to be amazed at the child's confidence. The M'hir heaved and slapped and stormed, but she simply rode with it.

There he is.

Yao didn't—couldn't point. Instead, part of the M'hir settled, pulled away from a shape. No, not a shape, Aryl realized, but a voice. A voice of shadow rather than sound. Words billowed outward, like a curtain's tattered edge ... *Myris* ... *where I* ... *hands* ... *Myris* ... *I* ... *I* ... *where I* ... *Myris* ... *hands* ...

Words and nothing more. Sickened, Aryl pulled back. *That's not Ael.*

Yes, it is.

The child had no way to sense his loss. The voice, to her, must seem *real*.

It's only an echo, Aryl sent, frantically offering memories of mountains and shouts and laughter. *Don't follow it. Never follow such things.*

The glow beside her brightened.

... the murmur of voices, real voices, was a welcome shock. Aryl hugged Yao, pressed her face against her soft, fine hair. "Clever, clever Yao," she praised, making sure only *approval* and *affection* passed her shields. Inside, her stomach twisted. What lay ahead for Yao, for Juo's baby, for Lymin's? For her own? To only sense each other through the M'hir ... to hear a voice and not know if it came from the living or dead? "We'll have to spend more time together."

"I could show you how to play 'port and seek!" Yao offered, squirming free. "I'd let you catch me sometimes. I let Ziba. She says I don't, but I leave her a trail sometimes." Aryl was shocked by a *tugging*, deep in her mind—no, in the part that could *reach* the M'hir. "Or I do this."

HEREHEREHERE!

Aryl winced.

"Sorry."

No one else reacted to the mind-numbing *shout*. Aryl knew what that meant. It had been sent to her through the M'hir, with a precision few matched in normal sending. "Thank you, Yao," she said numbly, gesturing gratitude. "Now go tell your mother I said you were clever and helpful. She'll be pleased."

The child disappeared with a giggle.

To reappear in front of her mother, who let out a not-so-pleased shriek before gesturing apology to her startled neighbors.

Too late, Aryl abruptly realized, to debate whether Om'ray belonged in the M'hir or not.

Their children were already there.

Interlude

WATER GLINTED IN THE LIGHT from the oil lamps, black and slippery. Enris boldly stepped in and lowered his. "See?"

"The wet boot or the foolish Om'ray in it?" Yuhas asked. He'd caught up to them on the roadway.

Worin snickered.

"The water. See how it builds up behind the boot."

"And over it."

Enris smiled to himself. "Because the boot's not big enough." Before his brother found this funny, too, he sent a fond *Behave, youngling.* "That's why you're here. All of you."

The Om'ray he'd summoned stood with him on the dry pebbled floor of the river, each carrying as many small lamps as they could manage, doubtless wondering if he'd lost his mind. Worin. Yuhas. Fon, Cader, and Kayd. Kran with Deran, leaking *distrust* through their shields. Though they'd come. Anything to do with secrets and Power, Enris thought ruefully. The Licor sisters, Josel and Netta.

Steps away, in the dark, Naryn di S'udlaat. Uninvited. He spoke knowing she listened.

"We'll use lights to mark our line. Put them on the ground, spread out. We don't have very—" The unChosen, delighted to be out when most of their elders were heading for bed, bolted to the opposite bank, lamps waving. "Watch for moving rock," Enris shouted after them. Not that the hunters would risk the water, but he felt a twinge of Chosen responsibility.

A small twinge.

He resisted the urge to look up; clouds obscured his stars. He'd have to trust Marcus had been able to give them privacy. There was no way to know.

Enris took his lamps and placed them on either side of the narrow New River, splashing across and back with noisy relish. Yuhas met him, having placed his.

"What now?"

The unChosen returned, led by Worin, and stood waiting. From their *anticipation,* they'd decided this was a game worth playing. "Now," Enris said, ruffling his brother's hair, so like their mother's, "Sona stops wasting water."

Some things were better shown than told. Having picked his prize beforehand, he walked to it as briskly as the loose footing allowed. Confidence. That was the key. This would work.

Or he'd look like a fool.

Wouldn't be the first time.

The chunk was a broken piece of Sona's bridge. A disturbing reminder of the Oud's strength. Enris patted it, stepped back, put his fingertips together, and concentrated. You, he told it unnecessarily, *there.* And concentrated.

Power answered.

The chunk quivered, then moved. Not through the M'hir—he didn't dare risk where it might reappear—but through the air, graceful and slow. Larger than it first looked, having dug its own hole in the riverbed. He tried not to grunt with effort. Confidence.

When over the water, he let go. The chunk dropped and tilted and came to rest with a grind of rock to rock. And, he thought with glee, a much bigger splash than his boot.

The river spread and spread, before it found the way around.

"That's the idea," Enris added unnecessarily.

"Like the vat in our shop," Worin said excitedly. "How our father—" his voice faltered, but he recovered. "It's how we kept the melted metal flowing where we wanted. Into the right molds."

"Or stopped it altogether."

Yuhas leaped to the top of the chunk and let out a whoop that echoed out into the surrounding darkness. "This time we stop the river!"

Hush, Enris sent hastily. He'd prefer not to have the rest of Sona—and Aryl—arrive until this worked. The Yena couldn't move a pebble with Power; on the other hand, nothing would move nearby he wouldn't notice. *Go be our scout.*

To the rest: "Line them up on this side of the—" A loud *chink!* "—lights." Enris turned with the rest to see a second chunk of stone, big as a home, sitting where one of the oil lamps had been.

"Sorry," Fon said.

"Try to save some of the lights," Enris suggested. "Husni will count them tomorrow."

They moved the largest chunks and boulders first. Josel was steady and controlled; Netta's rocks tended to swoop from side to side, prompting the others to dodge out of the way. Kran, silent and determined, worked as hard as anyone, but Deran's control was worse than Netta's. For the sake of everyone's toes, Enris soon moved him to the far bank.

As he should have known, it quickly became a contest between Fon and Worin. Cader and Kayd, without this Talent but there because Fon was, busied themselves running through the dark to find the biggest possible hunk of bridge for him. Worin, Enris noticed with an inward grin, wisely picked smaller ones, so he moved more. There was laughter and a good amount of teasing. Kran edged closer while this went on, something wistful about him. Enris, between his own efforts, told himself he should speak to Worin and Fon, help the young Grona find a place.

His sister wasn't his fault.

All the while, water found its way between the chunks, as if to mock them.

When they ran out of broken bridge, they began *pushing* smaller boulders into line. Many were still half the size of an Om'ray. Not so many laughs now. Enris wiped sweat from his face with his sleeve, wondering at Fon. The slight young Yena stood in the circle of light from one lamp, face composed and peaceful, while rock floated toward him from the darkness.

From where Naryn watched. He could almost feel her eyes burning the back of his neck. Why she was here was beyond him; it wasn't her habit to seek him out, knowing he tolerated her solely because of Aryl. The Oud were easier to bear, despite what his Chosen might think. The not-*real* were beyond understanding or trust or blame, like bad weather. Naryn . . .

Suddenly furious, Enris almost released the boulder he was *pushing* too soon. He made himself focus and placed it with extra care.

This was why he avoided her, he thought bitterly. Naryn undermined his self control. Just standing there, in the dark, alone . . .

Always alone.

How did she bear it?

If it weren't for the warmth of his link to Aryl . . . today's loss, Ael and Myris . . . it had felt like losing Tuana all over again, his mother and father, all of them. If it weren't for Aryl, he couldn't imagine existing with that terrifying emptiness. That pain. His next heavy breath was closer to a sob. He *reached* for the link that held him to the calm clarity of Aryl di Sarc's mind, and steadied.

Naryn had to feel the same. But she endured it alone. Because she'd offered him Choice.

If he hadn't been able to reject her, they'd be Joined now.

Enris stood very still. That was it, wasn't it? The reason Naryn so thoroughly unsettled him. She'd never blamed him. Not for the baby, not for her fate. She'd accepted responsibility for what had happened to her, because of him. She'd done nothing since arriving but help his Chosen and their new Clan. The one Om'ray he'd considered utterly selfish proved herself otherwise day after day.

No unChosen should have been able to reject her Choice, as he did. How could she have been prepared for that? Could she have stopped herself? Was it even possible for a Chooser, once committed to Join?

Questions he'd never thought to ask, until feeling the irresistible Power of Aryl di Sarc, until being Joined himself.

Until now.

"Enris?"

"I'll be right back, Worin," he said, turning away. "More rocks."

Naryn waited as he approached, invisible to his inner sense, a silhouette against the lights of the village. He halted a few steps away, finding himself in the unfamiliar situation of not knowing what to say.

She drew her own conclusion from his silence. "I'll leave."

"No. Wait. What do you think?"

Glints marked her eyes, as if she'd tilted her head. "Of a dam? Clever. If it held enough water, some would overflow into the ditches to the fields. But it won't work."

"Why?"

"See for yourself."

Enris looked over his shoulder at what was now a wide wall of stone and rubble, taller than two Om'ray, and growing. He was impressed. The water, however, was not. It still escaped easily through the gaps between stones. "We need more rocks," he said stubbornly. "Smaller ones."

"You could add them for the next fist and it wouldn't stop the flow." Before he could protest, Naryn added thoughtfully, "Or you could try something else."

Enris gestured toward the useless dam. "I'd appreciate your help."

"My help?"

He understood the astonishment in her voice. Deserved it. "I never thought you were stupid," he said finally. "I'm—"

Don't you dare pity me! With sufficient *fury* to sting.

Clear enough. "What do you mean by 'something else'?"

* * *

Naryn went to one knee in the pebbles, brushing them aside to expose the hard-packed dirt beneath. "This is what I mean."

The rest stood around, at a distance. Naryn appeared not to notice. She did a great deal of that, Enris realized. Being neither Chooser nor Chosen made others uneasy from the start; being quick to take offense and powerful did the rest. Only Aryl was completely comfortable near Naryn.

Then again, she was powerful, too.

"You saw how the Oud used dirt as well as rocks," she said, looking up with a frown. She pressed with her fingers. The fine-textured stuff was almost like rock itself, but cracked under pressure. "The river didn't sink into the ground because of this. It's what we need in the dam." She stood.

"How can we move it?" Worin asked.

Good question, Enris fretted, scuffing the toe of his boot against the ground. When he *pushed* something, he could see its size and shape. Touch it. This? How did you *push* grains too small to see?

"We should have brought shovels." This, from Cader, brought nervous laughter from the unChosen.

They could dig the dirt, Enris thought bitterly. If they

had a thousand times their number, or were willing to become like Vyna, where unChosen toiled deep underground for a lifetime, using blocks of black stone to hold back the molten rock in Vyna's Heart . . .

We have until firstlight, he sent to Naryn. *The Human protects us from their eyes until then.*

"I see." Beneath, *disapproval.* Aryl had said Naryn no longer tried to convince her to avoid Marcus; it didn't mean a change of opinion. "Then it should be done now." And she walked away.

No, not away. Naryn followed the course of New River, away from the wall but staying in the middle of the original riverbed. Into the dark. Alone.

He sensed when she stopped.

Get out of my way.

Power built. Raised the hairs on his arms. "Go!" he shouted, waving his arms at the unChosen. He grabbed Worin by the shoulder and shoved. "Up the bank. Hurry!"

When Fon hesitated, staring back at Naryn, Josel and Netta took his arms and carried him.

Power. No one could be deaf to it. He could barely breathe through it. Enris threw himself to the top of the bank and whirled around. "Naryn!"

For Aryl's future.

The ground roared.

Chapter 5

DUST AND SOOT SHIVERED from the rafters above. As the floor trembled and Om'ray cried out in surprise, Aryl pulled out the device Marcus had given her. Nothing. *Not Oud,* she sent, making sure it reached everyone, knowing that was their first fear.

The trembling stopped, ending her next one. The Grona had shared memories of shaking mountains and, while Aryl didn't mind a branch moving under her, she was not happy about the ground doing the same.

"Check the hearth and lamps," Haxel ordered, mindful of fire when they had no means to fight it.

Aryl!
You're all right?
Come to the river—quickly.

Aryl ran, hearing the pound of feet behind her. They all came. To her *inner* sense, Sona moved as one.

None were faster.

Some had grabbed lights. She needed none, ran without regard to the tilted stones or chance of injury. Enris called, and nothing else mattered.

From no lights, to a confusion of them. A wavering

line of illumination stretched across the empty river. There were gaps. As Aryl came closer, a light winked out, then another. Then more.

Enris!

"Down there!" A shout. It wasn't her Chosen, whose mind was preoccupied. Worin. He met her at the river's bank. "They're on the other side."

Other side of what? Then Aryl's eyes adjusted. As more Om'ray came up beside her and raised their lights, it became clear.

Enris' idea.

If she wasn't so alarmed by his call, she'd have been impressed by the wide wall of rubble. As it was, the wall— and the dust cloud above it—were in her way. *Enris!*

Here. Look out for the hole.

What hole? Aryl ran down the bank, one arm back for balance. Ran farther down than she remembered, the footing softer. Wrong. Her feet began to slide more than step. Suddenly, she found herself *lower* than Enris.

The "hole," she told herself in disgust, unable to slow until she came to its bottom. Dust filled her mouth and nose. She sneezed and spat. Why was there a hole?

A light from above—from the river's bed. Yuhas held a lamp out to show her that side of the hole, then shrugged helplessly. "No rope."

And a rope it would take. For the hole was a pit, three Om'ray deep, running as far as the light showed, possibly all the way across the riverbed. The material of its sides was a fine dirt, laced with pebbles still dropping and rolling around her.

It wouldn't, Aryl judged, hold a biter's weight, let alone hers. There was only one thing to do, despite who might be watching. She concentrated . . .

. . . with admirable presence of mind, Yuhas grabbed her as she staggered at the brink. She wrenched free, already running to Enris.

There. On his knees, supporting a crumpled figure. Yuhas, having followed, lifted the light.

Naryn?

Her friend lay as pale and still as Myris, as death. Aryl *reached*, unsurprised to find Enris already *there*, pouring his own strength into Naryn. She dropped down beside them, took hold of Naryn's hand and did the same. *What happened?*—unsure if she asked about Naryn, the dam across the river, or the hole.

The memory Enris immediately shared answered it all.

The ground roaring and *lifting!* Naryn, throwing Power into one incredible effort. A rain of dust and dirt and pebbles on the wall, coating it in a thick layer. More Power, to *push* and *push* at dirt until it packed every crevice and space. Everything she had.

Until she had nothing left for herself.

FOOL! Aryl sent, furious. Her hands were shaking as she stroked Naryn's arm, tried to replace the lock of red hair that had escaped from its net to lie with horrifying limpness along the other's cheek. *Don't leave me.*

"She won't. We were in time." Enris eased his position, so Naryn's head rested against his chest. "She's recovering."

He was in little better shape, drenched with sweat, panting with effort. Aryl sent strength to her Chosen, too, along with a snap of *annoyance.* "This would be your fault."

"Oh, yes."

"And when the Strangers look at their vids? See Om'ray moving rocks the size of buildings through the air?" When they see her 'porting out of a hole, Aryl added to herself with an inward wince. "What then?"

Under *worry* for Naryn, a definite flavor of *smug.* "They won't see a thing till firstlight. And then? It's the work of our helpful Oud neighbors, of course. What else could it be?"

Meaning Marcus was involved. She would never, Aryl vowed, leave Enris alone with the Human again. Ever. Then the enormity of what he'd done—what they'd done—sank in. "You've stopped the river."

"With Naryn's help."

"She almost killed herself."

Just to her, as grimly as she'd ever felt him.

I'm sure that was the idea.

If staring could move water, Aryl thought, amused, then the ditch would already be full. They'd all taken turns here, beside where the wide pebble-filled ditch scooped out the riverbank. It had been a curiosity before: easy to see from the exposed side, if less to imagine how it might work.

Firstlight and, at last, water lipped the bottom line of white pebbles, turned them dark, covered them. Rose to the next. Gurgled along. All down the bank, Om'ray—who'd laid on their bellies to lean over and watch, cheered and patted one another. *Warmth* and *affection* surged from mind to mind. A tinge of *awe.*

As if Enris needed any encouragement. Aryl leaned against him. "It worked," she commented, gazing out at the rippled surface of what was, undeniably, becoming a lake. Only firstlight, but water filled the former riverbed from bank to bank, lapping gently against the wall of stone and dirt. "If it overflows into the courseways, the Oud will complain." She wouldn't. The courseways flowed first through the dead grove of nekis. Watered, perhaps they'd grow again.

"It won't. The ditches from Sona drain back into the river below the dam and before the courseways." Brimming with *content*, Enris wrapped his arms around her middle and pulled her into his lap. The sun was warm on her skin. The lake made the air softer, somehow.

The lake was deep. A new worry. She'd been in water over her head before. "We'll have to warn the young ones."

His deep laugh vibrated through her spine and he nuzzled her hair. "Tai can teach everyone to swim."

"Not me," Aryl countered, then had to smile. His *joy* was impossible not to share. "If he can convince Husni— I suppose I'll have to."

Husni. The other elders. She needed to talk to them all today, find some answers about the Cloisters, resolve what to do with Oran. She shifted, loath to move, no longer at peace.

Or was it something—someone? With very poor— make that no shields. Aryl frowned. *WORRY ... WORRY!*

"Hello, Aryl. Enris." With a bright smile that fooled no one, Seru dropped down beside her. Ezgi didn't even try to smile. He sat, crossed his legs, and began digging morose little holes in the dirt.

"Cousin," Enris greeted him with that "why are you bothering me?" tone he usually saved for his little brother.

There's a problem, Aryl sent privately.

We were enjoying a moment alone. Of course there's a problem.

She elbowed his ribs, gently. "Seru, what is it?"

She didn't expect Seru's green eyes to fill with tears, or for her cousin to wail, loudly: "Naryn's b-baby—!!" *WOEFEARGRIEF!*

HUSH! Aryl sent without thinking.

Seru covered her face with her hands, and Ezgi abandoned his digging to cradle her in his arms, giving Aryl a reproachful look. "She's upset."

"Which the entire world knows," Enris informed him, but kindly. "Help her!"

Ezgi blinked, as if the notion hadn't occurred to him. The handsome young Chosen might have more Power than his beloved Seru, Aryl reminded herself, but he had a fair bit to learn about using it. "Strengthen her shields," she advised, grateful as the pressure of Seru's emotions against her own subsided. "Much better." She touched Seru's arm. *What about the baby?*

Seru worked her face free of Ezgi's shirt. "What she

did—what Naryn did—it took strength from them both. Naryn's recovering, but her baby isn't. I don't know how long—the baby's dying, Aryl. I can't help either of them!" This with an outburst of *DISTRESSDESPAIR-GUILT* not even Ezgi could contain.

It didn't matter, they all felt it. Aryl sighed, looking out at the sparkling water. "It was going to happen," she heard herself say in a strange voice. "This is sooner, that's all."

Neither Tuana were prepared for the Yena swiftness with which Seru threw herself from Ezgi to pounce on Aryl, taking her by one leg to yank her from Enris' lap, grabbing her shoulders to give her a hard shake. "Don't say that!"

"Don't be a fool!" Aryl shoved free. The two sat on the dirt and glared at one another.

Seru didn't back down. "We have to do something!"

"Aryl. Seru's right. We have to help Naryn."

She twisted to look at Enris though, to her *inner* sense, he held no shield against her. His concern was real. As was his determination.

He'd stopped a river, but there were some things no one could fix. Aryl's own *despair* welled up. If only Oran had been in control of her dreaming, could access the knowledge of Sona's Cloisters—even that, she admitted, was grasping for too small a branch. *Tuana's Adepts couldn't do anything for her.*

Her Chosen spoke aloud, his eyes glittering like sunlight on water. "I know who could."

Of tasks not to envy, Aryl decided, she'd pick Seru's and Ezgi's. The two would explain to the rest of Sona—at the last possible moment—why three of their number, including their Speaker, would leave in the midst of, well, of everything. Those with the most pressing concerns were Haxel, Bern, and Oran. All three would be looking for her. A discussion and problem that could wait, in her opinion, so long as Oran wasn't in the Dream Chamber. Naryn couldn't.

Maybe she should suggest Ezgi let Seru's shields fail again. Their Birth Watcher's passion for what they hoped to accomplish would send the others running. Especially Haxel, Bern, and Oran.

An unworthy thought, however appealing.

"Explain to me again why I have to wear this?" "This" being Oran's Adept robe. Naryn held it up to herself. It would fit.

"Because it might help." Because Enris tried to anticipate everything that might sway Vyna's Council in Naryn's favor. Borrowing the robe had been Aryl's task.

What they would take to trade was his. She was careful not to *reach* for him; he'd sense her impatience, her not-unreasonable worry he'd linger with the Human to relate every detail of the new dam and the lake growing behind it.

They'd no time to spare. She didn't need to be a Birth Watcher to know that. Naryn's skin was an unhealthy color; the *feel* of her was wrong. "Will you hurry?" she suggested.

Naryn raised a brow. "You didn't ask Oran for it, did you?"

Had Oran been with the robe at the time, she might have. "I'll apologize later. It's not as if she needs it right now. Please, Naryn," Aryl said, more gently. "Enris will be back at any moment. We have to go before—" Before the baby died, taking Naryn with her. They weren't to tell her; Seru had insisted. "—before we're missed."

The other slipped the robe over her head, running her fingers along the textured threads of embroidery. "I wondered for such a long time how it would feel," she mused, straightening the front panels.

Aryl's lips quirked to one side. "How does it?"

Naryn held her arms and turned slowly. "Heavy," was

all she said when she stopped, but there was a faint pink to her cheeks.

They were prepared, but where was . . .

"I have them." Enris was grinning as he appeared, as if fully aware of her worry. The white crate under his arm was familiar. And not-Om'ray. "Didn't need to wake our friend at all."

She'd apologize to Marcus, too. As for the ease of all? It left an unpleasant *taste*, like a warning. "We can't use that," Aryl decided and grabbed a pack. "Here." She held it open.

Her Chosen's grin disappeared. He took the pack from her hands. "Don't get too close to these. Either of you." He poured the clear wafers in, tossed the empty crate aside, and slung the pack over one shoulder. Careless, no. Disrespectful, yes. "Are you ready?"

"There's no need for you to come." Naryn pointed to the pack. "Give me that. I have the memory of their Council Chambers." She had more. Memories of how the Vyna had treated Enris. How they trapped and killed unChosen from other Clans who came on Passage, calling them "lesser Om'ray" unfit to Join with their Chosen.

Aryl looked forward to meeting them in person. She'd promised to behave, but if they gave her any reason . . .

But what mattered about the Vyna wasn't their isolation or the threat they posed—it was how they managed to give birth without having Chosen at all. Like Naryn.

Who wasn't going alone.

"Together or not at all." Aryl took Naryn's hand, sent *reassurance,* and—

Before she could form another thought, Enris grabbed her free hand and the room disappeared . . .

"—Enris!" Aryl's protest died in her throat. She threw up her shields, felt the other two do the same.

They were in Vyna.

Naryn stepped up on the dais and took a seat. "So how long do we wait?"

The show of frustration was just that, a show. Naryn was exhausted and frightened. Not, Aryl knew, that she'd reveal either.

"They'll come," Enris said grimly.

Aryl nodded to herself. No hiding their arrival. They would be *felt*, as she *felt* the Vyna above her. Vyna who had to be wondering how three Om'ray could suddenly appear in the heart of their Cloisters. It shouldn't be long.

Strange, a Cloisters not only below ground but underwater. Like the buildings Marcus had shown her with his flying vid device, beneath the Lake of Fire.

The wall of arched windows that in Yena looked out on green life, and in Sona, piles of dirt, here revealed a darkness as star-filled as truenight without the Makers in the sky.

Stars that *moved*.

Fascinating. Aryl walked to the nearest window. Not stars, of course. They might, she judged, be eyes of some kind, if eyes varied in size and shape, and were all white. She drew her short knife, flipped it in her hand, and rapped the hilt firmly on the transparent surface.

"Did I forget to mention the rumn are attracted to noise?" Enris commented, carefully not approaching the window.

"I want to see one." Aryl rapped again, more firmly. The "eyes" swirled in an outgoing spiral from the point of contact, then rushed back again with powerful grace. Markings on a body, she decided in triumph, peering closer. A very large body. Or several.

She'd watched water hunters eat an osst alive. Aryl shrugged and put away her knife, losing interest. Simple to avoid such a threat. Stay out of the water.

Then, they were no longer alone in this part of Vyna's Cloisters.

The Council Chamber doors were wide open. A sparkling blue cap, sprouting a growth of twisted yellow threads knotted with tiny black beads, appeared at the left side of the doorframe, followed by a single eye as a Vyna contorted to see them while keeping as much of himself unnoticed as possible.

With that on his head? Aryl tried not to smile.

Etleka! Enris greeted cheerfully, for some reason running his hand through his thick black hair. *Aryl, Naryn, meet my old friend—*

The cap and eye were gone.

Friend, is it? Naryn commented.

Enris grinned. *Watch this.* "Etleka Vyna!" His deep voice rang from every corner of the vast room. "You know I'll do this as long as—"

HUSH, Enris! The Vyna scuttled around the corner as if chased, coming to a panting stop. *Fool!*

Starvation couldn't explain an unChosen so pitifully frail. Ill, perhaps, Aryl thought. His face wasn't right either. Beneath the brilliant cap and tassels, his eyes were sunken pits, his jaw too long. Dirt lined the creases at his neck and forehead. He wore a simple shirt and pants held up by a rope belt, the stained yellow fabric worn through at the knees and thinned at the elbows.

He looked as out of place in the gleaming chamber as they must.

Enris no longer smiled. He gestured a grave apology. *What happened, Etleka? I thought you were to—*a trace of *revulsion*, hidden so quickly Aryl might have imagined it—*serve one of your Adepts.*

You happened. No effort to hide the emotion there. *Anger* curled around *dread*.

Aryl stepped closer to her Chosen, wary of threat, however unlikely the source. Enris glanced down and gave a tiny shake of his head. His problem, that meant.

She scowled at him, then at the Vyna. Her problem, if he made any move at all.

I meant you no harm, Enris sent. *You or any Vyna.*

No harm? Etleka's palms slapped the front of his

pants, once. Twice. Hard, furious blows. *Contaminated, they call me. Fit only to clean waste. And talk to* you. *I don't care how you got here this time. Go away, Enris. You aren't welcome here. Go away!*

He hadn't looked at her, Aryl realized. Not at her or Naryn. As if Enris was all he could see.

Enris spread his arms. *Blame me. I won't argue. Once we see your Council, we'll be gone and never come again.*

The young Vyna's mouth gaped, showing too few teeth. If it was a smile, Aryl thought with a chill, it was the most horrifying one she'd ever seen on an Om'ray's face. *No other Vyna will come near you. Go!* He waved his filthy hands, as if shooing biters.

They will when you tell them we've more of what I gave Tarerea Vyna.

The hands stopped moving. Etleka licked his lips. *Give it to me. I'll take it. Show them.*

"Think we're fools, unChosen?" Naryn snapped from her seat on the Council dais.

Etleka drew himself up and looked at her for the first time. *You are* lesser *Om'ray, unworthy and foul. I, least of Vyna, am beyond your comprehension.*

"That I agree with—"

Naryn! Aryl admonished. To the Vyna, *We will stay here and wait for your Council's decision.* Then, as she'd learned from her mother, she swept her hands in the gesture of gratitude. *Thank you, Etleka Vyna. Be well.*

Then she turned and went to rap on the window again.

There was a flicker of *astonishment,* as if the scruffy unChosen couldn't believe he was being dismissed by a "lesser Om'ray." She kept an eye on his reflection against star-flecked black as he whirled and ran from the chamber.

"He and Daryouch looked after me. Taught me to catch denos. Fed me too many." Enris stood beside her and reached to almost touch the window, but didn't. "I never meant them any harm."

Aryl dropped her hand to take his, felt his *remorse* and wished she could rap the hilt of her knife against heads, not the window. *Peace, beloved. None of this was your fault.* Aloud, "Any harm here belongs to the Vyna. And that Tikitik." Thought Traveler, if he'd known the consequences to the Vyna as well as Enris, probably enjoyed both. Meddlers, the Vyna called them.

Never without their own motives. They'd stirred this pot. Why?

"We wait," Aryl decided. As long as it took.

Agreed. His fingers closed around hers.

Naryn tucked her feet under the Adept's robe and her chin into the palm of one hand. She closed her eyes. "This was your idea. Wake me when someone interesting shows up."

Without the sky, there was no way to measure how long the Vyna kept them waiting. Enris leaned against a wall, big arms crossed and eyes closed. She might have thought he dozed, as Naryn quietly did, except for the awareness of his mind where it touched hers, making sure he knew where she was, following her steps. Not trusting, her Chosen. Not trusting at all.

She smiled to herself as she paced.

The size of the chamber was familiar. It was immense, able to accommodate all of Vyna many times over. Her *inner* sense felt this as the smallest Clan other than Sona, but she'd been surprised to find only ninety, and those spread out, as if few lived or worked together.

Yena's Council Chamber had the same narrow dais in front of the wall of towering windows, the same row of tall-backed, pale green chairs for Councillors. Chairs for ceremony, not everyday business. There'd been a cluster of comfortable, mixed seating on a homely mat to one side of Yena's, a practical clutter of tables and mugs. Sona's had been stripped of all but the dais; they'd yet to find the ceremonial chairs among those tossed into rooms. Vyna's?

The magnificent expanse of floor was bare of anything but polish and reflection. She might have walked on the lights above, the windows with their moving glints of white. Aryl stayed to the walls, knife in hand and reversed, tapping once in a while. In Yena, the ceremonial doors weren't the only way in. There'd been another entrance, smaller, covered by a curtain. A convenience for those entering from within the Cloisters: Councillors, Adepts, the Lost. In Sona, an open arch, barely head high. There seemed to be none here.

The Stranger camp had taught her not to rely only on her eyes. Sona itself had hidden doorways, many of which they had yet to find despite Oran's promotion to Keeper and Hoyon's boasting.

Tap, tap. Didn't matter to her if the Vyna disliked sound.

And, Aryl thought, walking another soundless few steps before stopping again, it passed the time.

There was a great deal of wall.

Tap, tap.

Almost back where she'd started, the next tap produced a more interesting *clank*. Metal. On a section of wall exactly like the others. She didn't try to find the opening mechanism, satisfied to know where the Vyna would come.

Aryl went to wait by the ceremonial doors, her eyes fixed on the hollow portion of wall.

Her stomach suggested it was after the midday meal before any Vyna came toward them. At last. She'd begun to fear Etleka had gone back to cleaning pipes instead of taking their message. "Someone's coming."

Several someones.

"The Council," Enris guessed.

Naryn unfolded and rose to her feet, smoothing the panels of her robe. Aryl resisted the impulse to do the same. Thanks to her impulsive Chosen, she hadn't had time to grab a flask of water, let alone change into anything remotely impressive. She wore her favorite, thus well mended, blue tunic, of a loose comfortable fabric from Sona's storerooms and deep pockets. A belt held her knives. Her feet were in a tough pair of the light Sona footwear she found didn't interfere with climbing. At least the tunic was clean and her hair was inside its metal net. Most of it. What expressed itself behind her back she couldn't worry about.

The Speaker's Pendant—she'd meant to leave it behind. Aryl started to tuck it inside her clothes. Clans didn't talk to one another through delegates. Unless it would help the Vyna deal with her. On that thought, she left it out.

Be careful. From Enris to both of them.

Your idea, Naryn *snapped* back. Then added, *For which I thank you, Enris d'sud Sarc, in case there's no chance later,* with the faintest possible touch of *hope.*

Enris looked at her and gave his slow smile.

Aryl resisted the impulse to drop her hand to the hilt of her longknife as the section of wall cracked along four lines and silently turned open. These were Om'ray, she told herself firmly.

But shared memory hadn't prepared her for who came through the doors.

First came six Chosen, all in transparent robes that showed the swell of pregnancy on their too thin bodies, their hair shaved or absent, replaced by caps that sprouted colorful threads and beads. Vyna's Council. None matched Enris' memories.

As they took their seats, sparing not a word or look for the three Sona, another group entered. Aryl hid her astonishment. Nine chairs, each floating a hand's breadth above the floor, their occupants the oldest Om'ray she'd ever seen. Vyna's Adepts. They were wrapped in white blankets and attended by unChosen males, ready to give them strength. The future Etleka had wanted so badly.

Yorl sud Sarc, her mother's uncle, had taken her

strength to heal himself. Had Vyna begun thus? Aryl shuddered.

Like the Councillors, Vyna's Adepts paid no attention to them, though Aryl guessed this had something to do with the concentration needed for such Power. For Power was here. She could *feel* it, knew from the stiffness of Naryn's body beside her that she did, too. Enris, on the other hand, looked relaxed and welcoming. From his shields, he was neither.

The Adepts settled into place, a line before the platform. An instant's shifting and rustling, then they were still.

And all the Vyna looked directly at them. Without surprise or question on their faces.

Oran's dreams.

So. Their Adepts had received them, too. Aryl glanced at the row of nine seated before the platform and dismissed them. If they valued their lives so much as to spend others' to keep them, they wouldn't risk the M'hir.

Keeping her eyes on the Vyna Councillors, she grasped her Speaker's Pendant and took a firm step ahead of Enris and Naryn.

Keeping her mouth firmly closed, too. Manners first. *Greetings.*

You are not welcome here, lesser *Om'ray.*

They believed she wouldn't know one sending from another. Few could. Aryl quite deliberately turned left, to face the Councillor second from that end. *We don't intend to stay. We have what you want. Enris?*

He slipped off the pack and opened it. The clear wafers sparkled.

The glows in the water outside the window went into wild motion, swirling into clusters as if their owners would peer over the shoulders of the Vyna. The Councillors leaned forward; the lips of the wizened Adepts worked, as if they longed to speak. *Lust* and *greed* and *envy* flooded past their shields.

Aryl's stomach twisted.

Enris deliberately closed the pack and hung it from his shoulder. As if any here would try to take it. Compared to her Chosen, these Vyna were brittle twigs to snap in one hand.

The Councillor who'd rebuked their presence rose and came down from the dais, every step graceful despite her swollen abdomen and breasts. She stopped in front of Aryl. *What do you want in return?*

"To live." The unChosen flinched, wide-eyed, at Naryn's voice. The rest, Aryl noted, did not.

The Councillor didn't look at Naryn. This close, Aryl could see blood pulse beneath her skin. Sparkling dots lined where she should have eyebrows. The bones of her face jutted like stones through snow, and her lips were the blue of death.

Om'ray to her *inner* sense.

Stranger than the Human, in every other way.

If we help this one, you will give us the Glorious Dead. You will leave. You will never return in this or any way.

There were hunters in the canopy from whom you couldn't back away, who attacked any weakness. Like this Vyna, decided Aryl. *Take them.* A gesture to Enris sent the pack sliding across the floor to the Councillor's feet, spilling its contents. When she looked up from it with dismay, Aryl smiled her mother's smile. *Help Naryn di S'udlaat*, she sent, *or I will take you to meet the Clans of the unChosen dead in your traps.*

The deep-set eyes narrowed. The glows pressed to the windows pulsed, their light shifting the shadows.

Coming to a decision of her own, the Vyna held out her hand. A hand with four fingers and two thumbs, each bearing paired rings of green metal.

Aryl, no. From Naryn, not Enris. Her Chosen was quiet, a brooding presence deep in her mind. Aryl pitied the Vyna if she meant betrayal. She calmly laid her scarred, callused palm over the other's cloyingly soft one and waited.

I will show you what binds your friend *and her unborn.* This sending was shockingly intimate, delivered to a layer of her mind where Aryl had only felt Enris before. And, she admitted, Bern when he'd been heart-kin. Though repugnant, Aryl endured it. This must be how the Vyna managed private conversation when all spoke mind-to-mind.

There. The Vyna thrust her through Naryn's shields as if they were gauze, and with as little care. How was it possible? Aryl fought to remain calm, to learn what she must and no more. Worst of all, the Tuana was blind to her intrusion, focused on the Vyna, her concern for Aryl, her fear for herself. *Do you see it?*

Aryl had traced the links between Om'ray before; it was a Talent she rarely noticed or used. When Naryn had first revealed her condition—her mind Joined to that of her unborn instead of an unChosen in proper Choice—she'd touched their link only enough to assure herself it was true.

What the Vyna showed her now was something *else.* The link wasn't between two minds. It was between Naryn's and *nothing.* Aryl heard her own gasp. The Vyna pulled her out again.

She was not Watched properly. A powerful Chooser can become pregnant without a father—as if this were unremarkable—*but what must be prevented is a Joining before the new vessel has been filled. If that occurs, they will both die, as even* lesser *Om'ray know.*

Vessel? She had to mean the baby. Filled by what? How? The Vyna, Aryl thought with disgust, sounded like the Oud—or worse, like Marcus. She pushed confusion aside. *Help her!*

The Vyna Councillor's hand dropped to her side and she stepped away. One of the wafers rose from the floor. The other Councillors rose from their seats, hands outstretched as if it was being offered to them. But the wafer flew to hover before Naryn.

Press it over the vessel. Over the unborn. DO IT!

Naryn, as if stunned by the Power of that sending or seeing no harm in it, took the wafer.

"No!" Enris shouted. "Wait!"

Too late. Pressed against the swell of her baby, the clear wafer turned milky white and glowed.

The Adepts began to chant, thin, unused voices breaking with the words. Spit ran down their chins. "Take her, Glorious Dead! Take her! Be born again!"

The other Vyna chanted as well. More and more stars-that-weren't jammed against the windows, distorting the colors within the room.

Naryn's face changed, mouth opening as if to scream. But no sound came out.

Wrong! This was wrong! Aryl *reached* for Naryn and Enris, concentrated on being *away* . . .

. . . But the M'hir was impenetrable, woven through by lines of seething *force* that disrupted Aryl's every effort to hold her locate . . .

She flung herself free of the M'hir, grabbed for Naryn. They'd run from this place.

The wafer turned black and fell from Naryn's limp hands. It shattered on the floor, spreading a dust that glistened in the light.

The chanting stopped.

Naryn looked at Aryl, blinked, then the oddest expression settled over her face. She cupped her abdomen in both hands. "Her name—her name is Anaj. Anaj di Kathel."

What have you done? Enris' mindvoice held an undertone of *horror.*

What we were asked to do. The Vyna Councillor beckoned and the unChosen scurried forward to collect the wafers from the floor. They ignored the pack and picked each one up in two hands to carry to their particular Adept. Slowly. Tenderly.

The ancient creatures stroked the wafers with their bent hands, cuddled them in their laps, heads bent so the tassels of their caps hid their faces.

They were probably drooling on them, Aryl thought with disgust. *I can't 'port,* she sent to Enris, felt him concentrate, saw him shake his head as his effort failed, too.

Something's wrong.

What wasn't?

Why are you still here? The Councillor demanded.

It wasn't the Vyna somehow stopping their 'port?

A touch on her arm. *It's them,* Enris sent, just to her. *The rumn. They're partly in the M'hir.*

The windows were full of them, whatever they were, their luminous markings almost pretty. A good disguise, Aryl decided, unable to make out any identifiable body parts. No gleam of teeth, but life in the canopy taught that not all threats came with an obvious mouth and jaws.

She did not *reach* for them.

The other Councillors gathered beside the Adepts, like eager children forced to wait on their elders for their share of dresel cake. Except for the one still confronting Aryl. *You are not welcome here,* lesser *Om'ray,* she sent, with a *flash* of cold impatience.

Aryl scowled. "We are not *lesser* Om'ray—"

We'll find our way out, Enris broke in, making an extravagant gesture of gratitude. To her: *Once we're above the water, maybe we can 'port. Unless you want to stay here?*

Anything but that.

Aryl took Naryn's arm, gently; urged her to follow Enris through the ceremonial doors. She appeared dazed, blue eyes large and unfocused. They had only the Vyna's word she'd been helped, that this "Glorious Dead" inside Naryn would mean both would survive childbirth. She wouldn't risk checking that link here. She'd risk nothing here, where Om'ray invaded one another's minds as casually as she'd swat a biter.

Instead, Aryl looked over her shoulder at the Vyna, saw her standing tall and superior, her hands folded just so, mouth pursed with pleasure. Enjoying the spectacle of the three "lesser" Om'ray running away, was she?

Aryl *drove* into the M'hir and forced a connection between their minds. As the other fought and wailed, her *terror* of the *darkness* threatening them both, she sent a promise.

If Naryn dies, this is where I'll leave you.

Let the Vyna remember that.

Black stone stairs, steep and beaded with moisture, led up from the Cloisters. Enris led the way, taking the first few three at a time. Aryl stayed with Naryn. "I should take this off," Naryn muttered, awkwardly holding the stiff panels of Oran's robe as she climbed.

Enris slowed and glanced back. "No time. Do your best, Naryn. The doors above are open. We have to hurry. They won't let us go if they can help it. And . . . there's a bridge." As if some final doom awaited them instead of a path.

Aryl shook her head. "Don't worry. I'll help—"

A gasp as Naryn staggered, her hands clenched against her middle. Aryl caught her before she could fall. Beneath her hands, the robe flared, then flattened, its panels twisted over a swelling that *moved* as if trying to force its way through. As Aryl stared, Naryn gave an involuntary grunt of pain. "It's Anaj! Help me—"

Aryl had her arm around Naryn; now she poured *strength* through that contact, all she could spare. Enough to steady Naryn on her feet, put some color in cheeks that were too pale.

"We have to hurry," she agreed, meeting Enris' worried look.

Smash, BANG!

Clatter, clatter . . . something ahead . . . something that rolled and bounced down the stairs. Enris shouted a warning, and dodged to one side. Aryl drew her long-knife and put herself in front of Naryn.

Down, down.

Ping!

Aryl frowned and put away her knife, placing the sound. "It's only a rock."

A rock of fair size that bounced into view, then careened off the wall behind Enris and flew over Aryl's head. She didn't bother moving, but watched it come to rest in front of the door below. "Why a rock?" she puzzled out loud.

Enris, who'd flattened himself against the wall, laughed as he pushed away. "Because the Vyna prefer their visitors dead. Can we hurry, please?"

Aryl kept frowning at the rock. "It's not black." She drew her knife again. "I thought all the rock here was black."

Smash, BANG!

Clatter, clatter . . .

Another rock, similar in size. This time, Enris held his ground, but Aryl pulled Naryn to the side. She watched it land beside the first. Watched both tilt, tip, and roll toward them.

"Not rocks," she announced unnecessarily.

Smash. Smash. Smash. BANG!

Even Naryn managed to run up the stairs.

Chapter 6

VYNA WAS AN ISLAND of black rock within an encircling mountain, like a rough-edged seed inside a pod. Sturdy bridges connected the two, but the water between—

Aryl drew back from the edge, pulled Naryn with her.

—the water was vile. A musk of rot, like that of the Lay Swamp, but what she'd glimpsed through the billowing mist suggested nothing as natural. Its smooth surface glistened like metal, flaring purple and red when disturbed.

And it was being disturbed.

SPLASH!

A surge of motion, hints of stars against darkness, and the curved back—or whatever—of the rumn disappeared below again. They, at least, were enjoying the rain of rock hunters.

And other things. As their feet hit the platform beyond the Cloisters bridge—a crossing the normally height-wary Tuana had managed at a run, cries echoed behind them in the mist, desperate and horrified.

Enris sighed.

Aryl tried not to *feel* as the Vyna caught in their floats died.

The next SPLASH was followed by a hideous, drawn-out scream from overhead. "Esan!" Enris shouted to be heard over it. "It's the Tikitik!"

Which makes no sense at all, Aryl sent, not straining her voice. *Why would Tikitik attack the Vyna?*

Though their method was effective, if wasteful. Vyna rose in a great vertical spiral, low-walled ramps wrapped around its core of buildings like a wing around dresel pods. Most rocks bounced off walls or rooftops into the water. Those that arrived on ramps or skidded against an edge began a slow grind and roll away from water to the safety of shadows. Since Vyna had almost no doors, most of those shadows were inside their buildings. She'd already watched several rock hunters roll through a nearby arch. It would take time for the Vyna to find and remove every one, time when they'd be wise not to fall asleep or leave babies untended.

Unfortunately, the rumn remained at the surface, attracted by the splashes. Impossible to tell if they ate the rocks or merely milled around in hope of more tender flesh. The effect was the same. The M'hir remained impassable.

As long as the rocks kept falling, the bridges—though wide and perfectly safe, in her opinion—were, too.

Mist billowed downward again, propelled by something above. Another, more distant scream.

Aryl looked up. They'd taken what shelter they could beside a wall. "I can't see it," she complained. Enris had shared his memories of immense size, claws, and unusual wings, but with woefully inadequate detail—being more interested in the ground below at the time.

"Good," he asserted, back against the wall. "Trust me, if you could, you'd be too close."

Aryl made a noncommittal noise. She wanted to see one. Especially in flight.

"No more running," Naryn said weakly, and eased herself to the ground. She let out a small moan. Immediately, a trio of rocks that had been aiming at a shadow changed to tilt in her direction. Aryl kept her eye on them. They'd be easy to push into the water—it was how close she dared get to the water to do the pushing that was the problem.

She could see one feeding pile of rocks; the unfortunate Vyna beneath hadn't made a sound. Doubtless the mist hid more. Those out in their floats had fared the worst. The rest of Vyna—she *reached*—most sheltered deep in their island or stayed within the Cloisters. Had the Councillors and Adepts noticed their Clan was under assault, or were they still huddled over their prize?

Would their metal doors hold?

More screams from an unseen creature. Another series of rocks clattered to the pavement, to stop and begin to roll toward them.

"Is it me," Enris asked mildly, "or are they starting to aim them at us?"

Whether they were or not, Aryl thought grimly, there were too many rock hunters nearby for comfort. "Maybe they'll run out."

"We could go back to the . . ." Naryn's voice faded in and out. "Aryl . . . I . . ."

You wore the pendant here, didn't you? Fool.

"Naryn?" Aryl knelt by her, put an anxious hand on her sweat-chilled brow. *Naryn? What did you say? Why the pendant?* She hadn't told anyone, not even Enris, what the Oud had said. It had made no sense, anyway, babbling about Tikitik counting all life, waving a pendant and token at her.

I said you were a fool. Are you mind deaf, too?

Not Naryn. Aryl glared at the rock hunters, who, being noticed, pretended to be a natural heap of rocks in the middle of perfectly smooth pavement. She *reached*.

Naryn's mind was closed behind her strong shields, other than a whisper-thin presence. She saved her strength, was close to unconscious.

And was not alone.

Of course she's not alone! Now get me out of here.

Aryl rocked back on her heels. "Enris?"

"I *heard*." He came to Naryn's other side. All around, the splash and clatter of rocks being dropped.

The sendings were powerful.

More than that, Aryl realized with dismay.

They were not from a child.

Anaj?

Unfortunately. A hint of *amusement. I hope Teso put himself in one of those things, too. Serve him right. He convinced us only our knowledge would be stored. Not who . . .* nothing amused now . . . *not who we are . . .* grimmer still . . . *Kynan?* The sudden overwhelming awareness of *LOSS* was quickly buried under layers of shielding. Aryl might have imagined it, if not for the tears spilling down her own cheeks. Naryn curled as if to protect what she carried.

Enris said gently, "Your Chosen."

Dead. Flat and cold and final. *They're all dead. As we'll be if you don't start acting like a Speaker instead of cowering here.* A *snap* of authority. *Think rocks are all they can drop?* An image, terrifyingly clear, of baskets filled with what belonged to truenight, to the utter dark, to the nightmares of Yena.

The swarm.

Aryl shuddered.

"What's wrong?" Enris demanded. He hadn't *heard*? *Negotiate, young Speaker, before it's too late.*

"Aryl—"

No time to explain. Aryl looked desperately at Enris. "Protect them!" Then she slammed down her shields and began to run.

Up the ramp, jumping rocks, stepping on them. Too slow. Too slow. More screams, more CRASH.

Aryl grabbed the next light pole and swung herself atop the railing wall. Better. She hit full stride, leaping across where the wall angled back on itself as it climbed. Higher and higher. She passed heaving piles of rock hunters, doorways choked with them as too many tried to enter at once, and knew it could be worse.

The swarm hated light. That wouldn't save anything in their path.

How high did she need to be?

Only one way to find out. Aryl kept running.

The ramp wall widened, its top becoming a dirt-filled hollow choked with vines and other growth she crushed underfoot or jumped. The air finally smelled of life. Behind her, the grind and click as rock hunters excitedly worked to reach it, piling on each other. They'd be a hazard on the way back if they succeeded.

Though, Aryl thought with sudden cheer, easy to kick off.

Enris was directly below again. She'd circled the island.

Where were the Tikitik? The mist and black stone swallowed the light from Vyna's glows, smudged shadows, refused any long views. That much was familiar from the canopy. Her shadow ran with her along the steep buildings, doubled, disappeared, caught up again.

Aryl jumped the next sharp angle and stopped, balanced on her toes. Something was here. Something other than the rocks rolling in the shadows.

A stretch of ramp, floored in black with white lines for ornamentation. Beside it, an upward thrust of building, with an abundance of narrow, empty windows. Thin vines trailed down between. No Vyna to her *inner* sense. Unlike a Yena, they ran down from danger.

Poor choice, she thought absently, busy searching for what alerted her.

There. A patch of mist ahead, darker than it should be.

A darkness that shifted.

Up, then. The vines Aryl knew better than to trust, but the window openings were as good as a ladder. She took advantage of a series of glows shaped like swimmers along the lower portion of the building to reach the first line of windows, then it was a simple matter of picking those which would take her to one side of whatever shaded the mist.

From the smell emanating from the first window, this wasn't a building normally in use. Enris had said the Vyna were more numerous once. Yena had been; its outlying bridges served empty homes. She hadn't paid attention then. Hadn't imagined the past mattered, or that it stretched beyond living memory.

They could, Aryl mused as she climbed, compare the numbers of children born to each Clan; such information was recorded in its Cloisters. Perhaps that had changed over time.

Marcus would be proud of this un-Om'ray notion.

Haxel would consider it a thorough waste of time.

Aryl snorted. At the moment, they'd both be right.

A louder *snort* answered. From above.

Slipping inside the nearest window had appeal. Aryl kept climbing.

The mist shifted around her, a warm thick breeze she'd enjoy under other circumstances. Shifted and darkened, as something leaned down through it to inspect her.

Now she did stop.

Two pairs of eyes appeared through the mist, blinking alternately. Each was larger than her head. They disappeared behind the yawning chasm of an enormous mouth, yellow-tongued, abundantly toothed. The mouth closed again. Good sign. The neck she could see beyond the long head was swollen. Recently fed.

Better still.

The head shook with a splatter of drool and lifted back into the mist. She climbed after it, passed a foot with claws that could easily span her body but presently gripped the sill of a window, then another, and another. The finely scaled legs supported a long, narrow body, covered with hairs, each tipped with a tiny sparkling drop.

Enris might have exaggerated the narrowness of Vyna's bridges; not so the esan's size. Haxel would want her to find out if it was edible.

Where were its wings?

Short of climbing a leg, she couldn't see past the body, so Aryl worked her way from window to window until she found herself at the top of the building.

The sixth foot crushed one of the Vyna's wall-top gardens. The head reappeared as she jumped from the wall to the ramp below, swinging down to regard her past its front knee.

As did other heads. They clustered here, the esans, clinging to the wall she'd climbed, standing on this ramp. More above. Like flitters roosting on a nekis, as close together as manners allowed.

There were, Aryl realized belatedly, no more splashes. Just the esans' overlapping *huffs,* as if they took in her scent and rejected it.

Huffs and a muffled *clinkclattergrind* from over her head.

Aryl glanced at the swollen neck drooping above her. Round shapes pushed against the skin. The esan gave an irritated shake and *huff.* Something *rattled.*

Explaining how they carried the rock hunters. She was almost sympathetic.

Mist swirled around paired legs, then revealed a single figure standing by itself. Watching her.

Tikitik.

More came out of the mist, gathered in groups, stared. Something Tikitik were well equipped to do, possessing four eyes: two large, a smaller pair behind, all on mobile cones of flesh. Instead of a mouth, writhing gray protuberances moved as if tasting the air. They wore nothing but a belt to support a longknife and strips of cloth patterned in their symbols to wrap ankles and wrists. Their skin, more knobby plates than hide, was pale gray, the color of mist. No surprise. It could change, she'd seen it for herself, to match a background. For Tikitik were skulkers, hiders, loving to surprise.

When they couldn't get something else to do the work for them.

Aryl's fingers itched for her longknife. With an effort of will, she turned them to touch the Speaker's Pendant instead.

Aryl?

He'd felt her reaction. She sent an image of what, or rather who, faced her. *Peace, Enris.* He subsided, watchful and worried.

The solitary Tikitik was different. It wore a black sash from shoulder to hip, ending in a fringe that brushed the stone pavement, and held its head higher than the rest on its long down curved neck—though not at shoulder-height. It gave a soft, guttural bark. A laugh. "Greetings, Apart-from-All."

She didn't need the symbols on its wristband. Using that name for her—that laugh? This was one of the Tikitik outside any faction, who wandered Cersi to gather information for its kind and, she was beginning to fear, stir trouble at whim. It might be one she'd met, or another. They were all dangerous. "Thought Traveler," she acknowledged coolly. Courtesy first; knife if necessary. "What are you doing here?"

Esans stirred uneasily at her voice; one uttered its scream. The Tikitik at their feet grunted something at them; they stilled at once. She hid her distaste. Their way, to control beasts. Why the beasts allowed it was a mystery she'd rather not solve.

That familiar sly tilt of the head. "I would ask you the same, Little Speaker, if it mattered. I'm here to bestow a remarkable honor. You will be the first Om'ray to visit Tikitna, the Place-of-Bloodless-Meeting. There you will explain." It pranced forward with its disturbing quickness, clawed toes snicking on pavement, then stopped. "You will explain so very many things."

She could try to 'port. It might work this far above the still-restive rumn. All four of Thought Traveler's eyes were fixed on her, as if daring her to do exactly that: flaunt this profound *change* in Om'ray in front of it. Prove everything it suspected.

End the Agreement.

"I look forward to it," Aryl said. *Enris, the Tikitik want me to leave with them.*

Instantly: *Not alone.*

Not alone, she agreed, as though there was a choice. Vyna was no place for Enris and Naryn. Or Anaj. "There are Sona Om'ray on the lowermost level," she informed the Tikitik. "They come with me."

"Of course." Thought Traveler gestured toward the mist—or was it to the encircling mountain beyond? "The Vyna, however ill-mannered, must be protected."

"By killing them?" And she thought Oud spouted nonsense.

"A few nonbreeders." An amused bark. "Which brought you straight to me without exposing Vyna to a more intimate intrusion."

"I'm no threat to the Vyna." Not if she could help it.

"Apart-from-All. You are nothing but threat to the Vyna. How I would enjoy explaining matters to you ... but you could not comprehend."

Aryl comprehended one thing quite well, as attendant Tikitik busied themselves for departure, attaching baskets to the legs of the esans, barking softly.

Thought Traveler had enjoyed "protecting" the Vyna.

Under other circumstances, their flight by esan would have enthralled her. In Yena, Aryl had spent fists building models of wastryl wings she'd called fiches; her triumph a shape able to glide great distances on a wind. The esan's two pairs of wings, once opened from their fold over the back, were like those of most flitters, being clear with dark veins. They stiffened like one of her fiches as the esans flung themselves from Vyna's walls, gliding down through the mist toward the platform below. To rise over the mountains, the stiff wings beat in powerful strokes, then began to vibrate in place, like a biter's.

The gliding, Aryl thought with a certain satisfaction, she could do.

The basket suspended between the middle pair of legs wasn't uncomfortable, mostly because Enris held her in his arms. They'd protested when Naryn had been put in one of her own, but the Tikitik were surprisingly gentle with her. There'd been some kind of cushioning within.

Not enough.

Anaj. Her distinct mindvoice made it easy to forget she wasn't standing with them. An oddly familiar voice. Like, Aryl decided, unexpectedly amused, an older Haxel.

"More like my grandmother," Enris countered, and their esan shook vigorously. His deep voice irritated the creature more than hers.

Mountains swept beneath them, their shapes muted. The sun was hidden behind cloud. She shivered in the chill and Enris rearranged his grip so his warm forearms covered hers. A Tuana's skin must be thicker. *This is much better than my first flight,* he sent cheerfully. *Think they'll let us keep one?*

She eyed the body above dubiously. Thin and muscular. An abundance of long bones beneath the skin when it flexed. *Looks tough.*

His laugh rumbled through her. *Not to eat, my blood-thirsty little Yena. To carry things. Us, for one.*

It wasn't often he managed to shock her. *There are machines for that*, she countered, and found she quite liked the notion. Machines that weren't Om'ray, that was the problem: the Strangers' aircars, the Oud's version, which required an Oud willing to fly it. Unless . . . *I could ask our Oud for one,* she mused, snuggling against Enris. *We could take it apart, see how it was made, change it to suit us.*

We'd need tools, a metal shop. She'd surprised him in turn, but his clever, bold mind took hold of the idea and began to puzzle at it.

Anything was possible, if they survived this day. On that thought, she opened her shields, let her *inner* sense *reach*. She didn't need the Vyna's revolting intimacy or to intrude into the other's mind. This was her Talent, Aryl thought gratefully, and sought Naryn.

There. A solitary glow, no longer knotted to another by Joining. Aryl sighed with relief as she traced only the connections natural among Om'ray: Naryn to her, to Enris, to the rest of their kind . . .

. . . to Anaj.

She sleeps at last, child. Let her be.

And you? Enris sent. *How does it feel in there?*

Trust her Chosen to ask what she hadn't dared, Aryl thought with an inner grin, waiting for the answer.

Suddenly, her body felt too small, too warm; the arms about her too tight; the sound of wind and breathing replaced by the POUND of a stranger's heart. She couldn't see, couldn't feel, couldn't taste or smell, could only squirm and struggle futilely against—against—

STOP! His sending was intended to sting. *That's enough!*

You asked. Not contrite. If anything, the old Adept's mindvoice sounded pleased, as might Haxel after a lesson successfully delivered.

Aryl had been imprisoned within a rastis once; had fought her own inner battle for sanity. The memory tasted like Anaj's sharing: terrified, abandoned, alone. She'd have given anything to have help. *I could try to let you see through my eyes.*

Aryl!

Hush, young hothead, Anaj told him. *I can* hear *if I wish. I don't want to see. I don't want to be here. Bad enough* sensing *where we are.*

Where they were was passing over Rayna, aimed at Amna, though Aryl doubted that was their final destination. Sona was farther away every moment, a temptation easy to resist. They couldn't abandon Naryn—or Anaj. *We'll get you to our Birth Watcher as soon as possible,* she promised.

I don't need a Birth Watcher. I need OUT!!

A blinding flash of *AGONY* from Naryn.

What's happening? Anaj?

LET ME OUT!

The sac opened to the baby's demand. They couldn't allow Anaj's desperation to rip it open inside Naryn. They'd both die.

Anaj, stop, please. Aryl pulled away from Enris and clenched her hands on the basket rim, trying to see under the other esan, to see Naryn. *If there's a safe way to free you, we'll find it. But it can't be here. You know that.* Healing used Power to push the body's growth beyond normal. Could they hurry a pregnancy?

I will be free. There was something implacable in the sending. *I don't belong here. I can't survive here.*

The Vyna's help was like a rotted rope, Aryl thought bitterly, one that would snap if you trusted it. *Wait, Anaj. Until we're home—*

Where do you think the beasts take us, child? Not even a token grants safe passage through Tikitna. Home? More likely when they're no longer entertained by you, they'll drop us in the Lake of Fire. Trust me, I intend to be free before dying again.

Enris gripped her shoulder, bent to whisper in her ear. "Baby Grandmother knows something of the Tikitik's meeting place."

Aryl nodded. She forced down her fear for Naryn, concentrated on being Sona's Speaker. *Anaj. Tell me about this place. About the Tikitik.*

Frustration. *Cersi has changed. This is no longer my time.*

The past matters, Aryl sent, confident of this if anything. *The Tikitik pay attention to it. Om'ray must. You warned me about the swarm in baskets. It's something they've done before.*

Yes. Bleak. *That's how they move them to a new grove. Without warning. As if hoping to kill Om'ray. Or Oud. They can't be trusted. They don't think like we do.*

They have a purpose, Aryl sent back, feeling Enris agree. *Thought Traveler said I was a threat to Vyna, that Vyna must be protected.*

They won't lie, Anaj admitted. *Not directly. Confuse and avoid and never say the whole of a thing, always.*

Another who'd been Sona's Speaker, Aryl realized abruptly, flattening her palm over the pendant. *You wore this.* Adept and Speaker, like her mother. She let out a sigh of relief. *I need your help—*

Remember what *I am.* Bitter. Bitter and afraid and hollow. *I'm scrapings from when Sona flourished, when we were the largest of the ten Clans. Nothing more.*

Ten? There were eight, counting newly restored Sona.

Which are gone? Enris asked.

A moment's silence. The old Adept must *feel* the change in her world, know what was missing. Aryl held in her compassion; she didn't think Anaj an Om'ray who'd value it.

Nena. None came to Sona in my lifetime. My grandfather . . . he remembered an uncle from Nena who did clever rope tricks. Extra thumbs.

The other . . . Anaj's shields tightened, dampening her emotion. *Xrona's gone, too. My sister's second Chosen was from there. Their children had his curls. He'd talk all truenight about his Passage, how he'd climbed through the canopy and dropped his glow when she Called so he had to wall himself inside a giant thorn bush to escape the swarms but nothing would stop him—*

'Second Chosen?' Aryl interrupted. *I don't understand.*

What's to understand? With a return of the old Adept's asperity. *Her first drowned in the river. Fool never did swim as well as he thought. As for the rest of Cersi—*

She survived his death? Enris, this time.

This time, Anaj hesitated a long moment. Then, *Why does this surprise you?*

Aryl steadied herself, then shared her memory of Myris at the instant she was Lost. Enris put his arms around her waist, shared inner *warmth* through their link. *That's why, Anaj,* he sent. *Our Chosen end together. Joining is for life.*

Your link does feel different . . . it goes—startled—*it goes through the Dark as well! How is that possible? What* are *you?*

Something new, Aryl admitted. While the other was off-balance, she sent, with all the *confidence* she could, *Which is why you should trust us, Anaj. Please. We will find a way to help you. Stay where you are. For now.*

No answer. For Naryn's sake, she hoped the old one listened.

A whisper in her ear. "I wonder where they were. Xrona. Nena. What is it?" As she stiffened.

"Nothing." Aryl tried to relax.

But said aloud, she *knew* those names. Marcus Bowman had said them, parts of them. He'd claimed they were Hoveny words, spoke them in an order: Vy. Ray. So. Gro. Ne. Tua. Ye. Pa. Am. Nor. Xro. Fa.

She'd never forgotten the shock of that first time, hearing real sounds come out of his not-Om'ray mouth. Ye-NA. Tua-NA. Hearing him say the names of Cersi's Clans.

Eight now. In Anaj's Cersi, ten.

Had there been more once? A Norna? Fana?

What other names did Marcus know?

It was as well for her peace of mind that the drone of the esan's wings ceased just then. The ground began rising. They entered air full of a tangy scent, unlike anything she'd encountered before.

The basket tipped forward with the esan. Eager to

see, Aryl leaned well over the edge; Enris grabbed for her belt, holding onto the opposite side. "Careful!"

The esan shook irritably and continued to plummet.

She ignored them both. What was below took her breath away.

Paired curves of white held back an expanse of glittering green-blue water, water that swelled and tumbled and roared toward them in matched lines without beginning or end. The curves edged a flat land, shaped like an open pod and covered in unfamiliar growth. Too even to be a grove, Aryl judged. The land stretched into the water, the border blurred as brown spilled into the water to stain it in thick bands.

The ocean.

She'd heard of it, tried to imagine it, failed. Undrinkable water she could comprehend—the Lay was foul. Unlike the Lake of Fire, the ocean had life; Amna Clan harvested swimmers along its edge. She lifted her gaze.

Like her first view of the sky, of stars at truenight, what she saw made no sense at first. Clouds like puffs of winter breath marched away to the horizon, smaller and smaller until they were dots. There, the water lost all texture, became dark as it collided with the sky and clouds in a ragged edge that refused to let her eyes focus. She could see forever. Too far. Too much. *Enris* . . . now comforted by his hold on her belt, sharing his *awe* at what confronted them . . . *Enris, how big can the world be?*

How small is ours?

Calm yourselves, Anaj sent. *What you see is illusion, the mind's trick to fill the emptiness beyond. Om'ray are the world. How could there be anything beyond us?*

Not a question she should answer, Aryl decided.

Poor Anaj had enough to bear.

Tikitna.

The mauve-green growth, solid from a greater height,

proved to be riddled with gaps as they descended. Some glinted, revealing a multitude of narrow, twisting streams; their brown water was sluggish, as if reluctant to enter the ocean and be lost. Other gaps bustled with movement: Tikitik and their beasts. No structures, but Aryl ran out of time to look. Their esan settled on top of the growth, cracking branches and stretching its long neck to snap and scream at its fellows as they arrived in turn.

"Hang on!" Enris shouted. His voice didn't appear to bother the beast this time. Good advice, Aryl thought, hoping Naryn heeded it. Their basket swung below, still tied to the middle legs. The esan didn't appear to care about that either, continuing to vigorously defend its chosen spot from all comers.

Remind me to stay home next time. Naryn's mindvoice, steady and, if not strong, then reassuringly normal.

Anaj must have listened, Aryl thought with relief. "I'm going to climb down and find Thought Traveler."

Her Chosen peered over the edge of the basket, probably assessing the height. *You can't do it without a rope,* she sent fondly.

Enris straightened, rocking the basket, and laughed without humor. "Which one?"

"What do you mean?"

He jerked a thumb over his shoulder; Aryl looked down.

Black Tikitik sat in the lowermost branches of the growths around them. Fifty, perhaps more.

Every wristband she could see bore the symbol that meant "Thought Traveler."

She really should have changed before leaving Sona, she thought, brushing shreds of green-mauve from her tunic, plucking one from her hairnet. The basket was full of shattered plants, courtesy of the esan's flailing about. She looked like a child caught playing in the canopy. Where was dignity when she needed it?

Probably, Aryl told herself, hiding someplace safe.

"If they all have questions," her Chosen commented, "make sure they give us lunch first. We missed it."

Make sure we aren't lunch first, Anaj added.

Naryn was silent, but let Aryl feel her *confidence.*

They believed in her.

She wished she did.

Interlude

THERE WAS LUNCH. Too much of it, Enris thought queasily. The sinuous stepped construction that was the Tikitik version of a table was crammed with bowls of varying shapes and sizes. Bowls of the revolting dresel jelly, shiny and purple, that Aryl and the Yena prized, bowls of swimmer flesh floating in a brown sauce exactly as his uncle from Amna had remembered for him, bowls of what Anaj proclaimed to be fresh rokly, bowls of this and that, even a bowl of denos cakes, steaming hot.

Sweetpies that might have been his mother's. He tried not to look.

Favorite foods from different Om'ray Clans, some he didn't recognize. Proof the Tikitik knew more about his kind than he did.

Of course, it wasn't only the food and its implications that ruined any appetite he'd had.

It was the audience.

Tikitik surrounded them, silent, attentive. Most squatted on wide branches, branches that curled down to a convenient height, that aligned to provide the best view, that made easy steps to upper levels, that walled away secrets. Overhead, finer growth interlaced to make roofs, with short, stubby leaves tilted to direct sunlight where it was wanted and shade everywhere else.

They'd seen the Tikitik buildings from the air, Enris thought with disgust, and not known it.

These Tikitik were hard to recognize as well. He'd expected them to be mottled mauve and brown to match their surroundings, or black like the Thought Travelers. Instead, their knobby skins blazed with color. Yellow pulsed along pendulous throats. Heads were bright blue and more of that color flared along the short spines of each arm. Eye cones were more variable.

Did they have to come in fleshy pink?

Fur brushed his hand and Enris managed not to flinch. Another loper. The things had no fear or caution. And weren't alone. Everywhere he looked, something moved. All to a purpose. Lopers used their clever paws and teeth to carry objects. What he'd at first thought were biters after his blood—and promptly swatted, to the amusement of the Tikitik—turned out to be busy picking up wastes. An assortment of them had almost finished removing a spill near the denos bowl, flying off with flecks of yellow on their tiny limbs.

Another reason he wasn't hungry.

"Mothers must be strong." Thought Traveler—the one who'd accompanied them here—stretched its fingers toward the bowls. "Any of these contain what your bodies require. You should eat." This close, its skin wasn't black, Enris noted, but a blue so dark as to lose its color. The cones were startling white, the eyes themselves black beads sitting on top. To draw attention where it looked? Its mouth protuberances, like those of the rest of its kind, were gray.

As far as he was concerned, those looked more like a meal trying to escape than body parts.

Another reason.

"Something more familiar, perhaps." A tall gourd stood beside one bend of the table. The Tikitik lifted its lid and indicated Enris should come closer. "Young Oud? These are quite fresh."

The gourd was full of small pale rocks. Moving rocks.

Young . . . Oud?

Familiar indeed. Remembering that taste, Enris swallowed bile. Never eating again, he decided. Ever.

Naryn eyed the selection, then chose rokly. Enris guessed Anaj had a share in that choice. Aryl merely lifted an eyebrow. "How do you know what we need?"

"We know what everything needs." Thought Traveler lifted its head. Its smaller rear eyes moved ceaselessly, as if it was as important to keep watch on its fellows as on them. "And that is the last question I will answer in Tikitna."

By the look on Aryl's face, it wouldn't be the last one she'd ask. Enris kept his smile and his *pride* to himself. It would take more than all of Cersi's Tikitik to stop his Chosen if she saw a path for her people. She didn't seek to lead others—didn't believe herself capable of it. She didn't need to; her vision and courage, the pulse of her extraordinary Power, these drew Om'ray to her, gave them strength.

Other than the Vyna—and maybe, given time, them as well.

If Om'ray were metal, Aryl would glow like a finely crafted knife being tempered by flame. Beautiful, stronger by the moment, deadly if necessary. A sensible Chosen would fear for his life, she so willingly risked hers. Unlike Anaj's sister, he wouldn't survive to Choose again.

He wouldn't have it any other way.

Except . . .

Enris strengthened his shields. Fear for Sweetpie would choke him, then spread to smother them both. Aryl fought her own constant battle with instinct; he could sense it. All he could do to help her was control himself and keep shields between them at the deepest level.

Though something must have *leaked* through. She glanced up at him with those wide gray eyes, a softness in their depths. A loose strand of hair tempted him to touch it.

"Don't miss the sweetpies," he ordered gravely and took three for himself. He ate them without tasting, enjoying far more her hesitant yet trusting nibble, then dazzling smile as she reached the filling.

"You were right. These are good."

He brushed a crumb from her chin. "I'm always right."

The Tikitik stirred around them, hissing softly, some giving their bark. Naryn came back to stand with them, looking uneasy. "Something's happening."

Aryl nodded. Enris could see nothing but branches and squatting Tikitik. "Lunch" had been waiting for them in an area otherwise identical to where they'd walked from the esan's landing. Paths no wider than his shoulders wound between the low branches, and nothing of the sky could be seen. It was like being inside a living tunnel. A crowded one. And the smell? Between the musk of the Tikitik, the fresh and plentiful droppings of the lopers, and the food, his nose should have been unable to smell another thing.

But it did.

Enris turned his head toward the source, only to find Aryl already gazing the same way. A path, like the others, twisted so they could see very little of where it led. "What is it?"

"Rot. The kind that lies beneath dark water. Something's stirred the bottom."

The Tikitik surrounding them were no longer restless. Thought Traveler was also still, except for the slide of its eyes. If he had to guess, they waited for the Om'ray to do something. What?

What are they waiting for? Anaj sounded annoyed. *Why are they keeping us here?*

Aryl's full lower lip was between her teeth, her habit when puzzling through a problem. Usually Enris found it set him thinking of things that weren't problems at all; here and now, he felt sudden anticipation.

The lip came free. "I don't believe they are," she stated. Then, *Come,* as she started walking briskly.

How did he know it would be the path with the rot?

"It could be worse, Naryn," he assured her as they trailed behind. "There could be climbing."

There were Tikitik in Aryl's way, their shoulders towering over her head. Enris tensed as she simply walked straight at them, but at the last possible instant, they took a step to the side, raising their heads sharply as if offended.

"You need not accompany Apart-from-All." Thought Traveler pranced up beside him, clawed feet silent on the soft ground. "Here will is measured, not imposed or opposed. You could stay here and wait in comfort."

"Our will is to follow our Speaker," Naryn snapped.

"That is up to you."

"Alone," Enris suggested.

A soft amused bark. "But that is up to me, Enris Once-of-Tuana. I find myself with the will to follow. I admit to being curious how Apart-from-All will explain herself."

Knowing his name didn't make it the same Thought Traveler who'd dropped him in the midst of the Vyna . . .

"As it is my will to return this."

. . . the thin leather strap dangled from its three clawed fingers, twisting as the fingers rolled it to and fro did. A knot of hair was tied to it.

The thong was from his pouch; the hair Aryl's gift, a Highknot, as she'd explained it. Yena children, on their first climb away from their mothers, would tie one to the highest point they reached. Accomplishment and a promise to return.

Definitely the one. Enris took the thong from the smug creature and tucked it in a pocket, sensing Naryn's *curiosity*. Or Anaj's. No questions, was it? "I hope you had a better reason to drop me on the Vyna than the fun of watching me die."

A bark. "This is why I so enjoy our conversations. Consider it a test of Vyna's will. I knew you'd be a temptation."

He hadn't missed Tikitik gibberish.

"I'm gratified you survived, despite refusing my excellent advice, Enris Now-Sarc," Thought Traveler continued. "The opportunity for your stimulating company shouldn't be wasted."

Meaning there'd be no getting rid of the creature. Enris gestured a grim apology to Naryn.

They entered the path. Like the others, it was too narrow to walk side by side, though lopers squeezed past, carrying or dragging bags. Enris let Naryn go first, then put himself ahead of Thought Traveler. Underfoot, a dense twisted growth, like a mat, deadened all sound; its faint spice when trodden on did nothing to counter the miasma of decay. The path's center was lower—worn, he guessed. Otherwise, there was nothing to give a sense of age.

The plants to either side met over their heads. They were inhabited. He could hear Tikitik voices, distant, sometimes moving. Once, the clatter of what could have been dishes. Rustling. The living walls were inhabited, too. More biters-with-tasks; something that seemed to swim through the foliage, stopping to stare at them with its triplet of stalked red eyes; what he assumed were yellow flowers until one jumped to the path beside him in a flurry of limbs and teeth to pin a squealing loper and drag it away to the shadows. Aryl, ahead, didn't turn around. Naryn flinched and walked faster.

"It's necessary to cull the old ones," Thought Traveler volunteered, raising his voice to be heard over growls and squeals. "They forget their routes." *Crunching.*

Wonderful place. His skin crawled as he imagined all four of the Tikitik's eyes watching for any reaction.

The path kept twisting. All he could tell after the first few turns was that they most often walked toward Amna, its many Om'ray a comfort, if out of reach. Aryl set a quick pace: confident or happier in motion, no matter where she was going. Both, Enris thought fondly.

Maybe their unwelcome companion could be of use. "Is this the way we're supposed to go?"

"Questions are forbidden in Tikitna. They impose will."

Or maybe not.

What would Aryl do? Though it rankled, with this Tikitik especially, Enris decided to apologize. "I meant no offense. This is an unfamiliar—" ridiculous and highly annoying, "—constraint on our conversation."

"We don't expect Om'ray to know our ways." Its head appeared over his shoulder, the nearest cone eye almost touching his cheek, fleshy protuberances brushing his jaw like soft moist fingers. With an effort, Enris managed not to leap away or, what would doubtless be worse, swat the things. "You've never been curious about them before."

Not a question, Enris realized. Yet it could express interest. He tried to look the other in the eye, without tripping over his feet. "To most Om'ray," he admitted, "you aren't *real*, so your ways don't matter."

Another eye swiveled his way. This close, the movement made a sound like chewing on ice. His stomach protested. "You, like Apart-from-All and this other one, no longer need to adjust to our presence. You consider us real, then."

Another not-question, he was sure of it. He began to see what compelled Aryl to try and understand not-Om'ray. The slightest success was rewarding.

Though he could have done without the head over his shoulder.

And it was right. He couldn't point to the moment he'd stopped fighting his *inner* sense, when he'd accepted the not-Om'ray as being—as being people, too. The Human? No doubt there. Oud? He wasn't ready for that. Not yet. That they had their own will and desires that affected his kind and their survival?

That he believed, Enris thought grimly.

"We're learning," was all he said.

"Another dangerous choice." Thought Traveler's head bobbed, then retreated. "You continue to entertain, Enris Mendolar."

"Enris d'sud Sarc," he corrected, turning to look over his shoulder at the creature. Its use of "Choice" was no accident. What had it said, that day outside Vyna? "You told me, 'This would not be a match we favor.' Sorry to disappoint you." Quite the opposite. Could the Tikitik grasp the nuance?

That amused bark. "Far from disappointed, Chosen of Aryl di Sarc. Your match was not favored because we deemed you unfit. We would never be in favor of a lesser mate for Apart-from-All, an Om'ray of such . . . interesting . . . potential. I'm gratified you exceeded yourself."

Thought Traveler excelled at mixing flattery with insult. Enris dismissed both. There was a truth here. Something he should know. He stopped and faced the creature; the narrow path forced the Tikitik to stop as well. "It couldn't have been my hair," Enris commented mildly. "My mother claimed it was my best feature. Of many."

Not humility?

He ignored Naryn.

"This is Tikitna, where explanations may be given." Four eyes regarded him; something rustled in the shadows. Another something squealed in pain. "Consider, Enris Chosen-of-Sarc," Thought Traveler said at last, "that some are best not received."

"That's my choice," Enris informed it, and crossed his arms. "I'd like to know."

"We deemed you unfit because of your birth-sib." The Tikitik held out a hand and turned it palm down. "We observed him fail to adapt."

Falling felt like this, Enris decided numbly. As if the ground beneath his feet had been 'ported away, leaving him over nothing at all. Words forced themselves through his lips. "You're telling me you watched my brother die."

"Yes."

Enris?? Aryl, alarmed.

Blood pounded in his ears. He couldn't answer her, dared not.

"Another Mendolar for your entertainment?" Hands

balled into fists, Enris advanced on the Tikitik. "Did you laugh at him? Did you?"

Enris!

Instead of retreating, Thought Traveler squatted, knees higher than its head, and spread its arms. "A blow to my neck would cause the most pain," it advised calmly. "Though if you prefer permanent damage, strike any eye."

Enris froze.

"We did not laugh when Kiric Mendolar stepped off the bridge," the Tikitik continued. "That which would survive must be strong. Your brother was. He completed an arduous Passage. He endured the canopy until we believed he would adapt and find a mate, but we were wrong. There are peculiarities in how Om'ray interact with one another that we do not and probably cannot comprehend. We concluded Kiric's inability to find a Yena mate made it unlikely you could succeed."

"Wrong again."

Thought Traveler's head lifted slightly. "Which does amuse me."

All four eyes, Enris told himself. Blind it. Then kill it.

I have my knife. Aryl's pragmatic offer startled him to sanity.

What was he thinking? Kill Thought Traveler for the truth?

Kiric wouldn't live again.

Om'ray violence here would end any hope of negotiating with the Tikitik.

No. As much to himself as his fearsome Chosen. More calmly, *though I do appreciate your willingness to slit throats for me.*

"We're falling behind," he told the waiting Tikitik, and turned back to follow Naryn.

* ✳ *

Watch your step.

The sending from Aryl came before they caught up to her.

"What—?" Naryn's foot skidded sideways. Enris lunged for her, only to have his boot sink deep, black mud bubbling over it. Bubbles that released fresh rot.

I told you to be careful.

You call that a warning? Naryn sent indignantly, pulling free to take a second lurching, sliding step. Her boots sank in as well. After a few steps, the white hem of her Adept's robe was thoroughly stained. *You get to explain this to Oran.*

Mild dismay fading as Aryl's concentration shifted.

No Aryl-sized footprints marred the path ahead. Enris glanced up at the branches and shook his head. "She cheated."

Thought Traveler passed them, barking good humor, its long-toed feet spread wide and not, Enris noticed, sinking at all.

Leaving him alone with Naryn. "Wait."

She looked at him, raised one dark-red eyebrow.

Enris dug into his inner pocket and drew out the sleep-teach device. "Take this, Naryn. Put it somewhere safe."

He might have asked her to touch an Oud. "What is it?"

"We don't have time." He thrust out the hand with the device. "Keep it safe. And don't let them see it. Or Aryl," he added.

If anything, the eyebrow went higher, but Naryn took it in her long-fingered hand. He wondered belatedly where she could put it, but she simply slipped it within what had looked a seam. Why was he surprised? Adepts needed pockets, too.

They were still alone—but not for long, he was sure. Aryl would take what risks she must; he was only as safe as his Chosen. Someone else had to know, be able to use it. He offered his right hand. "Naryn, please," as she hesitated, her expression strange. "I have to show you how it works."

She crossed her arms, rejecting any touch. Of course, he realized, chagrined. He'd offered the hand of Choice. Cold, distant. *It's from the Human, isn't it?* Just to him.

Yes. It can teach us their words. If his feet hadn't been stuck in mud, he'd have bounced from one to the other with impatience. Not a good idea, with Naryn.

Show me, she sent at last.

Enris *shared* the memory of how the device was used. Not enough, he realized. He lowered his shields to let her feel his *conviction*, his *urgency. Naryn, if anything happens to us, 'port to Sona. Warn them. If the Tikitik come after you, use this. Go to Marcus for help—*

Her *revulsion* hit like a blow. *Never!*

Impossible, stubborn Om'ray. Shields back, Enris grabbed her hand, ignoring her wince. *Do you think an empty Cloisters can save us?* Naryn tried to pull free; he held tighter. She had to listen. *The Strangers have technology beyond anything on Cersi. Marcus is the only hope left if the others turn against us. You can trust him—*

The only one I trust is Aryl! She threw *PAIN* at him. *LET ME GO!*

Enris opened his hand and she flung herself back, glaring at him. With an effort, he made himself not glare back. *Aryl trusts Marcus—*

The stir of *concern,* from a mind occupied elsewhere. He sent a quick *reassurance* and felt Aryl's focus ease and shift away.

What I know, Enris, still with force, *is I will not risk Sona. I will not reveal our ability to the Tikitik. I will not run home and draw them after me. I will not—will not!—trust Sona to a being who isn't even of our world. I'll die first.*

And she would. Hair lashed against her shoulders. Her dark eyes defied him.

Aryl, for all her fondness for Marcus Bowman, refused to add any of his technology to their daily lives. Now here was Naryn, ready to die before seeking the Human's help.

Was he the only one to grasp the superiority of the Strangers' technology? The only one to see it might be better to reach beyond Cersi?

Then let's hope all goes well. Enris held out his hand for the sleepteach device.

No. Naryn smoothed the panel over her pocket. *Aryl must know about this. You can't use it without her consent.*

She was right and he knew it, much as the realization galled him. "Keep it, then," he said aloud, unwilling to trust *inner* speech. "But I tell her when I'm ready, not you."

If Naryn *felt* the warning beneath the words, she didn't react to it. "You're her Chosen."

Which wasn't a promise, but the best he'd get. Enris gestured ahead.

Without another word, Naryn turned and left.

Enris followed.

Tried.

His right foot wouldn't move.

He pulled.

And pulled.

Finally, his boot came free with a *splot,* mud flying in most directions. Enris heaved that foot forward, relieved, only to find his other foot glued to the ground. *How much of this is there?* he sent to Aryl, dismayed.

You're almost here. A sense of *awe.*

Enris stopped struggling and looked up, trying to see ahead, but the path took another of its twists. *What?*

Hurry up.

He muttered to himself about Chosen who didn't have to walk the ground like normal Om'ray, about the additional layer of mud his boots accumulated with every step, about the appalling STENCH, while Naryn, some-how less attractive to mud and stench, vanished around the twist. Sweat stung his eyes.

The harder he tried to move, the deeper each step sank.

On the bright side, Enris told himself, he no longer wanted to wring a certain Om'ray's delicate neck.

A loper carrying a bright blue bag ran by, its tiny feet

not breaking the surface, and stopped to chirp at him. A laugh, person or not. Enris fumed and made it three whole strides before his boot went too deep again.

Don't be startled—

A scream, from Om'ray lungs!

Somehow, Enris found the strength to break into a sloppy, halting run. He followed the path around the corner, leaving ruin behind him.

He broke into sunlight and came to a stop beside Naryn, who wasn't moving at all. Her hands covered her mouth, and she stared ahead.

At . . . he didn't scream.

But only because Aryl stood grinning in reach of what was, most certainly, a monster able to swallow her with one gulp. "Look what I found."

Four monsters. With more moving knee-deep along a muddy stream, a muddy stream that splashed over each time one lifted a foot and dropped it down again.

A muddy stream that stank.

Why was it always monsters? Enris took a second, calmer breath, wiped sweat from his brow, then looked down. Black mud coated his pant legs to the thighs and liberally streaked everything else. He didn't remember getting any on his left arm, but the evidence was there. His boots looked like strange growths and he casually kicked one against the other, spraying mud on Naryn. "You said hurry."

Beneath, through the M'hir, only to his Chosen: *They measure your will. That's what this place is about. That's why no direct questions are allowed, only hints and statements. Be careful.*

Games. With a *resigned disgust* that made Enris smile. *I hate games.* Aloud, "These are esask." As she might have said "rastis" or "dresel" or any other word that meant more to Yena than anyone else on Cersi. "Young ones. I think."

Young? Something as tall as two Om'ray?

Like the esan, these had six legs and narrow bodies, with heads carried low on a curved neck. The head boasted the same four large eyes, but the nostrils were wide and open and there were two curves in the neck, the first lumpy.

Fed, he hoped.

Only the upper half of the body was covered in hair: thick, shaggy, and pale brown; the rest, including the legs, bore heavy black scales. A short brush of stiff hair followed the neck, to end at the snout. One esask yawned, displaying twin rows of needle teeth.

The heads of those waiting moved restlessly from side to side. Others passed, going upstream, disappearing around more branches and foliage. They had riders.

Thought Travelers.

The Tikitik sat astride, their thin legs dangling. They paid no overt attention to the three Om'ray, though they hissed at one another. If it was conversation, one guess, Enris decided, about the topic.

"His" Thought Traveler appeared perfectly content to stand on the shore and be passed by.

As was Aryl. All she said to it was: "I will wait for you." *I'm sorry, Enris, Naryn. Anaj. Patience. I ask your patience. This could*—a hint of *irony*—*take a while.*

What's she up to? Anaj, a hint of *frantic* in her voice.

She didn't know them, Enris reminded himself. She had nothing to trust. *Aryl is Sona's Speaker, but she's of Yena. She's dealt with both Oud and Tikitik before. She won't let us come to harm.*

He eyed the tall, narrow esask and sighed inwardly.

Of course, insisting on the uncomfortable and terrifying wouldn't bother Aryl di Sarc at all.

Chapter 7

THE ESASK POUNDED ITS FOOT into the water, splashing the backs of her legs. They could move silently; this was a display, of temper or warning. Or both. Aryl didn't react, her eyes on the Thought Traveler who'd brought them to "lunch" and then followed them here. She was gaining a feel for this place and its rules, enough to test it. The Tikitik wouldn't impede her movements; they wouldn't direct them. As usual, they waited to see what others would do.

To some consequence. That, she didn't doubt. It had goaded Enris, possibly to discover the extent of Om'ray self-control. Had that sparked his dispute with Naryn? UnChosen Yena who clung to anger were put on a branch to resolve their differences. Maybe this was the Tuana version. She'd kept her distance. They weren't shouting anymore, at least.

The impatient esask was part of the Tikitik's game, there to take them wherever they must go next. She could easily scale its side; so could Thought Traveler, his kind being marvelous climbers. Naryn, unlikely. Enris, with his greater bulk? He'd likely pull the poor creature's hair out trying.

The esask she'd seen before knew to crouch for a rider to dismount or mount. What signaled this convenient cooperation was a Tikitik secret. So. Wait. Watch. Without looking away from Thought Traveler, not even to feast her eyes on Enris or check on Naryn, already weary. If it wanted a contest of will, Aryl smiled to herself, she was ready.

Child, do you know what you're doing?

No.

That set the Old Adept back for an instant, but only an instant. *Are you a fool?*

Sometimes. Not this time, she sent, keeping it private as the other did. Power granted such fine touch. *It waits for me to break the rule here, to ask a question. Or to abandon you. It tests my resolve. The Tikitik were Sona when you were its Speaker, Anaj. You know them. Can I afford to appear weaker?*

No. Immediate and sure. *Never back down from them. Never allow them to ridicule or offend you. They respect determination, when used to a purpose.* Something eased between them. *I knew a Yena, once. Fierce, like you. Strong. I remember he made a room smaller by being in it.* Her sending expanded to the others, became light. *You wouldn't be from Pana, would you, giant Chosen of Sarc? My cousin's son took Passage there. Big, too. Bit of a dreamer. Good at making things, but always eating.*

Sounds right, this from Naryn, bravely trying to keep the conversation going. Her shields were tight. *But Enris and I came from Tuana.*

Thought Traveler's smaller eye cones had begun to track the esasks and riders moving down the river. Aryl didn't need to look to know they were now fewer, with longer intervals between. The sun beat down on her head. Nice to be warm for a change.

I had a great uncle from Pana, Enris added cheerfully. *Chosen by my grandmother's sister. Dama claimed he ate so much they had to make a new door to the metal shop.*

Aryl made a point of shaking her head. To joke about food—sometimes she didn't understand these Om'ray.

Images, then, from Enris. A very large door, wide to

allow a cart full of fragments of green metal scavenged from the Oud, a short ramp into a vat that burned with fuelless flame. The metal, melting, flowing, becoming what was new and useful. The images abruptly stopped. *It was a good door.* Despite shields, his *grief* tolled through her mind.

No more Tuanas, Aryl vowed, no more Clans destroyed. If it took staring at this Tikitik until her legs collapsed under her, so be it. She'd know every bump and knob of its skin soon. Blue-black skin, white spines and cones. Bold, unique coloring. Why? Not for Om'ray benefit. What did it mean to other Tikitik? Importance? Age? Or was it their neutrality, for Thought Travelers insisted they belonged to no faction and spread their news to all. To help Tikitik decide what to avoid, she remembered. To stay away from any course likely to be wrong. A Thought Traveler had told her that.

This one was scarred. Fractures crossed several of the hard knobs. Perhaps old, for its kind. A survivor. The wristbands were of the finest weavings she'd ever seen, as was the sash across its shoulder. Important. Or particular.

There were tiny hairs on the protuberances that obscured its mouth, hairs like those on the backs of her fingers. Sensitive. She'd had such thrust into her mouth to suffocate her into unconsciousness; she'd had them feed her dresel.

Of course, the Tikitik stared back. The large hindmost eyes never left hers. Without eyelids, it didn't blink, but the eyes themselves rolled back and forth in their sockets, replenishing their moist coating.

Remind me to tell you how beautiful you are.

Aryl smiled, shared it inwardly.

Chosen could do that.

At some point, no more esasks traveled by; their own waiting mounts were sound asleep, lips loose and backs sagged in two places. Enris made a nest of sticks to keep Naryn out of the mud and took turns sitting with her or pacing where the ground was firmer, careful not to cross Aryl's line of sight. If there was a will stronger than hers, she thought fondly, it was his. Stubborn, that was her Chosen.

He'd never let her leave alone.

He and Naryn were busier than they looked. Anaj was full of questions. Who were the Sona now? What did they mean, the river had been emptied? Which buildings were rebuilt? Why hadn't they trimmed the *nipet* vines to encourage more blossoms? As for rokly, everyone knew it started underground each new season.

And the purple plant was a weed. Naryn laughed out loud at this.

Harder questions; Adept questions. What was the M'hir? How had Om'ray come to use it? How did Yao manage, blind to her own? What were the Lost?

They didn't tell Anaj about the Strangers or Marcus; they couldn't help it, Aryl thought. A Speaker, an Adept, an elder—she'd read the awkward gaps, understand there was more to know. Perhaps she waited for a time Aryl wasn't preoccupied.

Preoccupied. She was that. Tikitna told her there was more to know about the Tikitik than she'd imagined. Their control over beasts was nothing compared to what they could do with plants. The wood here grew as the Tikitik required. It explained the pieces they used to build Yena's homes, shaped rather than cut.

That was only the beginning. The buildings here, for they were true buildings, were a blend of many different plants somehow convinced to grow together without choking. She'd seen sweetberry vines growing in polite rows, recognized flowers that opened to glow through truenight, but here arranged to form symbols, even small round balls of tasty *plethis*—a scarce find in the canopy—in easy-to-harvest clusters.

Costa would have loved this place.

As for the life that ran, crawled, or scurried everywhere? This was more than a bargain to carry a rider or provide blood. This was technology, every bit as impressive as the Strangers', if not more so. The plants were meticulously cared for, not by Tikitik but by a host of crawlers and biters. Some were familiar, normally fond of Om'ray flesh. Some were rare, in her experience, or ate one another. Here they worked together, gathered to a purpose other than their own survival.

For all Thought Traveler's talk of will, here theirs was imposed on everything else.

What did that mean for Om'ray?

The world moved around them, the world as she could *feel* it. An unChosen made the journey from Rayna to Amna. She wondered what he thought, sensing Om'ray where no Om'ray should be, and wished him a safe Passage.

Shadows crept over the esasks, dulled the reflections in two of Thought Traveler's eyes. No chill yet, as there would be in the mountains. Anaj slept. Naryn and Enris argued silently about how best to improve their dam. At some point, this involved building small dams in the mud to make some point.

Before today, she'd accepted there'd be no more than cold courtesy between the two closest to her heart, for Naryn was that. Oh, she loved her family, had close friendships within the Sona, but Naryn ... ? They were of a kind. If things had been different, they'd be heartkin. If her Chosen hadn't good reason to despise her friend ...

At this rate, maybe they'd all eat at the same table one day.

Fool! You wouldn't know a good idea if it cracked your thick skull!

One day.

Aryl hid her amusement and watched Thought Traveler.

Had it shifted?

She braced herself, knowing the not-Om'ray quickness of its kind. Stiff, she'd be slower than usual, though she'd tried to flex what muscles she could.

But Thought Traveler merely swiveled its eyes to the esask, took a leisurely step as if it hadn't stood motionless for the better part of an afternoon, and smacked the first leg. The tall creature shuddered awake, then bent all six knees until its belly touched the muddy water. The Tikitik gracefully stepped on a knee, grabbed a handful of hair, and swung itself astride. A smack on the neck and the esask thrust itself up and began to walk upstream after its fellows.

The remaining three esask, now awake and seeing themselves left behind, pounded the water to a froth. But when Aryl smacked the leg of the nearest, it crouched quickly and waited, as if relieved she'd come to her senses. "See that?" she asked Enris.

He laughed. "I thought everyone knew that trick."

Congratulations, Speaker.

The game's not over. Aryl stepped on the esask's knee and lifted her leg over its back, settling on the hair.

Anaj's reply chilled her to the bone.

It could have been.

Unlike the lumbering osst she remembered all too well, the esask glided along the stream, the lift of its legs barely perceptible to a rider. Easy to see why they were effective predators, Aryl thought. The head was in constant motion. This close, she could see the short stiff hairs on its neck were as well. If they were hairs. Every so often, they went still for a moment, then rippled in perfect order from snout to body, like the many small limbs of an Oud.

Curious, she wanted to touch them; she didn't, and

warned the others. These were somehow sensitive to something other than light, making the esask a predator of truenight as well.

As if truenight needed more.

The esasks set their order. Hers quickly caught up to Thought Traveler's and persisted in staying alongside. Enris followed, Naryn's trailing behind his where she couldn't see her. Naryn *felt* confident. The substantial body hair, however uncomfortable against bare skin, did offer a good grip; the creatures moved smoothly. The water in the stream's midst came no higher than their scaled bellies.

Nonetheless, a fall from even this low height—

You call this "low?!"

I call this prying. But she smiled to herself. *Do you think she's all right?*

Which one? She felt him grow distant and waited. A moment later, *Anaj says you know what to do, and I should leave you in peace. Also that she's most emphatically not interested in what's happening at the moment so long as Naryn sits up straight, so would I leave her in peace, too.* There was a growing *fondness* to his sending, as if something about the Old Adept's feisty nature appealed to him.

Naryn?

She's not as strong as she wants us to believe, but she won't fall off while I'm watching. You could ask about me, you know. I'm stuck on one of these towers of flesh too. Did you see those teeth?

Rather walk?

She imagined him looking to the side, where very few paths broke the solid vegetation. Up was the same. The sun shone through the occasional gap, a gap that revealed the plant buildings had more than tripled in height. The water itself was sluggish with mud and scraps of floating vegetation. With the occasional v-ripple against the current she didn't bother mentioning.

I'm fine riding.

"We approach the Makers' Touch."

Aryl started, having grown used to Thought Traveler's silence. She swallowed her question and waited.

An eye swiveled her way. "The Makers' Touch is where Cersi's name was carved into the world's skin by its creators. All Tikitik come here at least once. It's supposed to encourage strong progeny. Some believe . . ." A pause.

She could swear it looked smug. The despicable creature knew how hard it was for her not to ask. Aryl gritted her teeth.

". . . most do not," it continued. "But we won't kill each other here, which makes it a useful place. Tikitna was built over the generations to house those who come to trade, to exchange information, and, of course, what's most important of all, to explain themselves in such a way that those listening won't kill each other upon leaving."

From no information to an ominous tangle of it. Thought Travelers were consistent. "I'd rather know what you want from me," she pointed out, keeping her voice level with an effort, "than the consequences."

"The consequences stay the same," it countered, "while only you, Aryl of Sona, know what needs explanation."

It had her trapped; by the serene cant of its head, it knew. By not asking questions, by giving her nothing more than the opportunity to speak, the Tikitik left her no way to judge how much explanation would be enough.

Aryl fell silent, inwardly and out, watched the stream for ripples, and wondered for the hundredth time if they wouldn't be better to 'port home now, admit the reality of it, and be done. What stopped her?

Taisal's reaction. Her mother refused to accept moving through the M'hir, for herself, for Yena. She'd warned trying to spread this knowledge would divide Om'ray into those who could and those who could not—and worse, those who would not. They needed a place like this, Aryl thought desperately. A place where she could explain her ideas and others would have to listen in peace.

Have to? That was the other lesson here, she thought suddenly, staring at Thought Traveler. What gave her the right to impose her will on all Om'ray? Was she so sure 'porting through the M'hir was the only possible future?

Nothing...

And yes.

The plants that encompassed the stream abruptly spread apart, creating an entry every bit as impressive as the ceremonial doors in a Cloisters. Flowering vines framed it—not flowers, Aryl realized, as the bright red suddenly dropped away, to reveal themselves as flitters rising and circling into the vast opening beyond.

To announce their arrival?

The esask continued forward, its feet silent in the water. For water floored the space ahead. Living wood, taller than any she'd seen here yet, arched high above and met in a weave of branches tight enough to bar the sun. Glows provided light, glows like any at Yena—except these were underwater.

Dark, murky water flowed around the outside edge, blurred, and escaped through the weave of plant structures that surrounded the open space. It was kept from mixing with the water in the center by a barrier of—she had no name for the material from which it was made. The top edge, the width of her hand and polished, barely rose above the water. What she could see of it was as clear as a Cloisters' windows. The water in the center—

"It's like the Lake of Fire," she said involuntarily.

Thought Traveler bobbed its head. Agreement or surprise—she couldn't tell.

Like that lake, this water was impossibly clear. From the esask's back, she could see to what had to be the bottom of the world, lit by floating glows somehow held at varied depths. That bottom was pale and smooth, with muscular curved lines like the flow of an impossible river, a river that didn't move.

Enris, do you see this? What could it be?

He surprised her with a calm answer. "Melted rock, gone cold and solid again." His esask and Naryn's moved up beside hers, then all three mounts stopped, perhaps because Thought Traveler's had. "I saw the same outside Vyna. Melted rock used to make a dam. I thought they'd made it." She felt his *unease*.

Made. The barrier was a made thing, too. Aryl let her gaze follow its shape, how it outlined the clear, lit water. Inward there, out again. Another sharper curve. On the far side, narrowed to no more than a few strides wide, wrapping back around to almost touch the larger portion. Another such protrusion, circle back, and narrowing. Around it all, the brown muddy, natural stream. "It's a symbol," she said in amazement. The full shape would be more obvious from above, but still . . . it looked familiar.

She twisted to look at Thought Traveler's wristband. The paired wavy lines meant "traveler"; the trio of widening circles, "thought." The rest of the complex markings she'd been told represented important names and tasks from an individual's "kin-group."

One, set by itself above the rest. One that matched the shape she saw here.

Four eyes locked on her. Then, a long clawtip touched the shape. "Cersi."

"CERSI!! CERSI!! CERSI!!" Aryl and the others looked up at the cries. There you are, she thought, very carefully not reaching for her knife. All the Thought Travelers who'd preceded them.

And more. From the overlapping voices, more Tikitik than she'd known existed.

Interwoven branches roofed the huge space. Thin shapes walked within its shadows, bold with color or shadow-black themselves. Some lay flat, dangling an arm, the tasseled end of a sash. Others sat with feet hanging through. All at a height she envied.

To see this, she realized. The symbol for Cersi. The name of their shared world. "Can—I want to go up there," she told their Thought Traveler, changing from a question just in time.

"No, you don't," Enris objected.

Hush.

NO. YOU DON'T.

"Some other time," Aryl said, gesturing a discreet apology to her Chosen. He was right. She shouldn't think only of herself, not now.

Though this structure—it was the first thing about Tikitik she envied, the first indication of something common between them and—if not Om'ray—then those Clans who lived high in the canopy. Yena. The long-ago Xrona.

The echoes of "Cersi, Cersi" were swallowed by the still, humid air. The canopy was like that, the warmth of midday stifling sound.

Then her esask stamped its foot. Slowly. The result was more expanding ring of ripples than splash. With a side-long twist of its long neck to stare at Thought Traveler's. Which did the same.

If they started squabbling like esans, Aryl intended to smack hers. Though maybe that would make it crouch—not a good idea, away from any solid surface other than the narrow barrier. Not a good idea at all.

Thought Traveler, this one, continued to watch her with all four eyes. For once, the protuberances writhing around its mouth stilled. Waiting, she thought. For what? She hoped it wasn't another staring game; she may have won the first, but she'd looked into its face more than anyone should.

"Aryl. Aryl!"

She glanced over her shoulder to see the esasks of Naryn and Enris moving away. Naryn looked desperate. Enris, grim-faced, had his big hands on the short-bristled hair of his, pulling hard enough to raise its neck. The creature opened its toothed mouth in a soundless protest, but kept walking.

"There is food and drink," Thought Traveler informed her. "An opportunity for cleanliness."

Having experienced the Tikitik's notion of a bath—which involved the application of *things* to bare skin that ate any dirt, as well as some skin—she hastily called out to the others, "It's all right. They're offering more food. Just don't take a bath."

Enris drummed his heels into the sides of his poor esask, kept pulling. *I WON'T LEAVE YOU.*

Must you shout? Anaj's mindvoice, with a pronounced *snap* of *irritation. Let the Speaker do her work! You Chosen can be such a nuisance.*

As this was unlikely to do more than increase *her* Chosen's resolve, Aryl turned to the Tikitik. "I thought you wouldn't impose your will on others here."

"I do not." With a bark of amusement. "It is their choice to stay on the esasks. Or not."

"Or not" meant the water. None of them could swim; no telling what hunted beneath the muddy surface.

You must go, she sent to Enris, with all her *love.*

He stopped punishing his mount, but his shoulders were hunched.

Enris?

Not hungry. Not leaving.

Stubborn, annoying Tuana.

By this point, their esasks were between the wide lower supports of the outer wall, brown-and-black bodies merging with the shadows.

Aryl wasn't the least surprised when her Tuana, who so hated climbing, stood on the back of his moving esask, caught his balance with a wild swing of his arms, then leaped to one of the wide overhanging branches.

Tikitik scurried out of his way. Not the most graceful landing. He hung half over the branch, kicking the air, then hauled himself up by brute force.

She was a little surprised when Enris reached down to pull Naryn up with him. Their esasks disappeared into the shadows, probably relieved.

I'm always right, he sent smugly, taking a seat. *What's next?*

As if it somehow heard, Thought Traveler smacked his esask. As it lowered itself into the water, hair spreading around it, the Tikitik stepped from its back to the barrier and began to prance along that edge, one foot ahead of the other, clawed toes spread to hook over the sides.

If she hadn't been close enough to see the barrier, she'd have believed it walked on water.

Its right side was bathed in soft light, filtered up from the clear depths; its left was shadowed and cast a dark reflection that jostled and moved over the dark, turbid stream. Things rose to that reflection, snapped at it, thought it prey. Things she didn't want to see more closely, like what lived within the Lay Swamp and devoured Yena's husks.

Her heart began to pound in great, heavy beats.

Her esask stomped the water, impatient to join its fellow now wandering after those of the other Om'ray. The Tikitik hissed to each other and leaned down, eyes catching fire from the lights below. The smell of wet wood mixed with that of stirred rot.

Gorge rose in her throat.

I can't do this.

Enris might have held her, so *real* was the sensation of his strong arms around her, his breath in her ear, his warmth. *You won't fall.* Not teasing, not a goad. What he truly believed.

A ground dweller's opinion. This was no healthy branch or trusted braid of rope. The Tikitik, superb climber that it was, stepped carefully and used its long clawed toes, a natural advantage. At a guess, the smooth surface was slick with moisture. There'd be no second chances if she lost her footing, no grasp for safety.

A short fall, but into what might as well be the Lay, for her chances of survival. Would she be eaten alive or drown? She'd almost drowned twice; had drowned and died once, according to Marcus, who'd somehow revived her.

He wasn't here now.

There was no one else here who could do this.

Aryl took a deep breath. She sat cross-legged atop the esask to undo her sandals and tie them to her belt. She rubbed her bare feet against the creature's long hair to rid the soles of mud and sweat.

Acting on a less practical impulse, she unclasped her hairnet and tucked it safely in a pocket. Her hair took a heartbeat to realize it was free, then spread in joyous waves. Red-gold obscured her left eye and she batted it away, but before she completely regretted her decision, the mass settled over her shoulders, soft, warm, and thoroughly Om'ray.

Now that's not fair. With gentle *heat.*

Not fair. But if it was for the last time?

Later, my Chosen, she sent, refusing fear.

Cold. That was her foot's first impression of the barrier. The chill sent a shudder up her leg.

Cold, and curved. Higher in the middle. Without conscious thought, Aryl turned her foot slightly, let its curve follow the barrier's. Turned her other foot the opposite way. Found her balance.

Easier, once committed. Now that she could fall into the water at any moment, Aryl no longer paid attention to it. The Tikitik above were silent. When she'd looked up, all she could see were heads, all eyes reflecting points aimed at her. For some reason, they pressed their long necks against the nearest wood. To brace themselves?

Her Thought Traveler walked one way around the world's name. She would walk the other, for no better reason than she wouldn't follow anyone else. Not on this journey.

If she was wrong—well, this could all be wrong.

Paired v-ripples followed her shadow. Let them.

See? I told you it'd be easy.

Don't distract her! Naryn, doing her best to keep her own dismay and fear to herself. *The sooner she's done, the sooner we can be out of this appalling smell.*

Done.

Done what? So far, she was walking around the symbol. Surely the audience above expected more, even if they'd doubtless be entertained by a fall.

A fall . . . unlikely. Aryl gained confidence with every step; the motion helped warm her. If they wanted to watch Om'ray drown—or be eaten—they could have had the esasks throw them from their backs. This place, this symbol. These were important to the Tikitik. To share them with another species?

They believed they had good reason.

She was here to offer an explanation.

Of what?

Start somewhere, Aryl told herself. Anywhere. She slowed and cleared her throat, choosing words with care. They were more dangerous here than any lurker underwater.

"My name is Aryl di Sarc. You named me Apart-from-All, and once it was true, but no longer. Now I am Chosen, a mother-to-be, and Speaker for Sona's Om'ray. Sona's new Om'ray. Yena's exiles."

They knew, of course. Three factions claimed Yena: one willing to follow the Agreement, one too cautious to change, and one eager to seize the Strangers as an excuse to end it. There'd been Tikitik laughing in the grove that truenight. Laughing as Yena's homes burned and her people were divided. Because of her.

"We stayed at Sona where Oud, not Tikitik, made

us welcome. We would not have wanted any to die on our account, but the Oud protected their claim on Sona. One of you came and insisted on the Balance being maintained. If we'd known—" her hair rose and snapped, "—if I'd known that meant destroying Tuana, I would never have permitted it. We would have left Sona first."

She reached a point where the barrier turned back on itself and had to stand on tiptoe to make the turn. The next section was straight, and she took longer strides, possibly gaining on Thought Traveler, though one thing she grew sure of: this wasn't a race. They moved together, somehow, it and she.

"There are Tuana with us. Most, including my Chosen, came because of the Oud. They value us for their own reasons. You know that, too. The others—some escaped the reshaping."

Clear water, lit from within, swept a gleaming curve ahead of her, matched by a curl of thick brown stream. The two began to seem less like water as she walked between them, and more like symbols themselves. Was the brown the M'hir; the clear, the real world? Or was the brown what lived and the clear what did not, but rather was made by the will of intelligence? Which made little sense when the Tikitik made what lived—or at least so some factions claimed. Perhaps, Aryl thought, she made it all too complicated. Maybe the two simply represented life or death. Survival or failure.

Both had to exist, to write the name of the world. Was that the true meaning of Tikitna and the Makers' Touch?

If so, she wasn't here to explain Sona or Tuana.

She was here to explain herself.

Why not?

Why, she thought fiercely, not.

Their attempts at secrecy were worse than futile. The Tikitik could follow them—somehow—no matter if they walked, climbed, or 'ported. They'd been caught in

Vyna, traveling as no Om'ray could, where no Om'ray Chosen would.

If she could explain its value to Om'ray, to peace and safety, this might be a chance to gain acceptance for their Talent.

And she'd feared to walk over water?

Courage. From Enris. From Naryn. Even from Anaj. Her *anxiety* must have spilled through her shields.

Encouraged, Aryl wrapped her fingers around the Speaker's Pendant. "All my life, I've been told the Agreement forbids change." Were her words lost in this space, deflected among the branches above or smothered in moisture?

She refused to doubt. The Tikitik made this; they brought her here. They wanted to hear her.

They would.

"I've been told change was forbidden so that all races would stay as they were. That the Agreement preserves the peace of our world. But Om'ray exist in more than what you see. There is another place we—some of us—can sense with our minds." A hint of *shock* from Naryn or Anaj, quickly hidden. They still trusted her.

Would they?

Aryl walked, her toes out, balanced along the callused edge of her arches. "Some Om'ray call it the Dark," she continued. "To our inner sight, it's like storm clouds building against truenight. Or sometimes like water, black and turbulent. The minds of Chosen Join through it. That's why the death—" she fought the tightness in her throat, "—the death of one dooms the other. It wasn't always so. I believe this change must have been happening inside Om'ray for a long time, where no one could see or notice."

Thought Traveler was heading toward her now, on the same side of the symbol. A time limit, she guessed. When they met, she must be done.

When done, she must succeed.

"No one noticed, until me. I found I had the Talent to move not only my thoughts, but my body through the

Dark. It was nothing I intended. It's part of what I am. Something new. Because of that, because my change couldn't be hidden, I was exiled from Yena." Because of that, Costa, Leri, so very many . . .

Aryl forced away the past. "Because change risks the Agreement, I knew using my ability again would be the worst thing I could do—not only for Yena but for Cersi." Step. Step. A larger ripple than most followed alongside, then sank away. "But when my people were in danger, I didn't think. I acted. I used my ability to help us survive." Survive the Tikitik attack on Yena, something else they knew.

"I tried to keep it a secret, but it isn't only me. There are other Sona with this ability—to 'port through what we call the M'hir or move objects through it. Because Om'ray continue to change inside."

Her path wove back toward its start. Thought Traveler matched its steps to hers. Closer. Closer.

"We value the Agreement," Aryl stated firmly. "I value it. But this change isn't something we control. All we can control is what we do with our new Talents." Its eyes angled downward in their cones to meet hers, expectant.

What else could she say?

The truth.

Aryl let go of the pendant and lifted her chin. "My Clan wants to live in peace. But we won't allow Om'ray to die at the whim of another race again. Ever. We have the means now to survive—and we will."

Her next step took her to Thought Traveler. They both stopped.

"The whims of Oud kill Om'ray," it reminded her. "We do not."

"I see no difference." Aryl frowned. "You make it impossible to survive."

"We make it difficult. A profound difference." With a bark of amusement, Thought Traveler gestured to their surroundings. "Life must struggle, Little Speaker. Which is why we regret losing Sona as it becomes interesting. I only hope Tuana's survivors prove as resilient and entertaining as your Chosen."

Enris . . .

For a wonder, his sending felt *amused*. Almost. *I'm fine. Imagining breaking its neck keeps my mind off where we are. Why did I think it was a good idea to perch like a Yena?*

Her lips twitched, but she concentrated on Thought Traveler. To stand on the narrow edge was "difficult." She bent her knees slightly, settled for however long this took. Aryl wished she could sense its emotions, read meaning in how its eyes shifted or its mouth protuberances writhed. It was, she thought glumly, easier talking to the Human.

Or a chair.

Nonetheless, this being was the one she had to convince, and through it, the rest of its kind. "With you as neighbors," she began, "the Tuana will be forced to change, too. Change is against the Agreement—"

"It is not."

The water, clear and mud-stained, suddenly loomed closer. Regaining her balance was easier than believing what she'd heard. "I don't understand."

"Perhaps you can't." Thought Traveler tilted its head to regard her from another angle. "Om'ray have never grasped the essence of the Agreement."

She glowered at the creature. "We aren't stupid."

"I never said you were. To you, the world is Om'ray, the past a few generations long, and time moves into the future with each birth. Without comparison, without history, you cannot observe how change is part of all life, including yours. You said it yourself, Apart-from-All. When Om'ray discover something new among themselves, their reaction is to conceal or stop it. Unsuccessfully, let me assure you, though we may appear oblivious. Watching for change," a grand and meaningless sweep of its arms, "is what we do."

What it did was be confusing. Aryl's hair lashed its agreement, stinging her cheeks. She should have left on the net. "Cersi is divided among the Tikitik and Oud," she recited grimly. "Om'ray may trespass outside their Clan only during Passage. Change is forbidden, for all sakes. What 'essence' do you think we miss?"

It didn't protest the question. "You say the words, Little Speaker, but apply them only to yourselves. The change the Agreement forbids is in the Balance among our races, not within any one." Thought Traveler leaned so close, the writhing worms of its mouth brushed her chin. Her hair retreated; Aryl did not. "The Balance keeps the world fit for us all. Think of it, Apart-from-All. A Cersi perfect for Oud would be too dry for us." A gesture to the living building overhead. "A Cersi perfect for Tikitik would not only be too wet for Oud, but swarm with life beyond even a Yena's ability to survive. While a Cersi perfect for you—could not exist here without Oud to drain the ground and Tikitik to replenish it. Without the Balance, none of us survive."

Aryl's breath quickened. If she understood, the Adepts were wrong. There was no reason to fear new Talents among Om'ray, to forbid them. If she understood. Don't ask a question, she reminded herself. Don't fall in the water. Don't make a mistake.

"If what I learned was wrong," she said carefully, testing the concept, "then it's not against the Agreement for Om'ray to be different from one another."

A feathery touch across her eyelids, then the Tikitik drew back slightly. "You continue to impress, Aryl di Sarc. I wonder if you could possibly grasp the source of our delight at Sona."

Another Clan? A restored Clan? That wasn't it, Aryl thought, frustrated. The Tikitik had lost Sona to the Oud.

It said they watch for change. What's Sona if not the biggest one of all?

You're brilliant, she informed her Chosen, receiving

a thoroughly deserved *smug* in return. Aloud, "It's not only differences between Om'ray you care about. It's differences between our Clans, too."

This brought its head bobbing upward in its double nod, then down to stare with all four eyes. She could hear hissing above, but didn't dare look away. "Astounding. Few of your kind could reason thus. Fewer still would trouble themselves to try."

She bristled. "If you talked to us, instead of pushing us into 'difficult' situations for your amusement, you'd find we reason as well as you."

"Point taken. Though to be fair to my predecessors, you're the first Om'ray to endure our attempts at serious conversation." A chill ran down her spine. "We do indeed care—a great deal—about the differences between Om'ray Clans. Every one is unique. Every one must stay distinct to promote the diversity of your kind. Your understanding is not required—" proving it could read her gathering scowl. "Your cooperation is."

A promising turn. Cooperation implied a future, didn't it? "If it means we can live in peace . . ." she let her voice trail away.

"It means you have become dangerous, Little Speaker. Your people now walk the name of the world, as we did here, and to either side is death. For the first time in our shared history, Om'ray could disturb the Balance. By accident. By design. And we cannot survive without one another."

Like the stupid Oud, she decided in frustration. Trying to enlist her, or Sona, or both, against a rival. "Then leave us in peace—"

It pushed her. Quick and hard.

Even as she cried out and slipped toward the brown water, Thought Traveler caught her arm in a grip that hurt. It pulled her upright again, held until she tugged free. "None of us," it insisted, "survive alone."

Aryl!

She sent *reassurance* to Enris, to the others, wishing she could do the same for herself. She was missing something here. Something vital. The Tikitik wasn't trying to annoy or scare her. It was—it was trying to make her understand. What?

Words. Words weren't enough for Om'ray. How could she get more from such a being?

The Yena game. The trust game.

Using her left hand, Aryl took hold of Thought Traveler's left wrist, below the band of cloth with its name. It didn't avoid her touch; it didn't resist when she tugged the wrist toward her. Their balance so connected was precarious; both had to use their opposing arms to compensate. "Cooperation," she said.

"Yes."

The Tikitik's skin was cool and dry, almost pebbled. More like stone than the covering of flesh, except for the pulse beneath her forefinger and thumb. Too quick.

Might be normal. Hers raced, too. She'd never imagined playing with it, nor any game for such stakes. The world itself? What could it want from her?

They, not it. Thought Traveler spoke for more than itself. So must she. How could Om'ray be dangerous?

It had taken them from Vyna, said it was to protect the Vyna.

Why?

Unless . . . "Our new Talent lets us travel to other Clans, not just at Passage. Or instead of Passage. That's the danger," Aryl guessed with a surge of triumph. "You want us to stay away from each other, to keep the Clans as different as possible." So much for Enris and his plans for trade. "We can do that." She'd be glad to keep Sona to itself. They'd have to be sure Oran's dreams truly stopped, but she'd be glad of that, too. Life would be simple. Peaceful.

Thought Traveler moved its left arm outward; Aryl adjusted automatically. "Vyna knows it must not be contaminated by other Om'ray, Little Speaker. For the rest, change is essential. We would not impose restrictions on your Talent, even if we could."

Bubbles disturbed the brown water beside her, as if something hung below the surface and laughed at her. "The Vyna can drown in their own poison," she said coldly. "They're hardly Om'ray anymore. But if you don't care about our Talent or what we do with it—" how she wished her mother listened to this, "—I don't know what else you could want."

"Stability. Numbers matter, Little Speaker. Your numbers. Clans are supposed to stay together. An unChosen here or there is accommodated by the Agreement. You've seen the result when several Om'ray move from one Clan to another at once. The Oud react in reckless fashion. The Balance changes. Too much change and—"

She was ready, barely, for its sharp pull. Knew to bend her knees and resist, to ease the pressure as it suddenly moved toward her again. Thought Traveler played the game well, for all it was something Om'ray, something Yena. She didn't let go. She didn't dare.

"Sona won't happen again," Aryl protested. "We prefer to stay with our Clans, with our families. We must. Like Chosen, we're linked to one another, inside." Except Yao, she thought suddenly. Except Yao and the new babies.

Tomorrow's problem.

Today? If all the Tikitik wanted was for Om'ray to live as they normally would, of course she'd agree. "If we're left in peace, I promise we'll stay where we are." She offered her right hand, her left still locked on Thought Traveler's wrist. The final stage of the game: commitment.

The bubbles increased, as if what watched them from beneath sensed they would fall any moment.

Aryl. More than her name. Everything Enris saw in her, believed about her, felt for her. Hair caressed her neck, slid over her shoulders.

Rippled down her arm to where the Tikitik's clawed hand closed gently over hers, and explored that black strangeness, its shining red gold like a glove. Thought Traveler canted its head to watch, eyes swiveling in their cones, until her hair relaxed to lie against her body as hair should.

All four eyes lifted. "Then we understand one another, Aryl di Sarc, Speaker for Sona and all Om'ray of Cersi."

A loud rustle overhead made Aryl look up. The branches had emptied. They were alone.

Thought Traveler, its balance as sure as her own, released her hand. She let go its wrist. Then it barked. "Congratulations, Apart-from-All. You've exceeded every claim I made on your behalf, and I was most extravagant in my belief. There were those," in a confiding tone, "sure you'd try to kill me on the way here, a breach of Tikitna that—it doesn't bear mentioning, now."

Oh, there'd have been no "try" about it.

Not a thought she'd share when all was going well.

More than well.

Aryl felt giddy as she stepped back. The future she'd imagined as a dim possibility was here. Now. They could 'port without fear. Be whatever they were to be. Stay together? What could be easier to promise?

Being together was life to Om'ray.

She'd done it!

Her *joy* threw itself to the others, came back threefold. *Joy* with an underlying *distrust* doubtless from Anaj. The old Speaker thought she knew the Tikitik. But she'd admitted this wasn't her time.

It was theirs. Hers. She'd done it!

Now can we go home? Naryn asked.

Home it is. Aryl gestured gratitude to Thought Traveler, then drew the locate of Sona in her mind and . . .

NO!!! The hysterical protest broke her concentration. She almost fell into the water.

It's safe, Anaj. Naryn shared her sending with the rest

of them, as well as her own weary longing. *Relax. You don't have to do any—*

NO!!! You can't know it's safe!

It doesn't hurt our babies, Aryl interjected. She felt Enris keep his distance from the conversation. Coward.

I am not one of your babies! NO!!!

Naryn shared her *loathing* of Tikitna, all things Tikitik, and of sitting on a branch over filthy, swimmer-infested water. *Do you want to stay here?* Memories of soft Sona blankets, fragrant soup, and crisp mountain air.

Walking was good enough for your parents. It's good enough for me.

With real fear.

Justified, Aryl decided ruefully. They couldn't promise travel through the M'hir was safe, not for Anaj, not until they knew more of what she was. At any rate, they couldn't 'port if the powerful Old Adept continued to resist Naryn's efforts to concentrate. Or leave Naryn behind.

Aryl sighed and looked at Thought Traveler.

"We need a ride."

Chapter 8

THE WHITE SAND WAS WARM and soft and glistened in the sun. Enris sprawled on his back beside
her, one big arm over his eyes and his feet—free of his
ruined boots—buried to the ankles in the stuff. Naryn
paced where the water frothed up on the beach, her
Adept robe dragging. Aryl supposed this was her way of
protesting what they were doing; it wasn't going to wash
the mud stains from Oran's robe.

She licked her lips, savoring the hint of dresel that
lingered. Thought Traveler had pressed food upon them
before they left, insisting mothers-to-be must eat. Enris.
Dresel. Warmth without rain or biters. The future—the
right future—within reach. What more could she want?
She stretched luxuriously. "I could stay here all day."

"That's good. We may have to," her Chosen commented, his voice muffled. "Or longer."

The esasks had brought them out of Tikitna to the
sand; they'd refused to step on it. From this vantage
point, the Tikitik village—she could use a word for something much more imposing—looked like any dense, wild
growth. Another name she needed, Aryl pondered, was
for the plants they used for their construction. Not nekis.
Not rastis. Something that willingly grew strong, thick,

and twisted, with roots drowned in bitter water. She'd learned so much today.

Not least, that rock hunters were Oud young. Haxel would love it, Aryl grinned to herself. The canopy crawled with creatures whose offspring looked nothing like them, as well as parents who abandoned the next generation to fend for themselves. To be fair, the Oud did do something for their young. The adults had done their best to dry out Sona's valley and argued with her to keep it that way.

Though since their young killed Om'ray without concern, well, Om'ray would continue to return the favor.

Aryl squinted at the sky toward Sona, a more comforting direction than out over the limitless ocean, the direction that mattered. Two tenths until firstnight, she estimated. Three at most. Had they left for Vyna only this morning? It felt, she decided with another stretch, more like a fist.

"It won't be much longer," she assured Enris. "He'll answer." And he would. The sun rose every morning; the Human wouldn't fail her. His gift, the geoscanner, was on her lap. Silent as yet. She'd pressed the control as Marcus had shown her, said the special words he'd given her if she needed his help: "*Two. Howard. Five.*" Howard was his son. She'd seen a recording of him, tall for a child, as well as images of the rest of the Human's family: a daughter, Karina, little more than a baby. Kelly of the long red hair. His Chosen. Cindy, his sister, with a pleasant smile. Family he'd left to work here; kept close using his clever devices.

Devices that included an aircar. Much better, Aryl thought cheerfully, than walking across most of Cersi and around the Lake of Fire.

"At least we shouldn't have to worry about Anaj's reaction. Since her view is of the inside of Naryn's belly."

Aryl poked a finger into his ribs, unerringly finding the spot to make him squirm. "A little respect for the Old One, if you please."

Enris peered at her over his arm. "You know I'm right. The best way to cope with our not-Om'ray friend is not see him in the first place." Inwardly. *Relax. You know the instant we're back, Haxel will have us in the fields. After,* this with a *glee* that burst through her very bones, *we can play 'port and seek all we want without breaking the Agreement. I may not walk anywhere again.*

He lifted his arm; she came close but instead of curling at his side, Aryl propped herself with elbows on his broad chest and stared down at him. "This doesn't mean we can be careless. The Strangers—"

A sandy finger crossed her lips. "I insist. Celebrate. You've accomplished a greater understanding of our world than any Om'ray before you. You've made us safe! Can you never just enjoy a triumph?"

They never came this easy, Aryl thought, but only to herself. Her Chosen was right; this was a moment for joy, not worry. "Of course I can—"

"Aryl? Aryl? Aryl?" Her name erupted from the device now resting in the sand.

They both lunged for it, ending in a tangle that otherwise Aryl would have relished. "I'll answer," she told her overeager Chosen firmly, and sat up. Grinning, Enris leaned on his bent arm to watch.

There was another button to be pressed, so. "Yes. It's Aryl, Marcus," she said. Awkward, giving her name to the device. "We need your help to get home. We—"

"Where— Never mind, I've locked your *coordinates*." He was distracted; she could hear it in his voice. "Turn off the 'scanner and stay where you are. I'm almost there."

He was?

The device's clear dome covered its array of tiny glowing parts. Staring at it did nothing to ease her disquiet.

"Almost here?" she echoed. "Why?"

"Turn off the 'scanner. Bowman out."

Aryl did as he demanded; the lights faded, the device lifeless in her hand. She tucked it away carefully. Some Om'ray could *taste* change about to happen. She could.

And did. A thoroughly unreliable sense, giving little more than a vague sense of *dread*. But she paid attention to any warning in the canopy. And here.

Enris chuckled. "I thought we'd get to laze about till supper at least. Who'd have guessed . . ." His smile faded as he looked at her. He sat up. "What's wrong?"

The *taste* of change.

"Marcus hasn't left the valley since the last snow. He lets the others come to him. Why would he be flying about? Why this way?" Her hair strained against its net. "He must be leaving Cersi." Aryl drew her knees to her chest and hugged them. "I thought he'd warn us first." Had she offended him? Missed some vital Human courtesy? Made him sick with the turrif after all?

Or had she misunderstood their friendship all along? There was hurt in the thought. That didn't make it wrong.

"You're the one who says look before you take hold," Enris soothed, one hand shading his eyes. "Marcus wouldn't go without telling us. And when he does leave, he'll be back soon. He wants to see our beautiful Sweetpie."

"Will he be back?" Aryl countered. "What do we know of his kind, beyond the few here?"

They were few, she thought, because their technology did so much for them. Site One, the Lake of Fire, held only the three of its Triad. Site Two, the mountain near Grona, had Henshaw's Triad and the flitterlike being who'd helped Marcus rescue the exiles. Marcus, with a vague wave toward the sunset, referred to Site Three as *inactive* and explained they used it now for *re-supply*. Six lived there, two *comtechs,* the pair of archivists sent to help him pack, and the non-Humans who comprised the rest of Marcus' new Triad. She hadn't paid attention to his babble of incomprehensible—and unpronounceable—names, but she had to the numbers. The camp at Sona was called Site Four, implying no others. Four sites and fourteen Strangers were, in Haxel's dour estimation, four and fourteen too many.

From what else Marcus had said, and not said, there were far more involved in his work. They lived on other worlds. Gave orders by comlink. Traveled between in ways he'd never quite explained. Which had been fine, Aryl thought in frustration, until now.

"He told us he answers to others. Coming back might not be his decision to make." She dropped her head to her knees. What if she hadn't called Marcus? What if they'd 'ported home, only to find him gone from the world?

Enris traced the back of her hand with a sandy finger. "Don't underestimate our resourceful Human," he said gently. "Even if you're right—and I'm not saying you are—he talks to his family from here, doesn't he? So he can talk to us from there."

She raised her head to glare at him. "Where, Enris? Where is 'there'? We don't know the full shape of this world, let alone his!"

What's wrong? Naryn had stopped pacing. Too far away to hear, not far enough to escape carelessly spilled emotion.

Nothing. Aryl tightened her shields. *We'll be leaving soon.*

Her Chosen freed his feet and brushed them off, shedding sand like snow. "I should have known." He pulled on a still-damp boot with a grimace. "A peaceful Cersi isn't enough for my wild little Yena." Utterly sincere, if not for the *teasing* beneath the words. "But I've the answer. Om'ray-sized fiches. We've no lack of cliffs to jump from."

Cheering her up, was he?

She should be happy. The future she wanted for her people was here, now. That could be the change she *tasted.* Not a warning, a promise. Aryl managed a smile. "You hate cliffs."

"I wasn't volunteering to try the things," with an exaggerated shudder. "I'll leave that to those with less sense."

"Meaning me."

He laughed. "Hoyon comes to mind. Might inspire him to 'port."

"And you call me bloodthirsty?"

His grin, the *relief* beneath it—they only added to the guilt she was careful to keep to herself. How could she care so much for a not-Om'ray? She'd known Marcus would leave. If not today, then one day. One day, he'd leave forever.

Wasn't that for the best?

Of course it would be, Aryl told herself sadly.

For everyone else.

"There he is."

The sun sat over Grona. Naryn and Enris shaded their eyes, gazing where Aryl pointed. She was sure the glint in the sky could be nothing else. Nothing living moved that fast, or in a straight line against the wind.

Fast? Aryl frowned as it approached. Too fast. The glint became a machine that plunged at them like a rock falling. She and the others flinched as the aircar came uncomfortably close overhead before it dropped to rest, throwing a stinging cloud of white almost at their feet.

The opaque roof lifted before the sand settled again. Marcus popped up like an Oud from a tunnel. "Let's go!" he shouted at them, beckoning with both arms. "Hurry!"

Fear of the Tikitik?

Naryn scowled but followed Aryl and Enris. Her displeasure aroused Anaj, silent for some time. *Naryn? What's happening?* A pause as they climbed into the air-car, then: *ANSWER ME!*

The Old Adept, Aryl winced, had very little patience and a very loud mindvoice.

"We're flying home," Naryn said aloud, her face like ash. Aryl took her arm, poured *strength* through that link. Her friend gave her a determined smile. "Hopefully a quick trip," she added fervently.

More esans? I suppose they brought us here. But I hope this is the last time!

It will be, Aryl sent, smiling at Marcus. "Thank—"

He didn't smile back. "Hurry," he insisted, moving out of the way to allow them to climb in.

Funny voice for a Tikitik. But after the observation, Anaj's presence faded behind her shields.

This aircar had two seats, facing front, with padded benches along each side. No packs or crates cluttered the floor, Aryl noticed with relief as she took one of the forward seats. She'd been wrong. The Human wasn't dressed for a journey either. He wore his favorite pretend-Om'ray clothes: pants, shirt, and boots of the right shape and color, if wrong fabric and fasteners. The boots were covered in dried mud and had left tracks and clumps everywhere. The shirt was stained with sweat. "Sit, sit," he urged, throwing himself into the seat beside Aryl's and stabbing the control buttons.

Naryn and Enris hadn't reached their seats before the roof closed and Aryl felt the machine lift.

Her relief evaporated. In haste. And alone? Something was wrong.

"Any reason for the rush?" Enris asked, a little too casually.

"Busy day." A little too glib. "Always busy days. Are you comfortable? Aryl? Naryn?" In that distracted tone. "Enris?"

Not "What are you doing on the other side of the world?" or "Why didn't you 'port home?" Reasonable questions. Important ones.

Leave this to me, Aryl sent. "We're fine, Marcus. We were

visiting—" he wouldn't like this, she knew, but continued, "—the Tikitik."

But instead of the wild-eyed flinch she'd expected, the Human merely nodded. "*Scanned lifeforms.* Many Tikitik, many other *organisms.* Busy place, *saltmarsh.*"

He didn't know about Tikitna, she realized with surprise. Perhaps living buildings couldn't be detected by machines designed to search for ruins of metal and stone.

Right now, he wouldn't care. She didn't have to sense the Human's emotions to read the tremble of his hands on the controls or the sheen on his forehead. His green-brown eyes flicked constantly between two small screens.

Trouble.

The day had been going so well.

The aircar leveled. Marcus sat back with what was more shudder than sigh. Aryl put her hand on his arm, careful to keep her shields tight to avoid any painful contact with his mind. "What's wrong?"

His eyes lifted to hers, brimming with worry. "Take you home," he said faintly.

She tightened her fingers to get his attention, not to hurt. "What is it?"

"Might be nothing." He collected himself with a visible effort, managed a wan smile. "*Autosurveillance* didn't resume this morning. Not what I did. I only set for last 'night." A slide of his eyes behind her. "Only for that one time."

She didn't need to ask why. Enris and his dam. She'd been right to suspect something going on with the two of them. It didn't help her know what troubled him now. Aryl nodded encouragement, hoping the Human would begin to make sense. "Go on."

"Should have been fixed with *nextroutinesweep.* Back up at dawn. All working. But not on. Not right. Not normal. Nothing—" Now the words came too fast, but she didn't try to slow him. "Dawn comes, all systems go dead. No com. No security field. No autodefense. No one comes to see why. *Securityprotocol.* Someone should have come."

Too much sense. She might not understand the machines, but any Yena knew what it meant to post scouts, then have them fail to report. "So you're doing it. Going to them—to the other sites." Her heart started to pound. Why him? Why alone? "Couldn't the others do that?"

He shook his head vigorously. "Need them to stay and secure the artifacts. I'm First. My responsibility, everyone on Cersi. My fault."

"No," Enris objected. "I asked you to turn off your vids."

"My decision," Marcus said simply. In that moment, Om'ray or not, he was the elder. He shrugged, that gesture they had in common. "Should have been no problem. Should have come back on."

She'd never seen the Human quietly desperate, not even when the Oud were burying them. "This isn't about machines being broken."

Marcus covered her hand with his, stared down as if fascinated by the contrast between her tanned, scarred skin and his, white and smooth. "Aryl reading my mind?" he asked with an odd smile.

"You know I—"

"I know." Softly. The smile disappeared, replaced by something grim. His thumb rubbed hers, then he looked up. "You're right. Not about machines. About danger. Here. Because of our work."

Tension. She tried not to show her own. "What do you mean?"

"The search for the Hoveny—important. But many Triads search, on many other worlds. Most look for years and nothing worthwhile. Our families forget us. Those who sent us here, they send supplies and wait for reports. Forget us." A hand pressed to his chest with the word. "Security checks, back at First. Offworld protocols. Good enough, understand? No risk, no one cares, forgotten. Unless we find something. Or think we have. Once find confirmed, every protection sent." That desperate edge to his voice. "Reports secret. Go only to the office of the First. No one else should know."

"Why?" Aryl narrowed her eyes. "Who shouldn't know?"

"Those who take what isn't theirs."

Why had she thought his vast Trade Pact would be safe from greed and thieves? Maybe, she realized, because the alternative was terrifying. "You think that's what's happened." She licked dry lips. "That someone's come to Cersi, to take from you."

"I could be wrong." Marcus lifted his hand from hers; guessing he worried about the contact, she released his arm. "No *leak* in history of First—no secret exposed. None they admit," this heavily, as if he, too, had suddenly found an alternative difficult to bear. "If happened, maybe my fault, too. I delayed reports, kept some information out—" a faint blush on his cheeks. "I could have drawn attention. Wrong attention."

What does this mean for us? Naryn sent.

She was right to ask. "You said 'danger.' What kind of danger? What would they do?" Whoever "they" were.

Marcus consulted his screens—not, Aryl judged, because they told him what to say. Finally, he gave her that uncertain sideways glance. "The bad kind. I flew over Site One on the way here. The tower is damaged. I thought—hoped that explained the com silence. A broken machine, not—not— Then you called. Coms work, Aryl. No one's using them. No one."

And she'd worried he was leaving.

A physical threat. To him. To those who worked with him. Something that could disrupt the Strangers' seemingly invincible technology. "Do they threaten us?"

"I'll take you home," he said as if he hadn't heard. "You get everyone inside the Cloisters. Stay there until I come. Promise me."

Haxel would have her blade against the softness of his throat by now, demanding answers. Not that it would

work, Aryl knew. No threat would move Marcus Bowman to say anything he didn't want to say.

And she'd never allow it.

"We'll go with you." Two of the Triad sites were between here and Sona. He wasn't a fool.

Not a fool; not happy either. Marcus frowned. "No."

"You need to check on your people. You've already
wasted time coming for us."

Behind her, Naryn sighed, but Aryl could feel her
agreement. Naryn might not care about Marcus, but she
knew they had to learn about this mysterious threat.
Enris? She sensed his presence close to her thoughts,
careful, wary.

"Bad idea!" Marcus lurched around in his seat. "Enris.
Tell her."

"I like it." Her Chosen leaned back and put his massive arms behind his head in a show of ease. "The sooner
we're home, the sooner Haxel puts me to work."

"I'd—" Naryn bent double, her hands holding her abdomen. "Leave me be!" she gasped.

She didn't protest to them.

Anaj! Aryl sought the other through the M'hir. *Stop!*

Interesting. The other's mind was a solid spot of light,
their connection locked instantly. Trained Power; practiced control. *So this is your version of the Dark. You
look like flame, Child of Power.*

*Anaj. Please. Leave Naryn in peace. We must learn
more.*

Not an esan.

No. Aryl risked the other's reaction and shared a
quick image of the aircar and Marcus. *Not-Om'ray, but
a friend.*

Interesting, Anaj repeated. *What you wish to reveal
and what you think you can hide about our new companion, this Human.*

Aryl checked her shields.

Don't worry. I'm in no position to argue. A ripple

through the M'hir; it might have been laughter. It might have been despair. *I'll be patient as long as I'm able.*

She knew what Anaj meant. *If I can help—*

Save your strength. Find the truth, then get us home.

Aryl blinked herself free of the M'hir to the sound of the Human's voice, loud and vehement. "—go home. This is Trade Pact problem. Triad problem. Not Om'ray. Not yours! What of babies?"

What would he think of the acerbic old Adept currently living inside Naryn? She was *real* to Om'ray, but would she be to the Human?

Some things, Aryl reminded herself, Marcus didn't need to know.

One he did. "If you take us to Sona, we won't get out of this machine. Unless you think you can force us out? And our babies?"

Enris made a choking noise.

"Aryl," the Human pleaded. "Not safe!"

Her grin faded. "Did you think we were friends only when it was?"

Marcus stared desperately at the screens. A muscle jumped along his jaw. She waited.

"Promise to stay in aircar, no matter what," he said finally, not looking at her. " 'Port away if I say so. Promise."

She'd do no such thing.

When she didn't answer, a glance assessed her expression, then the Human sighed. He dug into a pocket, brought out a small disk she'd seen it before, the one that held images of his family. He handed it to her. "Keep this safe for me. Promise that?"

As a trick, it wasn't up to his usual standard. Aryl took the image disk and put it in a pocket. "What I promise is to give it back when we're all safe."

"Stubborn," he commented, but almost smiled.

Behind them, Enris chuckled.

The Lake of Fire took its name from strange clouds, like curls of smoke, that often rose from its still surface. Aryl pressed her nose to the now-transparent side of the aircar but could see only one. She'd meant to ask Marcus if the Strangers knew what caused the smoke, if it was something to do with the structures beneath the surface.

Today wasn't the time for curiosity.

Marcus wouldn't talk to her, busy with the controls when he wasn't staring at the small screens as if their flow of color and symbol offered some final hope. She'd seen him afraid for his life, but this was different.

Odd. The solitary curl of smoke was taller and darker than those she remembered. "Marcus?"

He lifted his head and looked out. "Site One," Marcus announced grimly, his face set in unfamiliar lines.

Meaning the smoke was from the Strangers' platform over the underwater ruins, where Marcus and his Triad had been working when she'd first met them. The aircar veered toward the nearer shore.

If the buildings were still on fire, why was he heading away? For their safety? "Don't worry about us," Aryl said quickly. "We'll help. Go back!"

Marcus tapped the small screen. "No one to help," he said. "No *lifesign*."

Enris got to his feet, loomed between Marcus and Aryl. "Who did this?"

The Human looked up. "No proof who. Could be accident, *malfunction*. Artrul—her Triad. *Evacuation-protocol*. Means they go to Site Two. Damaged tower. Local coms down, that's all. Confusion." A too-casual shrug. "See? Take you home now."

He tried to get rid of them again. "Site Two," she insisted. It lay a ridge beyond Grona.

"Not safe."

Now the truth, or some of it. "What is?" Aryl said gently. "You waste time arguing, Marcus."

At last, the hint of a smile in his eyes. "I should know

better by now." He slumped in his seat. "Stubborn Om'ray." One finger pushed a button and the aircar shot forward, faster than Aryl had known it could go. "Sit." This to Enris, who put his hand on the Human's shoulder and squeezed gently before returning to the bench.

Naryn closed her eyes and put her head back, hair fretting across her shoulders. This flight wasn't going to improve her opinion of Marcus Bowman or his kind.

Aryl checked her longknife.

For all the good it might do against what could bring fire down in the midst of a lake.

They flew over the canopy. Over Yena, her inner sense told her. Aryl kept her shields tight and felt the others do the same. Taisal could have reached through the M'hir, demanded an explanation; that her mother ignored their passing overhead was one less worry.

Eyes fixed to his screens, Marcus ignored the view. They were higher this time. Higher than wastryls flew or wings could rise on the M'hir. Higher and faster. Without her *inner* sense to give her perspective, she wouldn't have recognized the Sarc grove, or spotted the ring of old rastis that surrounded the Cloisters.

How high could they go, she wondered, before they reached the end of the sky?

Site Two was carved into the side of a mountain ridge. Though Aryl had only seen it in truenight, the Strangers had stuck glows everywhere, turning the darkness to day. Easy to remember the long sharp ledge where they landed their machines—she trusted Marcus was capable of landing this one there—then the short walk up a slope to a second, higher ledge where the Strangers had set up camp using the same plain white constructions as at Sona. Why? Because here they'd dug into the mountain itself. They'd freed a series of massive structures, exposing them once more to light and air. She'd had the barest glimpse at the time, busy planning to escape with Enris, but the buildings had been like those under the Lake of Fire, smooth curves and unfamiliar angles. Perfect, undamaged. Not like the ruins of Sona.

The Hoveny Concentrix.

The Strangers had made a discovery. Something important enough to draw Marcus and his Triad—and her—here.

"Marcus, what did they find? At Site Two."

He gave her a bemused look, as if this was the last thing he'd expected. For a moment she thought he'd evade the question, as he most often did when it concerned his work, then he replied, "A door."

Doors, in her experience, were only useful under one condition. "A door you could open?"

"Could? I think so. But we're not ready yet." He cupped his hands tightly together. "The inside has been sealed a very long time. Still intact. We want to know about the *internalenvironment*—the air—inside. Vital to detect any systems still *operational.*" He lifted his thumb to make a small opening. "Tyler's Triad made *controlledaccesspoint, lockdown* rest until ready. Send tiny vidbots to look for us. They'll finish the first level soon, then move to the next. Takes time." His gloom lifted as he spoke. "Hoveny structures are almost always empty, as if the owners moved out and then locked the doors. Best finds so far have been what was missed. Objects left on a floor, perhaps dropped in a hurry. Artifacts. Tell us little alone. Have *nocontext.* What we really want to find are *workinginstallations.* Parts of building that couldn't be moved. Remarkable *preservation* inside. They might still work."

Aryl thought of the tables filled with objects she'd seen being sorted. "You have artifacts at Sona."

He grimaced. "Oud don't respect doors. Make big mess."

Enris laughed.

TRILLLLLL!!

The noise burst from the control panel. Lights flashed. Marcus bent over it, muttering in his own language. He did something to silence the sound, but the lights reflected on his pale skin, turning it red, then blue, then yellow. Red again. He stood to stare through the clear ceiling at the scattered clouds overhead, then dropped back into his seat. "Watch," he ordered. "Tell me if you see anything approaching."

"From above?" Naryn asked in disbelief. Aryl shared her reaction. What was the Human thinking?

"From anywhere."

The aircar began to descend, quickly.

"Don't crash this time," Aryl reminded the Human, her hands gripping the edge of the seat.

For some reason this made Marcus choke on a laugh of his own.

Down. Down. The lights played over them like biters hunting a spot to bite. Aryl did her best to ignore them, staring out as Marcus directed. Enris and Naryn did the same.

They had to be close to Site Two by now, Aryl thought. Looking down, she could see the slope of the mountain, littered with loose rock. Loose rock with an appetite. A patient, seldom rewarded appetite—not much wandered here.

"Something's behind us." Enris. *What is it?* he asked her, sharing the image of a distant speck.

Wastryl—or not.

Marcus didn't look around. "Is it getting closer?"

"I can't tell."

TRILLL!!!

The aircar swung violently to one side and back again, like a branch pulled and released with a snap. Aryl clung to her seat, her eyes on Marcus.

Who now looked furious.

"What was that?"

"A suggestion." Unhelpfully. "Don't talk now."

A suggestion? Enris sent. *What's going on?*

Maybe he avoided a wastryl. She'd seen a vidbot explode when attacked by the flying creatures.

Can he land at this speed?

Aryl glanced out the side and flinched. The mountainside roared by, too close, a blur of shadow and jagged edge. *We have to trust him.*

Privately, through the M'hir, their link as solid as flesh touching. *No, we don't. We could leave, now.*

I won't risk Naryn. Or Anaj.

This doesn't?

We must know what's happening to the Strangers. Aryl pulled free, refused to be distracted. Some risks had to be taken. She focused on Marcus. His hands were sure on the controls, as if anger had burned away all fear. Anger at what?

The aircar tipped to one side, answering her question.

No one spoke as they flew past what had been Site Two. Wisps of smoke marked the remains of buildings. Crumbled machines, scorched and useless, lay on what had been the landing ledge.

No one had escaped that way, Aryl thought.

The Hoveny buildings were unscathed. Rock lay shattered around them, mixed with bits of machine, but the structures were as flawless as she remembered.

Marcus did little more than glance at the devastation before turning back to the small screen. A muscle along his jaw twitched. It was the only expression left on his face. He sent the aircar upward again; faster than before.

This time, no talk of taking them home first.

Or of accidents.

Site Three, Aryl told the others. She didn't know where it was, what it was.

I don't want to meet what could do this, Naryn protested.

We must. Enris, as grim as she'd ever felt him. So he shared her dread. Ruthless, coordinated attacks. Technology equal to or superior to that of the Strangers. What chance would Om'ray have, if they became the next targets?

Or Oud.

Or Tikitik.

Courage, she sent, wishing for more of her own.

Marcus headed away from Grona and Yena, choosing a path that, to Om'ray sense, led to where the sun dropped out of sight, leaving darkness behind. Mountains passed beneath them, a monotonous landscape of ridges and deep valleys, browns and grays. Rarely, a glistening thread marked what must be a river. Proof, Aryl thought, that the world continued beyond Sona's waterfall.

Didn't it?

Uneasy, she turned the bracelet around and around on her wrist.

The proof passed beneath. She could see for herself. The world continued . . .

Didn't it?

Aryl . . . something's wrong.

I feel it.

Like a branch with hidden rot, the floor of the aircar suddenly grew soft, untrustworthy. She lifted her feet with a cry.

The air she breathed turned too warm, then too cold.

The Human takes us past the end of the world! Naryn, *fear* leaking past her control. "Turn around!" she shouted. "Take us home!"

Marcus didn't look around. "Almost there."

Aryl had walked away from her kind before this—so had Enris. They'd been able to leave other Om'ray behind, prided themselves on their strength.

They hadn't gone far enough. Hadn't gone this far . . .

Too far . . .

"Marcus," she gasped. "Naryn's right. You have to take us back."

"Site Three here."

Mountains rose beneath them, the sky squeezed downward, there was no room to breathe, no room for them.

Somehow, she managed not to grab for the controls or the Human's neck. "We—can't—be here!" Hard to form words. To think. "Turn around!"

He turned then, something rousing in his eyes, a spark. "Aryl? What's wrong?" Even as the Human spoke, she knew it was already too late ... another instant ... any further ... they would become ... *nothing*.

NOOOO!!!!!!!!! the inner scream came from them all. No. It came from outside. It came from everywhere.

She knew that sound.

The M'hir Wind was coming. It blew through the great pipes of the Watchers, set into the mountain. Time for the Harvest. Time for change. She could hear their moaning, feel it through her flesh ...

Calling her *HOME*.

Aryl threw herself into the M'hir ...

Interlude

ALIVE. THAT WAS GOOD. Surrounded by the warm glow of Om'ray. That was better. A head thudded against his chest, small arms wrapped around him, strong enough to threaten his ribs. Aryl. All was right with the world, then. But . . . how?

The Watchers. He'd heard the drums, felt them. Hadn't he? Had to answer. Hadn't he?

Enris took a shuddering breath. He didn't know about the others, but he most definitely hadn't formed a locate before that desperate 'port *HOME*.

Which was . . . where?

He cracked open his eyes, careful not to move. There could be branches involved. And heights, knowing his Chosen.

He sighed with relief. A floor. They were on a floor. In a room.

More than a room.

Enris blinked, and the size and platforms formed into sense. Aryl had shown him images of Sona's Dream Chamber. She must have directed them here, to the safety of the Cloisters.

Where—another blink—they were surrounded by Om'ray.

Too many Om'ray.

Drowning in the glow of his own kind, dizzy with *belonging*, he closed his eyes and fought for calm.

The world had changed shape.

Someone stirred against him. He stretched back a hand, found a knee that pulled itself away. *We're all right.* Naryn, shaken, but aware. And amazed. *Do you feel it? The Power here?*

Anaj: *Speak for yourself, child. I'm not the least all right. What's going on?*

WE LEFT HIM!

Aryl. *Hush!* Enris winced. *We have company—*

WE ABANDONED MARCUS!

He took Aryl's shoulders; moved her so he could see her face. Oh, he knew that fierce look. It usually preceded an act of spectacularly careless bravery. He tightened his grip. "We can't help him. Not now. He's—" Where did someone go, when they left the world behind? He hadn't understood. None of them had. Human and Om'ray were not the same. The Human's world wasn't theirs.

Couldn't be.

Enris took a deep breath, steadied himself, offered *strength* to his Chosen. "He's gone. And we have company." Then, as if she was as deaf to other Om'ray as Yao. "Look for yourself," drawing her to her feet with him.

The chamber was meant to hold an entire Clan.

It now did.

Hundreds stood and stared at one another. No one spoke. Shields were slammed tight.

Not any Om'ray, Enris realized with a jolt. Naryn was right. Power. The white robes of Adepts were everywhere. Even those who weren't shielded their inner selves with confidence.

The fierce look turned to a safer wonder. *What's happened?* "I'm the Speaker," Aryl muttered aloud. "I suppose I have to say something."

Enris couldn't help but chuckle. "Good. What, exactly?"

She dug an elbow into his ribs, but the *feel* of her eased

slightly. "I'll make it up." With that, Aryl jumped on the nearest platform.

Everyone turned to look at her. Too small. Too young. Unknown to most. Aryl shouldn't have seemed impressive.

That she was, standing there waiting for their full attention, made him smile.

"Welcome to Sona," she began. The words—he *felt* as well as heard them. Aryl was sending through the M'hir as well, making sure everyone heard and understood. Preventing panic. Good. Beyond the *pleasure* of being within so many of his kind, Enris was reasonably sure panic would be his next feeling.

Because they shouldn't be here at all. The Sona, maybe. Having the advantage of height, he'd spotted them already, at the near end of the room, a tight knot with Haxel at their core. Perhaps Aryl's desperate 'port had somehow drawn them, too.

Which didn't explain the group of dappled Amna closest to him. Or any of the rest.

Aryl spoke again. "Are there other Speakers here?"

Not what he'd expected. *Why?*

Later.

Points of movement among the rest, Om'ray stepping aside to let three approach Aryl.

One with a familiar fierce look on her face.

"Hello, Mother," Aryl di Sarc said, seeming not surprised at all.

❋ ❋ ❋

Over seven hundred Om'ray had arrived in the Dream Chamber of Sona's Cloisters at once. They'd come from every Clan but Vyna, including three from Tuana who carefully avoided Naryn. Everyone told a similar story: they'd been about their normal affairs when overwhelmed by a sense of loneliness, a need to go *HOME*. They'd *heard* the Watchers in whatever variation existed for their Clan. Descriptions of the M'hir itself varied too; some hardly noticed their journey through it, a few were still shaking. Others thought it a calm and peaceful place.

It might have been, compared to here, Enris thought wryly. Who'd have thought there was such a thing as too many Om'ray in one place? Even Husni had appeared daunted by the bewildering array of strange voices, faces, and clothing. Briefly. Before she and Haxel had taken charge of what they called "the necessities," enlisting the rest of Sona—more accustomed to dealing with strangers—to assign others to tasks.

There'd been no arguments, no attempts to leave, no fear. Strangest of all, he had to admit, everyone *felt* they belonged here, in Sona. This was their Cloisters, Om'ray whose names they'd yet to learn were their Clan, this was . . . this was home.

Which was fine and natural for Sona's few, but he had yet to grasp why it was so for the hordes of strangers peacefully milling through their Cloisters. They didn't speak of families left behind or of a future anywhere but here. It was as if the assortment of young, old, unChosen, and Chosen had arrived on Passage, committed to live with their new Clan, dead to their old one.

It wasn't possible, Enris decided firmly. None of them had planned this; none of them should have accepted such a drastic change without question.

Not that everyone had. The new Adepts might *feel* Sona as their home as much as any other arrival, but they were curious. They'd gone to the Council Chamber almost at once, to "discuss" the new Sona and discover what had brought them together and how. A discussion that had been going on for tenths.

With Aryl di Sarc.

". . . scan me if you don't believe what I say. We had nothing to do with this."

"You had everything to do with it. Maybe it wasn't your intention," as if a huge concession, "but who here doubts we'd be still in our original Clans if not for your reckless behavior?"

Enris tried not to listen. Chairs. Anything to sit on. That was his job. As if the precious Adepts needed anything more than their rears.

Not his problem.

Aryl depended on him in other ways right now, including keeping his *frustration* to himself.

"Fools," he grumbled once safely past the Council Chamber doors. "If they'd listen instead of making accusations, they might learn something."

Of course, most of the Adepts were no longer doing that much. They'd sorted themselves, how he couldn't guess, until the majority sat in their Clans as far from those with Aryl as they could. Which made no sense.

Except for one who'd nipped through the doors after Enris and Naryn, Rayna, by his appearance. While some wore the stiff white robes of their rank, others were dressed in soft layers of bright fabric, with twists of more tied to the bottoms of sleeves and hems to flutter when they walked. Aryl thought it ridiculous to wear something that would not only catch on every twig, but draw attention. A shame, Enris decided. She'd look lovely.

The Rayna themselves were small and slightly built, with skin darker than a Yena's, striking against their fair hair and pale blue or yellow eyes. Their female Chosen left their hair free, but had somehow convinced it to hold colorful fabric twists in loose knots.

Somehow, he couldn't wrap his mind around Aryl's hair being that cooperative.

As for the Rayna Adept himself? Enris scowled. "Why aren't you staying?"

"Karne d'sud Witthun," the other replied stiffly. "I could ask you—or them—" with a nod to Naryn, "—the same question. Your place is with the rest."

"Chairs."

"Chairs?"

"Someone has to make you Adepts comfortable."

Don't mind him, Anaj sent. *He gets irritable when he's hungry.* Unharmed by the 'port, the Old Adept had been remarkably calm since arriving at Sona, perhaps because she was the only one of the hundreds here in her proper place, however that place had changed. Her home, not theirs.

Theirs now, too, if Enris could believe it. Without asking any of Sona's present members if they wanted more. He'd have said yes in a heartbeat to another twenty or so. Seven hundred?

Including Adepts who paid no attention to Aryl di Sarc's leadership?

He growled deep in his chest, and Karne gave him a worried look.

Noticing, the former Tuana gestured apology. "Welcome to Sona. I'm Enris—" he stopped there. Among the many things yet to be explained to the new arrivals was the clever way Aryl had convinced Sona's locks to open for them all. It hadn't seemed the right time to say they'd simply given themselves the 'di' of Adepts. Instead, he nodded at the doors. "Why do you think we belong in there?"

Because we DO! came from Naryn. *I do!!*

No, I said. I need a rest, Anaj answered firmly. *Find us a bed before you fall on your face.*

Enris hid a smile. Poor Naryn. Anaj might *be* her baby, but the Old Adept left no doubt who was eldest and in charge. "While I'm off to hunt chairs," he informed the Rayna. "So why are you here and not there?"

"I'm lesser." From his tone, Karne was beginning to wonder if Enris was capable of understanding anything but chairs. "They don't need me."

"Ah. Another body to carry chairs. Good."

Don't be mean to the child, Enris, Anaj sent, just to him. *Once trained, Adepts sort themselves by individual Power. The strongest act as Council for the others. Only First Level Adepts will gather close to Aryl—hers is the greatest Power here. Karne can sense yours. He's brave to speak to you at all.*

Like Dama. Chastise and compliment in the same

sending. A laugh bubbled up from his chest and Enris sent a rush of *affection* to Anaj. *Grandmother.*

Charmer. Then, with *worry. Naryn can't take much more.*

He knew. The only rest they'd had was after Tikitna, and she'd wasted it pacing the sand. She knew it herself. She might protest, but hadn't Naryn listened to Anaj and left the meeting?

The Rayna wasn't done. "I thought you'd have some answers." Karne stepped closer, his arms waving at the corridor. "What happened to this place? Why are you living like this?"

"We don't actually live inside—"

The young Adept didn't stop. "You're both Tuana— that Clan was attacked after you came here. Why? Is that going to happen to our former Clans?"

The last came with such *fear,* Enris strengthened his shields to keep it out. "We don't know," he said. "Not yet. But you're safe here." Before he could say more, like a flash of light, Ziba appeared in the corridor, laughing. At the sight of them, she covered her mouth and disappeared.

Yao appeared in the same spot, disappeared. Followed by three children Enris didn't know, holding hands. They giggled and were gone.

Karne looked dazed.

Worin appeared next.

"No, you don't!" With a lunge, Enris had his brother by the arm. "Who said you could 'port in the Cloisters?" He'd *looked* at the M'hir. It remained coiled around itself like a towering summer storm. Complete with lightning. "It's not safe yet. Even if Ziba thinks so," he warned at the beginnings of a rebellious frown.

"Husni sent us to look for benches," Worin announced virtuously, black hair tumbling over his bright eyes. In other words, Husni had had enough of the mischievous pair.

They thought of the M'hir as another playground.

What had Aryl told him? The M'hir was already part of their children. With an inward shudder, Enris brushed back Worin's hair, ruffled it. "Why benches?"

"For beds. Did you see how many Om'ray have come?" He radiated *joy.* "We found a whole room of benches, but they're fastened to the floor."

"If they're fastened, they serve some purpose where they are," Karne warned. "You'd better check with your Adepts first."

Enris shook his head. "They'd debate it all 'night." Making it pointless to find beds. *Anaj?* he sent.

Show me, child.

Worin's eyes widened. "You're Naryn's baby!" *You can talk already?? Can you play?*

Enris snickered. Naryn gave an impatient sigh.

Not with children who don't mind their elders, Anaj replied. *Now show me these benches. You can.* This as Worin hesitated.

Enris gestured approval. His brother had never shown this particular Talent, but he had the Power for it. *Like this,* he sent, offering a remembered *view* of Sona's new dam. *Think about the place you want to show us—*

Like this? Images spilled out, vivid, overloading the senses. *The uppermost level. Dimmed light. A slice of dark sky. Giggles. Shouldn't be here. Running along curved benches. Jump! Can't catch me. Can. Can't. Let's play 'port and seek. Husni won't know* . . . The images stopped there. Worin gazed at the floor, the ceiling, anywhere but at his brother.

Mischief indeed. Enris bit his tongue.

You can't move those benches, Anaj sent calmly. *They're part of the floor. Let some sleep up there. It won't be the first time.*

And, hopefully just to him, *Try it when the moons are overhead. Kynan liked their light on my skin.*

Old, not dead. Enris laughed so hard, Naryn began to frown. He gestured a mute apology. "Hungry. We missed supper." Most of the new arrivals had finished their evening meal before being summoned. He hadn't, something he planned to fix.

"Sorry, Enris." Worin's face fell. "Husni said there's nothing to eat here. There's water, though. Fon and the other unChosen went for it."

Sending out the youngsters wasn't a decision he'd have made, not when they didn't know what was happening outside. The Human had warned them to stay in the Cloisters until he contacted them; he'd had a reason.

Contacted how? Enris wondered suddenly. He hoped the Human didn't plan to knock on the Cloisters' doors. Explain that face to their new Clan?

Explain how a being could fall out of the *real* world and return . . . not something he could do, Enris thought, swallowing hard. He'd thought he'd begun to grasp what the Human and Thought Traveler meant when they said Cersi was only one world, one place, of many; he'd prided himself on his imagination when he looked up at the cliff and told himself there could be more mountains and rivers beyond it.

Then he'd almost left the world himself.

The effort to reconcile what his mind remembered and what his *inner sense* knew upset his empty stomach. Impossible.

"Why did all these Om'ray come here, Enris? What's so special about Sona? No one's saying."

About to reassure his brother, Enris noticed Karne's attention and changed his mind. "No one knows," he admitted. "Not yet."

The young unChosen straightened his shoulders. "Don't worry," he said solemnly. "What matters is that everyone made it. Even Seru, who couldn't reach the Cloisters before."

Enris stared at his brother. Worin was right. All of Sona had 'ported. There'd been no time to comprehend what was happening, to help one another. The two newborns had been in their mothers' carryslings, but the older children had been roaming free. Yet they'd come, too.

The urgency of the summons chased along his nerves as he remembered it. Was that the key?

Naryn spoke, her voice low and urgent. "Enris, remember watching the plows dig the fields? The second pass was easier because the soil was broken. Maybe having so many aimed at the same destination through the M'hir opened an easier path. Something the 'lesser'—" with a dismissive glance at Karne, "—could use."

It made sense. "I—"

"But I think I should sit now." With that, she began to sink toward the floor.

Enris threw an arm around Naryn's waist to draw her up again. "You need a bed, not debate." Without hesitation, he tried to give her *strength* through their contact, but she shuddered free of his hold to stand, barely, on her own.

"I just need to rest," she snapped. *LEAVEME-ALONEDON'TTOUCHME!* Karne and Worin backed a step.

"Can you walk to the Dream Chamber?"

"Can you?" Her scornful look would, Enris decided, be more convincing if her face had any color at all. Between that, and the filthy Adept robe Oran had adamantly not wanted returned, Naryn di S'udlaat looked disturbingly like a corpse. An ill-used one.

He stepped smoothly in her way before she could try to move—and likely land on her face—and held out his left hand, palm up. "For Anaj. Take what you need. Or—" as he *felt* her resistance, "—I will carry you, like it or not."

Temper flared her nostrils and narrowed her eyes. "Without supper?" Disdain.

"I'll manage." *You'd let Aryl help.*

"I won't be hauled through the Cloisters like a bundle of sticks!"

Let me help.

You hate me. You've reason to. With all the *despair* she'd never revealed, betrayed by her own weakness. *I don't trust you.*

Why should she? Until last truenight, he'd tolerated her presence for Aryl's sake. Since then, he'd given *strength* to her unasked, *shared* what she didn't want to learn, and brought her to the Vyna to be forced to accept a Glorious Dead.

Oh, and hadn't he finished by hauling her up on a branch in Tikitna like a sack of scraps, then flying her out of the world with a not-Om'ray she feared?

Which, though not his fault exactly, probably hadn't helped.

Nothing had gone as it should since the dam. His Chosen had known better. He'd felt her distrust but ignored it, sure he was right about the Vyna, assuming Aryl was being her Yena-self, prone to worry over anything that worked the first time or looked easy to walk.

Enris gestured apology with both hands; it wasn't only to Naryn. "What do you want me to do?"

About to speak, Naryn tilted her head as if listening. The strain in her face eased slightly. "Anaj asks," almost a whisper, "for some of your gift."

Silently, Enris offered his hand again.

Her fingers trembled as they approached and she clenched them into a fist, eyes flashing to his. He pretended he hadn't noticed, smiling at Worin who watched in fascination.

A little too much fascination. Might be time for a Chosen to unChosen talk. Especially with Ziba around. You could never start too soon.

Fingertips.

He ignored them.

A palm against his.

Only then, easily, gently, Enris let *strength* flow through that contact. He kept his shields in place, offered no other sharing, let the outpouring continue until she lifted her hand away.

Their eyes met. For that instant, he saw a Naryn he'd never known, perhaps the Naryn only Aryl knew: vulnerable, scarred, passionate.

With the cool lift of a brow, her guard returned. "I know my way." She pushed past him and walked down the corridor, red hair uneasy on her shoulders.

She'll do. Anaj, to him.

Enris half smiled.

"I thought you didn't like her."

He ruffled Worin's hair. "It's complicated."

"Is Naryn still going to die when her baby is born?"

"How did you—" Apparently there were no secrets left in Sona. "She won't die."

Not if a brave old Om'ray could endure until summer.

Not if the world itself endured.

How had everything become fragile? There was nothing he could make or fix; nothing all the questions and answers being traded in the Council Chambers could change. This was the life Aryl had led in Yena: every step over certain death, any day the last.

He hadn't understood, until this moment, what it took to keep walking.

The other two were staring at him, eyes wide and afraid. Enris found a smile. "Come along, Karne," he invited, his voice light. "Let's see what we can find. On the way, you can torture me with tales of the delicacies Rayna would offer a starving guest. Which I trust are better than Vyna."

"You've been to Vyna?" This with *awe.*

Much better than fear, Enris thought, tucking his own away.

Much better.

Chapter 9

ARYL SHOOK HER HEAD, a gesture without meaning to her present companions. She shouldn't be here. Marcus needed her—she was sure of it. Whatever he'd find at Site Three, it wouldn't be help. She could call him. The geoscanner sat in its pocket at her waist, turned off as he'd ordered. If the Strangers could talk across the unimaginable void between worlds, surely this could reach the mountains beyond this one.

It might as well, she thought glumly, be at the bottom of the Makers' Touch in Tikitna. The existence of a Human, of others capable of attacking him, of other worlds and races and languages was easier to believe than this, that she sat cross-legged on the floor of Sona's shabby Cloisters with her mother and Sian d'sud Vendan, while Yena's Adepts seemed completely at home and argued M'hir terminology with Oran.

As for their audience?

If there were any Adepts left with their Clans, it was hard to tell from the hordes in white in Sona. Twenty-seven surrounded her, argued with one another as much as with her. The twenty-seven possessed shields so strong they almost disappeared from her *inner* sense, except for the Power they pressed against each other when making a point, like *nirts* baring teeth when they met on a frond until the smaller closed its mouth and sidled away. The rest pretended disinterest, sitting in small groups. They waited for commands, she guessed. Games of Power. This was how Adepts ruled themselves.

How they'd always ruled their Clans.

She should have seen it before, but she'd believed what she'd been told. About too much.

Three Speakers in this circle: her mother, for Yena, and those for Amna and Rayna. As she'd feared, each wore their pendants. If the Tikitik could detect those, they'd know what had happened.

Of course, she told herself grimly, all they'd have to do was count. The shift in their numbers had been anything but subtle.

Every Om'ray—except Yao and the babies—would have felt the extraordinary change in the shape of the world. The other Clans had diminished to Sona's gain. Gain? Their names alone . . . it was like listening to Marcus babbling in his own tongue. Bowart, Nemat, Paniccia, Eathem, Prendolat, Friesnen. On and on they went. Sona's handful were overwhelmed.

These new Om'ray didn't need her. Didn't care for her opinion, once gathered in numbers. They took on their accustomed role as Adepts, mighty hoarders of secrets. Did it reassure them to be equally ignorant?

She grimaced inwardly. Oran might enjoy this pointless babble, but surely even she knew they wasted time debating if 'port was a useful word. The Adepts left the larger questions to fester in the space between minds: what had happened? Why were they here? What might be the consequences? What should they do next?

As far as the newcomers were concerned, next would be the establishment of a proper Council for Sona. Her Sona. Theirs, for all they asked her advice. A Council, and plans to expand the village to receive their numbers. As if they were welcome to stay and the world would let them.

Aryl drummed her fingers silently on the floor.

Why did they want to stay? These were no unChosen on Passage; these were individuals who—a few tenths ago—had been part of larger families, who'd had roles within their Clans. Most had never left those homes before. Why did they *feel* that home was here, in Sona's stripped Cloisters and a mountain valley yet to feed its few Om'ray?

Each time she broached those questions, the others looked at her as if she'd grown a Tikitik's extra eyes.

They were the ones grown bizarre. Something about them had changed, whether the Adepts admitted the possibility or not.

Convenient, she thought, that the present discussion ignored her completely.

Aryl loosened her shields and dared *reach* for her own answers.

Names became familiar.

Deeper. She found and followed the bonds between Chosen, between mothers and children. They were intact. It would have been more of a surprise if those had stretched to allow one to 'port here without the other. *Deeper . . .*

. . . *the M'hir encircled them all, like the swarm waiting for truenight, impatient, eager, hungry . . .*

No. There was no threat.

. . . *they were trapped . . .*

No. They weren't confined.

. . . *the M'hir was* held *as it was . . . strings of glows against the swarm . . . a net to hold a Chosen's hair . . . the sun against truenight . . .*

Aryl fought to comprehend . . . Power? No. And yes. Nothing aware, nothing of effort. But every mind she touched was . . . *connected!!*

She pushed free of the M'hir and stared at those around her, seeing them for the first time. No wonder they *felt* at home, that they weren't strangers.

Quickly, she *reached* again.

The bonds connected her to them and back. Enris,

Naryn, Anaj, Seru, Haxel, Worin . . . every glow she *knew* had become tied together.

Aryl *paused* in the M'hir, its tumult nothing more than noise in the distance. She'd seen such a weaving before . . .

Her mother.

Part of Taisal had been left in the M'hir when her Chosen died; she'd bled Power ever since to keep from being drawn into it. Power that wove connections with other minds, connections she could hold, like the hand lines of Harvesters that ran between the great rastis of a grove.

Thinking of Taisal brought them close in the *darkness*. Aryl *looked*. Surely these stronger connections would help—

—instead, Power poured from Taisal as if from a death wound. She'd been wrong. The new connections weren't holding her mother from the M'hir—they helped ensnare her, pulled her deeper!

Her Mother used Power to resist, but for how long . . .

Aryl jerked back to herself with dismay. "Mother!"

Taisal turned to look at her, her frown at the interruption fading. "What's wrong?" She looked slightly weary, nothing more.

It wasn't fair, Aryl cried to herself. Others of Sona were comforted by their visitors, families reunited when such a thing had been beyond anyone's imagining. There'd been tears of joy. And of disappointment. There were children, babies in arms—only natural that Seru would hope for her little brother. But no other Parths had left Yena, and Seru had buried her face against her Chosen.

No other was put at risk like her mother.

"Aryl?" a softer question, concern in those eyes, so like her own.

"It's—I don't know." They sat together. They hadn't had a moment to speak in private; private sendings except between Chosen wouldn't be tolerated by this group.

How long could Taisal hold?

Not the question that mattered most. Not a problem Taisal would accept as more important than their Clan. She couldn't worry, couldn't interfere. Their bond was real, their love, but her mother, Aryl thought with a pride like sorrow, had taught her well. "It's about the links between us, between Om'ray," she said instead. "Can you sense them?"

"No."

Who can sense the links between Om'ray? Aryl sent loudly.

The rude interruption drew frowns and a few puzzled looks.

"I can," Sian replied.

"Me," offered Dann d'sud Friesnen of Pana. Murmured agreement from several more.

"Look at ours."

Silence. She sensed Power *reaching.* Aryl waited, aware of her mother's wary curiosity. These were the best of their kind.

Would they see it? Could they?

It wasn't only the world that had changed.

"We're linked to one another," Sian declared. Even in Yena, he'd stood out: more slender, darker, with thick lines of silver through his black hair. His eyebrows drew together; there was worry in the look he gave Taisal. He knew, Aryl thought. "Somehow, our minds remain connected within the Dark."

"The M'hir," Oran corrected sharply. Aryl winced.

But the Yena Adept gestured a gracious acceptance. "I defer to your greater experience, Sona's Keeper."

Oran flushed with pleasure, though Aryl doubted Sian meant it as a compliment. Sona's Cloisters had used her. It had somehow known its new Keeper was different from other Om'ray. It had sent Oran's knowledge of the M'hir not only to the Adepts, but to all who'd come here. How and why? More questions in urgent need of answers.

Gur di Sawnda'at spoke up. "Nothing has changed our Joinings to our Chosen, our bonds with heart-kin and children. We still *sense* all other Om'ray." The Rayna shared her *relief.* "We're part of Cersi."

"It doesn't matter. We've been caught by the Dark!" Aryl couldn't see who spoke. "It won't let us go!"

Before she could reply, others did. The Council Chamber erupted, those who'd sat surging forward, their *anxiety* spilling through the rest.

Aryl went to rise to her feet, but Taisal captured her hand and leaned close. "Wait," she said in an urgent low voice. "The Sona Adept—the one the Vyna implanted in an unborn. Anaj di Kathel. Does she have memories of this Cloisters?"

Aryl threw a desperate look at those around them, most shouting at the top of their lungs. "I should do something—"

"Let them howl. It's one thing to accept travel through the M'hir—quite another to accept it as part of us. Calmer heads will prevail soon. Tell me about Anaj."

"She remembers her life. Why?"

"Because this," Taisal laid her hand on the floor, "is more than a home for Adepts and the aged, more than a place to store records. A Cloisters is what makes a Clan, Daughter. Remember Cetto's proposal, that we trade Yena's to the Tikitik for safe passage? It would have ended us."

"Because without a Cloisters, Adepts could no longer dream." Which might, Aryl thought grimly, be for the best.

"Dreams only let us share knowledge between ourselves and with those gone before us. Dreaming together—" Aryl might have imagined her hesitation; Taisal must have decided secrecy no longer mattered between them, "—can produce new approaches to a problem."

"Like exiling us."

A sharp look. It wasn't denial. "Dreams aren't essential. This is." Again the hand on the floor, now a caress. "Cloisters are part of what binds us together and shapes the world itself."

Aryl was used to the Human bending her perceptions of reality. Her mother? "What binds us is inside us," she objected forcefully. If it was somehow the Cloisters, Yao and the babies wouldn't be alone, would they?

"Yes. But the strength of that binding within a Clan lies in the Cloisters." Taisal tapped the hilt of the long-knife at her side. "And it can be undone."

"I don't understand." She was afraid she did.

Sian had stayed silent, though Aryl knew the Adept listened. Now he crouched beside them, careless of his robe. "We're healers of mind as well as body, but there's nothing we can do for Om'ray of great Power who lose the inner battle. Such can't be left a risk to the rest, but to toss them into the Lay is not enough. Their minds would drag others with them. The device your mother means lets us cut that mind free of the world first." He turned to her mother. "Taisal, even if Sona's Maker is still usable, we don't know if it can be set to sever only connections through this M'hir. We could risk losing ourselves."

"Maker." The word dropped so casually from Sian's lips chilled Aryl's blood. " 'Maker' is Tikitik," she said numbly. "They use it for everything that matters to them. Their ancestors. The moons. Holes in the ground."

The looks on their faces, the *astonishment* leaked through their shields was almost funny. Almost.

"They do?" Taisal asked. "What do Tikitik know of Makers?"

Anaj, from another time, hadn't reacted to the Tikitik's use of the word; today's Adepts were shocked. More knowledge, Aryl thought bitterly, lost to the past. Thought Traveler had been right. They existed within too few years, within too little space.

Om'ray were trapped in themselves.

"It's time I told you about Tikitna," she said.

I can almost see it . . . an *inner* caress as tangible as any touch *. . . how your skin would glow if the Makers were out.*

Aryl flinched.

What did I say? What's wrong?

Nothing. She eased her hip on the bench. *The sun will be what's out and soon, Enris. Get some sleep.* Not to mention they weren't alone. Every bench held an Om'ray, most strangers. The new Adepts had proved useful at last. They'd known how to dim the lights in the areas used for sleeping.

Makers.

No chance of sleep with that word in her head. She'd told the others about Tikitna, including the Makers' Touch and her promise. Amna and Rayna had the Tikitik for neighbors; their Speakers had grown quiet as she *shared*, too quiet. They'd gestured approval when she finished. Approval, but beneath, in every mind, shivered the same *apprehension*.

How would the Tikitik react to the new Sona? How would the Oud?

The Adepts, no surprise, dismissed the Strangers and the destruction of their camps as irrelevant.

They were wrong, but Aryl didn't waste her time trying to convince them, not when she couldn't offer more. Where was Marcus? He'd promised to contact her. Did he find promises impossible to keep as well?

Was he . . . ?

She struggled to quiet her thoughts, to keep her mind as still as her body; Enris, at least, should rest. Husni had imposed this effort on them all. Being eldest, other than Anaj, she'd even quelled the Adepts. Hadn't hurt that

she'd brought their fretful, overtired children into the
Council Chamber to make that announcement.

Aryl smiled to herself.

I felt that.

Sleep.

Makers. The Tikitik. Whatever their connection to
Om'ray, Aryl knew Thought Traveler would come. It
would demand to know the worth of her promise. She
couldn't force the others to leave. She didn't know what
she could say.

You'll think of something.

Stop prying.

I didn't have to. He might have been pressed, warm
and comforting, along her back, instead of lying on the
floor. Enris was, unfortunately, too big for a bench. *You
need to relax. What should we name Sweetpie?*

Of all the odd . . . *You know perfectly well the Cloisters will give her a name when she's added to the records.*
Seru had insisted Juo and Lymin should introduce their
babies to Sona's later today. It would ease tension for
them all.

Her Chosen was amused. And more awake than ever.
*You? Follow tradition? Sweetpie deserves more than the
next name on a list.*

He tried to distract her. Aryl stroked the gentle swell
at her waist and let him. *How else would you name a
child?*

Hesitation and a certain *shyness.*

She grew intrigued; not such a casual topic after all.
You've a name in mind?

We could call her Ridersel.

A Tuana name. His mother's. *Ridersel di Sarc.* Aryl
mouthed the words to herself. *If you like. It's better than
Sweetpie.*

Aryl! Feigned outrage. His *joy* ran through her
bones.

She smiled and thought of a deep, lingering kiss.
Sleep.

After that?

Her hair slipped over her bare arm. Aryl brought a fistful of the soft stuff against her cheek. *With that.*

The sun rose over Amna, spilled its light across the world, and nothing else, Aryl thought, was certain today.

"You tell the children there's no breakfast! Haxel has to listen!"

All right. Maybe one thing. She shook her head at her indignant cousin. "Seru. We can't risk going to the mounds for supplies before the scouts report back. You know that."

"Then they can bring something back."

Enris, walking beside them, chuckled. "I'd help."

He'd come to tell her Haxel and her scouts were preparing to leave for Sona. Aryl had excused herself from the Adepts—already up and deep in discussion. Last 'night, Enris had *shared* what little they knew about the Strangers' troubles with the First Scout. According to him, she'd taken the news very calmly.

That couldn't be good, Aryl fussed to herself. She had to talk to Haxel first.

As for food? If Haxel expected trouble, her scouts wouldn't carry packs, empty or otherwise. "Being hungry won't hurt them. Or you," to her Chosen.

"It will hurt Naryn and Anaj," Seru declared, green eyes flashing. "They're weaker than the rest."

"I don't need—" *We'll be fine, child—*

Once assured Naryn's pregnancy was "normal," Seru had put herself firmly in charge. Now she was unmoved by either the former's sharp temper or the Old Adept's superior tone. "I'll say what you need and what's fine around here."

Aryl hid a smile. How her cousin could think of Anaj as an unborn she couldn't begin to guess. For her part, she was constantly tempted to look for the Old Adept, so *real* and strong was her *inner* presence. She imagined her standing straight, the only sign of age the wrinkles playing around keen eyes and firm lips. With hair confined by metal links.

Even Naryn, who'd shed Oran's filthy robe for a mismatch of clothing from several different Om'ray, appeared cowed by Seru's determined responsibility. "We slept," she offered.

You call that sleeping?!

"I'll mention the food," Aryl said hastily.

Gesturing gratitude, Seru smiled. Before she turned back, she reminded them. "Don't forget the naming ceremony. At firstnight. Cetto's agreed to speak for the new ones. Don't be late." As if nothing could matter more.

Life as it should be, Aryl thought, warmed by gratitude of her own. That's what Om'ray like Husni and Seru gave the rest. "We'll be there," she promised.

Ridersel, Enris sent privately.

I'll let you tell her, she replied, amused when his *smug* faded to mock *dismay.*

They reached the section of pale yellow corridor marked by dusty footprints. Ahead, the tall arched windows to either side of the metal doors were obscured. They didn't bother cleaning them. Fresh dust arrived with every breeze, spattered into sticky rounds when a stronger wind carried droplets from the waterfall beyond the grove. Only the frames on the walls looked as bright as they had in Yena, with their inexplicable arrangements of rectangles and disks. A puzzle for another day, Aryl told herself firmly.

Haxel leaned against one of the doors, arms folded. Syb, Veca, Gijs, and Yuhas, along with four of the Tuana runners, stood nearby. Only Sona. All were armed as if going after stitlers, with extra longknives in their belts. All were waiting.

For her? Aryl slowed. "What's wrong?"

The First Scout rolled her head, leaning an ear against the door. "Listen."

Aryl walked forward, put her ear to the chill metal.

taptaptaptap . . . TAP . . . taptaptap

Marcus. It had to be. Eagerly Aryl grabbed for the door.

Haxel blocked her way. "It isn't your friend."

"How do you know?"

By way of answer, the other pulled her knife and rapped the hilt on the metal.

SMACK! All but Haxel jumped back as a huge dark form crashed against the nearest window and slid down out of sight. "It doesn't like that," she said calmly, replacing the knife in its sheath.

An Oud.

taptaptap . . . TAP . . . taptaptap

Knocking on their door, as it had on the Human's.

"It's a Visitation," Aryl heard herself say in a remarkably normal voice. "It wants to talk to me."

"Or wants a way in." Haxel scowled, the scar white on her cheek and jaw. "They tried it before."

"I'm sure." And she was.

But where was Marcus?

A lake stretched at her feet, not clear or dead, but a rich blue, with clusters of floating yellow-and-pink flowers, and flitters that snatched gleaming swimmers in their fingers. Water tumbled over rocks to rejoin the great river. Something sang from the grasses nearby. Children tried to find it, laughing, splashing. The sound would stop when they came close, to start again at a short distance; willing to play, if not be caught.

Reflections, where the water grew still. The soaring white petals of the Cloisters, the dark, red-streaked stone of the cliff behind it, nekis and vines and shrubs adding their softness between. The sky itself, the glow of the setting sun.

Everywhere, Om'ray. Leaning on the platform wall

*to admire the view, conversing in quiet voices or none at
all, hurrying or taking their time along the stone roadway
that followed the lake's far edge and led to the villages
beyond. Peace. Prosperity. Happiness.*

Long ago and gone.

Aryl pulled free of Anaj's memories to see her Sona.

The lake was an expanse of small pebbles, here and
there drifted in dust, streaked by late-day shadow. The
roadway was cracked and heaved. Nekis grew, stunted
and alone. The Cloisters squatted in the dirt.

And Om'ray huddled in fear.

What went wrong? The Old Adept asked, drawn by
her thoughts, sharing what she saw. *What did we do?*

We changed, Aryl told her.

The Oud, as she expected, had humped itself away
from the opening door. Syb had slipped through first,
Yena-fashion, but their care wasn't necessary. It had
moved off the platform completely, to wait below.

Be wary near the Oud. She'd felt Enris remind the
others, warn them back. He, of course, stayed with her.
They were one, always.

No vehicle this time. The Oud Speaker had surged up
through the ground, leaving an open wound coated with
whirr/clicks. Urgency or carelessness? Neither boded
well.

Aryl walked down the ramp to meet it. The instant
her feet touched the dirt, it reared to speak. "Why Sona
less!? Where is!? WHERE IS!? Why? Where? Why?"

The empty village. So it did watch them, somehow.
Stupid creature. The other truenight, they'd gathered to
give their names to Sona and remember Tuana's dead.
It hadn't been upset then—or had it tried to find her, to
express that opinion? She thought it approved of their
'porting. "We're here," she assured it, puzzled. "In the
Cloisters."

"NONONO!" It swayed from the top, side to side.
"LESSLESSLESS! Where? Why?"

"Here. Inside," Aryl insisted. "There's nothing to worry about. Sona—"

"Aryl!" Haxel jumped down from the platform wall to land bent-knee beside her. "We've company," as she straightened, pointing toward the cliff. The Oud reacted by dropping to the ground. It ran backward a short distance on its little legs before it stopped.

Aryl looked up. From this distance, the shapes clinging to the massive rock face behind the Cloisters appeared small and insignificant. Fronds, opening to the sunlight. Wastryls, waiting for heat. As if they'd waited to be noticed, they began to fall toward them.

Enris gave a grim laugh. "Getting crowded, isn't it?"

Esans. They circled overhead, descending slowly, growing larger. She counted five . . . more. They carried baskets, not that she'd thought they'd come alone.

One let out its shuddering scream, answered by another. *Steady!* she sent quickly to the others, driving her own fear down until she felt only calm certainty. The confrontation would be now, before they'd been able to return everyone to their Clan. There was no choice.

"They've come to talk to me," she told Haxel, who gave her a stare of disbelief.

Not to drop more rock hunters? Enris asked. *I'd like to be sure about that, since we're standing out in the open.*

No.

Not that they were in any sense safe.

Some of the esans tried to land in the surrounding nekis grove, but the too-slender branches and stalks cracked under their weight. They rose again, screaming, to join their more experienced fellows who hovered above the dirt to let their passengers climb out. Aryl and Enris shielded their eyes against the dust generated by the huge paired wings. Haxel squinted, as if determined to

see all she could. The Oud Speaker scurried back and
forth, back and forth, kicking up its own cloud, half sinking into the ground.

Clean clothes and a drink of water. Time. That above
all she needed and couldn't have. Aryl spat to clear her
mouth and waited.

The esans lifted away and headed back to the cliff.
Thought Travelers appeared out of the settling dust,
their blue-black skins losing color with each step until
they stood before her like clouds themselves.

Silence, except for the rapid clatter of the Oud's limbs,
the slither of stones across its body and cloak. The thing
appeared frantic.

Sona's neighbor.

Useless creature, Aryl thought in disgust. "Stop that!"
she told it, to no effect.

A rock thudded off its back. The Oud slid to a stop
and reared, facing the wrong way. After an instant's hesitation, it bounced in place, flesh shaking, limbs loose and
clicking together, each bounce turning it slightly. Until it
faced her. "WHATDOWHATDOWHATDO?"

Aryl glanced at Enris, who gave a charming shrug
and dusted his hands.

One Thought Traveler pranced ahead of the rest.
She didn't have to guess which one that would be. Their
"friend." "What do you believe has happened here,
Speaker?" To the Oud, not to her.

The Oud stilled. "Sona less." Almost sullen.

"Is that so?" Two of the Tikitik's eye cones swiveled to regard Aryl, the others remain fixed on the Oud
Speaker. "Apart-from-All. Humor me. Have those with
you step on the ground."

Come, Aryl sent to the Sona waiting on the platform.
They climbed down the ramp, Yena as reluctant as the
Tuana.

"More!" the Oud exclaimed joyfully, then slumped.
"Less than. Where rest? Balance!!! WHERE REST!??"

The other Thought Travelers stirred uneasily at this, fingers flexing, eyes turning.

We could bring out the rest of Sona, Enris suggested. *Make the right number.*

We don't know it would be. And she wouldn't risk more Om'ray on ground Oud could churn to liquid—or within reach of the too-fast Tikitik and their predatory mounts.

" 'Where are the rest?' " Thought Traveler repeated. "How can you not know? You are the ones who demand Balance, who insist on it, who trammel all those in your way to achieve your version of it." Its head bobbed sharply up and down. "Count for yourself, fool!"

"Count one. Count one. MeMeMe. Sona Less."

"Idiot." With no other warning, the Tikitik lunged at the Oud, knife out. Aryl stepped in its way, hands up. "No!"

ARYL!

The Tikitik stopped in its tracks and stared down at her. "It's insane," it argued in a reasonable tone. "Once I kill it, they'll send a new one to talk to us. That's what Oud do."

"No more," the Oud protested weakly. "One." It folded its speaking limbs and waited.

Waited, Aryl realized with cold settling around her heart, for them to understand. For her to hear what it said, not guess at meaning. "It's not counting Om'ray." Her voice came out too high and she lowered it. "It's counting Oud. Something's happened to them."

An image of twisted machines and scorched buildings slipped into her mind. *The Strangers.*

Why would they harm Oud?

Do we know they wouldn't? Enris replied, letting her feel his *dread.*

The Thought Travelers hissed to one another. One went to the hole in the ground through which the Oud had arrived and squatted. It picked up whirr/clicks, discarding some. Those it kept, it brought to its mouth protuberances, patting the body and wiggling legs thoroughly before dropping it. Why, she couldn't guess. Enris had told them the rock hunters were a young form of Oud. Were the whirr/clicks another stage or just biters with a taste for Oud?

After the fourth, it stopped and stood. "The Oud is accurate," it announced. "Sona's colony has been decimated. This is the only Minded left."

Sensing her confusion, Enris supplied another image: a naked Oud, upside down and oblivious, using its limbs to polish the rock ceiling of a tunnel. *Not all think.*

How many could? If most "Minded" were dead, did this make Sona Tikitik again?

Following her negotiation with them, the Oud lived at the head of the valley, under the Stranger camp. Marcus' camp. It was steps away, behind the grove. She threw a despairing glance. The illusion still disguised the opening. What was behind it now?

Marcus?

I'll go. He'd followed her thought.

No, Enris. She held herself in place with an effort that tore at her heart. *I need you. Here.*

"Then we are finished." Thought Traveler beckoned. Before any Om'ray could move, the nearest of its companions had swarmed over the Oud, blades flashing.

The Oud Speaker died without sound. It sank down, its soft body spreading wide beneath its cloak. Green stained the hem.

"No!" Aryl drew her knife, heard the others do the same. Would they be next?

"Minded cannot make sense alone," Thought Traveler stated in its infuriatingly superior voice. "And we have little time. The world is broken, Apart-from-All. It will not recover from the foolishness of Om'ray."

Never appear weak or ignorant. Aryl stiffened. "I don't know what you mean."

"You can believe we know." It bent to the Oud corpse,

ripped the Speaker's Pendant from its torn cloak, and held the dripping object fastidiously away between clawtips. Without waiting for her answer, it flipped the pendant into the hole.

Every Tikitik turned its head to follow that motion.

"We, too, have a unique sense," Thought Traveler continued. "The Makers' Gift, if you like. It resides here." Straining its neck upward until she could see the pale underside of its head, the Tikitik pressed its thumb deep into the soft tissue between its jaws.

A vulnerable spot.

It returned to its normal posture. "The Gift *sings* of healthy rastis, draws us home through darkness or heavy rain. The pendants, Om'ray tokens ... all such were made from a substance that also catches our attention. We have but to *listen*. I assure you, we *hear* the pendants of Rayna, Amna, and Yena inside your Cloisters, where there should be none. If you open its doors, would I find the many missing from other Clans, where there should be Sona's few?"

The pendants betrayed them to the Tikitik. The Cloisters hid them.

Caught in the possibilities, Aryl hesitated too long.

"I would, I see."

"We'll send them back—" If they'll go, she added to herself.

"To their Clans?" It stepped closer. "They cannot go home. They've been changed forever, little Speaker, and only belong here. Did you not realize this?"

It couldn't know about their new connections through the M'hir. But it was right, she realized, feeling her blood turn to ice. Those who'd come to Sona, who knew how to move through the M'hir, were no longer the same as the rest of their kind.

She wasn't.

Closer still, with menace, forcing her back. "They cannot leave. And the moment your Om'ray set foot on the ground, the Oud beneath—busy as we speak, producing

new Mindeds to make their decisions—will know how
many now live in Sona. More than should. They'll want to
keep you, prattle about 'Oud, best is,' and to do that—"
it moved again; she retreated, stumbled in loose dirt,
waved Enris back, caught herself, "—to do that, they'll
go to their lists and they will reshape as much of Cersi as
they deem necessary to redress the Tikitik for this *Gift*
of Om'ray. One Clan? Two? Three? Tikitik factions will
be split, some favored, others not. Our Balance will be
changed."

Thought Traveler stopped. So did she, near enough to
smell its musty breath, to see its body soften and bend
as if too weary to stand straight. "The moment they step
outside, Apart-from-All, your Om'ray destroy both our
peoples. And, though it matters not," a careless flick of
its fingers, "the Oud will not long survive on their own."

"We'll live inside the Cloisters," she promised desperately. "Only come out in the same numbers each time."

"Do you believe that's never been tried? Ask yourself,
Apart-from-All. Why did Sona's Adepts die outside?"

Its face approached, filled her sight. Eyes swiveled on
their cones to bore into hers. A whisper, so quiet she
doubted anyone else could hear: "Prepare, as we must,
for the doom of the world."

One heartbeat there, the next, gone. The esans, respond-
ing to no signal Aryl could see or hear, swooped down like
a storm to pick up their passengers. The Thought Travelers didn't look back, didn't speak again. They climbed into
their baskets and sent their mounts climbing.

Leaving only Om'ray.

They were looking at her, Aryl thought wildly, sick
inside. At her. Haxel and Galen sud Serona, the grizzled
runner from Tuana. Her Chosen. Naryn. Everyone. As if
somehow she could save them. As if she knew anything
at all to do.

"Marcus," she heard herself say. "We have to find
him."

Chapter 10

AVOIDING THE PATH, Haxel led them through the grove. If there was a trap, it would be along the wide, flat, easy route the Human had made. Aryl came next, Enris behind her. To one side, out of sight if not beyond their *inner sense,* Syb and Yuhas, followed by Galen. To the other, Veca, Suen d'sud Annk, and the Licor twins.

Naryn? She'd returned to the Cloisters, her thankless task to tell the others what had happened to the Oud. With Anaj's help, she hoped to find those among the new arrivals with more experience with the other races, who might have answers, a plan. Aryl wished them success; she didn't expect any.

Om'ray had never paid attention to the not-*real.*

Which would have been reasonable, she thought wryly, if the not-*real* had cooperated and not paid attention to them.

Her nerves settled as they moved through the grove. A hunt. Finally something normal, something Yena. Where their skill mattered.

Even Enris moved quietly.

SnickCrack! A faint *apology.*

Quietly for a giant Tuana with big feet. Aryl almost smiled.

Where the grove thinned, Haxel stopped. She glowered at its unclimbable sticks as she waved Aryl to her
side. Their hands touched. *What do you think?*

Aryl pressed herself against the nearest stalk, sank
below Om'ray height, then eased around until she could
see between the young leaves.

The buildings were intact; the ground its familiar mo-
rass of mud and vehicle tracks. No burning. No destruction as at Site Two.

All wrong, she sent. The buildings stood white and
exposed, their illusions gone, doors open. A shirt, socks,
other belongings were strewn before the one Marcus
used as a home. The rest . . . Aryl eased back and touched
Haxel. *The storage buildings are empty.*

Before or after? Not waiting for an answer, Haxel
slipped to the others, brushed hands, gave her orders.
Syb, Yuhas, and Galen went one way, fading into the
grove; Veca, Suen, and the twins the other. They'd circle
wide. Haxel flickered in and out of sight, choosing her
own path.

What about us? Enris asked, crouching beside her.

Aryl stood and brushed at her no-longer-blue dress.
"We," she said calmly, "are here to visit our friend."

"You mean walk out there and be Haxel's bait."

She shrugged. "That, too."

Deliberately casual strides took them across the
opening to Marcus' door. Strides during which Aryl's
shoulders tensed and her eyes searched for the telltale
shine of a vidbot or other watchful machine. Shadows
shortened as the sun moved higher overhead. Her feet
sank in the loose dirt.

Once there, she paused beside the inviting doorway.
Lights were on inside. These weren't Om'ray, she reminded herself. Her other senses had to do. She listened,
not breathing.

Nothing.

Aryl danced in and to the side, crouching with her

knife ready. Enris burst through behind her, an intimidating bulk. But they were alone.

And everything was broken.

They moved through the mess. The mattresses, used or not, were torn apart, the beds ripped from their wall supports. Cupboards and crates were open or upended. Marcus' jars of dirt were smashed. Not a struggle. Something else. Aryl frowned. "If this was a hunt," she wondered aloud, "did they find what they were after?"

"Wasn't these." Enris pointed to the devices on the counter. All looked as if someone had taken a hammer to their faces—or used a body part suited to violence. There were Strangers, Aryl remembered, who could do such damage with a limb.

"Or they didn't want them used . . ." At the thought, Aryl pulled out the geoscanner and turned it on. Its glow was reassuring, though the red display wasn't. Oud below. But she knew that.

Not the "Minded." Not decision makers. Not yet, somehow.

They had time.

She thumbed on the device. "Two. Howard. Five."

Is that a good idea?

"He answers or he doesn't."

"How long do we wait?"

She propped the 'scanner on what had been a table. "As long as we can," she said quietly.

"Well, then." Enris used his arm to clear a section of counter, brushing debris to the floor. When he sat, it creaked under his weight but held. "We wait." He smiled with a cheer she didn't believe for an instant. His shields were at their tightest; without an effort, she could only sense their connection, nothing of how he felt.

"You don't think he's coming back."

"From beyond the world? Do you?"

Aryl found her own perch. *I must,* she admitted. Aloud, "Don't underestimate—"

Come. A summons.

"Galen's found something." Enris stood, his hand out to her. *Aryl.*

"I'm all right." She retrieved the 'scanner, her hand wanting to shake.

There'd been a *warning* with the sending. What Galen found hadn't been good.

Aryl . . .

"Let's go."

"Oud?"

The middle building had been stripped clean, leaving only overturned tables. The far building was empty, too, but not for the same reason.

Aryl stood with the rest outside the open door. To enter meant stepping in the churned green mud that had replaced the floor.

Haxel knelt, brought a fingertip of it to her nose. "Oud," she confirmed after a sniff, wiping her finger on her leggings as she stood. "Last 'night."

"They collect their dead," Galen told them, his gruff voice low as if afraid of being overheard. No need to point to the wide hole gaping in the center. "We've never seen where they take them. Somewhere deep."

"Why would they be here at all?" Aryl asked. The wide door could accommodate an Oud, but Marcus had never let the creatures inside. Too many breakables, he'd said. "Why were they killed?"

"The artifacts."

She looked at Enris.

"That's what this is all about," he said, gaining confidence with every word. "Marcus told us he'd left his people here, to secure the artifacts. The Oud must have understood that much. Maybe they tried to protect them."

As one, they all stared at the hole. The deep, black hole.

"The Strangers could be down there?" Haxel asked tensely.

Aryl understood. The hole was as appealing as the waters of the Lay. All the Yena looked uncomfortable.

"It'll lead to a normal tunnel." Josel didn't appear to notice the dreadful ooze underfoot as she walked to the opening. "I'll go."

Syb stared at her. "In there?"

"I'll come with you."

Enris? *No,* Aryl protested.

YES! His friends might be alive. I owe him this. Someone waited their chance and I gave it to them when I asked Marcus to turn off his machines. The *fury* turned gentle. "Wait here. Tunnels aren't for Yena—ask Yuhas."

"I'd go," that worthy protested.

Enris put his hand on Yuhas' shoulder. "Of course you would," he said, giving the other a gentle shake. "But Aryl needs you here."

Aryl ignored this last. "Not your fault. The trap was set first. It had to be," she insisted when he looked doubtful. "Marcus told us there'd be extra protection soon. Whoever this was must have planned to ambush him as he left with the artifacts, before that protection was ready." Vulnerable prey, out of its normal place, alone. "When a better chance presented itself, they sprang the trap early, that's all." She might not understand trading and the value of things; this, she did.

"What are these Strangers?" Suen was appalled. "They kill each other. They kill Oud. Why do you want to help them?"

"Because we hope they can help us," Haxel said grimly.

Because they were friends . . . Aryl kept the words to herself.

In too short a time, the Tuana were ready. Aryl stood where she could watch. Galen went first, eldest and most experienced—and toughest, in Haxel's estimation. Instead of trying to climb, he simply sat on the side of the hole and let himself slip down with the crumbling mud. She *reached* through the M'hir. Galen had the Power to answer. *As I thought. There's a proper tunnel in sight and a nice easy-to-follow mess where they've dragged the bodies. And there's some good wood down here.*

Enris' uncle. She shouldn't be surprised, Aryl told herself, that her Chosen's family was every bit as blithely cheerful going into danger as he was.

As if he'd heard her thought, Enris laid his palm against her cheek. *Back soon.* Then, with a ridiculous "Whoop!," he jumped and slid into the darkness.

The twins went together, holding hands. Suen last.

Don't make me come down there to save you, Aryl sent.

We'll 'port from the merest sniff of trouble, I promise. Despite his light tone, she knew better. Enris wouldn't leave Marcus or anyone else with the Oud. And he believed in the Strangers' superior technology.

"And now we wait," Haxel said grimly.

"We wait," Aryl agreed.

She went to the open door and leaned her back against the frame, taking deep breaths of air free of the stench of dead Oud. The others gave her space.

Because, she thought wearily, they believed. They believed she'd calm the Tikitik, return Om'ray where they belonged, and prevent the Oud from reshaping the world.

What she'd give to throw one of Ziba's tantrums, to scream at her elders and demand they find their own solutions. To be . . .

To be young again and home.

Self-pity. And she called herself Yena? A Sarc? Would she rather be ignorant and powerless?

Aryl's lips twisted.

She'd fall first.

Waiting was pointless. She dove into the M'hir, and *reached.*

Naryn.

Aryl. Their connection locked at the instant of recognition. The Tuana appeared like lightning, an eye-burning brilliance within the storm. Not peaceful, in any sense. Naryn never would be.

It didn't help that she was furious. *Good thing you left. Rayna and Amna are arguing about the seniority of their Speakers, as if any of them could do better.*

She'd love to hand the job to either, Aryl thought. She couldn't. *Listen, Naryn. My mother talked of a device in the Cloisters, called a Maker.*

Yes. Anaj's been discussing it with the Adepts. A fleeting *wonder*, supplanted by *dread*. *To cut an Om'ray's binding to the rest? If it weren't for Yao and the babies, I wouldn't believe it possible.*

Can the Maker do anything else?

That isn't enough? She could almost see Naryn's eyebrow lifting.

Can it remove a memory? An idea she hadn't shared, not even with Enris. Wrong, desperate, doubtless Forbidden.

A chance.

Their connection thinned as Naryn fell silent; Aryl poured Power into it to keep their minds together. *Can anything?* she insisted.

Faint. Troubled. *You want the others to forget the M'hir.*

Yes. Then we send them home to their Clans. They'll have questions, but no way to learn the truth.

This isn't what you wanted for us. For all of us.

She'd wanted too much, too soon. Now, Aryl thought bitterly, she'd settle for survival. *The Oud and Tikitik will be at peace. Sona will keep apart from the rest. Safe.*

Like Vyna. A lash of *scorn*. *That's good enough for your daughter?*

She flinched. The grove in front of her, across the clearing, was stunted and unhealthy. Vyna was a worse blight on the world. *Then what?* Aryl demanded angrily. *What would you have me do, Naryn? Give up, like the Tikitik?*

Use the strength around us. For us.

What do you mean?

You saw what the Strangers did to each other. They could easily destroy Tikitna. They may have killed Oud already. As Aryl hesitated, stunned, Naryn went on. Her Power reinforced their link now. *Do you want to live in fear? Enris was right and I hadn't seen it. These would be formidable partners. Last truenight, I learned the Strangers' language.* An image formed of a device Aryl had seen before: the machine Marcus had claimed taught him Om'ray words as he slept.

We learned, a caustic mindvoice intruded. Anaj had attached herself to their thread. *Not that I had a choice, you understand.*

Naryn pushed her aside. *I can talk to them now. Any of them. Ask for their help.*

Though the other couldn't see it, Aryl shook her head violently; her hair lashed her shoulders. *It won't work.* Marcus had told her the Trade Pact wouldn't let the Triads interfere; he wore his costume and pretended to be Om'ray, rather than draw attention. As for those who'd attacked the Triad sites? *The Strangers won't help us.*

They would for the ability to travel through the M'hir.

Tuana were traders.

She hadn't realized, until now, that they could make anything a commodity.

No, Naryn.

Spread their problems across countless worlds and races. What had Marcus called it?

War.

Aryl...

NO! Don't mention this to anyone again. Either of you.

Aryl severed their connection so violently, the M'hir slapped back at her as if she'd tossed a mountain into the ocean. Stung, she fought to *see* reality, to hold her sense of self. Finally, the waves ended and released her. She hoped Naryn and Anaj hadn't felt that. Not all of it.

Enough, Aryl thought grimly, to help them understand.

The Oud, wanting her help against the Tikitik. The Tikitik, against the Oud. Now Naryn, proposing Om'ray and the Strangers against both.

Never, Aryl vowed, while she lived.

"Anything I should know?" Haxel asked in a quiet voice.

Checking her shields, Aryl made herself relax as she turned. "We're in trouble, and the Adepts argue about my age."

The First Scout chuckled. "They don't know you." Her smile faded. "What does that mean?" She pointed at Aryl's hand.

Which still held the geoscanner. Startled, Aryl raised the device. A blue light pulsed beneath its clear dome. "Something new," she admitted.

Haxel stiffened. "Dangerous?"

The blue pulse flickered faster and faster.

"Not the Oud." She could think of only one thing to try. Aryl lifted the device near her mouth. "Marcus? Are you there?"

A loud burst of jumbled sounds answered, none understandable. The voice—was it a voice?—was shrill, higher than any she'd heard. Shrill and threatening.

Aryl turned off the 'scanner, shoved it in its pocket, and met Haxel's pale eyes. "Not a friend," the First Scout decided. "Inside."

The hole was, if anything, darker and scarier than ever. Aryl avoided looking at it as Haxel began to speak. "Syb, you and—" The rest was drowned out by a deep rumble, rushing toward them.

Closer . . . closer. On them!

The building shook.

Mud loosened around the hole, sliding down but not filling it.

Enris!!!

We're all right. Are you?

Last time it had been Naryn, digging out the riverbed.

This? Was the mountain shaking? Should they 'port to safety? Before she could do more than consider it, the sound and vibration passed overhead and diminished.

It's leaving, she sent, astonished.

"Find it!" Haxel ordered. "Stay out of sight!"

Be careful! This from her Chosen, with a certain *irony*.

The rumble went behind the buildings, to where the Oud toiled to disturb what some Tikitik called the "Makers' Rest." Om'ray didn't go there, not anymore. Aryl followed the sound, running close to one wall. She stopped before breaking into the open, paused to *sense* Haxel and the rest nearby in the grove.

They would let her take the lead; she was their Speaker, and there were no other Om'ray here. What might be here, Aryl thought with an odd catch in her breath, none of them could guess.

The Oud had been busy since she'd last been here. The landscape was torn open—not torn, she realized with amazement. They'd stripped away what had lain on top to uncover roadways and stone stairs. A set lay before her, winding and worn, and of no use to Oud, which likely explained why they'd continued to dig deeper to either side. Aryl could imagine Marcus being grateful to have something easier for his feet.

Easier and better cover. She took the stairs, careful to keep to shadows. The rumble was coming back toward her.

Aryl showed her teeth. Good. Now to see. She eased around an exposed rock wall.

Busy indeed. A structure had been partially freed from the cliff face, curved and elaborate, as flawless as those she'd seen beneath the Lake of Fire and uncovered by the Strangers at Site Two. Hoveny ruins.

Things left by the long-dead didn't concern her.

What came toward her, its low rumble vibrating through the soles of her feet, did.

She'd made fiches the size of her hand glide through the air, of dresel wing, thread, and sticks. She knew the amazing aircars of the Strangers, the noisy winged fly-ers of the Oud, had been carried by an esan's doubled wings.

How could anything like this fly?

Aryl clutched her pendant, almost deafened. The machine descending before the cliff was larger than the buildings behind her. Twenty—more—aircars could have fit inside it. Like the Oud flying machines, fire came out of it. Like the Humans' aircar, there were no wings.

Her eyes narrowed. Scars marred its skin. There were objects fastened to it, or protruding from it. Along its underside, what must be feet. On its back? Those objects were sharp and aimed forward, like horns or knives. Best to assume they were as dangerous as they looked.

The fire ceased, as if turned off like a glow; with that, the rumble ended, but the machine wasn't silent. It whined as it came to rest, feet adjusting to the uneven ground with a series of metallic clangs. Suddenly, even the whine stopped.

Silence. Aryl's ears buzzed.

A ramp extended like a tongue to taste the dirt. Above it, a door opened into the belly of the machine.

And out they came . . .

Interlude

UNTIL THIS MOMENT, STANDING TOO CLOSE to the sky in Yena's canopy or on a mountain ridge—closely followed by dangling from the claws of an esask over a mountain ridge—had been the former Tuana's idea of situations to avoid repeating at all costs. Enris dropped his hand from the now-stable tunnel wall, tested his legs, and moved being underground when the ground itself shook to the top of his list.

Trust Aryl and the Yena to chase after the cause.

Be careful, he'd sent, as if she could. Or would.

"That was—unpleasant," he commented.

"That?" His uncle chuckled, not unkindly. "Always happens when Oud run their machines in nearby tunnels. Shakes up some dust, nothing worse. Josel?"

The hole had opened into a well-lit tunnel; a tunnel which promptly and unhelpfully branched in four directions, all strewn with Oud gore. Not for long, Enris noticed queasily. Normally skittish iglies clustered around the larger splots of green, paying no attention to Om'ray and their boots as they crowded to get at the stuff, shoving one another vigorously with their jointed legs. Those pushed out of place flashed alarm and complained with *wet-smacks* before jumping back in.

"Through here," the unChosen announced, pointing to one of the identical tunnels.

All Josel had done was quickly step inside each tunnel mouth and back again. Having been lost among the Oud once, Enris hesitated. "Why that one?"

Netta bumped him forward. The twins, also identical, were his height and strongly built, even for Tuana. "She knows."

"She does," Suen assured him. "Josel's Talent tells her where there's been movement lately—and how much. This was the busiest tunnel."

A useful Talent for a Runner, who would normally avoid any space in use by Oud. Enris gestured gratitude and was rewarded by a shy smile.

Galen waved Josel ahead; the rest of the Tuana followed. But Suen delayed a step to let Enris come beside him. "I want to thank you." He spoke quietly. A Runner habit, not to risk mindtouch near Oud.

"Thank me?"

"For what you did for Naryn."

Suen d'sud Annk was once S'udlaat. The family resemblance was there, in the fine lines of his face, the thick red-brown hair. The difference was in the openness of his face. Suen was not an Om'ray of secrets, though he had Power. And he was the closest family Naryn had left, cousin to her mother, heart-kin to her father's brother. The closest she'd ever had, Enris thought. Suen had not only sheltered Naryn when she'd fled the Adepts; every time she'd had run off in tears, furious or petulant or both, it had been to him.

Enris shrugged. "Glad I could help." However complicated the result.

A frankly doubtful look. "She doesn't make friends."

A not-question, like the Tikitik. "Not easily," Enris agreed, but something made him add, "She's found one in Aryl. You know that."

The *feel* of Suen grew warmer. "I know. But, no offense, they're two of a kind. It's having you take her side that's made the difference. Naryn's life in Sona will be better for it."

Not pleasant, hearing his dislike might have influenced the rest. Not that he need accept all the blame, Enris told himself more cheerfully. At her friendliest, Naryn was as safe to approach as a starving esask.

They walked on a rough floor, their way lit by glow-strips hanging from temporary supports. How new was this tunnel? Enris wondered suddenly. That the Oud might have dug it to reach the artifacts quickly was not reassuring. Not reassuring at all.

Neither, he thought, was that *smell*, and wished the iglies could slurp faster.

Iglies.

But no Oud. Rock or adult.

"Where are they?" he whispered. Voices echoed here, found their way back from unexpected directions.

"Where they need to be," Netta said. "I've watched—" her wary look at Galen's back suggesting a lack of Chosen permission for this activity "—Digger Oud. Only one starts a tunnel, but it doesn't take long before there's a crowd of them, pushing and shoving to get at the work. They don't notice us at all."

"Until the Minded one showed up." Her twin.

"There's no need to—" Netta closed her mouth quickly as Galen glanced over his shoulder. Her lips were as dappled as her skin. An Amna trait, making it easy to pick out those newcomers from that Clan, if not foolproof. Some were so thoroughly speckled their skin looked dark.

Aryl liked the effect. She'd told him it made her think of sunlight filtered through leaves.

Aryl. The tingle along his nerves wasn't fear of this place, though he could, Enris grimaced, do without dead Oud goo on his boots or the squirt of it when he couldn't help stomping an iglie. The tingle came from Aryl's state of mind. It affected his; she couldn't help it. *Hunter*. Her outer senses were incredibly alert; her thoughts, if he let himself *reach* too deep—as had happened once or twice—an emotionless sequence of decisions, rapid and sure. This far. Step there. Ignore these. Danger!

While such focus revealed much about a Yena's ability to survive, he preferred not to share it. Probably, Enris reminded himself with a rueful inner grin, Aryl preferred that too.

He himself was more distractible. He liked to think as he walked. Not that he had anything in mind at the moment, but it had been his habit to wander through the fields at home, ponder designs, look to the world for ideas.

They passed an opening; Josel didn't turn aside but Galen stopped. "Wait."

Josel looked a question at the older Runner, who pointed to the floor. Enris felt a sudden chill.

A small puddle, without iglies. A puddle of dark red, thickened but still reflecting light.

Suen squatted for a closer look. "Om'ray," he said grimly.

Enris shook his head. "Human."

A different kind of day, sitting in the sun by the waterfall, a too-curious finger on Aryl's longknife, a moment of shared wonder at a drop of innocent red.

Nothing innocent about this puddle on the floor of an Oud tunnel.

Without waiting for the rest, Enris walked through the opening beside the blood into what he found wasn't a tunnel, but a circular room. The ceiling was twice as high and more openings pierced the walls above, a reminder that Oud had no trouble running underneath a ceiling or down a wall.

The floor of this—was it a room, or another kind of tunnel?—was what mattered.

The floor, and what the Oud had dumped on it.

There was no other word for the shambles. Crates of the Strangers' white material formed a jumbled pile higher than his head; its base almost filled the room. Some had toppled and rolled to lie with what weren't crates, but fragments of bodies.

Not Marcus. Not Marcus. Enris said it to himself over and over as he searched, his shields as tight as he could make them to protect Aryl, hand over his nose against the reek. Strangers. Of varied shapes and sizes. Cut into bits.

Once sure, he relaxed. Strangers, yes. Two . . . he spotted another piece of head . . . three. But none dressed as if pretending to be Om'ray.

"This one's different." Galen rolled a limp torso over with his boot. "Look at the clothing."

The torso had its head. It was Om'ray-like—or Human—save for short yellow bristles where ears belonged. What remained of the body wore a one-piece blue garment with no fastenings or seams. A nearby leg bore the same fabric.

The other two wore Triad work clothes, complete with a line of symbols on their shirts. Names, Enris thought, and used his knife to cut the scraps free. He tucked them deep in a pocket. Marcus would want names.

There was nothing to identify the bristle-eared Stranger. Enris stared at its face, hoping the memory would be enough.

The twins hovered nearby, not overly concerned by the mess, but curious. Suen, meanwhile, followed him patiently from body part to body part. He was quiet, but there was a growing *unease* coming through his shields, so when Enris finished, he looked curiously at the former Runner. "What do you see I don't?"

"There's a story here. Galen? What do you think?" Suen pointed to an arm coated with green, then at a hunk of what was more meat than—than whatever it had been alive, Enris decided.

After his own examination, Galen went to the crates. He moved a couple of smaller ones aside, studied others with care. When he turned to face them again, his craggy features were set and hard. "I agree. These Strangers killed the Oud."

"You can't know that," Enris protested. There wasn't a Talent to show past events, was there? His uncle, formidable in his own way, was no Adept.

"I can. Only Oud juice on the crates means they died carrying them, or were nearest to them." Galen indicated the arm. "Being dragged spread more of their goo around, but see this? The only splashes are high on the Strangers' bodies. They were standing when the Oud died, close enough to be the cause." He pointed to the meaty piece. "And that's what a Digger can do. I don't know," flat-voiced, "the why of any of this. But Diggers rush to protect their Minded, like stingers boiling out of their nest. I'd say they did this time, but were too late."

What had Marcus said? That it took two to turn off the defenses. Things began to make a terrible sense. "That's why the Human's camp was left intact," Enris said numbly, remembering the smoke rising from the platform on the lake, the destruction on the mountainside, Marcus' grief and worry. "The thieves knew what they wanted would be here. The two working with the artifacts were part of it." Marcus had trusted those he'd left. They'd betrayed him.

For what lay inside these crates.

"I don't understand. Why would they kill Oud?" Netta was pale. "Didn't the Oud invite the Strangers here? Didn't they work together?"

"The Oud worked with Marcus. They knew the artifacts were important to him; that he wanted them kept safe. And what does 'safe' mean to Oud?" Enris gestured to the pile. "Underground. My guess is the Oud decided to take all this into their tunnels and the thieves had to stop them. Try to stop them."

Silence, inside and out, as the others absorbed this. He understood. This wasn't good, on any level.

Josel spoke first, radiating *worry*. "The dead Strangers

look like Om'ray. What if the new Mindeds think we did this?"

Her twin answered, her eyes widening. "They'll attack us, like Tuana!"

Hush! Galen projected *confidence.* "You forget. Aryl di Sarc is our Speaker. Leave the Oud to her."

More loaded on Aryl's small shoulders.

Enris would have winced if he hadn't agreed completely. "Let's get out of here, before we're the ones who confuse the Oud." Above ground, and with his Chosen.

"What about the artifacts?" Suen asked, eyes flashing. "If they're valuable, we should take them with us."

Galen frowned, but gestured agreement. "You're right."

Maybe to a Runner, used to grabbing whatever could be moved in hopes of future gain. Enris fought for patience. "Their value to the Strangers caused this problem. We can't risk bringing them to Sona."

"We could 'port them to a hiding place," Netta offered eagerly. Josel nodded, coming to stand beside her twin.

About to argue the goo-stained crates were well hidden right here, Enris felt a *stir.* Aryl. An alert, not quite a warning. "Something's happening above ground." Something *astounding.*

Aryl, he sent quickly. *We found the crates. And Marcus' people. Dead.*

How? The Oud?

Yes, but . . . There was no easy way to say it. *We think Marcus' people were part of it.* He shared the image of the bristle-eared Stranger. *This one was with them. They killed the Minded for trying to protect the artifacts. That aroused the Digger Oud. Marcus was betrayed by his own.*

She grew distant.

Aryl? Enris stared down the tunnel. *What is it?*

Marcus is here.

Chapter 11

THE PITTED SURFACE of the old wall was warm beneath Aryl's splayed fingers, returning the last of the sun's gift. The air itself was cooling rapidly; mountain spring, colder than any season in Yena. Her coat hung on its hook in Sona. As if cold or coat mattered.

The ramp from the machine to the ground was metal. It rang with their careless steps. The cliff echoed their voices. The four who glanced beyond their fellows from time to time carried thick black objects in their hands. She marked them as threat.

The remainder were not. Aryl counted five, then a final two came out of the shadowed top, each holding a tether to a platform that floated in midair.

No faces at this distance, but the figure who led the rest wore Om'ray clothing, but wasn't.

Marcus.

Was this rescue?

Something kept her close to stone, held her still, uncertain.

He'd gone to Site Three. Maybe that was a bigger place, with more resources. Maybe this was help coming.

Or it was something else. Her Chosen's sending burned through her mind, left a foul *taste*.

Aryl eased around for another quick glance.

On the dirt now. Walking as if they didn't know or need care what lay beneath. Coming this way.

To the buildings. Where the artifacts would have been waiting, except for the ever-unpredictable Oud.

They could know she was here. Marcus had had devices to sense the presence of others. But none looked her way. A pair continued to talk in their incomprehensible words to one another, their tones easy. Triumphant.

Enris. Haxel. Aryl sent the image of the Strangers, then of the buildings. Received instant *assent*, before all the Om'ray tightened their shields. They would be ready, out of sight.

She smoothed her rumpled, sorry dress and moved to where she could be seen.

Instant chaos. The four pushed the others aside, aimed what must be weapons at her. They were tall and thin, skin scaled like a Tikitik but with heavy fanged jaws that were likely their preferred armament in a fight. Crests rose over their heads and behind where ears might have been.

Aryl kept her hand from her longknife and waited.

A sharp command stopped their rush forward, lowered weapons, produced what sounded like a laugh. Naryn's new knowledge would have been useful, but not essential. This, Aryl understood perfectly.

Someone didn't think she was dangerous.

Fools came, she mused, in every shape.

Not in a hurry; not tarrying either. They reached the long shadow of the cliff and kept moving toward her. Toward the stairs, Aryl corrected to herself. Marcus was still in front. She couldn't explain to herself why she waited without a smile. Why she didn't call out a greeting or expect one.

Then Marcus stepped onto the first rise of stone and sunlight washed across his face.

Across bruises and blood.

Aryl whirled and ran, abandoning the stairs for the wall, dropping to the uneven ground to hit that in full stride. She ran for the grove, her heart hammering in her ears and shouts behind.

Marcus led the way because a terrible thread cut deep into the flesh of his neck, a thread held by the Stranger behind him. He led the way—Aryl dodged by instinct and a stone *burst* where she'd been, shards stinging her side—he led because a weapon pressed into his spine hard enough to bow his body.

He led—she was in the grove and threw herself forward as nekis *flamed* behind her— because there was nothing alive in his eyes.

Aryl drew her longknife, *knew* where she had to be …
… and was there.

The brush of fingertips. The shift of hand and blade. They moved no more than this. They had no need.

The Strangers had the technology to save themselves. There was no need to walk noisily into a trap even a stitler would have suspected. But that technology, Aryl judged coldly, was their weakness here. Having beaten their own kind, they felt themselves superior to the "vestigial populations" left on this world …

NOW.

… and they died for it.

Enris caught Marcus as he crumpled forward, Aryl's first cut having been through the thread that bound him.

Her second severed the head of the creature at the other end.

It was over, of course, in paired heartbeats. The Tuana held unused knives, giving the Yena startled looks. Being traders, Aryl thought curiously, had they planned to offer a warning?

You didn't warn what could kill you.

Haxel wiped her blade on the nearest husk. "Enris, take the Human to Oran." Declaring Marcus one of them without hesitation. "We'll deal with what's left in the air machine." She picked up one of the dropped weapons. Nothing happened when she pointed it. She gave it an irritated shake.

"Only wor—" They turned at the faint, pained rasp of a voice. Marcus didn't try to smile. Aryl doubted his mashed lips could have formed one. "Only—works—for owner," he managed.

The First Scout shrugged and dropped the weapon on that body. "Shame."

"Can—can't—"

"Hush," Enris said kindly. He cradled the Human in his arms with no obvious effort. "Haxel can manage."

"That's not what he means." Aryl stepped closer. "What is it, Marcus?"

A gleam in the open eye. Gratitude or tears? "Think five more—in ship. Seven, most. Can't let—any go," he struggled. A finger scratched at Enris' arm, lifted to point at the headless husk in its spreading orange-yellow pool. "Mind—mind—crawler—" He turned to press his face against Enris, his body convulsed in quiet sobs.

Pity later.

They scanned his memories, Aryl sent to the Om'ray staring at Marcus, her *rage* ice-cold beneath the calm. *They could know about us.*

Haxel's scar whitened. "We were going to kill them anyway. It's—" She broke off as Josel leaped from where she was standing and stared downward. "What is it?"

Footprints blurred. The dirt softened!

"The Oud!" Enris. "To the Cloisters. Now!" He and his living burden disappeared.

GO! Aryl sent. And watched the others vanish.

Windows broke the smooth side of the building, made an easy climb to its rounded top. A breeze slipped by her cheeks; she couldn't tell if it was chill or warm. Didn't care.

ARYL! Her Chosen was not happy. Not happy at all.

I know what I'm doing.

Safe or not, she couldn't leave.

Not without seeing for herself.

Not without being sure the rest died for what they'd done.

The bodies of the not-*real* went first. Aryl lay on her stomach to watch, ready to 'port if the building began to sink. But the Oud left it alone and churned only the ground between.

Quiet fell. Like the still of the canopy before the M'hir Wind, when the world took that final breath.

Aryl stood and walked to the end of the building, balanced on the top of its domed roof. She looked down at the air machine. Sun streaked its surface, shadowed the weapons on its humped back. The tip of the ramp remained exposed, a convenience for those expected back with what they valued.

She smiled.

The first sign of attack was a darkening in the dirt all around the air machine, a *stirring*.

The next?

As if a mouth opened in the world, the ground fell away beneath the machine. As it toppled and dropped, fire erupted with a roar from its end. If it was an effort to escape, all it accomplished was to obscure the hole with smoke and violent flashes of light. Aryl flinched, threw her arms over her face, began to concentrate . . .

kaBOOM!

. . . she was in the air, flying backward amid dirt and stone and scorching heat . . .

. . . then, she was on the floor of the Cloisters.

Flat on her back on the floor. Surrounded by legs.

Where, she thought giddily, was dignity when she needed it?

And why was everything spinning into darkness . . . ?

"Aryl. Beloved. Aryl?" A deep, gentle whisper in her ear. It tickled and her hair lifted to find the source. "Awake? It's about time." This not gentle at all. Aryl opened her eyes and blinked.

Still on her back.

Pushing off the blanket, she sat up, ignoring the complaints of various abused body parts, and swung her legs off the platform. Enris stood nearby and watched, arms folded, shields tight.

Not tight enough. Waves of *anxiety, dread,* and a not -insignificant *OUTRAGE* beat at her. "Stop that," she grumbled, rubbing her forehead. "I'm fine."

The waves eased slightly. His ferocious scowl didn't. "You aren't fine. You were close to an explosion."

Explaining the sore head.

Aryl rose to her feet, pleasantly surprised to be clean. Her hair tumbled free around her bare shoulders and she fought it back with both hands, looking for its net. "What's been hap—" The rest was smothered as Enris wrapped her tightly in his big arms. Aryl patted him comfortingly, though she winced at what was, by the feel, a bruised rib. Or two. *Never do that again,* he sent.

I didn't know it would blow up, she said reasonably. Though this was the second time, in her experience, which didn't say much for Stranger technology. *Enris, love. My ribs?* Not to mention she couldn't talk while he squeezed her like this.

He changed his hold to cup her face in both hands, studying it while she waited. Hair coiled around his wrists, looped its red-gold up his arms to stroke along his jaw. Finally, his scowl faded. He planted a firm kiss on her forehead, then her mouth. "Oran did a good job."

Oran. The Healer?

Aryl pushed away. "How long have I been lying here?" And where was here? She looked around for the first time.

One of the Cloisters' small rooms. She hadn't lain on a platform—she'd been on their bed, from Sona. The weathered wood and rock looked wrong against the pale yellow walls. There was more, all wrong. Supplies, blankets, baskets of clothing.

The steady light from the ceiling strip shone on their home.

"What have you done?" she demanded as she grabbed clothes and began to dress.

Enris chose to answer her first question. "You've been lying here, scaring me, for two days."

She froze, her head halfway through the neck of her tunic. "Two days?"

The corner of his generous mouth twitched. "The world hasn't ended and no one's come knocking."

Two days . . . finished with the tunic, Aryl fought hair until Enris tossed her hairnet to her. "As for what we've done—"

Hair secured, Aryl shook her head impatiently. She reclaimed the Human's disk and 'scanner, tucking both into pockets, then threw her knife belt around her hips and secured it with a quick tug.

"I can see for myself." Done? They'd settled in, that was what they'd done. They'd had time to 'port the entire village here, plus probably most of the supplies from the mounds. She picked up her Speaker's Pendant. Put it down. Everything else could wait. "Marcus?"

His shields locked tight.

Not good. Not good at all. "Enris?"

"We've done all we can—"

Worse. "Where is he?"

"I'll take you." He gathered her close again, this time gently, and ...

... they were outside.

Outside?

A damp breeze chilled her face as Enris opened his arms to let her go. Aryl stared around in shock. This was the Cloisters' platform, still covered in dirt and dust. There was the wall around it—

—a wall that looked over a wide, dark lake. At its far edge, where there should be nekis, only a few scattered tips showed through water laced with white foam. Its near edge was the wall. Water slapped against it, sprayed into her face. A log tumbled past, roots helplessly in air.

She was still unconscious, Aryl thought numbly. This couldn't be real.

"We think it was the explosion," Enris said. "Whatever the Oud did to divert the waterfall isn't working anymore. The upper part of the valley is flooded like this, though by Sona the river returns to its old path." He didn't mention his dam; it couldn't have withstood this, Aryl realized with an inner pang. "The Stranger camp was destroyed," he finished.

"Why did you bring me here? Where's Marcus?"

Enris sighed and gestured apology, his hand raised to point left. *The others refused to let a not-*real *inside.*

She didn't reply to this, didn't do anything but turn and walk along the platform, following the outer curve of the Cloisters. She passed window after window and dared not think of those inside, who'd leave—who'd leave—

"Aryl!"

There. A cluster of white crates for walls. Sona blankets for a roof. This was all they'd done for him?

"Wait!"

Aryl broke into a run, hearing Enris behind her. She burst through the blanket that made a door and stopped in her tracks.

Warm and dry. Dim; the oillights couldn't match daylight. A faint, unfamiliar smell. Two narrow crates were tables; one held an untouched meal, the other an assortment of items that belonged in pockets but not on Cersi. Other crates for seats. A bed. The breeze wafted the blanket overhead.

Like their first shelter at Sona, when they'd had nothing.

Sian surged to his feet at the sight of her; so did Naryn. Little Yao stayed where she was, snuggled in the curve of the Human's arm.

While he—while Marcus lay against pillows, a shadow that smiled and coughed and wasn't right. Wasn't right.

"What have you told her?" Naryn demanded.

Enris, who'd entered at her heels, spread his hands in an eloquent gesture. "She didn't wait."

Aryl didn't listen to them. She walked to the bed, found a smile for Yao, lost it when she looked at Marcus. "I'm sorry—" Her voice failed, too.

"Are you all ... right?" the Human asked. "They told ... me you ... were hurt."

Perfect words, quietly spoken, the small pained gasps for breath the only sign of effort. Why he wasn't already dead, she couldn't guess. Bones stood out on his face and hands. The skin of both was purpled by bruises, pale yellow where it wasn't. His neck had been neatly bandaged; fresh red stains marked a still-open wound. "They took better care of me," she told him, and planned to 'port their precious Healer into the floodwater at her first opportunity.

"Oran tried. So did Sian." Naryn was standing on the other side of the bed. She drew the child from Marcus with a gentle hand and handed her a cup. "Yao, our friend's run out of his drink. Please go and ask Rorn if there's any sombay left."

Yao gave Aryl a too-adult look, but disappeared obediently.

"What do you mean 'tried'?" Aryl asked.

Sian. *Healing won't work, Aryl. Nothing does.* With *compassion.*

Marcus looked anxious, as if he'd transgressed. "Everyone . . . has been kind. Aryl. Don't . . . be . . . angry."

Was she that easy to read? Probably. Aryl forced her expression into something calmer. "You haven't been eating."

His eyelids had healed, the eyes themselves were unutterably weary. "Left . . . for the big guy. Not . . . hungry."

"The real hurt is inside." Sian touched a forefinger to his own head. *Any mindtouch causes pain. He's severely damaged. There's nothing I can do.*

The mindcrawler.

Aryl sat on the bed and put her hand close to, but not touching, the Human's.

Aryl? Caution, no more, from Enris.

I have to try.

She waited. Marcus met her gaze for a long moment, then tipped his head on the pillow, the way he had when about to ask one of his odd questions. "This . . . not your fault. You know . . . that."

"I know." They'd left him to confront whatever waited at Site Three, alone, because the summons had been impossible to resist. They'd left him a captive, to be abused and hurt, because she'd had no way to find him. They'd saved him as soon as they could, and been too late.

Words. None of it helped. None of it mattered.

But his eyes brightened at her agreement, just a bit. Which did.

Aryl leaned closer. "Marcus, let me try to help you. Please."

"Problem is me," he replied. "My fault . . . this, too."

"No. None of it."

"You're a . . . good friend," this with almost a real

smile. "But this is ... important. The truth between us. Mindcrawler no threat ... to most Humans. Understand? Only to ... some. Only to Human ... *telepaths.*"

Aryl frowned. What was he saying? He had no Power.

Marcus continued. "Strong Human telepath ... can talk like you do. Not teleport." This with relief. "They can protect themselves. Others—" his hand lifted to his own chest "—vulnerable. Understand me? No ability. Only weak mind ... easy target ... weak." A tear slipped from one eye, left a glistening trail along one cheek.

He wasn't weak, in any way. "I cut off its head," Aryl assured him. Whatever "it" had been. Not Human. Ugly. "Did they tell you?"

Enris leaned over her shoulder. "Made a mess," he added. "You know Yena."

The Human's eyes widened, then he sputtered a laugh. "Friends," when he could talk again. "Good friends."

Now, she urged him silently. While trust was greater than fear.

As if he'd heard, Marcus shifted his hand until their fingertips met.

Aryl had touched his mind before. She knew, as the others didn't, where the danger of trespass lay within the Human, the whisper-thin distance between emotion and intention, between memory and self. Careful to stay away from his thoughts, she lowered her shields and let her *inner* sense float outward.

No room for doubt. Sian was trained in healing a mind; she'd done it only once, in desperation, to help someone she loved. Myris.

Well, she loved this not-Om'ray, too, this Stranger who mangled words and smiled with his eyes, who'd set aside his life's work to protect a people he hadn't known existed a year ago. Who lay here in trust, more alone than anyone or anything in the world, while she was surrounded by the glow of her kind.

... Something.

There. Aryl didn't *reach*. She paid *attention*.

More. *Pain* ... *confusion* ... fragments of emotion unwound, like a dresel wing unfurling from its stalk, slowly at first.

Memories came too, rattled like pods drying in the wind, bound in *fear* and *pain*. His capture. Rough hands. Waiting ... waiting ... knowing the worst was to come. *Revulsion. Despair.*

Aryl let the memories slide past, didn't react even to her own face, hair wild, eyes calm, the blur of a knife. Though she smiled inwardly, *sharing* a *joy* as fierce as any Yena's.

More.

Her breathing wanted to flutter like his; she *moved* somewhere else.

Here!

Discord! NOISE! Every biter in the canopy, buzzing in her head at once.

It wasn't sound at all.

Aryl *stayed*. This was important, whatever it was. Her mind raced through words and images, tried to comprehend what wasn't *real*. Noise or silence? Old bone or rock? Om'ray or Human? Differences fought each other, weakened her concentration. She became desperate for anything familiar.

Here. Safely distant from Marcus, a presence solid as the buttress roots that held the great rastis so they bent to the M'hir Wind but didn't fall. *Always.*

He shouldn't be with her, not here; that he was meant everything. Aryl steadied, sent sincere *affection* to her Chosen, then returned to what confused her.

Not-*real*. And not-Marcus either.

Tracks in moss. V-shaped ripples in a stream.

These—these were the wounds left by the mindcrawler as it ripped through the Human's mind!

Her mother had scanned her. This wasn't the same. This was no trained intrusion after a secret, an unpleasant invasion that left its victim whole, if exposed. This was the swarm consuming what it touched, full of greed and heedless of harm.

With mounting horror, Aryl followed the damage. She tried to grasp its extent, to find a place to attempt healing, but the more she *looked*, the more she found, as if the wounds festered and spread.

Or did they spread because she *looked*? Is this what Sian meant?

She *backed* away.

What to do? She had to do something . . . what? She didn't know how to help an Om'ray with such hurts.

How could she help a Human?

Aryl. Her name; his *grief. Stop. There's nothing we can do.*

Enris was right. She knew it, though it was agony to be helpless. She tightened her shields and opened her eyes.

Marcus' eyes were still closed. He trusted her. Had he believed she could help?

All she'd done was learn she couldn't, Aryl told herself bitterly. "Marcus—"

He opened his eyes, appeared dazed, but before she could say anything else, a small figure appeared. Yao flung herself on top of the Human and whirled to face her, teeth bared. *DON'THURTHIMDON'THURTHIM!!!!*

Aryl wasn't the only one to flinch from the raw Power of that sending.

"We didn't hurt him—" Enris began.

LEAVEHIMALONE!!

Marcus eased his tiny protector to the side, where she crouched like a quivering stitler about to launch. "Aryl would never . . . hurt me, Yao," he soothed. "No . . . one here would . . . hurt me."

Unimpressed by words, Yao continued to glare at Aryl. *I won't let them.* Quieter, more polite, but with no less *determination.*

She should have expected this. Yao was the only one of them who wouldn't see a not-Om'ray lying here. All

she saw was the truth: here was someone kind, like a
father, who suffered. Aryl nodded to herself, then consciously thought of Marcus, of her feelings for him, and
shared them with the child.

"Oh." Yao's eyes opened wide and she settled back.
"You're his friend, too." She grinned, as content as she'd
been furious an instant before. Her tiny hand found
the Human's. "Have you tried Comspeak yet? I'm very
good at it."

"You are." Marcus smiled happily at the child, then
looked at Aryl. "Aryl, too? Good! Aryl—" A stream of
gasps and babble came out of the Human's mouth.

"I don't—"

Aryl stopped as the babble *reshaped* itself into
words. "—understand me now? I . . . worried sleepteach
could affect . . . *fetal* development . . . but Naryn . . .
found an Om'ray way. All Sona can talk . . . to me . . . to
anyone who . . . comes here. Amazing . . . You, too?"

Sona's Dream Chamber. They'd used it to *teach* the
language of the Trade Pact?

And she'd worried about supplies from the village.

The Strangers will be back. Naryn, flat and sure. *We
all know it.*

Not in time to save Marcus. *You should have
waited*—

Till you *woke up?* With a flash of *irony. Tell that to the
other seven hundred.*

Marcus enjoys hearing it, Enris pointed out.

Indeed, the Human, oblivious to the emotions of the
Om'ray around him, was still smiling. "Aryl," he urged,
"say something!"

She had to smile back. "How do—am I—I am speaking it!" The movements of her mouth and tongue were
strange, like trying to shout and whisper at the same
time, but he took her hand and squeezed it.

"Comspeak," he assured her. "Wonderful to hear . . .
in your voice, Aryl. Wonderful."

This in two days, Aryl told herself, appalled. What else could they have done?

"Keep an eye on him, Yao. I'll be back soon," she told Marcus.

Once she knew.

Chapter 12

"WE'VE BEEN WORKING, young Aryl," Husni said, with a look that suggested Aryl could be better employed than asking the obvious. The elder walked between tables dragged into one of the corridors, as if supervising the storing of dried dresel. She had a group of unChosen busily wrapping flat pieces of some brown material in strips of what had been the fabric Sona used for shirts.

Decisions were made. Enris had followed her inside. *They had to be.*

Right or wrong ones?

That, he didn't answer.

The pieces were covered in neat rows of symbols. Aryl glanced at them, then stared. "Those are words. Names." Written in Comspeak. Which she could read!

She wasn't sure which astounded her more.

"Why are there names?" she asked.

"Did you get her out of bed too soon?" Husni asked Enris, her wrinkles creasing deeper.

"It's—"

"He did not," Aryl objected, suspecting her Chosen had let her sleep so long for reasons of his own. "What are these?"

"Parches," the elder said unhelpfully. "Anaj told us

where to find them. As for the names," Husni correctly read Aryl's scowl and gave a wrinkled grin, "the Adepts added everyone to Sona's records, but this Cloisters wouldn't accept the rest."

"Rest?" They weren't, she hoped, expecting more.

"The names for families—in the other Clans. Our Adepts need to know who shares grandparents before they can decide which families should send unChosen on Passage. Everyone's given us all the names they know. We've made two sets, one to leave here, and one ready to take with us—in case we ever leave. These," Husni waved a hand over the parches, "record the birth of the M'hiray."

Pride welled from all those in earshot.

Her head threatened to pound. "The 'M'hiray'?"

"I thought of it," Enris said modestly. "We needed a name for people like us. What do you think?"

That the world, and her Chosen, had gone mad while she slept? "We're Om'ray," Aryl managed to say between clenched teeth. "What nonsense is this?"

"No Om'ray can do what we can!" The outburst came from one of the unChosen at the nearest table. Since all quickly put their heads down to concentrate on folding, Aryl couldn't tell which.

She didn't care. She clamped a hand on Enris' wrist and concentrated ...

... as she'd hoped, the petal-roofed chamber was empty of all but sunlight.

" 'The M'hiray,' " she repeated acidly. "No more surprises, Enris."

"Promise to stay still longer than a moment, then."

"I—" Aryl deliberately sat on a bench and put her hands together, though every nerve screamed to *move*. Which worked much better as a way to find answers, she thought ruefully, in the canopy. "I promise."

This gained her a doubtful look, surely deserved, but her Chosen sat across from her and leaned forward to rest his forearms on his thighs. His face was thinner than she remembered. A lock of black hair shadowed his dark eyes. Or was it something *grim* she felt?

"After the explosion, the water rose quickly," he told her, *sharing* images at the same time. "Within tenths, we were trapped inside. There was no choice. We had to 'port for food. That was what everyone was waiting for—proof the M'hir was safe. Since then?" A laugh without humor. "I thought I was used to Ziba popping in and out. Wait till you're in a room and fifty Chosen appear out of the air. 'Porting's become—" his lips curled, "—remarkably casual."

She'd ignored the oddly quick *shifts* in her sense of place; she had, as her Chosen said, been too close to an explosion. But they were real. The newcomers were 'porting from room to room instead of walking! Frivolous, wasteful ... Aryl kept her temper with an effort, concentrated on turning her bracelet around and around on her wrist. "You'd think," she said more calmly, "some would have gone home."

"Apparently this remains home," with a shrug that invited her to share the irony. "But you're right. Once in a while, someone 'ports to their former Clan. For belongings, to check on those left behind, curiosity. Whatever the reason, no one stays long."

"Aren't they welcome?" She'd been afraid of that. How did "M'hiray" appear to ordinary Om'ray?

And when had she accepted the distinction, too?

"Welcome?" Enris looked thoughtful. "No one's said. That's not why, though. It's the connection you discovered, through the M'hir." His hand sketched a link between them. "Turns out to be stronger than the link to other Om'ray. Anyone who leaves is drawn back."

"You tried." He wouldn't take another's word for something this significant.

"Yes." His face turned bleak. "At first, I thought it was simply the instinct to return to my Chosen—not that I had to worry about your getting up to risk yourself anytime soon."

Aryl snorted.

"But it was different," Enris went on. "At Sona, with the others, I felt—it was like being back in the aircar. I *needed* to return. Though not as strong. Nothing," he said soberly, "could be."

That moment, that feeling. Aryl caught her breath. Was that when Om'ray had split in two?

"It has to be," she said aloud.

"Has to be what?"

She could see it as surely as his dear face. "Stretch a rope too far and it becomes weak. When Marcus flew us over the mountains—what if it weakened our connection to other Om'ray? Enough so this new bond took over when we fell out of the world and were about to be—" What? Lost? Was that what lay beyond the world? Nothing but minds and selves dissolving in the M'hir? Aryl forced away the terrifying image. "When we went too far," she finished, proud of her steady voice. "Without a strong link to other Om'ray, only our connection through the M'hir could save us. And it did. By pulling us together. All of us. Here."

His eyes lit with comprehension. "Of course. The Cloisters where we practiced 'porting. Where Oran was the Keeper."

"The Cloisters that shared her dreams with all of Cersi." Aryl shook her head, but it wasn't denial. "My mother told me a Cloisters affects the binding within a Clan. Sona's is the only one tied to the M'hir."

"Meaning we're tied to it?" Enris shook his head. "I hope not. As it is, we'll have to keep 'porting for supplies. We've nothing to trade with other Clans." An abrupt, bitter laugh. "We'll need those coats." He hesitated. "Any chance you can tell the Oud to drain the lake?"

Aryl didn't bother to point out that only her Chosen would think she'd remain Speaker with three older ones already vying for that position. Or that they had no idea if any Oud survived to do the repair. "If they don't," she told him, "we'll have Tikitik for neighbors."

"Tikitik?" He scrunched his face. "Wonderful. I doubt they'd let us go back to the old ways here—fire, living on the ground. Oh, no. There'll be climbing. Next there'll be biters. You know they prefer my skin to yours."

He kept it light for her sake, Aryl thought. She moved to sit beside him, rested her head on his chest, and wrapped her arms around his middle. Her fingers didn't meet. Their minds did, a deep mingling that couldn't hide the truth.

If they were now M'hiray, not Om'ray . . . if their children would be . . .

Enris laid his hand over the swelling below her waist, spread his fingers as if to hold the small life within safe from the future, but neither of them could.

What would be the shape of their daughter's world?

They wanted her in the Council Chamber. Haxel could have used her at Sona, gathering supplies. Husni, Aryl thought with wry amusement, would probably let her help with the interminable parches.

This was where she belonged. Aryl unhooked the blanket from the opening, letting in the warm midday sun. Only good sense, she'd told Enris, to find a quiet task that would let her body finish the recovery started by Oran.

He'd agreed without any remark about Yena durability or Yena pride. Meaning she hadn't fooled him at all.

Asleep, the Human wasn't peaceful. His mouth worked silently. His head rolled from side to side so she had to replace his pillows often. As for the tremble in his legs?

Understandable, for a broken mind to dream of danger and flight, Sian had told her. He'd relinquished his bedside place with reluctance. Her mother's former heart-kin, like Yao, saw not a Stranger or a not-Om'ray, but someone in pain he couldn't help.

She'd gestured gratitude with a sincerity the Yena Adept appeared to find startling. She should have trusted Taisal's judgment, Aryl thought, embarrassed by her younger self.

Sian hadn't left her much to do. Aryl rearranged the Human's belongings on the crate-table: the sum of his possessions. A couple of small devices of unknown function, an ordinary-enough comb, a handful of the Human's dreadful rations.

She pulled his image disk from her pocket. "I promised," she whispered. Not that any of them were safe.

"What's that?" Yao's chin lifted from her knees. She sat on a pillow in a shadowed corner, so quiet and still Aryl had almost forgotten her presence.

"It holds images of his family." Not knowing how to make it work, Aryl set it carefully by the comb. "His sister. His Chosen. Their young son and daughter." His Chosen, being Human, wouldn't die or be Lost when Marcus was gone. She'd have to live with her grief, and raise their children alone.

"Karina and Howard," Yao said promptly. "Marcus told me. Howard gets into mischief all the time, like Ziba. Karina behaves. Like me."

How well a baby could behave was an open question, Aryl thought, smiling to herself, but didn't doubt the affection between Human and child. Or why Yao stayed by Marcus tenth after tenth, instead of playing with her friends.

Healers were rare among Om'ray. That important Talent showed itself first as an ability to *sense* who was injured or ill, a need to be near them. Costa's Chosen, Leri, had been drawn to an injured scout, when only a child herself. Even if distressed their daughter was drawn to a Human, Yao's parents should be glad for her future.

If Hoyon looked beyond his hooked nose, Aryl grumbled to herself. "You missed lunch," she commented.

"Lunch?" Yao leaped to her feet, then looked at

Marcus. "I'm not hungry," she said bravely, sinking back down.

Unlikely. "Go." Aryl made a shooing motion with her hands. "I'll be here."

The child disappeared with a grin.

Going back to the crate-table, Aryl laid out the scraps of fabric Enris had given her, the ones with words in Comspeak on them: *Archivist Second Class Tomas Vogt, Archivist Second Class An Tsessas.* She agreed with her Chosen; Marcus would want to know about them. She added the geoscanner. It was his, too.

"Don't turn . . . on here, Aryl." An urgent whisper. Brown eyes watched her. Had he been asleep at all?

Anxious eyes. "You're safe," she soothed. Something made her collect the fabric scraps before she sat beside him. "Those who took you are dead, Marcus. All of them. Their machine exploded like the vidbot." If louder.

"Good," with venom. "Thieves . . . killers." Marcus made an effort to calm himself. "The machine is . . . called a starship. Aircar that . . . flies between . . . worlds."

"Starship." He'd used the word before. Aryl wasn't sure she liked the sound of it, stars being among the untouchable confusions the Human so casually added to her life. "It wasn't the starship you expected—the one to take you home?"

Definite offense. "No! Not mine!" A terrible cough. "*Pirates*!"

His language might sound *right* to her ears now. That didn't, Aryl thought with some frustration, give her every meaning. She left the topic of "pirates," sure it was a word to give Haxel later, and put the 'scanner on the bed. "Can you use this to call for help?"

"No one . . . to call. All dead . . . Artrul. Tyler. Their Triads. P'tr sit 'Nix . . . He tried for . . . Site Three . . . *shutdown*." He strained to get the words out. "Site Three . . . attacked first, Aryl. First . . . to stop . . . off-world alarm . . . should have known . . . I found . . . They died in their beds, Aryl! . . . Josen and Meen . . . my—my

new Triad ... Harmless! Helpless! ... No need to kill—"
He began to cough.

She gave him a drink from his cup. "Easy."

He swallowed, eyes dull. "Try to fix ... com. No
time ... Pirates followed ... they find me ... they take ...
they take ..." His lips worked in silence and he gave her
a helpless look.

"I know." No need to explain, she thought. The swarm
might eat you alive, but theirs was honest hunger. The
mindcrawler? "The pirates are dead," she reminded
him.

Marcus rallied. "Site Four ... still intact ... Vogt?
Tsessas? You save ... them too?"

"We were too late." She opened her fist and let the
scraps fall on his blanket. "I'm sorry, Marcus."

He fingered the names gently, smoothed them flat,
then sighed. "They died to ... save history." With a gesture to the crates that walled him on three sides.

She didn't correct him; he deserved better memories
than their suspicions. "The Runners went back for the artifacts when the water began to rise. Some Tuana," her lip
curled, "can't resist what might be of value." A "value"
that had done this to Marcus. At least the others hadn't
allowed the foul things inside the Cloisters. She couldn't
help but add, "They should have left them to rot."

"Aryl." The Human gave her a distressed look. "History ... not to blame. These ... these are important.
These ... yours now. Keep ... safe."

"If you say so," she said to please him. She'd trade
them all for his survival. "What about your starship?
Can you contact it?"

"Local com only ... starship too far ... but ..." a sudden gleam in his eyes, "... when they get here ... they'll
send down ... search parties." Marcus reached for the
'scanner, only to pull back. "Not here. You take ... to my
camp. Close as water allows ... Set distress beacon." He
showed her how to turn the dome, then press it down.
"Away from Om'ray," he insisted.

Even now, he wouldn't draw the attention of his people to them.

There were cracks in the cliff—better still, she'd climb the Hoveny structure and put it on one of its wide ledges. Aryl took it and stood. "We'll watch for an answer," she promised. "Bring you to them as soon as—"

"Aryl. No hurry."

"What do you mean?" she bluffed, knowing full well. "The faster we get you help the better."

"There is no help." This with such calm certainty, she sat back down, the 'scanner clutched in both hands. "I know this," Marcus brushed trembling fingers across his forehead, "can't be . . . fixed. Best my people . . . do . . . is keep me . . . breathing. Not enough. . . . Not enough . . . Already I don't . . . always know where . . . I am or . . . who. I . . . can't taste . . . can't smell. Things . . . things I know," with a hint of desperation, ". . . slip away. To speak . . . hurts . . . to think . . . hurts . . ." His gentle brown eyes pored over her face. "Aryl. Only one . . . thing left . . . I need you to . . . do it."

She'd known this, too.

With a heavy heart, Aryl drew her longknife and laid it across her lap.

Marcus pressed back into his pillows and raised both hands to fend her off. "Not that . . . !" He didn't relax until she sheathed the blade. "Should know better . . . what I ask . . . a Yena," he said, making a croaking sound and wiping his eyes. A laugh?

"Your choice," she told him, trying not to show her relief. "How can I help?"

"I . . . want to . . . leave a message. To put with . . . the beacon . . . for my family." He pointed to the image disk on the crate.

She gave it to him and waited, curious. Marcus half smiled. "Alone."

"Of course." Sensitive as an osst, Aryl chided herself. He wanted to say good-bye to his Chosen, his children. "I'll be outside. Call when you're done."

"Then ... you can tell ... me all about ... you and Enris and Sweetpie. I want to ... know the ... future of my other family."

Aryl managed a smile.

So did she.

Water was more trouble than winter. Aryl glared at the flood. The dirt-heavy waves rolled a bloated Oud corpse past the Cloisters, one of many. Nothing feasted on them. She never imagined she'd miss underwater hunters. Maybe a rumn or two would ...

"How is he?"

Aryl glanced at Naryn, then put her chin back on her crossed arms. She was watching a particular nekis stalk, hoping to see the water level go down. It hadn't, as yet, cooperated. "Leaving a message for his family."

Her friend joined her at the wall, shoulder against hers. After a long moment, "So he knows he's dying."

"Marcus isn't a fool!" Aryl snapped, then gestured apology. "Yes, he knows," she sighed, counting corpses. Three. Five. "Did they agree on a Council yet?" Decision makers. She'd wanted to be free of that responsibility, Aryl reminded herself. Another good reason to be here and not in the Council Chamber.

"Done." Naryn snapped her fingers.

"That was—" too fast. "How?"

"The Adepts. They sort themselves by strength and desired Talents. When they proposed that reasoning for our Council, argued it was the M'hiray's best chance for survival, no one objected."

She'd have objected. Power wasn't everything. "Adepts, then."

"Some. They wanted the Speakers. Gur di Sawnda'at and Dann d'sud Friesnen agreed. Your mother declined. You," with a nudge at her shoulder, "weren't there."

"Which would be declining," Aryl nudged back. The

Speakers were obvious choices. Adepts who knew how to talk to other races, they would understand the difference between sensible risk and outright folly. As for Taisal?

Her mother was more concerned with the M'hir than the M'hiray.

"Who else?"

Distaste. "Two from Tuana. Ruis di Mendolar, Mia d'sud Serona."

Both powerful Adepts. Mia had come on Passage from Amna, so he knew that Clan as well. But ... Aryl frowned and kept her voice low. "Weren't they the ones—?"

"Who declared me ruined?" Naryn's shields opened to share *irony.* "They had to accept me if they wanted who I carry."

"Anaj."

They insisted. The Old Adept sounded more pleased than otherwise. *Quite flattering, considering the state I'm in.*

Considering the strength and experience of that mindvoice, Aryl thought, they'd have been fools not to.

"And a final two, from Yena." Naryn watched for her reaction. "Cetto and Seru."

So Power wasn't the only factor. Good for them, Aryl thought, feeling better by the moment. Cetto d'sud Teerac, the former Councillor from Yena, had always been a bold and courageous thinker. As for her cousin? "What happened when Seru heard her name?"

"I thought Ezgi would have to pick her up off the floor," Naryn chuckled. "But she's our only Birth Watcher. The Adepts felt strongly about including her knowledge."

"She'll surprise them all," Aryl predicted. Easy words, but when she finished, something felt ... wrong. She turned to Naryn, who no longer smiled. "Something I should know?"

"Seru di Parth made the first proposal to the M'hiray Council. One they accepted unanimously." *Heart-kin, I'm so sorry.* "It concerns you and the Human."

If it involved Seru, Aryl assured herself numbly, it should be about the naming ceremony, or better slings for their babies. Shouldn't it?

Not when the new generation was threatened. She'd felt it; Seru must.

"What's the proposal?"

We cannot survive inside this Cloisters. The M'hiray must leave Sona, Anaj sent. *The* not-Om'ray *will help us find a place of our own.*

Of all M'hiray, Seru was the last one she'd expect to share her Chosen's high hopes for Stranger technology, or to convince others. "How?" Aryl countered reasonably. "He has nothing left."

He's done what none of us has. Seen past the waterfall. Gone over the cliff and seen what's there.

"Of course he has—" Aryl stopped, understanding at last. "No."

Naryn's hair whipped her shoulders. "Everyone's afraid for the future, Aryl. Afraid of what we might have to become. If we stay here—there's been talk of taking what we need from other Clans."

"No."

It's the Council's decision, child. We will use the Maker to cut the last link between M'hiray and Om'ray, freeing us from Sona and Cersi itself. We will 'port to a new home, taking what we can carry. All we need is a locate.

Which they wanted her to rip from Marcus' mind. She'd be no better than the mindcrawler. She'd be worse—she already knew the pain she'd cause.

She already knew he'd let her.

Aryl backed away from Naryn, from Anaj. Put herself in front of the "door" to the Human's pitiful shelter. "I'll take some Yena. We'll 'port to the cliff. Climb to the top, and come back with what we see."

"Haxel suggested that. Council—they argued if she only saw bare rock, we'd be no better off." Naryn lifted her hands in a hopeless gesture.

The Human loses more of his mind while we delay. Soon his body will die. Not callous, but with certainty. *This is the Council's decision, not yours.*

NO! Aryl didn't care that the sending stung, or that her *fury* disturbed Enris into an anxious question she ignored. *The M'hiray can rot here. No one touches Marcus' mind again. No one.*

Her Chosen appeared beside her, a storm ready to strike. "What's going on?!"

"Our new Council's ordered me to scan Marcus. To find a locate for the M'hiray."

At this, Enris planted himself beside her in the doorway and crossed his huge arms, a pulse beating slowly along his jaw. He'd been with her, in the Human's damaged mind. "There has to be another way."

I'll find it, Aryl sent.

She had to.

Two days was time enough to find chairs for the dais of the Council Chamber, if not to polish clean the floor or windows. Time enough, Aryl thought bitterly as she walked down an opening aisle of silent M'hiray, to go from being her people's leader to a solitary voice of dissent.

She'd never asked to be either.

The new Council waited for her. Naryn, with a woeful look her way, took the last chair. Cetto and Seru sat beside one another. Her cousin's skin grew blotchy when she cried; it was flawless.

So, Aryl thought. Seru was sure of this course.

Gur, Dann, Mia, and Ruis.

It changed them all, sitting up there, side by side. Their clothing was a mismatch; of the four Choosers, two wore nets, the others' hair wandered over their shoulders. Different ages, different faces, different Clans. But there was no mistaking common purpose, or that these individuals accepted their responsibilities.

They weren't going to listen.

Aryl kept her shoulders straight and kept walking. When she reached the cluster of Sona, hands reached out to hers, fingertips brushed her skin. *Encouragement. Belief.* Haxel scowled; Rorn looked weary. Oran wrapped offended dignity around herself like a coat; Bern didn't meet her eyes. Yao clung to her mother but reached out, too. Husni and blindfolded Weth. Syb and Fon. Gijs with Juo, their baby in her arms. Sona understood what Marcus had done for them: the rescue from Yena; the negotiations with Oud and Tikitik; keeping their secret from his own kind.

To the rest assembled here, the Human was not-*real,* not-Om'ray, and had only one remaining use.

Someone stepped close as she slowed before the dais. Ezgi, Seru's Chosen. He touched the back of her hand. *Aryl, Seru loves you. We all do. She doesn't see any other way. Forgive her, please.*

She glanced at his round, earnest face. Enris' cousin, Galen's son. He'd age well, she thought with an odd calm. The bones of his face were strong and clean, his brown eyes wise beyond their years. A Councillor himself, one day.

If any of them survived.

Peace, Ezgi, she sent. *This isn't about love or forgiveness.*

It was about duty to a friend.

Cetto rose to his feet. "Greetings, Aryl di Sarc." His rich deep tones filled the Chamber. Feet and minds settled. "We are the first Council of the M'hiray. Anaj tells us you have come to discuss—"

"I've come to refuse." She'd pitched her voice to carry, too. "And to tell you—all of you—that my Chosen and I will protect Marcus Bowman."

Naryn closed her eyes.

The Human would not risk our survival, Aryl di Sarc, Anaj sent, driving the words through the M'hir to them all. *How dare you?*

"Do swarms climb these walls?" Aryl sent *scorn* beneath the words. "Are we on rations and forced to starve our elders? No. We're safe and comfortable. We have the ability to get whatever we need. We will make a good future, here or elsewhere. We've time. Marcus doesn't." *Doubt.* She sensed it from someone on the dais and pressed the advantage. "Let him die in peace, with friends."

"Is it your opinion, Aryl di Sarc, that more Strangers will come to Cersi?" Gur asked.

They couldn't stop them if they wanted to. Aryl settled for a calm, "Yes."

Gur leaned forward, her eyes intent, gray hair twisting. "We can speak their words. Is your opinion, Aryl di Sarc, that we should greet these new Strangers? Befriend them? In case we do need help to create our good future."

Trapped. She could admire the skill of it, even as her pulse hammered in her throat. "No," Aryl said, having no other choice. Seru averted her face.

"Explain."

"We can't risk contact with any Strangers who might have been part of the attack against the Oud."

Gur sat back, touched fingertips to her pendant. "And is that the only reason?"

"No." Aryl stood straight. "We can't let any Stranger close to us. If they learn we can move through the M'hir, some might try to take that knowledge." War, Marcus had called it. "We have neither numbers nor technology on our side."

"By what you say, Aryl di Sarc," Gur said soberly, "And be sure that I—all of us—value your opinion in such matters above any other's. By what you say, there is only one Stranger we can ever trust. One Stranger innocent of harm, who has protected our secrets. And he is here. Now. Able to help us, in the small time he has left."

"Help who?" Aryl's violent gesture swept the Council Chamber. "Us? Who are we? No longer Om'ray. No longer anything. We're the threat to Cersi. What if Sona's Cloisters brought us together to keep us from harming anyone else? In your opinion, esteemed First Council of the M'hiray, won't the world be better off without us?"

Footsteps rang in the ensuing shocked silence. Everyone turned as Taisal walked quickly through the crowd to stand beside Aryl. Her face was like ash. "The Tikitik have left Yena."

"And Rayna!" Karne shouted. He followed at a run, skidding to a halt in front of the dais.

Rayna's Speaker, Gur di Sawnda'at, leaped to her feet with a look of horror. "What do you mean?

"Karne and I 'ported to Yena to examine its Maker," Taisal said quickly and firmly, a scout making a report. "The Adepts confronted me, demanded to know if the Tikitik had left because of us. I sent Karne to Rayna, while I went to the Tikitik grove nearest Yena to see for myself." Her eyes flicked to Haxel, then back to the Council. "It was deserted."

"There are towers of dirt all around Rayna." Karne tried to match Taisal's tone, but his voice quivered. "Everyone's locked in their homes or Cloisters. No one knows what to do! What does it mean?"

The Oud. Comprehension burned from mind to mind. *Oud. Oud. Oud.*

A memory shivered through her mind, leaving ice behind . . . *a mug struck the floor, splintered on contact, fragments sliding in all directions, connected by a spray of dark liquid that was the Om'ray . . .*

"It means the Agreement has broken," Aryl said quietly. "It means the end of the world."

"Whatever plan you had to leave this place," her mother told the M'hiray Council, "start it now, before Om'ray die because of us."

It wasn't until several moments had passed—moments during which the Councillors rushed down from their seats, during which voices and emotions and sendings surged like waves against sand until those with experience in running for their lives, Haxel foremost, began to bark orders—it wasn't until order began to shape itself from terror that Aryl realized Naryn di S'udlaat wasn't with them.

There was only one place she could have gone.

Aryl concentrated with furious speed . . .

Interlude

"WHAT'S . . . GOING ON?"

Enris turned and went under the blanket roof, giving the Human his best smile. "A difference of opinion between our new Council and Aryl. She'll win."

"About me."

Never underestimate Marcus, he reminded himself. "We have a small problem," he evaded, testing the crate the others had used as a chair. When sure it would hold his weight, he relaxed and sat. "It seems there are now two kinds of Om'ray. Those who can—" he fluttered fingers as Marcus would do to refer to 'porting, "—and those who can't. It wasn't just the three of us pulled to Sona. It was all the M'hiray. Over seven hundred. It's a bit crowded right now."

"*Stratification*."

He raised an eyebrow. "You've a word for it?"

Marcus smiled. "Not exactly . . . If you put . . . different things together . . . in water . . . shake hard . . . let all settle . . . layers of the . . . same kind . . . form. Stratification."

Probably the best description he'd heard, Enris decided. Especially the "shake hard" part. As for settling? "This layer," he commented dryly, "has a problem." He waved at the flood beyond the open doorway. "No home."

No smile now. "What say . . . Oud? . . . Tikitik? . . . Where you go? . . . What say, Enris!" with a rasp of urgency.

The Human knew their world. Enris shrugged. "As I said, we have a problem. Aryl did her best, but the Tikitik are in a panic—and the Oud?" If any were left in Sona who weren't floating corpses. "We don't know. They have their own ideas about where Om'ray should and shouldn't be."

"M'hiray—you—" a stab with a too-thin finger, "—can escape Oud. . . . Rest Om'ray can't." His eyes were like dark pits. "Danger . . . like your Clan . . . like Tuana. Everywhere."

There was nothing he could say to that, no evasion, no clever argument. Lost in fear, Enris dropped his head and shuddered.

A hand touched his, cold and dry. Shields tight, he looked up to meet a gaze as warm and compassionate as any *real*-Om'ray's could be. "I can . . . help, Enris," Marcus offered, the words gentle; the gasp for breath to speak them almost an afterthought. "On rest of . . . planet . . . on Cersi . . . no Oud . . . no Tikitik. Only . . . here. With Om'ray. . . . Do you understand? . . . Only here."

How could he possibly understand that? The world— he could *feel* its extent, *know* it—there was nowhere else.

Marcus saw his battle. "Enris. Trust me . . . what I know . . . Most of Cersi . . . empty . . . Safe places . . . Better places. I . . . have been to many . . . seen *planetarysurveys* . . . Trust me." He touched his temple with one finger. "All in here . . . for you. For Aryl . . . for Sweetpie. Take it."

Om'ray or M'hiray—his kind was tied together; to damage another's innermost *self* would endanger every mind in range. Madness would spread like thought itself. They couldn't do to one another what the mindcrawler Stranger had done to the Human.

Not to another of their own . . .

The Human understood what he suggested, better than any Om'ray could. Enris had never imagined such courage, never expected to find it here, in a creature who fought to breathe yet looked at him with such tranquillity in his eyes he was ashamed of his own fear.

"We'll find another way."

"Not in time . . . M'hiray need my . . . help."

Wiser. Older. Braver. He had to ask. "Are all Humans like you?"

"Better . . . same . . . worse. Like any . . . people." The hint of a smile. "Take what you . . . need, Enris. . . . My gift."

Better? Enris shook his head in disbelief, then gestured profound gratitude. "Thank you, Marcus. But no." He fought to keep his voice even. "Aryl's gone before our Council to make sure no one touches your mind again. She won't allow it."

"Someone must . . ." As if he was the only one being reasonable. "Aryl wrong . . . Can you?"

Enris was on his feet and almost backed into the wall of crates—which would have brought them down on their heads and be a fine way to care for their friend—before he could stop himself. "No!"

Marcus nodded. "Naryn can. You . . . bring . . . Naryn here." He moved his fingers on the blanket.

He'd rather be in an Oud tunnel beneath a shaking mountain.

"Trust me," the Human urged. "Let me help." His throat worked and a fresh stain of red marked the bandage. "Before I'm . . . not so brave."

Or in the canopy, with the swarm eating his knees.

The swarm. He'd burned homes to save Yena that 'night. Watched the smoldering wreckage fall into the dark, chased by embers like dying stars. The question in his mind hadn't been if he'd die. He'd been sure of that. No, Enris remembered vividly. He'd worried if he could bear to wait with Aryl to be eaten alive, or would his courage fail him and he'd jump like his brother.

It hadn't failed. But this? This was worse, so much worse.

Naryn. Through the M'hir, as tight and focused as he could. *NARYN!*

He had her attention. *Now isn't the best time—*

COME TO MARCUS, NOW. Would she feel his desperate grief? Would she . . .

She did. The sun coming through the doorway turned Naryn's hair to flame. "What's wrong?" she demanded, stepping inside.

What are we doing here? Go back to Council at once!

Hush, Anaj. "Enris?"

His voice wouldn't obey him.

"Take safe . . . place for M'hiray." Marcus offered his hand. "Take everything . . . to help. Hurry."

For the second time, Enris saw Naryn vulnerable. "No. Aryl—"

Do it. The Old Adept's sending contained *compassion* and *respect.*

"Do it for Aryl," the Human said, as if he'd *heard.*

Enris edged out of Naryn's way, brushed fingertips along her wrist as she passed him. No words; he couldn't speak. Only *support.*

She paid attention only to Marcus. Sat on the bed. Took his right hand in hers as if offering Choice. When her hair slid down her arm to touch his skin, he smiled in wonder.

She closed her eyes.

He closed his.

Enris held his breath, his shields.

And when the Human began to scream, Naryn bowed her head.

Chapter 13

THE WORLD, ITS END, HER LIFE ... nothing mattered as Aryl 'ported except speed. Something was wrong. Something was wrong ...

... the shelter took the place of the frantic crowd in the Council Chamber ...

A horrible scream filled her ears! Her longknife leaped to her hand, and she struck without waiting for a target. Hands gripped her arm, deflected its movement. There was a flash of *pain*, then a grip like stone.

On one arm.

Without pause, Aryl brought her second knife up to kill.

IT'S ME!

Enris?

Both knives dropped with a clatter as her eyes snapped into focus. Blood ran down his cheek. A superficial cut; she'd missed the eye. "You shouldn't get in my way," she reminded him calmly.

He grabbed her other arm. "Aryl—"

Another SCREAM, this ending with a rasping sob.

From somewhere, she found the strength to push her giant Chosen out of her way, or he let her pass.

Then ... she saw.

Naryn was holding Marcus! He writhed in agony as she held him against her!

"No!" Aryl lunged forward. Naryn's hair tried to evade her—whipped at her face to blind her—but she was too quick and grabbed handfuls, heaved to pull the other to the floor. "What were you doing?!"

But she knew. Even as she dropped to her knees beside Marcus—too still, too quiet—even as she didn't dare touch him but leaned close to use her open mouth to wait for his breath—she knew.

And there were other weapons than knives. The M'hir boiled behind her eyes; hers to command, waiting like the swarm.

Take her away, she begged Enris with her last shred of control, trembling on the brink. Kill a friend, for a friend?

She'd lose both.

As you love me, take her away. Go.

Because he did, because they did, Enris and Naryn vanished.

Aryl couldn't move.

Dark lashes bridged hollows of shadowed skin. Drying tears left a crusted stream.

Then. Warmth in her mouth. A stomach-sour taste.

A breath.

Life. What remained of it.

Blinking away tears of her own, Aryl eased back. She adjusted the blanket that had fallen. Her hands shook and left incomprehensible symbols on the fabric. Blood. Naryn's hair had sliced her skin. A clatter on the floor. The image disk. She bent to retrieve it, tried to think.

"He's not dead."

Aryl straightened so quickly the small form across the bed instinctively stepped back. But Yao wasn't daunted. "He isn't," the child insisted. "Look."

The Human's eyelids had partially lifted, exposing red-stained whites. Lips peeled back from his teeth in a rictus of effort, as if another scream tried to escape, but he refused it. His hands clenched spasmodically, his body shuddering each time. The bandage around his neck wept blood.

Not dead.

Not alive.

Aryl sat on the bed, carefully distant, and stared at him. "What can I do? I don't know what to do."

She hadn't expected an answer, but Yao offered solemnly, "I have a song. It makes me feel better. Marcus likes it. 1 could teach it to you and we could sing together."

Aryl didn't look at the child. "He wouldn't hear it," she said, lips numb.

"That's because he's thinking of bad things. You should make him stop. He'd feel much better."

She lifted her head. Huge eyes in a small face gazed back. "What a wise person you are," Aryl said gravely. She gestured gratitude. "I need you to leave us alone, Yao. Please."

The child walked to the doorway, then turned to look at Marcus. *I wish he was my father.* Then was gone.

Wise, indeed.

Aryl put the disk, warmed by her flesh, on the table. She covered the Human's hands with her own.

And dropped her shields.

. . . The mind, fraying along every pattern, memories dissolving into chaos. *PAIN* . . . rushing to fill every empty space. Worst of all, *awareness.*

Marcus knew what was happening to him.

That was all he knew.

"Hush. Think only of your world," Aryl urged gently, her *inner* sense focused on him, *sharing* his agony. "Your home, Marcus. That special place . . . a place you want to show me." Impossible to cause more pain than he felt, so she poured *Power* into the demand, forced him to *listen.*

With an effort, he *responded.* He may have uttered words aloud; she didn't hear, preoccupied with catching memories as they surfaced, holding them before they fractured and were lost.

She'd expected Marcus to think of home and family. Instead, her mind filled with *darkness* . . . then a sudden *light*.

Lights hanging from wires. Lights attached to walls. Lights on poles. Together they fought to illuminate a too-vast space, angled and rising away in polished steps. Steps with—another *memory*—*carved seats for those who'd never be mistaken for Human. One wall was lit, its surface dancing with more carvings, with eyes and forms, and postures that were and weren't beautiful but which*—another—*must have meaning to a different kind of mind.*

Here—another—*purpose. Here. Stand here, and whispers lift to the farthest corner, heard as if spoken by the one next to you. Whatever had been here, made this, had spoken, and listened. Commonality. A place to start understanding.*

All this, buried and ignored. Not of interest or value— another *memory*—*an old door, an older passage, then, all alone, a wall fell away.*

To reveal what flooded a young mind with the thrill of the past . . .

Peace settled around the memories. *Happiness.* It had been the best time of his life. This was his Yena. His canopy.

Aryl watched the memories transform his face: how the jaw lost its taut line, the eyes softened, then closed. She waited until he breathed more easily, more and more slowly.

And when she was sure Marcus Bowman had forgotten everything else, when there was no more pain or awareness, when he believed himself back *there* and had no sense of here or her, Aryl swept her knife clean and deep across his throat.

Chapter 14

BELLS RANG FOR THE DEAD. Aryl listened, but heard only the rustle of a blanket and the lap of water against the platform.

What was a Cloisters made of? she wondered idly. Not metal. Not wood. Another question of so many she'd meant to ask him.

Not Om'ray, not M'hiray, to linger by an empty husk, to lay her cheek against cold flesh, her hair still over her face. Was it something a Human might do, being unable to *sense* the disappearance of self?

Another unaskable question.

Aryl. Her mother's mindvoice. Her presence. Waiting.

Questions. Questions. Lacking bells, she picked one. *Why is his loss the hardest?*

Because it is. Grief adds to grief, Daughter, like the weight of vines on a rastis. His is not one loss. It's every one. Your father and brother. The Yena UnChosen. Seru's father. The Tuana. Myris and Ael. It's every grief you've known. It's every grief you know will come.

Not every rastis endured. Yena knew it. Add any weakness, be it damage from crawlers or rot, to the weight of vines? A canopy giant would bend to the M'hir Wind . . . and fall. Killing everything that lived within its fronds.

A warning to heed, for the life inside her, for the mind Joined to hers, for everyone she cared about. Aryl found herself sitting up. *I am not weak.* To herself as much as Taisal.

You never will be. Which is why we depend on you, Daughter. A burst of *warmth,* quickly replaced by *urgency. Are you ready? It's almost time.*

Aryl rose to her feet. "Yes."

She turned from the Human's husk and walked outside.

And found Naryn.

She stood alone, half shadowed by the wall of crates. Her hands were at her sides. Her hair, free of any restraint, had confined itself in a coil around her neck. Red, like blood.

Naryn, here's Aryl! She can help! Beneath Anaj's mindvoice surged *desperation. Aryl, something's wrong.*

Aryl couldn't move. She didn't dare. Rage choked her. Blinded her. Naryn had betrayed Marcus.

Hadn't they all?

Those who'd come in their starship to kill and destroy. Those who'd taken his trust and tried to steal his life's work. His friends. Who hadn't failed him?

Aryl. LISTEN! You have to help Naryn.

Who didn't move. Perhaps didn't dare. The edge was that close, Aryl thought with her own desperation. If either of them moved, there'd be no stopping—

FOOL! Harsh, with all the Power and fury of a full Adept. Aryl gasped at the impact, her thoughts scattered. *The Human was no victim, not in this. It was his will to be scanned. He told Enris you were wrong. Insisted it be done for the good of the M'hiray. For your good.*

"He was out of his mind!" Aryl couldn't take her fingers from her longknife. "He was dying!"

Naryn had to hear, but there was no change in her face,

cut in half by light. Her visible eye gazed into the distance, glittered blue with the lake's reflection. It was as if Aryl wasn't there at all.

Dying, he made more sense than the entire Council. Don't waste his courage.

"Why are you here?" She'd begged Enris to take Naryn away, to keep her away.

Because we need you! Naryn's trapped in the Human's memories. You have to help. It's your fault, Aryl di Sarc. You pulled them apart. What were you thinking?

"I wanted to kill you."

And almost killed your Chosen, Anaj chided. *What good would that have done, I ask? Bad as a Xrona, hands first and head second, if you use heads at all. Help Naryn out of this tangle. Or will you waste what Marcus Bowman suffered to give us?*

Stung, Aryl opened her mouth to protest, then abruptly closed it.

She knew better than anyone the Human's ability to persuade others, to convince them the very world wasn't what they believed. She knew his courage.

Enris and Naryn would have worried not only about harm to Marcus, but about her reaction.

Which, she flushed, came close to as thoughtlessly violent as the Old Adept said.

I am a fool, Anaj.

Yes. But apologize later, with an undercurrent of *fear* Aryl couldn't ignore. Whatever held Naryn in this state, it was beyond the Old Adept's ability.

Hopefully not beyond hers. Aryl took Naryn's limp hand in hers and *reached* carefully, lowering her own shields. Nothing of Naryn blocked her way.

Nothing of Naryn could.

For her mind was *crowded*. Blurred faces, bodies pressed one to another, voices overlapping in confused shouts and whispers. Too many to count. Too many to exist. There couldn't be this many Humans in the world,

Aryl thought in horror. There wouldn't be enough air to breathe! Not only Humans. Other kinds of faces and bodies tumbled and oozed and insisted they be remembered.

ENOUGH! Aryl shouted. Somehow, she pressed them back, sent them *away!* They tattered and spread apart, like spray from a waterfall, to disappear into the depths.

Until a single form remained, standing alone. Before he could turn, before she had to see him again, Aryl retreated, rebuilding her shields.

"Aryl?" Sanity in Naryn's eyes at last. And an understandable caution.

"It's all right." Aryl threw her arms around her friend, who stiffened as if expecting to be thrown to the platform again by a maddened Yena. "It's all right." *You did what I couldn't have done,* she sent. *Marcus was right. Heart-kin.*

Arms crept around her, tentatively squeezed back.

Sorry about the hair, Aryl added.

You should be. Naryn pushed away, but gently. "He saw beyond the mountains, Aryl. I have those memories." She rested her hand on the crate wall. "And these." This with innocent wonder. "The Hoveny."

If she remembered that, but not the unsettling mass of Humans, Aryl decided, well enough. "We're needed," she said quietly, feeling Anaj's emphatic *agreement.* "But first—" she nodded to the shelter.

"He's gone, then." Naryn's hair loosened from her throat to hang in limp waves. She touched the bloodstain on Aryl's tunic. "You didn't kill him, heart-kin. We all did."

Together, they went into the shelter. Aryl wrapped his few belongings in the Human's Om'ray-shirt, and put that in his hands. All but the image disk. Answering an impulse she didn't try to name, she tucked the device in her pocket.

Then Naryn *pushed* the husk of Marcus Bowman, their friend, into the M'hir.

As the blanket slumped flat, Aryl concentrated . . .

The urgency she'd sensed from Taisal and Anaj was everywhere. When Aryl appeared in the Dream Chamber, she could feel it *pulse* against her shields. Urgency, but no panic. The minds around her brimmed with purpose and determination.

The M'hiray were leaving.

She'd gone first to the small room with their belongings to change clothes, careful to transfer Marcus' image disk to a safe pocket. Now, she needed Enris. He was here, her *inner* sense told her.

And he was.

Complete with an angry red line scoring his left cheek, every bit as long as the scar on Haxel's.

"About that—" Aryl began as he approached.

The rest was lost against his mouth. They held each other as if they'd been apart years instead of moments, emotions surging back and forth between their minds until they blurred into one, filled with *grief* and *sympathy . . . remorse* and *understanding. Love,* most of all.

When they finally moved apart, Enris regarded her somberly. "You told me Marcus could change the world with his words. And he did. He said there were no Tikitik or Oud beyond the mountains. No Om'ray. Aryl, he knew where we could go. He knew we should. We owe him whatever future we have."

"A future he died for."

Her Chosen's dark eyes held hers. "There are worse deaths than the hand of a friend. A very quick friend," he added with a slight shudder.

"You were there?"

"For all of it."

Aryl scowled. "Prying."

"Being the Chosen of Aryl di Sarc." The hint of a smile. "Something that requires extraordinary ability and courage."

He could add good reflexes, she thought. Without them, that slice would have been something far worse. Aryl leaned her forehead against his chest for an instant of mute apology, then stood back. "What happens now?"

"Like everyone else, we," Enris laid his arm over her shoulders, "must pack. The M'hiray are leaving. Before," with *regret,* "supper."

Within a tenth, they'd assembled in the Council Chamber. Anyone could 'port what they carried on their person, so every adult had bundles in their arms as well as packs on their backs. Children carried what they could manage. Those who could *push* through the M'hir stood beside the bulkier items that would be their responsibility. Baskets of food and seed. Gourds of fuel for oillights and cook stoves. Stacks of tools to work the soil. They'd plundered Sona.

Because they weren't coming back. That was the new Agreement. The M'hiray would leave Cersi and its Om'ray—its Oud and Tikitik—forever and seek a new life.

Aryl was reasonably sure none of them knew what that meant. She didn't. This would be a leap into the M'hir with no way to know its end. They had no other choice. She wasn't the only one with the taste of change souring her *inner* sense. Either they took this chance, or stayed to witness the devastation sure to come.

Haxel had sent scouts. They'd 'ported to Yena. To Rayna. Everywhere but Vyna. They came back quickly, gasped worrying reports. Tikitik weren't to be seen. Oud continued to trespass: throwing up their mounds, flying low over villages in their noisy air machines. While Om'ray—Om'ray waited, helpless, while their world prepared to change its shape again.

The M'hiray made what preparations they could. Most wore coats and boots. Knives and hooks hung from the belts of those who knew their use. Mostly. Aryl noticed a pair of Amna unChosen admiring the Yena longknives they carried. "Those will remove fingers," she said as she passed by, "before you feel the cut."

"You didn't tell me that," Enris complained.

"Because you're 'extraordinary'," she reminded him and smiled at his *smug*.

Extraordinary was the sight awaiting them. The dais had been transformed. The chairs were gone, replaced by a smooth pillar of green taller than those beside it. Sian and Taisal. Oran and Naryn. The other Councillors were on the floor like the rest, complete with their burdens.

A tidy stack of familiar white crates were to one side. Worin and Fon stood self-consciously in their midst, hands on the nearest. Aryl slowed, scowled. "Why are the artifacts here?"

"They're too dangerous to leave behind. I did suggest sending them to the Vyna." Enris shrugged. "But no one listened."

Better still, Aryl thought, drop them in the M'hir. Not something she'd say aloud. She'd felt a stir of *resentment* when the others heard Naryn had *pushed* the Human's husk into the M'hir. As if the M'hir, no matter how dark or perilous, belonged to the M'hiray.

A foolish attitude, in her opinion. As well claim the sky and air. But with minds and tempers barely holding to calm, she'd no wish to stir an argument.

Enris gave her a quick kiss. "See you over the mountain. I'm to help Worin and Fon."

"But—" Taisal beckoned, so Aryl gathered her dignity. She didn't need to hold her Chosen's hand to feel his presence. Though, she thought wistfully, it would be nice. "See you soon," she finished. *Be careful.*

You, too.

Aryl stepped up on the dais. "The Maker," her mother said, gesturing to the featureless pillar.

It didn't look like much.

Though this close, Aryl saw it wasn't green—or was more than green. Colors played in its depths, subtle dark strokes that flickered and moved, brighter spots that pulsed like beating hearts.

Not hearts. She stepped back, startled. "It's a machine."

Sian gestured agreement. He seemed, Aryl thought numbly, to take all this as normal. "To use the Maker on one mind," he explained, *sending* the words through the M'hir to everyone, "it's left in its room. But as you can see," he pointed to the base, "it is also meant to be used here."

The base fit neatly into a depression in the dais, one that hadn't been there before. Or had it? She'd thought the differently textured shapes on the dais floor to be decoration. If each sank down to receive . . . *something* . . . what else could "fit" here?

And why?

Questions again. Meaningless ones. If there were no Om'ray where they were going, there'd be no Cloisters or "Makers." Aryl found she liked that thought.

"Is it time?" Taisal asked.

A *flow* of *assent.* They were willing.

Emotions flowed. Aryl felt suspended in *courage* and *determination.* The M'hiray sought a future. They sought to preserve those they would leave behind.

However they'd come to this, she'd never been so proud of her Clan.

Hear me. Anaj. *We don't know the full consequence of using the Maker.*

Understandable, Aryl thought wryly, if Adepts had only used it before killing those of damaged mind.

The Oldest Adept of all continued. *Our connection as Om'ray does more than define the shape of the world and where we are within it. It holds our names, for those who can read them. It holds our past, for only those minds we've touched do we remember as* real. *Once the Maker breaks that connection, we don't know what will be left.*

"The M'hir. It will stay," Oran said firmly. "The M'hir will keep our Clan together and take us where we must be."

Admirable confidence. Aryl wished she shared it. Though to Oran's credit, she was Sona's Keeper. She could be trying to encourage all those looking up at them.

Or herself.

M'hiray. Lower your shields and trust your Council. No matter what happens, wait for the locate. Go together to the future!

TOGETHER!

Naryn stepped forward, head high, face and hair perfectly composed. Her shields were impenetrable. "We will not forget the gift of Marcus Bowman to the M'hiray," she announced, then looked to Aryl. "I will need your help with the Human's memories."

Aryl nodded. His gesture.

Sian spoke next. "The two of you will choose where we will go. When you have the locate, hold that image. Oran, Anaj, and I will add our strength so all will *share* it. We 'port when—" he faltered. For some reason, he looked at Taisal.

Who finished smoothly, "—when the Maker completes its task and we are free." She turned gracefully and lifted her hands to the pillar.

"Wait." Aryl heard the word before she realized she'd said it, before she knew why.

Taisal glanced over her shoulder and smiled the most beautiful smile. *I did, Daughter. I waited for you to become who you are, who our people need. I need wait no longer.* "Don't let them fall."

She couldn't move, couldn't think. *Mother . . .*

A hand took hers. *An Adept must control the Maker.*

The locate, heart-kin. They're waiting. Naryn dropped her shields. Sent image after image of rock and water and empty spaces.

MOTHER! You can come with us!

"Then who'd pull up the ladder?"

Taisal di Sarc pressed her hands to the Maker and it began to glow. Brighter and brighter and brighter. Until . . .

. . . *the world flowed away,*
       Om'ray became as sand,
              and there opened a rift in the sky . . .

All she could hear was a voice. *The locate . . . Aryl . . . where do we go* . . .

All she could see was rock and water and strange twisted growths like bone . . . rock, water, bone . . . over everything crawled numbers and lines . . . *Site report 58323 . . . Site report 58324 . . . Site report 58325* . . . rock and water and growing bone . . . numbers and lines . . . rocks . . .

. . . *none of it was* real.

More voices. *Where do we go . . . ? Where can we go? DESPAIR.*

No more despair. She wanted peace. And happiness. Anything familiar. She *reached* with all her strength and will . . .

And there it was.

Lights hanging from wires. Lights attached to walls. Lights on poles. A vast space, angled and rising away in polished steps. Steps with carved seats . . . a wall danced . . . more carvings, with eyes and forms, and postures that were and weren't beautiful but which had meaning to a different kind of mind.

Happiness.

Peace.

Safe.

Aryl di Sarc poured Power into that image, felt others do the same, felt *confusion* become *purpose*.

With the others of her kind, she concentrated and let the M'hir take her . . .

... a bracelet turned around and around,
    became rock etched by water,
        became metal again and turned. . . .

As the M'hiray disappeared, Watchers roused to follow, became voice and force and purpose.

... While a mind became voice,
    Daughter,
        to be lost on the wind ...

Epilogue

THE M'HIR WIND BEGAN out of sight, out of mind. It stirred first where baked sand met restless surf. It became fitful and petulant as it passed over the barrens, moving dunes and scouring stone. Sometimes it sighed and curled back on itself, as if absentminded. But it never stilled.

It only grew.

It roared over the mountains and brought Sona a storm of hot, dry dust. Ditches hid their moisture beneath pebbles. Low walls and sturdy buildings protected the fields. But the harvest spoiled on stems and rotted in the ground.

The M'hir gave thunderous voice to Yena's Watchers. But no one danced among the rastis groves or lifted gleaming hooks to the sky. Dresel flew free on its wings, the prize of wastryls.

Cersi was not to change.

Everything had.

The Om'ray of Cersi

(Note: Names shown as first encountered in this book.)

SONA CLAN:
  Ael sud Sarc (Chosen of Myris, once Yena)
  Anaj di Kathel (Adept)
  Aryl Sarc (Speaker, once Yena)
  Beko Mendolar (once Tuana)
  Bern sud Caraat (Chosen of Oran, once Yena and Grona)
  Cader Sarc (once Yena)
  Caynen S'udlaat (once Tuana)
  Cetto sud Teerac (Chosen of Husni, once Councilor of Yena)
  Chaun sud Teerac (Chosen of Weth, once Yena)
  Cien Serona (Ezgi's mother, once Runner of Tuana)
  Deran Edut (Kor's brother, once Tuana)
  Enris sud Sarc (Chosen of Aryl, Worin's brother, once Tuana)
  Ezgi sud Parth (Chosen of Seru, once Runner of Tuana)
  Fon Kessa'at (Son of Veca, once Yena)
  Galen sud Serona (Chosen of Cien, Jorg's brother, once Runner of Tuana)
  Gijs sud Vendan (Chosen of Juo, once Yena)

Haxel Vendan (First Scout, once Yena)
Hoyon d'sud Gethen (Adept, Chosen of Oswa, once Grona)
Husni Teerac (once Yena)
Josel Licor (Netta's sister, once Runner of Tuana)
Juo Vendan (once Yena)
Kayd Uruus (Son of Taen, Ziba's brother, once Tuana)
Kor sud Lorimar (Chosen of Menasel, Deran's brother, once Tuana)
Kran Caraat (Oran's brother, once Grona)
Kynan d'sud Kathel (Chosen of Anaj)
Lendin sud Kessa'at (Chosen of Morla, once Yena)
Lymin Annk (once Runner of Tuana)
Mauro Lorimar (Irm's brother, Menasel's cousin, once Tuana)
Menasel Lorimar (Mauro's cousin, once Tuana)
Morla Kessa'at (once Councillor of Yena)
Myris Sarc (Taisal's sister, once Yena)
Naryn S'udlaat (once Tuana)
Netta Licor (Josel's sister, once Runner of Tuana)
Oswa Gethen (Yao's mother, once Grona)
Oran di Caraat (Adept, once Grona)
Rorn sud Vendan (Chosen of Haxel, once Yena)
Seru Parth (Birth Watcher, Aryl's cousin, once Yena)
Stryn Licor (Josel and Netta's mother, once Runner of Tuana)
Suen sud Annk (Chosen of Lymin, once Runner of Tuana)
Syb sud Uruus (Kayd and Ziba's father, Chosen of Taen, once Yena)
Taen Uruus (Kayd and Ziba's mother, once Yena)
Tai sud Licor (Chosen of Stryn, once Runner of Tuana)
Tilip sud Kessa'at (Fon's father, Chosen of Veca, once of Yena)
Veca Kessa'at (Fon's mother, once of Yena)
Weth Teerac (Looker, once of Yena)

Worin Mendolar (Enris' brother, once of Tuana)
Yao Gethen (Daughter of Oswa, once of Grona)
Yuhas sud S'udlaat (Chosen of Caynen, once of Yena
and Tuana)
Ziba Uruus (Daughter of Taen, once of Yena)

YENA CLAN:

Adrius sud Parth (Member of Yena Council)
Alejo Parth (Seru's brother)
Andace Vendan
Barit sud Teerac (Bern's father, Chosen of Evra)
Costa sud Teerac (Aryl's brother, Chosen of Leri)
Dalris sud Sarc (Taisal's grandfather, Unnel's father,
Chosen of Nela)
Ele Sarc
Evra Teerac (Bern's mother)
Ferna Parth (Seru's mother)
Ghoch sud Sarc (Chosen of Oryl)
Joyn Uruus (Son of Rimis)
Kiric Mendolar (Brother of Enris, Once Tuana)
Leri Teerac
Mele sud Sarc (Aryl's father, Chosen of Taisal)
Nela Sarc (Taisal's grandmother)
Oryl Sarc
Pio di Kessa'at (Adept)
Rimis Uruus (Joyn's mother)
Sian d'sud Vendan (Adept, Member of Yena
Council)
Taisal di Sarc (Aryl's mother, Adept, Speaker for
Yena)
Tikva di Uruus (Adept, Member of Yena Council)
Till sud Parth (Seru's father, Scout, Chosen of
Ferna)
Troa sud Uruus (Joyn's father, Chosen of Rimis)
Unnel Sarc (Taisal's mother)
Yorl sud Sarc (Taisal's great uncle, Member of Yena
Council)

TUANA CLAN:

Clor sud Mendolar (Enris' uncle, once of Amna)
Dama Mendolar (Ridersel's mother, Member of Tuana Council)
Eran Serona
Eryel S'udlaat
Gelle Licor
Geter Licor
Irm Lorimar (Mauro's brother)
Jorg sud Mendolar (Enris' father, Chosen of Ridersel)
Mia d'sud Serona (Adept, once Amna)
Mirs sud S'udlaat (Chosen of Eryel)
Olalla Mendolar (Enris' cousin)
Ral Serona (Enris' cousin)
Ridersel Mendolar (Enris' mother)
Ruis di Mendolar (Adept)
Sive sud Lorimar
Sole sud Serona (Speaker for Tuana)
Traud Licor
Tyko Uruus

GRONA CLAN:

Cyor sud Kaar (Member of Grona Council)
Efris Ducan (Member of Grona Council, Grona Speaker)
Emyam sud Caraat (Member of Grona Council)
Gura Azar (Member of Grona Council)
Lier Haon (Member of Grona Council)
Mysk Gethen (Member of Grona Council)

VYNA CLAN:

Etleka Vyna
Daryouch Vyna
Fikryya Vyna
Jenemir Vyna

Nabrialan Vyna
Tarerea Vyna (High Councillor)

OTHER CLANS:
Dann d'sud Friesnen (Adept, Pana)
Gur di Sawnda'at (Adept, Rayna)
Karne d'sud Witthun (Adept, Rayna)

Strangers of Cersi

An Tsessas (Archivist Second Class, Undetermined)
Artrul (Triad First, Site One, Undetermined)
Janex Jymbobobii (Triad Third, Site One, Carasian)
Josen (Triad Second replacement, Site Four, Undetermined)
Marcus Bowman (Triad First, Site One, then Four, Human)
Meen (Triad Third replacement, Site Four, Undetermined)
P'tr sit 'Nix (Pilot, Site Two, Tolian)
Pilip (Triad Second, Site One, Trant)
Tomas Vogt (Archivist Second Class, Undetermined)
Tyler Henshaw (Triad First, Site Two, Human)

Stonerim III

Prelude

A FIVE-FINGERED HAND, thick and spotted with age, brushed over plas sheets, tipped a mem-cube on its side, then turned palm up. "That's it?"

"Yes. Everything portable was gone. We searched for remains with orbital scanners and midlevel vidbots with no success. We're contacting next of kin based on staff records. Members of an indigenous population, the—" a slim, delicately scaled finger tapped a screen, "—the Oud, may have been involved although there's—ah—distinct possibility of scavengers. You saw the last annual report, I'm sure."

"No ground search."

"The Oud revoked permission for any offworld presence. It may be tied to an unanticipated territoriality. They're expanding at the expense of the other sapients, despite what early surveys described as peaceful coexistence." A pause. "In my professional opinion, the situation's unstable. Even with intervention by the First, I'm sure the planet will be closed in the next vote. This quadrant is still more Commonwealth than Trade Pact."

"The find?"

"There's no proof. Bowman played it close. He could, with his reputation. The funding committee did request a presentation next month, but expansion to a priority site and additional security was a given. For what, now becomes the question. Instead of supposedly productive excavations, we found landslides and sinkholes."

One thick finger pinned a plas sheet and jerked it free of the rest. "And explosive residue. Your thoughts."

"I couldn't speculate—"

The hand turned palm up.

"As you wish. The residue was inconsistent with local technologies, implying offworld origin. We recovered a handful of observation 'bots. They'd been shut down before any disruption. The authorization code was Bowman's. I regret to say there could be a connection."

"Elaborate."

"It wouldn't be the first time a field researcher found a more lucrative market for his work. As for the result? Deals go badly. They might have been surprised or met more than expected resistance onsite. My speculation, with your indulgence, is that considering the rarity of confirmed Hoveny relics, the goods weren't as advertised. Bowman could have used his reputation to entice a buyer who wasn't fooled by fakes."

"Murder and fraud. Serious accusations."

"Speculations. There is, of course, no proof." Scaled fingers met at their tips. "Other than Bowman's own report of being contacted by a representative of the Deneb Blues, which raises questions. Among them, why would a prominent criminal organization approach him, of all the researchers based out of this facility? And was his report sincere, or a clever attempt to throw off suspicion in case they'd been observed?"

"Insufficient."

"There is also the matter of his more recent reports. After the—accident—that killed the rest of his initial Triad, Bowman began encrypting all raw data, including vids. His submitted reports since have consisted of summaries and analyses. The support materials we have on file are inaccessible."

"Not unusual."

"Indeed not. Despite the First's impeccable security, many Triads keep their findings private until they are ready to share them. Still, for Bowman, this was a change in habit. Changes have reasons."

The flat of the thick hand swept the mem-cube aside as if offended. Dozens littered the long beige table. More waited in their racks. Potential finds, urgent demands, chances for glory, fool's hopes. "Enough of Cersi. The First has a lifetime's worth of stable worlds with as good or better indicators."

"No investigation? Surely we must tell the next-of-kin what happened."

An impatient wave. "Send out the standard condolences, hazards of pushing the boundaries of science, the First assumes no responsibility, et cetera." A finger tapped the table. "Inform the appropriate authorities the First considers Marcus Bowman a being of interest in the destruction of Triad sites and the murder of offworld personnel. See that Bowman's materials, encrypted or otherwise, are sealed, pending any internal review of the matter. Liquidate any assets and transfer to this office."

Slim scaled fingers collected the sheets and mem-cube. "I'll see to it personally."

"Next planet."

"No ss-sign of the artifactss-s?"

Slim, scaled fingers curled around a stem, lifted the preserved flower, held it to the light. Crystals lined each petal, sparkled like gems. "I have no explanation." A mauve tongue fastidiously removed a single crystal, brought it between nonexistent lips, waited for it to dissolve. The tongue's owner gave a delicate shiver as the sugar hit its bloodstream. "An excellent harvest. A shame you can't appreciate such flavors."

"A ss-scam is unlikely. Thossse we work with unders-stand the cons-ssequence."

"It's possible the information was flawed. Or Bowman suspected. He worked alone most of the past year, refused extra staffing of the new site. Our contacts put it down to a pretty local he'd taken an interest in, but . . ." another crystal, another shiver, ". . . but the Human may not have been the fool we hoped."

"If he ss-stole from us-ss, he was-ss!" Drops of black spittle landed on the vase of waiting flowers, drops that sizzled and spit and left holes behind. The stems bent, the flowers shriveled.

"Why don't I order another round?"

Chapter 1

. . .SHE TOOK A STARTLED BREATH, heard others do the same. From above, beside, below. Sighs afloat in darkness.

The air in her mouth was warm and dry and tasted of dust. A word settled in her mind, an awareness bathed in peace and happiness.

Home.

The skin of her hand cooled as fingers fell away from hers.

Hold still!

Curiosity stirred. Why?

A cough, not hers, quickly stifled.

A shuffle. Something fell and shattered.

Hold!

She obeyed the thought. She waited for more, hoped for sense.

There. There's light.

Light? She blinked to be sure her eyes were open, then turned her head slowly to find it. When she did, she blinked again to be sure.

Not much. Distant, like the gleam of a star through leaves. Below, far below where she stood. For she was standing. Steady, without flicker.

Don't move until I turn on the mains.

That couldn't have been her thought. Could it? Self became a new curiosity; she contorted her face, yawned wide, then pursed her lips. Rolled her head on her neck. Moved her shoulders and discovered weight on her back. Darkness pressed everywhere against her skin, soothing and close, except for the tiny gleam.

Except for the sounds of breathing, she might have been alone.

Breathing and now steps. Fumbling steps with frequent hesitations. The brush of fabric along a rough surface.

She tilted her head, tracking whoever moved with so little care. Step, brush, step. Until the sounds become fainter than her breath, so she must hold it to follow.

I'm at the panel! Shut your eyes.

She obeyed, then flinched at the dazzling brightness that spotted her closed eyelids, flinched but opened them as soon as she could bear it. Gasps of indrawn breath echoed her own.

"Hold still" had been excellent advice, for she stood on a ledge, one of many, one of—a glance up—the highest. At her feet, more and more ledges descended; they shortened and converged, like a three-sided staircase too large and awkward for use, scarred surfaces littered with crumbled debris and ash. Opposite, three facing walls, not as wide, similarly angled. Centered at the bottom, where the dim light had been, was a flat area covered in neatly separated stacks of—something.

Above was a pool of deep shadow. Where its edges met light, the darkness pulled away from shapes carved into the walls, shapes she didn't know, one supporting another all the way down, until they seemed not walls but crowds of watchers eagerly looking back at her.

At them. She wasn't alone. The lights—hanging, leaning, everywhere lights—shone on figures shaped like her. They stood on ledges, amid debris, looking as startled by the bags in their hands as they were to be . . .

Where?

Abruptly, *where* didn't matter as much as *who*. A visceral shock, the need to *know* one another again, a need more necessary than her next dusty breath. She joined the mutual *reach* for identity through the M'hir. Identity and *connection*.

There . . . Chosen to Chosen.

There . . . baby to mother, children to parents.

There . . . as more subtle connections overlapped the rest: family, heart-kin, friendship . . .

Above all, Power. Within the M'hir, the Watchers remained silent as the lesser M'hiray slipped aside while the stronger held their place, a natural sorting without word or conscious thought. And once they *knew* one another . . .

Everything became *real*.

Aryl di Sarc shuddered back to herself. *Enris!?* All around, a general shifting as everyone set aside burdens and hurried to be with their Chosen and family.

Here. Always. He was at her side that quickly. They touched each other with trembling hands. She worried at the angry scratch down his cheek, then forgot as their lips met.

Enris pulled away and smiled. Then, with growing wonder as he looked around. "Here being where, exactly!"

"Aryl!" A small figure jumped from ledge to ledge toward her. "We did it!" Yao di Gethen thudded into Aryl's hastily raised arms. "We did it! We're here!"

The next question. Aryl put the child down, tugged a curl gently. "Yao. Do you know where we are?"

"No," with a child's equanimity. "But it's not where we were. That's what everyone wanted, wasn't it? To go far?"

"It was." Another figure approached, one ledge below. "A new life, for all M'hiray. Welcome, Aryl! Enris!" Golden hair rose in a joyous cloud.

"Oran." Her heart-kin's Chosen. Aryl smiled a warm greeting, feeling better by the moment. "And Bern?"

"Here." From above.

Enris crouched by Yao to point. "There's your father." Hoyon d'sud Gethen was hurrying in their direction. Yao gave a happy cry and ran to meet him.

"Any idea where we are?" This to Oran and Bern as well as Aryl.

"Council will know." Bern shrugged. "The main thing is we're all here and safe."

Oran went to Enris. "Let me fix that," with a Healer's insistence.

"Nothing wrong with an impressive scar," he protested with a grin. Oran tsked at him before laying her hand on his cheek. She took great pride in her Talent. There'd be no scar, impressive or otherwise.

They were together and safe, Aryl thought, content, but where? She knew this place, she realized suddenly. Or a version of it. The lowermost carvings shouldn't be smeared with colors and black soot. None should be chipped away. The ledges were empty of all but refuse, but there should be—seats, she remembered triumphantly. Seats, oddly shaped seats, lining every ledge. The ledges should be polished.

Her content faded. How could she remember this, and nothing of *where* they were?

"What's Naryn doing?"

Enris wasn't the only one to notice the Chosen who'd left everyone else to walk to the flat area at the foot of the walls. Conversations quieted.

After peering into the nearest stack, and taking a quick step away, Naryn turned to face them.

"Welcome to Stonerim III." The words were as clear as if the other stood beside her.

That name ... Aryl's brief sense of familiarity was washed away by the flood of *confusion* and *dismay* from those around her. "Where is that?" "What kind of place is this?" More shouts. "How do we get out?!" "We're trapped!"

Hush! The same mindvoice that had held them still in

the dark, that had kept them safe until she turned on the lights. Lights she'd known were there. Because Naryn di S'udlaat knew this place.

She'd led them here.

Hadn't she?

The others calmed. Aryl's own uncertainty faded as Naryn continued to speak. "We aren't trapped. We're in Norval, the Layered City, on the highest of the pre-Arrival layers. This place—locals call it the Buried Theater. There's access to the surface." At this, a stir of *eagerness* traveled mind-to-mind. "Not yet. We can't leave until we're ready."

They couldn't stay. Why had she felt at peace here, in this ruin? What could possibly make a M'hiray happy here? Aryl controlled her impatience. Naryn was right. To rush into the unknown made no sense either.

A second figure dropped easily from ledge to ledge to join Naryn. Haxel di Vendan. Why the "di?" Aryl wondered. Her Power was less. She dismissed the puzzle. Power was a matter for Council, not ordinary Chosen.

"Naryn is right," Haxel said. "Scouts will go ahead, find a safe locate for the rest. Before that, let's get belongings and supplies on the highest ledge, at the back where they won't be easily seen."

No one moved.

Naryn's hair rose and snapped. "Do as Haxel says. She's First Scout of the M'hiray and responsible for your safety."

Shouldn't the full Council take charge? Enris sent privately, as they gathered their packs and climbed to the top with the others. *Why is Naryn giving orders? And why are we listening to them?*

Aryl met her Chosen's dark eyes. "Naryn knows what's outside this place."

"We don't. Why?"

It wasn't just outside they didn't know, she realized, feeling her heart pound. "Where did we come from?"

"From our home—" She watched Enris struggle to

find more to say, then give up. "We had to leave," he said at last, frowning in earnest. "I'm sure of that. For the good of everyone."

"We were better than the others," Oran offered. "More powerful. We didn't need them anymore, so they made us leave."

"If we were more powerful," countered Aryl, "how could they make us do anything?"

Bern chuckled. "Then we must have wanted to go. Home was too small for the M'hiray. We wanted something better." Oran smiled at him.

Aryl felt . . . doubt. She couldn't explain it. The words were right. They'd had to leave. They hoped for better.

They weren't the only ones speculating, Aryl noticed. Heads were bent in conversation, verbal or silent, as the others climbed with their burdens.

Enris. What do you remember?

Remember? His foot caught a loose bit of stone and he stumbled, a too-large pack not helping matters.

Aryl shoved the pack hard with her shoulder to restore his balance. "Careful!"

"You, too."

"I—" Aryl closed her mouth. After a look ahead for the best route, she could have run to the top with her eyes closed. Most of the others moved with excessive care, helped one another, lifted awkward bundles together; a few leaped from ledge to ledge with fluid grace. Why?

The reason slipped away, like the memory of a dream.

Enris paused and scuffed his boot toe where a seat had been attached then chipped away. "I remember this place being in better shape." With a tinge of *unease.* "How can that be?"

"It's been a while since Naryn was here, that's all," Oran explained easily, taking Bern's hand to help her to the next ledge. She didn't, Aryl observed, climb well. "If time mattered to a locate, we'd never arrive where we wanted to go. What's important is that she's familiar with all this—the lights, what's above. After such a long 'port, I'm just relieved we aren't confused."

"You aren't?" Enris gave his deep laugh. "Bern, you picked the right Chooser." But afterward, he looked at Aryl, as if his own words made him unsure.

As if, Aryl thought, dry-mouthed, he'd remembered a dream too.

"I'll be fine," Weth di Teerac protested, white hair straining its net. The blindfold across her tan face was no hindrance; a Looker could move effortlessly using her visual memory of a place. Which was the problem. Like all the M'hiray, Weth remembered the Buried Theater as it had been. To one with her Talent, the change from the memory of the locate was too sudden. Her hands clenched her belt to stop their trembling, but she fooled no one. She'd need time to recover.

"We've enough scouts," Haxel repeated, from her tone expecting no argument. "I want you ready when we all go."

For someone of so little Power, Aryl thought with admiration, the First Scout managed a fine air of authority over those who did.

Twenty groups of scouts waited, each containing one or more with Power sufficient to *reach* through the M'hir to the rest, all able to 'port back here to safety in need. The groups were small in number, none more than ten. They were to learn what they could about the city Naryn claimed lay above them. And find a way out for those who'd wait here.

To Aryl's surprise, she'd been one of the five Haxel selected to accompany Naryn, who would go first. Not a surprise, her Chosen stood nearby, clearly intending to be the sixth. Which he wouldn't be, she decided with exasperation, if he continued to poke his finger between the small bars to annoy those inside. "They probably bite," she warned him under her breath. Again.

"Haven't yet," he replied, bending in a vain effort to see what moved within the shadows. The stacks on the flat area had turned out to be full of something alive. Many small and lumpy somethings, that rattled when disturbed.

As they were now. *Enris!*

It got me! He sprang violently back, clutching his right hand, then held up only three fingers. When she gasped, he grinned at her and lifted the fourth, wiggling all of them. "See?"

"I see I'll have two children to raise," Aryl snapped back, but the corners of her mouth twitched. "You're as bad as . . ." The vague sense of a name slipped away. "Bad," she finished and pretended to pay more attention to the creatures than her Chosen.

They entertained Enris; they disturbed her. It wasn't the potent smell, or potential to lose her Chosen's fingers, but what the crates meant. The right height and no higher, they'd been designed for this use, with slots for air and light too narrow to allow the rattlers to escape. Each crate was wider than her outstretched arms, twice that in length, and every one full of moving little lumps.

Seventeen stacks, each ten crates high. A large number of still-vigorous creatures, with no sign of food or water. Left with a small light.

They hadn't been here long, Aryl said to herself, growing alert. They wouldn't be left for long either. "Haxel."

The First Scout looked her way.

Aryl nodded to the nearest stack. "Someone's going to come for these."

"Naryn?"

The Chosen gestured apology to the other Councillors before she walked over to Haxel. "What is it?"

"These." Haxel jerked her thumb at the rattlers.

"Someone's property. Aryl thinks this is temporary storage and I agree. The owners will be back."

Naryn's nose wrinkled. "*Offworld* vermin."

" 'Offworld?' "

"Not native to Stonerim III," the other clarified. "From another world."

"Like us." Enris looked inordinately pleased. "We're offworlders."

As if they didn't belong anywhere.

Aryl decided to ignore words she didn't like. "Only one door," she said. Something else she didn't like. Hundreds of M'hiray, presently waiting more or less patiently with their families, sharing the supplies they'd brought, the crude sanitation of a deep hole surrounded by a blanket, a hole from its stench, used by others for the same purpose.

To get their people out on foot would be time-consuming. To 'port out, they must have a locate.

Another reason to scout quickly.

Another reason *doubt* shivered down her spine.

Why come here, to such an unsuitable place? Not even their Council could explain it.

"We can't delay any longer." Haxel looked at Naryn. "You know it."

"I know. My fellow Councillors have a great many questions." For the first time, Naryn looked weary. "More than I have answers." Her hand sought the swelling beneath her tunic, as if for comfort.

Maybe she could *hear* her baby. Aryl's was a still-silent presence, a sparkling *glow* in the M'hir. "Seru said our babies are fine."

"Yes. She did." Naryn's eyes met Aryl's. For a heartbeat, there was such aching loss in their depths Aryl instinctively *reached* for the other, only to be rebuffed by impenetrable shields. Then it was gone. A lifted eyebrow. "I'll tell Council questions can wait."

"We go up?" Enris countered Haxel's quelling scowl

with his boldest grin. Aryl shook her head. The First Scout might as well surrender.

Coming to the same conclusion, Haxel curved her lips in what wasn't necessarily a smile.

"We go up."

Aryl ran curious fingers over the dusty stone, freed a chunk of lighter crumbly stuff to toss thoughtfully into a corner. This jagged tear in one wall wasn't the entrance intended by the long-dead builders of the Buried Theater, but Naryn remembered nothing else. They'd seen no sign of another passage.

There were, however, abundant and troubling signs this one was in regular use, putting Syb and Haxel in the lead, despite Naryn's knowledge. She came next, with Enris, while Aryl and Veca followed behind.

Veca wasn't happy. "No side corridors."

"None yet," Aryl replied, feeling the same. No way to avoid a confrontation—or slip aside and strike from behind.

Though why she'd thought of that strategy . . . Aryl shook her head.

Bright enough. Naryn had pressed a sequence of numbers into a box jammed between two stones, activating a series of small lights, themselves stuck in cracks or hanging from wires. The passage itself was hard packed dirt, with dirt and stone walls, and a ceiling that, though propped up by supports, showered dirt and dust at random.

Not the way to build things, Aryl decided, glad when Haxel picked up the pace.

They hadn't gone far when the passage made a sharp turn. Beyond were none of the small lights, but after a moment, Aryl's eyes adjusted and she could make out a rectangular glow ahead. They eased forward until they stood under what was the outline of a door.

In the ceiling.

Anyone bring a ladder?

Syb chuckled at Enris' plaintive sending. *We brought you.*

Sending instead of speech. Aryl approved. A closed door could hide any number of surprises, most likely unpleasant ones.

But this, Naryn remembered. "It's a *lift*," she informed them calmly. Silhouetted against the lights from the first portion of the passage, she slipped her hand *inside* the wall—Aryl rubbed her eyes—then grimaced as she felt around. "Substandard piece of—" Naryn muttered confusingly, then stood back with an exclamation of pleasure. "There."

The outlined section of ceiling lowered itself, spilling light and dust everywhere, and came to rest at their feet.

Haxel, who'd leaped aside, muttered something of her own as she returned to squint upward. "Good place for an ambush. Veca, wait here. Now, how do—" She fell silent as Naryn walked onto the piece of ceiling and gestured they should do the same.

Enris stepped on, grinning happily. One of them, Aryl thought grimly, should put sense ahead of adventure, but she followed her Chosen. Haxel and Syb drew their longknives as they did the same.

"Up," Naryn said.

And the section of ceiling rose into the air, carrying five M'hiray—one large—without effort. Aryl glanced down at Veca's dimly lit face, disappearing below, then resolutely faced where they were going.

The ceiling became floor, leaving them standing somewhere so different from the passage below, from anywhere she could imagine, that Aryl could hardly believe her eyes.

If not for the ceiling above, they might have stood out in the open, so vast was the space. The floor stretched, smooth and flat, away from the wall behind them. Wall?

It was more like the slanted side of a huge buttress root, but what could be above to need such support?

Root?

Aryl shook away the confusing image.

More isolated sections of slanted wall connected the floor and ceiling as far as she could see. Between, everywhere, immense pipes writhed like growths. White ones. Red ones. Black. Some narrow, some oval. Some looped up to a distant ceiling. Others flopped along the floor and headed in either direction as far as the eye could see.

They could see, Aryl realized, because one kind of pipe glowed. She stepped closer. The pipe was clear-sided; what produced the changeable bluish light was inside. And moving. Aryl averted her eyes quickly. What flowed within was more disturbing than this place.

"Maintenance Layer," Naryn informed them, and pointed left. "The next lift is over there."

"This one's the only access below?"

"To the theater, yes."

Haxel looked to have as many questions as she did, Aryl thought, but merely nodded. "Aryl. Call Karne, Galen, Bula, Josel, and Imi."

She nodded. An instant's concentration to send those names into the M'hir, less to find the five, and their groups, standing beside them. They looked around in awe, then focused on Haxel. "We're going that way," she pointed. "The rest of you fan out, look for a way to the next level. Naryn?"

Naryn used her hands to mark out a square. "Lifts are marked by a panel, this size. On a wall, or in the floor. Press it and the lift shows itself. You speak your command, up or down, to control it."

The others nodded.

"When you find one," Haxel took over, "check the next level. If it's promising, send for your next three groups and have them fan out. If not, keep going up on your own till you find something worth exploring. Understood? I don't want M'hiray scampering over each other or worse, being noticed. We need to see as much as we can, not take risks. Don't 'port where you could be seen. By anything."

Several looked uneasy at this. Karne d'sud Witthun among them. "What do you mean, 'anything'?"

"Stonerim III is more Commonwealth than Trade Pact," Naryn answered, making, in Aryl's opinion, no sense at all. "Most of the beings you'll encounter above will be Human. They look like M'hiray. But you'll see those who don't. Avoid conversations with either."

Haxel's scar gleamed white. "I'll want reports. Often."

Agreement. The scouts turned and left.

"Syb?" The First Scout turned to the grizzled Chosen. "Picked your spot?"

"Up there." His nod indicated a shadowed rise of gray pipe. He'd have a perfect view of anyone approaching the lift.

"Good."

Aryl nodded to herself. Haxel knew her people. If Veca and Syb couldn't stop would-be intruders—unlikely, but most of what was around them was unlikely—from here, they could 'port back to the others to deliver a warning and share the locate to this layer.

While she, Enris, and Naryn would receive the scout reports. Good news, she hoped.

Their own quiet footsteps were swallowed by the gurgle and thump of the pipes as Naryn led them across the floor to another slanted wall.

"Maintenance Layer," Enris commented. "So these carry water, heat, whatever's needed above us. Makes me wonder."

Aryl glanced at him. "Go on."

"What's above that could need so much?"

He didn't expect an answer.

Aryl wasn't sure she wanted one.

When they reached their destination, Naryn ran her hands over the featureless smooth wall, and gave a helpless shrug. "There should be a lift here. I thought there was. This is all—it didn't matter," with an odd desperation. "Only the theater mattered."

Aryl understood Haxel's somber expression, the *grim* that leaked through her shields. None of the other groups had found a lift yet. If Naryn's memory couldn't guide them ...

"We'll split up here. You try that way," the First Scout ordered, waving Enris right, Aryl left. "Make it quick," she added.

And careful, Aryl sent to her Chosen, who grinned back at her.

You, too.

Quick suited her. Aryl ran along the wall, eyes searching for a panel. When the wall ended, rather than follow it around, she sped to the next section, doing her best to ignore the sudden drafts of cold or blasts of heat when she passed under different pipes, listening for danger past the gurgle and occasionally loud thunks coming from the same source. Not a place for living things, she decided.

But living things were what she found.

Voices, ahead.

Avoiding one of the glowing pipes, Aryl veered into the shadow of a black one and crept closer. Closer. After a cautionary touch to be sure the metal wasn't of the too hot or too cold variety, she found a seam and eased herself on top.

There.

She grinned. Perfect.

Who needed a lift, when there were stairs?

Stairs currently in use by a raggedly dressed assortment of beings, some M'hiray-like—Human—others definitely not. The arrangement of poles and steps appeared solid, if clumsily built.

And not, she guessed, supposed to be here.

The beings had attached a cluster of small tubes to a yellow pipe's lower loop using some kind of disk. The tubes led to a droning machine that spewed forth a white liquid the beings were collecting in a variety of containers with every indication of delighted greed. Full containers were being carried up the stairs, while others carried down what Aryl presumed were empty ones to fill.

One tripped, its container spilling on the floor.

"That's outta your share!" shouted a Human near the machine.

The sloppy individual lifted its container. "Lemme refill. There's plenty."

"Get greedy and you'll get gone, my friend. Think this is a perm-tap? Them as work for Grandies will be down sooner than not. We'll all be locked then, won't we."

"I've a family—"

"Who don't need juice? Ack. Take your due and hurry it. All a'you." This as others on the stairs slowed to watch. "We need to wrap this."

The mess was ignored; the sloppy one refilled its container and ran up the stairs.

Good, Aryl decided. The sooner they finished their theft, the sooner they'd leave the staircase and the opening to the layer above they'd made through the wall at its top.

No reason not to encourage them.

Smiling to herself, Aryl slipped her hand through her metal bracelet and tapped it sharply on the pipe.

She might have poked her finger in a rattlers' crate. Everyone scrambled. Most threw away their containers and ran—or tried to run—up the stairs, disappearing through the opening. One fell—she winced—from near the top, to land with a sodden thud. It didn't move again.

The two nearest the machine dropped down behind it, which she hadn't anticipated. One leaned from that cover to point a small device in her direction. The other shouted in protest then leaped up as if running for shelter.

Aryl slid down, using the pipe as protection.

A *snap,* a flash of light and ...

BOOM!

As explosions went, Aryl told herself, that hadn't been much, but when she cautiously looked past the pipe, she saw it had been sufficient.

The puddles of white burned. The machine was in scorched pieces—as were those who'd been near it.

The staircase, however, was intact. Mostly.

I've found a way up, Aryl sent to Enris, Naryn, and Haxel.

You aren't serious.

Aryl blinked at Enris. "It's perfectly safe."

"A part just fell off," Naryn pointed out, her face pale. "How is that safe?"

The First Scout shrugged. "Wait here, then." She went to the staircase and began to climb, using the supports rather than the steps themselves.

As Aryl went to do the same, Enris protested. "Haxel can send a locate once she's reached the top. If she does."

Though made from scraps of metal and fastened with everything from rope to elaborate clamps, the stairs were solid. After all, they'd carried a multitude of beings and outlasted an explosion. They'd most certainly hold two M'hiray. He should know that.

How did she? The question distracted ... the answer eluded ... "Wait if you want," Aryl said more tersely than she intended. Turning temper to action, she swarmed up behind Haxel, quickly catching up.

Aryl!

Warned by Haxel's sending, she leaped through the opening at the top.

To find herself staring into golden eyes the size of her fist.

Chapter 2

ARYL WASN'T SURE WHICH of them shouted first, but she knew which took off at a run. She was giving chase before Haxel's exhortation to "Get it!"

Something in her responded to the speed, to following a target. She grinned as she hit the right pace, arms and legs pumping smoothly, focus narrowed to the figure ahead. Her surroundings mattered only when they presented obstacle or hazard.

Like the aircars filling this tunnel. Aryl stayed close to the curved wall, avoiding that traffic as it whizzed alongside. Not aircars, she noted absently. Most were the same size, and a featureless gray. 'Bots. Machines that could fly on their own. Moving too quickly to avoid, in both directions. At least some had lights on their sides so she could see.

One zipped across her path, aiming for the wall. Aryl dove and rolled, feeling her clothing lift in the wind left by the machine. There wasn't a collision. The wall simply opened a circle to receive the machine and then closed again.

Aryl!?

Interesting layer, she sent, breaking into a run again.

The one she chased kept looking over its shoulder, huge eyes reflecting the lights of the 'bots. Hardly wise,

Aryl thought. Not only did it slow by a stride each time, but exiting 'bots were a constant threat. A shame if one of those killed the creature before she caught it. They needed a guide.

A guide with special knowledge. Its trailing coat was tantalizingly close to Aryl's outstretched fingers when another 'bot zipped in front of it. Instead of stopping, her quarry whirled to follow the machine through the opening wall.

She leaped after both, the unusual door closing too quickly for comfort. On the other side, the 'bot darted into yet another stream of moving machines, one that curved upward within their tunnel.

The thud of footsteps heading right told Aryl which way to go. And that her quarry hadn't slowed.

Admirable. If annoying.

Immense pipes. Now thousands of machines. Just as well, Aryl decided cheerfully, she didn't have to worry about such things, only to catch one irritating creature.

Two legs. Two arms. A green fuzz of what might have been hair sprouting from its head. Those overly large golden eyes were all she remembered of its face. The flapping white coat disguised everything else. It had screamed in a voice like hers; presumably, it could talk.

It stopped without warning, slapping one hand against the wall. A lift! This one came from the floor, taking the creature with it. It turned to give her a mocking bow.

Until she jumped, fingers catching the edge, and was over and on top before it could react. "Got you," Aryl panted.

She'd startled, not stopped it. Her quarry jumped every bit as high as she had to reach the edge of the opening above them, hauling itself up and away.

A challenge.

Aryl jumped after it, only to find herself on yet another different layer of Norval.

Still no sky. Light spilled from the buildings that

rose on every side. None were very large; none stood alone. They were stacked on one another in no order she could find and shared walls with their neighbors. Doors opened on roofs. Instead of roads or walkways, steps led from rooftop to rooftop. The stack meandered upward to a distant ceiling, obscured behind the lines hung with wet clothes that stretched across every open area.

Water trickled along pipes cut in half. They met or poured into lower pipes, the pattern continuing to produce a minor waterfall. It disappeared through a wide grate, half choked with debris, close to where the lift had brought her.

Everywhere, people. Aryl hadn't imagined so many people could exist at once, let alone be in the same place. People leaning out windows. People sitting on steps. People walking along rooftops. Talking. Shouting. The sounds of work and life. Laughter and argument. Smells and colors and warmth.

Her mind said "people," but these weren't M'hiray. Human, most of them, if the similarity in shape mattered— though Human seemed to cover a remarkable array of possibilities—as well as a few, stranger, forms.

All this Aryl took in with one sweeping glance. Her quarry wasn't that far ahead. The white coat helped, but she knew how it moved, now. Even in a crowd, it couldn't hide from her.

As if it knew, it didn't stay in a crowd. Instead, it scampered up a wall, grabbing laundry lines and windows for handholds to a chorus of amused—or angry—shouts, twisting its body to fling itself onto the next roof.

This was more like it, Aryl thought gleefully.

Haxel wants a report. A barely contained hint of *worry,* which wasn't the First Scout's.

Still following our guide, she assured her Chosen, tamping down her excitement. *It knows this place.*

Send a locate. I'll help.

She looked up at the wall, but tactfully refrained

from sharing that image. *Too many would see. I'll find a place.*

And started to climb.

Messy. Cluttered. Busy. All things that made for hand-holds and footholds and a variety of ways to move through space without colliding with those who chose more predictable paths.

Aryl's feet and hands rarely touched the same object twice as she surged over the rooftops in pursuit. For the first time, she had the advantage. Her quarry might know its terrain, but every part of her knew how to move like this, when to use balance and momentum instead of strength, when to use strength to increase speed and distance.

The sounds and colors around her blurred as she focused only on the next hand- and footholds, blurred into something else, into a dream of fronds and vines and branches that gave extra spring to her leaps. Where anything that moved was a threat.

So when her quarry slipped and fell in front of her, Aryl drew her longknife with one smooth pull and—

ARYL! Enris, with an urgency that made her stumble. A stumble that let her quarry leap to its feet and throw itself through the nearest open door. *A guide, remember?* he sent almost too calmly.

He was right. She might have killed it. What had she been thinking?

Aryl wiped sweat from her forehead with the back of one hand, and went through the open door.

Stairs led down, steep stairs.

Enris. Be ready. You first.

Aryl took the steps without a sound, staying to one side, knife still ready. The air thickened around her, filled with eye-straining smoke and odors that might have been food—or food after it had been dead too long.

She was alone. Aryl paused and sent the locate. *Here.*

Enris appeared beside her, grabbing for her arm and the nearest wall as he realized where he stood. "More stairs," he complained.

Aryl chuckled. "I'll see if I can do better next time."

"So we have it cornered," her Chosen said hopefully, easing down the stairs behind her. She heard him sniff. "Wonder if that's edible."

She wondered why such a knowledgeable creature would pick this narrow dark stairway for its hiding place.

Until the stairs ended at a pair of sturdy, closed doors.

"At least it's private," she grumbled, sharing her memories of the chase. "I'll send the locate to the others."

"No need." He chuckled at her expression. "All our scouts are already on this layer."

"How?"

"While you, my dear Chosen, were running through tunnels and up walls, we found a lift right beside the door at the top of those stairs." A mock shudder. "Seeing it led to a nice empty building, Haxel took Naryn back to Council, I stayed to wait for you, and the scouts used that locate to get here." He lifted a finger and twirled it once. "Naryn says this is the lowest inhabited layer of Norval and the most densely populated. She suggested, strongly, we keep moving up."

Having seen the crowded buildings, Aryl agreed with that. "Have they found a way?"

"Not yet. Haxel suggested, strongly, we continue the hunt. In case your friend runs in the right direction." *As if she could stop you,* he added with *affection.*

Aryl grinned.

They both stared at the doors for a long moment, then Enris laid his palm against one. "Feel that."

A vibration against her palm. "Machinery," she hazarded.

"More like—" his voice became uncertain, "—drums."

"Drums?"

"I—it's gone."

"What is?"

Enris ran his fingers through his hair, the way he did when frustrated. "I don't know. Something I thought I remembered. It was almost words this time." A sudden grin. "Doesn't matter. Knock or go right in?"

"Wait." Aryl put her hand on his chest, felt her hair slide restlessly over her back. "I've been having moments like that, too. As if the past is a dream I've almost forgotten, but not quite. How can that be? What's wrong with us?" *How can we exist without a past?*

"By leaving such questions for a more suitable time." He kissed her forehead. Before she could object, *reassurance* filled her mind. *We don't remember being carried in our mothers either. Maybe this was a choice we made when we left our home—to save us from regret and make us look to the future.* "Which includes," a light rap on the door with his knuckles "this."

Aryl stood on tiptoe, took his shirt in both hands, and kissed him hard on the mouth.

A rush of *warmth.* "What was that for?" Enris asked with a small smile.

"I'll tell you later," Aryl replied, smiling back. She looked at the doors. "We go right in."

Her Chosen put out both hands and pushed.

The doors swung inward to reveal a disappointingly small, plain space and another set of doors. They stepped in. The vibration of machinery—or drums—was more pronounced here, as was the smell. Enris shoved the next set of doors.

"Careful there!" a loud voice complained. Its owner stepped out of the way of the still moving door, balancing a tray of drinks on four hands, a fifth carrying a rag.

Loud it had to be. The vibration here was a heavy pulse that hurt her ears, accompanied by other sounds.

Singing. Maybe. Loud, regardless. Aryl and Enris glanced
at each other. She put her longknife away. *We'll have to
walk around.*

That won't be easy.

Enris was right. It was impossible to see any floor
through the crush of people filling every available space.
A second level ran around the outside edge of the room,
also, from what she could see, crowded. She shuddered
inwardly. Not only at the risk of such close proximity
to unknowns, but at the thought of being touched—and
worse, by not-M'hiray.

Their quarry could hide here, without doubt. It could
be standing next to them and they'd miss it.

Giving up? with a hint of *challenge.*

Follow me. Only three areas had any opening at all, so
Aryl braced herself and headed for the nearest.

It was worse than she'd imagined. Not only touch,
but the stench of strange breath and the heat of other
bodies. Her feet were in constant danger and she
found herself unable to force her way through. Before she had to resort to a technique she saw a tray
carrier use, namely several elbows applied with force
to unsuspecting body parts, Enris took her by the
arms and turned them both around. *Let me go first,*
he suggested.

That did, Aryl had to admit, work better. Her Chosen
was larger than most and had a gift for finding the right
pair of beings to push between. Not that he had to push
most of the time. The Humans, especially the females,
responded to his smile with their own. At least until they
saw Aryl right behind him.

Friendly place.

Aryl poked him in the ribs.

The open area was surrounded by a rail. Enris edged
his way to it and made room for Aryl by scooping her
alongside.

While the rest was dimly lit, large lights were aimed
into the rectangular pit. Deeper than she was tall, the bot-

tom was filled with sand. Blue-stained sand. There were holes along the side across from her, holes with eyes glistening in their depths. Aryl's hand went for the hilt of her longknife. Enris intercepted it with a low chuckle. "I believe this is an entertainment."

"If you like *pox* fighting," the Human female on his other side volunteered. She leaned into Enris, red-gold beads rolling back and forth over her large chest. Aryl had noticed a wide variety of clothing and styles of hair among the Humans here, much of it brightly colored, making their M'hiray clothing inconspicuous, if drab by comparison. This female's face was colored in patterns that changed with her expression. At the moment, her cheeks pulsed with pink-and-blue spirals. "I prefer more—personal—pleasures myself."

"What are 'pox'?" Aryl asked, leaning forward herself. The free portion of her hair, well mannered till now, slipped forward to twine possessively over Enris.

"Pox? Attitude with teeth," the Human female replied, looking startled—enhanced by black-and-white stripes coursing over her skin—then intrigued. "How do you do that? An implant? I must know." She waved a length of lifeless black curl under Enris' nose.

She might not remember her own past, but Aryl found she knew more than she expected about Humans. For one, a female's hair remained the same, Chosen or not. "You're incapable," she said sympathetically.

"I'm—you piece of *crasnig* crust! Don't you know who I am?!"

Irritating? Aryl restrained herself. "No. Who are you?"

Surrounded by an unflattering blaze of yellow dots, the Human's bright blue lips flapped without sound coming out. That was entertaining, Aryl decided, but probably not a good sign.

"Look! Are those pox?" Enris interrupted with an air of desperation.

Balls of harmless-looking brown fluff were launching themselves—or being pushed—from the holes. They dropped on the sand, where they huddled in terrified-seeming clumps. A loud whistle from overhead drew everyone to press close, talking excitedly. Many slapped palms to black trays being passed around by the multi-armed servers. Each time, the black flashed a symbol in silver.

And each time the black sparkled, one of the pox did, too, only its silver symbol remained in place, hovering above its fur.

Aryl reached out to try for herself, but under her palm, the black turned a dull gray. The server shook its doleful head. "No credit, no wager."

"Crasnig crust," the female beside Enris repeated, her lip curled disdainfully. She slipped her arm into his, the skin of cheek and brow now flickering with cheerful pink-and-green spirals. "You're better off with me, gorgeous. I could buy this place for you."

Enris laughed. Aryl, too busy watching what was happening, missed his reply.

For a tall, thin door had opened at one end of the pit. At the same time, a bell rang out, loud enough to be heard over the hammering drums and din of voices. The pox stilled and oriented themselves to the opening.

Through which was shoved a—Aryl frowned. The bulky big-eyed creature with flopping ears and large back feet seemed completely harmless, unless it sat on the much smaller pox. If this was a contest of some kind, she couldn't see the point of it.

The creature lumbered forward, awkward in the sand. The surrounding pox shifted to face it, trembling in place. Those watching began to shout, as if exhorting some effort.

Their quarry wasn't among them. *Let's look over there,* Aryl sent. She tried to turn away, only to find a solid wall of beings behind them. Enris, his other arm encrusted with Human female, half shrugged.

We'll have to wait till this is over.

Aryl shared her *frustration*.

The shouts intensified. The fluff on the pox flattened against their bodies, revealing them to be long and thin, with small eyes, heavy jaws, and protruding yellow teeth. The symbols glittered above each, like bizarre decorations. Suddenly, the pox were in motion. As one, they scurried at the creature, kicking up little clumps of sand in their haste. Almost too quickly to see, they were on it, climbing, biting, eating.

Aryl watched in horror as the bigger creature bawled its torment. It reared and struggled, but any pox it dislodged jumped back. Tufts of fur filled the air like snow. Blue blood streamed from each bite.

Some pox weren't biting, but instead climbed the creature's back and sides, their target the eyes. They bickered as they climbed, snapping and pushing. Often they'd lock jaws and fall to roll in the sand. When one of those went limp, its symbol disappeared and someone among the spectators would cry out with disappointment.

The creature threw itself against the walls, tried to shake off its tormentors, but the pox gripped with their teeth. It wouldn't last long.

Nothing should have to face the swarm.

Aryl didn't stop to think. She threw herself over the rail, her longknife finding targets before her feet hit the bloody sand. The pox were slow to react, intent on their prey. They died with a little squeal, as if surprised, their symbols winking out. She slashed one way, then used the side of the blade to send a pox against the wall with a most satisfying crack.

They were slow to react, but more and more began to notice her, reoriented, scurried her way. Making it easier to smack them. Aryl bared her teeth.

Enris landed beside her, his boots squashing several pox. "This is not—" he said calmly, stomping another, "—one of your better ideas. The people up there aren't happy."

"I noticed." Raised fists and shouts. Objects thrown

at them—though most of those hit pox. She shouldn't feel satisfied, Aryl told herself with a smidge of guilt. Haxel would doubtless have something to say about such behavior. "I don't like them," she finished, taking out a clump with a sweep of her longknife. She didn't bother clarifying which she didn't like; her Chosen didn't bother to ask.

Abruptly, the symbols over the remaining pox disappeared. Red light shone from the holes in the walls. It was a summons; the pox stopped, fluffed out their fur, and scurried back inside.

Their prey, half stripped of its fur and bleeding from innumerable small bites, leaned against the door through which it had come and heaved a sigh.

A sigh she could hear, Aryl realized, because all other sounds had ceased.

Except for an approaching thunder of clanking metal, as if several someones fought with empty pots.

The spectators melted away from the railing where they'd been standing, to be replaced by a looming black shape.

Dozens of shining black eyes on stalks stared down at them.

Aryl and Enris stared up at the eyes.

Just as she wondered if she should say something, the silence ended in a deafening bellow.

"WHAT IN THE SEVENTEENTH SANDY ARM-PIT OF URGA LARGE ARE YOU DOING IN THE POX PIT!!?"

They were now the entertainment, Aryl thought glumly as she followed the huge black being through the crowd, a passage made easy by the space granted the creature. Its lower immense pair of claws might have been the reason, though it was equally likely the creature's imposing air of "move or I'll run you down" was responsible.

It did give her a better view of the place. She looked around for their quarry, knowing Enris did the same, but also marked possible escape routes, should they have to give up the chase.

There were several doors, like the one they'd come through, both on this floor and the one above. Interestingly, there was a lit dais, shaped like a licking tongue, filling the midst of this floor. No railing separated viewers from whatever they watched there, but tables with chairs were pulled up all around it. At the moment, the dais was empty. The air around it swirled with white smoke, though there was no open fire in sight.

More tables and chairs, most in use, filled the shadowy edges. The exception was a long curved counter that jutted out from one wall, its outer surface reflecting the legs and feet of those who sat on stools beside it. This turned out to be their destination. The giant creature used one of its smaller, more flexible upper claws to lift part of the counter, then snapped a lower impatiently when they hesitated to go through. "Inside."

Aryl obeyed, Enris behind her. The creature barely fit. It dropped the counter back in place with a bang: a signal to someone, for the loud drumming and singing resumed, and those who'd been watching turned away as if disappointed.

Explain to me again why we're not leaving.

We need help.

This is help?

She didn't know why she believed it, only that she did. The other scouts still hadn't reported success; Imi's group had retreated to the Buried Theater, after being chased by some kind of authority. Or a cook. The sending had been confused.

It's a Carasian. We can trust it.

The floor directly behind the counter was at the same level as the larger room. Three of the multi-armed beings stood there, busy wiping, filling drink containers, or taking away empty ones. They ignored the new arrivals.

The inner portion sank to form a ramp leading down to the back wall. A wall, Aryl saw with interest, covered with weapons displayed behind metal grids. She walked over to it, impressed. "Are these yours?"

Several eyes bent to look at her. "Their owners left them with me." Its voice was a deep rumble. "I suggest you do the same."

A hand slapped the counter before she had to answer. "Gurdo! Whaddabout our refund!?"

The tone wasn't one she'd use, given one of "Gurdo's" claws would span the Human's ample torso. But its reply was mild. "You'll have to take that up with Louli. I can call her for you."

The florid-faced Human lost all color. "No," he said quickly. "That's not necessary. 'S was only a little bet. Some fun. That's all."

"Generous of you. Yirs? Beer for this fine Grandie. On the house."

Once the Human was mollified, Gurdo tipped its big head back to Aryl. "Ordinary knives—no one cares. But any constable will seize that," a gesture to the longknife still out in her hand, "and throw you in jail for the privilege, first chance they get. Which will be when you leave the *'Dive*. You see, locals call this Tax Free Layer, but that's only because few here can afford to pay them, not that we don't get interfered with by the powers above. There's always a couple here. Yirs?"

One of the servers spoke without turning around. "End of the stage, as usual. Waiting for Brocheuse."

Aryl tightened her hand on the hilt. "They can try."

Enris coughed. *Leaving?*

"I do enjoy your grist!" The Carasian made a sound like rain on metal. Amusement, she guessed. Having bellowed them out of the pit, it had become a jovial host, its rage apparently a show for the disappointed spectators. Now it opened one of the metal grids and selected a disappointingly plain, stubby cylinder. "Try this. Force blade," it told her. "Has a number of advantages. Hides.

Intimidates," it announced as it pressed the fine tip of a claw into a depression, producing a thin glowing line that extended from the cylinder about the length of Aryl's arm, a line that hissed as it moved through the air. "With no inconvenient residue to worry about, if you get my meaning." It pulled a piece of white cloth from a stack behind the counter, tossing it into the air so it passed through the glowing line. Two halves fluttered to the floor. The Carasian turned it off. "Give me your pretty pox-sticker. I'll let you have this for twenty *rimmies*."

"A trade," Enris nodded.

"A fair one," as if her Chosen had protested. "Either way, you can't take that with you."

She certainly could, but Aryl didn't see the value in arguing. What she did see was the value in what it offered. "We'll need more of those," she said firmly. "Many more."

The eyestalks went in several directions at once. "I'm no dealer, friend. Just a bartender keeping the peace." With a little more volume than required, as if speaking for other ears.

Enris leaned forward, eyes aglow with interest, but not in the remarkable weapon. "What are 'rimmies'?"

"More force blades and a place for our people to live," Aryl interjected before Gurdo could answer. "A safe place."

Let me do this. "We're offworlders," Enris explained smoothly. "Arrived today. We could use some guidance."

It wasn't a lie.

Leaving most of its eyes on Aryl, the Carasian spared a few for her Chosen. Who looked, she thought, remarkably smug.

"You talk like Grandies," Gurdo observed after a moment. "Look like you can't afford a beer. Guidance is expensive. Especially the good kind."

Enris smiled. "Oh, I wouldn't judge us by appearance."

What was he doing? Aryl kept her mouth closed and shields tight. Her hair, however, writhed up and over her shoulders, reaching for her Chosen. Who lifted a finger to let a tendril wind itself around like a ring.

She did her best to smile and not grab it back.

"Amazing grist," the Carasian muttered. It shifted on its rounded feet, producing a muted clank, then came to a decision. "Can't talk here. Come with me. No promises, though."

A tap on a panel opened a door in the wall, splitting the weapon display into sections. The air wafting through was warm and damp. "But first." An upper claw opened and waited.

Impossible to read a face composed of what looked like polished metal bowls separated by a dark gap filled with restless stalked eyes.

Aryl.

She frowned, but gave the Carasian her longknife. Leaving her hand extended.

All eyes came to rest on her. Aryl didn't budge.

"Call it a sample," Gurdo grumbled, dropping the force blade in her palm. "Do not," with emphasis, "use it here." Her longknife went on the wall, the grid replaced over it.

Aryl tucked the cylinder in a pocket, satisfied.

"This way."

It wasn't, she discovered, an ordinary door. No sooner had Aryl stepped through than sprays of bitter water struck her from all sides. Sputtering, she hurried forward to get away from them, Enris doing the same.

The Carasian followed more slowly. While it appeared to enjoy the spray, the door wasn't wide enough for it, so it leaned to one side and pulled itself through by force, claws grabbing the door edge for purchase. From the deep scars in the doorframe, this was its usual practice.

Aryl spat out the bitter stuff and glared at the glistening Gurdo. "What was that for?"

"You were covered in sand." As if she should have realized. "I can't have sand in my home."

And as if the blue blood staining that sand didn't matter in the least.

As homes went, this wasn't much: a square room no more than five long strides wide in either direction, though two levels high. Quiet, dimly lit, its furnishings were four large polished rocks, speckled with gray, set into the floor. In the midst of the rocks, a small pool of dark water gurgled busily to itself. A set of stairs against a side wall led to the only other door, at the next level. There were no windows, but the wall straight ahead featured a framed image of water sliding over black rocks. Rocks with small black eyes. Eyes that disturbingly followed any movement, Aryl noticed.

The Carasian lowered itself over one of the chair-rocks, resting its pair of big claws on the floor. "Let me guess," it said briskly once the two M'hiray had sat. "You need idents. Certificates. For how many?"

Aryl pushed an impatient lock of wet hair back. "Everyone."

A flash of *caution.*

She understood Enris' concern; she had no time for it. Not while the M'hiray waited beneath their feet, trusting them to find the way out. "There are seven hundred and thirty of us. We need a place to live. Now." Aryl thought of the crowded roofs and buildings outside and shuddered inwardly. "Better than this. Private. Away from Humans."

So much for blending in. With a hint of *irony.*

It knows we aren't Human. Flat and sure. *Trust me.*

The Carasian dipped its head from one shoulder to the other. "If you picked this world, you know anything can be arranged for a price."

"A price?"

This is where you trust me, beloved.

She'd prefer to test her new weapon, but this was

Enris' knowledge, not hers. Though why was she so sure?

The reason slid away, leaving only belief.

Aryl subsided, crossing her legs on the rock to prove it.

"We've brought items to trade," Enris said in a casual tone. "Offworld items. Quite valuable."

We did?

I've asked Naryn and Haxel to check our belongings. There must be something. Any doubt of that Enris might have had—which Aryl shared—he didn't allow to reach his face or voice. "We'd be glad to show them to the right trader. Would that be you?"

Silence, then a deep, "No."

Aryl prepared to get to her feet. *We can still find the creature I chased.*

"That would be Louli," the Carasian continued. A smaller claw indicated the stairs.

"Lawren Louli. This is my place. *Doc's Dive.* Do you like the name? It's a little joke. Not everyone gets that. Gurdo tells me you have a problem that could mean profit. Profit I like. Wasting time, I don't. You look like a waste of time. You get that?"

Bemused by this rapid stream of words—Louli seemed to not need to breathe—Aryl missed the tiny pause that was her chance to speak.

"That's a lot of offworlders to settle. Private and safe, I hear. Quick, too. Why's that? Why quick?"

"We don't waste time," Enris countered, smiling. "Can you help?"

This Human female was different from the others Aryl had seen, beginning with her clothing. Every colorful section was a different eye-twisting pattern. There were two sections for each arm, and left and right arms didn't match. Each shoulder differed from the torso, which was itself, though shaped like a snug-fitting jacket, in four fabrics. The sleek pants were divided into three down each leg, neither leg coordinated to the other. Each foot, Aryl noticed when she snuck a peek under the table, wore a different kind of shoe.

The only item of clothing spared the battle of color was the white cap on Louli's short-cropped white hair. Was "cap" the right word? The object in question was taller than any cap Aryl remembered, and sat neatly on the back of the Human's head. It did add height, she decided.

Not that Louli needed help to dominate the conversation. Her bright blue eyes darted between them as if she suspected trickery. Between her quick incisive speech, and the way the Carasian lowered itself at her side— once it had forced its way up the stairs and through the door with loud rattling and complaints—Aryl was quite sure who felt in charge.

Here.

They overlooked the packed floor, with its "stage" and pox pit. The area around them was quiet except for their own voices and, though they could see the crowded tables to either side of this area, no one there appeared to see them. Aryl didn't know how it was done, but she approved. The three tables by the rail looked the same as the rest, but were of polished wood. Real flame burned in bowls of scented oil at their centers. Except where a second set of stairs led down, the floor was covered in a thick, rich carpet, its surface carved with an ornate design.

Marred with wet footprints. Aryl's hair had dried itself, but she and Enris sat at the Human's table in sopping clothes courtesy of Gurdo's aversion to sand. She sniffed self-consciously. The bitter water had left a smell behind.

Louli didn't remark on it. Perhaps because more carpets hung on the back wall and she'd have this one changed once her damp guests had left.

"Help you?" she repeated. "Depends. Depends.

Names would help. If you have them. Species. Gurdo says you aren't Human. Could have fooled me. Look it, both of you."

Her Chosen's silence said it all. Aryl felt her face grow warm. "I'm Aryl di Sarc," she said quickly, before Louli went on. "This is Enris d'sud Sarc. We're M'hiray. The only Clan—"

"Clan. Simple. I like simple. Start giving me glottal stops and nonsensical spits, and I won't bother remembering you. Now. Aryl and Enris of the Clan. I'm a busy being." Not that there was anything to be busy about in sight, but Louli sounded definite. "Tell me what you have to offer."

Something she'd like to know, too.

"I can do better." Enris was unperturbed. "I'll show you. There's a sample on the way here."

There is? she asked.

We can hope.

"Better not take long." The bright blue eyes snapped to Aryl. "You. Go enjoy the *'Dive* while we wait. Unless you have something against honest gambling."

" 'Gambling?' " Aryl echoed.

"Luck, chance, fortune, wagers, house always wins. Gambling."

"The pox," Gurdo rumbled helpfully.

Never back down, Aryl thought, and lifted an eyebrow. "I wasn't—" she said in her best imitation of the blue-lipped female's voice, "—entertained."

Louli stared, then laughed. "House won. I've no quarrel. Don't suppose you'd be interested in a repeat performance? Solid demand for pretties who'll butcher in public."

Before Aryl could attempt to decipher this, Enris spoke up. "Thank you for the offer, but we'll be leaving with the rest of our people."

"If I like what you show me. Otherwise, you won't be going anywhere."

Aryl's focus narrowed to Louli's fragile neck.

The Carasian slowly rose from its crouch.

Words, beloved. Only words. Go. This will be easier if I deal with her alone.

She was, Aryl decided, heartily sick of words. And of Humans who threatened what she cared about. "I'll wait down there."

Making it her idea to leave.

Interlude

ENRIS DID HIS BEST to look relaxed as his Chosen followed the giant Carasian down the stairs to the 'Dive's main level. Aryl had no concern about its company, though the bizarre creature could read her intentions in a way this seemingly clever Human did not.

Something to remember.

If only he could remember more, starting with the contents of the containers the M'hiray had brought to Stonerim III. Maddening, to be sure there was something of great value, without knowing what. Value they needed. Four groups had reported finding ways to go from this to the next level, ways closed to the M'hiray. Every lift and ramp way was guarded by those who checked for identification before allowing passage. Or took payment.

Payment they didn't have. They had to depend on Naryn and the others to find what they needed.

And this Lawren Louli to do what she implied she could.

Enris leaned back and smiled his best smile. "Tell me about this settlement you have in mind for the Clan."

"On this world? There's really only one worth considering—for those who can afford it. The Towers of Lynn, on the Necridi Coast. I'm not saying there's any left to buy, can't promise, but for the right price another purchaser might be convinced to step aside. We aren't talking cheap, Friend Enris." She tapped a forefinger on the table, nail tipped with white. "Sun Layer Grandies couldn't swing a Tower now. Offworld funds snapped up the first offering and the coming builds. Which makes it what you want. Private. Safe. Mostly non-Human."

"We'd have to see it first." He knew better than to seem desperate, even if they were.

Are you sure you don't need me there, Enris? A definite hint of *desperate* in Aryl's sending, too. She wouldn't enjoy the crowded floor below.

I'm sure, he replied, with a twinge of guilt. But his Chosen's honesty and passion were the last thing he needed when dealing with a trading partner like this Human. *Enjoy yourself and don't attract attention.*

A promise as her *presence* retreated from his, *I'll blend in.*

Unlikely, under any circumstances. Enris smiled to himself.

"A drink?"

His stomach remembered for him. "I'd prefer something to eat," he said gratefully. "It's been a while since . . ." Supper? Breakfast? ". . . I ate."

"What's your rating?" Louli smiled. "Wouldn't do to poison such a handsome guest." When he hesitated, she pursed her lips. "You really aren't local, are you? Are you First, then? Unaligned? Fringe?"

He had no idea. "Offworld."

"I got that. Don't want to say. Don't need to know. Fair enough. I'll screen your blood for something safe. If you Clan have blood? Not every being does."

"We do." Safe was important, Enris thought, though how his blood could tell a Human what would be, he didn't know.

Naryn? Anything?

Nothing yet. Seeds, of all things. Tools. Food. But we're not done.

Following Louli's guidance, he put one finger into a hollow cube she held out. Numbers and symbols swarmed across its surface. "Do I get to eat?" he asked hopefully.

"Anything the *'Dive* serves." Louli shook her head. "Wish I had your tolerance. Some of the hots Gurdo tosses in give me a rash. What's your pleasure?"

He had no idea. "Surprise me," Enris replied, feeling clever.

Enris. We found them. Naryn, *excitement* bubbling through her mindvoice. *The artifacts. I can't believe I didn't remember. What do you need?*

To know what an artifact was? Enris didn't bother to ask. *Something to impress our contact.*

Done. With reassuring promptness. *Send me the locate.*

Somewhere without a witness. *When you're ready, 'port here.* He showed Naryn the Carasian's quarters. *It will be empty. Come up the stairs.*

"Surprise you? Glad to." Louli pressed her palm against the tabletop. "Number Four, Suicidal," she said. "Pitcher of water. Bucket in case. Two beers, the good stuff."

Sitting back, the Human put her fingertips together, or tried to. The tips didn't appear to want to meet, and Enris watched in fascination. When they finally did, Louli regarded him over the cage they formed. "Don't you surprise me, Friend Enris," she warned. "You get hospitality because Gurdo's got a feel for opportunity and sees something in the two of you I don't. I expect to see merchandise worth the effort. Legal. Portable. Not alive merchandise. Anything else gets complicated. Complicated drops you a layer. Get that?"

"A layer?"

"Local expression. Cause me trouble. Lowers the value. Complications? You don't get so much in trade. Waste my time altogether, I won't be happy. You don't want me not happy. Fair enough?"

He copied her position, his fingers cooperating. "We won't be happy," Enris replied smoothly, "if you've wasted ours." *Naryn?*

Here.

"No time for food. Our sample's arrived," he added, as the door to the Carasian's quarters opened and Naryn stepped through.

Followed immediately by Haxel and Worin, his young brother.

Being outnumbered didn't appear to bother Lawren Louli. "Don't tell me. More wives. Bet that one doesn't share." A nod at Haxel, who might have been carved in stone after her quick assessing scan of their surroundings.

Enris ignored the obscure comment. *What do you think you're doing here?* he sent to Worin, with a lash of *worried anger.*

Though he paled, the younger Mendolar stood his ground. He lifted the small crate he carried against his chest. *They needed me to 'port this.*

So Haxel could have free hands and Naryn look impressive.

Despite the fear that things could spiral out of control, Enris took a deep breath and gestured approval. It wasn't Worin's fault. "Lawren Louli. This is Naryn di S'udlaat, Haxel di Vendan, and Worin di Mendolar."

Naryn did, he had to admit, impress. She'd taken the time to don her white Councillor's robe, and her dark red hair fell in a magnificent cloak over her shoulders and back, loose but under control. Haxel, as always, had hers tightly netted. As well Gurdo hadn't seen her longknife.

Though doubtless she'd want one of the force blades, too, once Aryl showed her.

Louli's eyes were fixed on the crate. "This the sample? What's inside? Let's see."

Your turn, Enris sent to Naryn, rising from his seat and giving her a small bow. *This Human claims to know of a suitable home for us. If we have something of value to trade.*

He hoped so, for all their sakes.

At a gesture from Naryn, Worin put the crate gently on the table and stepped back.

Louli rose to her feet as Naryn first pressed a finger to one corner, then tapped the remaining top corners in a specific pattern. The lid began to rise.

Enris held his breath.

Which was when Worin pointed to the floor below. "What's Aryl doing?"

Chapter 3

"THEY SHOULD MAKE THE DOORS your size," Aryl commented as Gurdo tilted its massive back, waved its claws vigorously in the air, and somehow maneuvered its bulk through the opening. The spectacle did clear a more than adequate amount of floor space, since anyone who'd been in the way moved quickly elsewhere. Spilling a few drinks.

A clawtip pointed up. "Lower layers support the upper; lower buildings support those above. Wide doors make the old-timers nervous." That rain on metal sound. "Louli prefers I make them nervous," it boasted.

Aryl carefully didn't smile, though Gurdo, despite its formidable natural weapons and loud voice, seemed more a threat to unwary toes and elbows than individuals. She glanced at the upper level. The window walls worked in Louli's favor. Where Enris sat with the Human was clouded from this side, allowing only blurred outlines to show. Her Chosen *felt* confident. He wasn't, she thought dourly, always right to do so. "I should have stayed there."

"Come. Have a drink. Enjoy the show." The Carasian dipped its head closer to hers. "That way you won't make me nervous."

Astute being. Aryl made a "lead on" gesture. The

stage, as they'd called it, was still empty. No one crowded them—crowded Gurdo, to be exact—but the rest of *Doc's Dive* offered no room to squeeze between anyone.

Or peace. Between their shouted voices and the heavy thumping—with occasional shrieks of song—that made shouts necessary, Aryl could barely hear her own thoughts. "Do Humans enjoy this noise?"

She decided the dip of head dome to either shoulder was the Carasian version of a shrug. "They don't have a choice," it rumbled. "When the musicians tried to keep their tips, Louli had a 'bot band installed. A used one. Only plays like that. Smokeheads tell me it's beautiful music, but they chew the ends of their fingers to pulp, so I don't trust their taste. The smart ones wear plugs in their ears. It's better when the show's on."

Probably no quieter, Aryl thought resignedly. *Are you sure you don't need me there, Enris?*

I'm sure. He sounded distracted but hopeful. *Enjoy yourself and don't attract attention.*

Aryl buried her reaction to that highly unnecessary bit of advice behind shields. *I'll blend in,* she promised.

She took his tinge of *disbelief* as a dare.

"When's the show?" Aryl asked Gurdo. Whatever it was.

"Now!" the Carasian bellowed unnecessarily.

White smoke billowed out from the stage edges and spilled overtop. It gave the illusion that the figures who suddenly appeared on the stage—to raucous shouts Aryl presumed indicated cheerful anticipation and not the blood lust of the pox pit, though the sound and facial expressions were quite similar—that those figures had 'ported there.

Except the swirling smoke around their feet made it obvious they'd come up on lifts.

The "music" changed at the same time, to something as loud, but more complex, almost pleasant.

A clawtip pointed to the curved counter. She understood. It had to get to work. There were stools there. An easy step from any of those, a leap, and she'd be at the door to Gurdo's room and the stairs to Enris. Satisfied, Aryl nodded and followed the Carasian as it lumbered its way through the milling crowd.

Not that there was a free stool until Gurdo snapped a claw and two scrawny Humans jumped off theirs and disappeared into the shadow and smoke. Aryl didn't bother trying to shout her thanks. Instead, she rapped her knuckles on the nearest part of the huge being, then took her seat.

About to turn to watch the stage, Aryl realized one of the many-armed servers behind the counter was asking her a question. "Yes?" she shouted.

The server's mouth moved again. Aryl cupped her hand behind one ear and shrugged helplessly. Obviously used to coping with the din, three hands appeared with empty containers of different shapes.

It meant a drink, but what? Aryl looked at her neighbors. The most popular beverage had an alarming plume of dirty yellow smoke; those drinking it used a long spoon to approach from the side.

"Let me," said a friendly male voice in her ear. "Two Pink Riders, Yirs."

"Coming up, KaeCee."

This KaeCee was tall for a Human. Aryl studied him warily as he took the stool beside hers. He smiled and seemed harmless. Seemed. "Thank you," she said politely, when the drinks arrived and he passed one to her. It didn't look daunting. A layer of pink froth over a green liquid. Fruit had been impaled on the stick rising from it, fruit cut in the shape of an implausibly endowed male. She glanced at her new companion to see where to start.

He pulled the stick and fruit from his drink and tossed it on the counter, then leaned closer. "Louli tells them to reuse the garnish."

Whatever that meant. Aryl dutifully tossed hers aside with some regret. Enris wasn't the only one to feel hungry. She sipped the froth, then gave KaeCee an appreciative smile. The pleasant taste included an interesting warmth down her throat. "This is good."

"Better than the floor show, that's for sure."

The figures on the stage? Aryl watched for a moment, nonplussed when all they did was sway in time to the music and shed their clothes. The fruit on a stick had been not only implausible in size, she noted, but the wrong shape. "Much better," she agreed, and turned away again.

"Personally, I'm more interested in beautiful strangers than dancing boys." He edged closer on his stool. "I'm KaeCee. Tell me all about yourself."

Aryl, busy taking another sip, glanced up in surprise. "No."

"Beautiful and mysterious." The Human licked pink froth from the hairs above his narrow mouth. All of his features were narrow, as was he. The hair on his head, an improbable blue, curled to his shoulders. When he ran one hand through it, Aryl noticed his fingernails were the same color. "Play nice," he urged. "You know my name. What's yours?"

Aryl put down the drink and frowned. "Go away."

Perhaps he couldn't hear her over the music, for he didn't move. Instead, his eyes traveled over her. "You have the most remarkable hair. And that net you wear. Old. A family heirloom? I've never seen work like that. Where did you get it?"

About to repeat her warning, much louder, Aryl hesitated. "From home . . ." she answered, losing whatever else she might have said. "Before we left." On impulse, she lifted her arm and showed him her bracelet. "This, too."

"Nice work. But new," in a dismissive tone. "My specialty is the ancient. The rare. Rare like you." The Human reached for her hair. "What is it about you?" he asked, his voice gone strange, his eyes not quite focused. "There's something . . ."

Don't attract attention. Blend in. Which precluded slapping his hand away, she decided reluctantly. Her hair promptly retreated, twisting itself into an uncomfortably tight knot at the back of her neck.

Encouraging that unwelcome hand to pursue.

Hair wasn't, Aryl realized, particularly clever. She slid off the stool and away from the hand before it touched. "I'll be leaving," she said firmly and did.

"Don't go!"

Aryl joined the others pushing their way into the crowd around the stage.

KaeCee, undeterred, followed.

Aryl?

Remind me to tell you how well I blended, Aryl sent, not holding back a snip of *outrage*. Which wasn't all because she was forced to run away. There was being surrounded by too many Humans, everyone with sloshing drinks and foul breath. There was breathing smoke and enduring brain-numbing noise.

Not to mention the floor was sticky.

Without warning, Aryl found herself pressed against the side of the stage by the crowd. She looked up naked legs and other parts to find herself staring into golden eyes the size of her fist.

"You!" she shouted.

"Wait!" KaeCee cried from behind.

There were times no action would end well. Aryl stared up at her quarry, quivering with the desire to leap on the stage and grab it, knowing she shouldn't. It, meanwhile, began a graceful gyration to the left, traveling away from her as quickly as it could given the lack of space between its fellows and their lack of cooperation getting out of its way.

Unfortunately, not moving gave the persistent Human all the time he needed to catch up and breathe down her neck. Aryl dug a discreet elbow sharply into his ribs. As he gasped, she took advantage of a gap between tables to go left herself, keeping the golden-eyed creature in sight.

Only wise, she told herself, to keep all options available.

A sweaty hand gripped her arm. Shields tight, proud of her restraint, Aryl glared into his flushed face and said very clearly, "I will break your wrist."

KaeCee let go, but didn't retreat. "If you want the *Aala*, I'll hire him for the night. Just come back with me."

Aala. The golden-eyed creature had a name. Was male.

Night? How could she know for sure, down here?

How could she believe anything this Human told her? Aryl forced the edge from her voice. "I don't need him all night. I need him to show me how to reach the top layer of this city." To free her people. To take them to the sun and sky. She hadn't realized the urgency of that need until now. Her breath caught. "Can you arrange it?"

This produced a beaming smile. Two of his teeth, she noticed, had been inlaid with tiny stones. "My dear beauty. I can do better. You don't need him. I can take you."

"You know the way?"

"Of course. You don't think I live here, do you?" He paused as if waiting for a reply, then continued more quickly. "My offices are in the Sun Layer itself. I come down occasionally. For the scenery." With a move closer.

Moved or was pushed. The music had increased in tempo, causing a mass shuffle toward the stage among the spectators. To express disapproval? From what Aryl could see, those who made it close to the stage either threw items to impede the footing of those on it or slapped them.

Then she noticed how those on the stage came perilously near its edge to provide flesh to be slapped, and how each slap left behind a patch of gold or silver.

Not disapproval. As for what it was?

Aryl shook her head. Watching pox eat their flop-eared prey made more sense.

"Here." KaeCee pressed something small and round into her hand. "Why should Brocheuse get them all?" With a wave at a nearby gyrating Human, whose bare skin sparkled with patches. Among other things. Flecks of metal pinched his skin along lines that suggested the seams of clothing. That had to hurt. Maybe those watching gave him the patches out of pity, Aryl thought dubiously.

"Go ahead," her companion urged. "Have some fun. Be daring."

The suggestion from one who belonged here was all Aryl needed. "I will," she said happily.

And leaped on the stage in pursuit of the Aala.

Chapter 4

AS CHASES WENT, it was over too quickly. The Aala spotted her approach, eyes dilating, but when he tried to flee, his limbs tangled with those of his neighbors, knocking several down. On rising again, they began, most unfairly, to strike him with fists and feet.

The spectators appeared to enjoy this even more than the movement to music, raising their own fists and shouting. Some started to hit each other. Drink containers and chairs began to fly through the smoke.

All of which didn't stop Aryl. She ran lightly along the stage, not touching anyone else, ball in hand. Once in reach, she grabbed the Aala from beneath a heaving pile of naked bodies, smiled happily at him, then slapped the ball against his receding forehead, leaving a gold patch. "Thanks for showing me the way here," she said.

"That's all you wanted?" the creature asked incredulously. "Directions to this place?"

"We're from offworld," Aryl explained. Before she could say another word, the Aala was pulled back into another skirmish.

She shrugged and jumped down, stepping over a body that crashed to the floor by her feet. Everyone was busy hitting one another. Or trying to. They weren't, Aryl decided, very good at it.

Humans.

Where was KaeCee?

"Hold it, *Femmine*."

The unexpectedly stern voice belonged to a Human male who wasn't fighting. Unlike KaeCee and the others here, he wasn't dressed in bright colors. Instead, he wore a simple black shirt and pants tucked into knee-high boots. Paired belts crossed his chest, with loops for various small objects. Another server, Aryl guessed. "I don't want anything," she told him, and moved away, looking for KaeCee's bright red jacket.

The server blocked her way. "You can't come in here and cause a disturbance."

Why, when it was so easy to do? Aryl thought with some self-pity, but gave more attention to the Human. Not a server. "I was told to enjoy myself," she explained.

"BY THE WORM-RIDDEN THIRD ARMPIT OF URGA LARGE, DON'T MAKE ME COME OUT THERE!"

Gurdo's bellow produced an instant of silence, then everyone erupted into movement and noise again. A table smashed nearby.

"A few drinks don't give you license to break the law, Femmine. You'll have to come with me."

Why did Humans believe simply saying a thing would make it happen?

They exchanged measuring looks. What he thought of her, Aryl didn't care. She judged him strongly built for a Human, but no more so than the performers on stage. If the objects he bore were weapons, she had her short knife and the force blade.

Which wasn't, she realized belatedly, blending in. She gestured apology and tried a smile. "I'm sorry if I—"

"There you are." KaeCee shoved his way past two females preoccupied with holding their shoes high above their heads, despite the risk to their bare feet. He had a bruise forming over one eye and his blue hair was matted with some green substance. "Let's get out of here."

"Not so fast, *Gennine*," said the Human in black. "There's the matter of a fine and—"

"Nonsense!" KaeCee stiffened, the good humor gone from his face. "What's your name? I'll have your badge!"

"Constable Gene Maynard." The other looked unimpressed. Aryl wouldn't have been either. "And you would be KaeCee Britain of Norval Antiquities and Otherworld Imports, looter of graveyards. Down to visit your suppliers, KaeCee, or for other diversions?" This with an odd look at Aryl.

Aryl—

At the faint *touch* from her Chosen, Aryl sent quickly, *It wasn't my fault. They started hitting one another. I haven't hit anyone,* she added proudly. Despite provocation. *I've found a guide.*

Triumph surged outward, so strong she wasn't entirely sure Enris had *heard* her. *I may have found a home. Louli's impressed by our sample. She's sent for someone to verify its value. You should be here. Come.*

She should never have left, Aryl told herself, eyeing a pair of Humans wrestling on the floor a little too close for comfort. *I'll be there as—*

"KaeCee! There you are." As the Carasian clattered toward them, it used its closed lower claws to shove oblivious combatants out of its way. "Louli wants you topside! Now."

"This wasn't my fault," KaeCee protested.

Aryl might have sympathized, but she had a sinking feeling the summons wasn't about the fighting at all.

The M'hiray would have to deal with this Human, too?

"Tell Louli," Gurdo said with some relish. "AS FOR YOU—" The "you" in question was apparently everyone else. It rattled away, shoving and pushing.

With a discordant wail, the 'bot band either died or gave up. The lack of deafening "music" did more to quench the participants' enthusiasm than the Carasian. Some headed for the exit doors. Most headed for the counter, or began righting tables and shouting for drinks.

The rest were on the stage, retrieving the tossed items despite outraged protests from the naked performers. Gurdo roared something and headed for them next.

"This won't take long," KaeCee said with a pronounced quiver to his voice. "Promise you'll wait right here for me?"

"I'll come with you," Aryl offered.

"No, no." He looked at the clouded window, not her. "Louli doesn't like surprises. Stay here." With a tug on his jacket, a brush of both hands through his dripping hair, he headed for the stairs with the air of someone about to face punishment.

Fine, Aryl thought. She'd go up the Carasian's stairs and surprise him.

"Hold on—"

She whirled to face the constable. "I said I was sorry. Explain what a 'fine' is so I can finish my business with you and leave."

Maynard tilted his head. He had nice eyes, Aryl noticed absently. Right now they were troubled. "Forget the fine," he said quietly. "Listen to me, Femmine. Kae-Cee's trouble. Not this kind," with a nod at the smashed tables and groaning patrons. "Another order altogether. Cross him, and you'll disappear without a trace."

He couldn't mean KaeCee. "Him?" Aryl's lips twitched.

The constable nodded grimly. "Doesn't look like much, I'll grant you. But somehow KaeCee dances a step ahead of the law. He's got connections, too. We can't touch him. Not yet, anyway. Don't let him touch you. That's all I'm saying."

This Human thought of her as one of his own, unaware she was something far more dangerous. Still, the warning seemed well meant. "I'll be careful," Aryl promised.

"You do that. But if you run into more than you can handle, or learn anything about KaeCee I should know, contact me. Here." He offered her a small brown rectangle, careful to keep it low as if no one else should see.

Aryl took it, then looked a question.

"It's a burst."

"A burst?"

"Pop it in any comport or reader on Stonerim III. It will send an alert to the constabulary. Where you are. That you need help or want to talk."

"Your help," Aryl countered warily. "To talk to you, no one else."

Maynard smiled for the first time. He reached to press his thumb against the rectangle. "Just mine."

Aryl walked away, the rectangle in her closed fist, fist at her side. With every step, she was less sure why she'd accepted it. Humans weren't M'hiray. They were too many, too different. Dangerous in number. Humans were to be avoided—or used, if safe. Her fist lifted when she passed an ownerless drink oozing yellow smoke at an empty table. She should toss the "burst" into it . . .

Instead, Aryl tucked it in a pocket. She'd discard it later, less obviously.

She wouldn't need it.

A warm flash of *gladness* filled her as Aryl stepped once more on Lawren Louli's thick carpet—in drier shoes. It had nothing to do with what was going on; Enris, her Chosen, reacted to her presence. His smile would have lit the darkest night.

She smiled back. *I missed you, too.*

Naryn. Haxel. Worin? She sent them each a greeting.

They were pleased to see her—well, Haxel had the look of someone planning a "discussion" for later, presumably about the bar fight which hadn't been, Aryl told herself firmly, entirely her doing.

KaeCee stood near Louli. He'd looked dismayed by her arrival, but quickly wiped any emotion from his face. Now, he kept glancing from her to Enris and back.

Maybe he wasn't a total fool.

"All here. Shall we get down to business, then? Sit sit." Louli had transformed into an effusive host. She beamed from one to the other, finishing with Aryl. "I've introduced the respected and renowned KaeCee Britain to the rest of your delegation, Aryl. KaeCee, this is Aryl di Sarc."

"I've had the pleasure," KaeCee said, with a slight bow. He'd decided to smile. It didn't reach his eyes. "Glad you could join us, Aryl."

Dangerous, this one, despite his appearance. She didn't doubt the constable.

Haxel had a way of going still when she picked up trouble. Aryl made sure to brush her fingers over the First Scout's wrist as she passed. *Watch him.*

Enris didn't need a warning. His relaxed stance covered an inner *alert*.

One of the M'hiray's white crates sat in the center of the table, its lid open. Though chairs had been added, no one sat. Worin stood behind his brother. Naryn faced the Humans, Haxel to one side. Aryl stopped on the other, across from KaeCee, beside Enris.

"Shall we continue?" Naryn suggested, gesturing to the crate.

"Go ahead, KaeCee. I've taken my look." Louli crossed her arms. Her fingers ran from elbow to shoulder and back as if restless. Aryl didn't let the peculiarity distract her. What could Naryn have found?

The Human tugged the crate closer with a casual finger, his expression bored. He tipped it forward and peered inside.

Then looked up, eyes wide. "Where did you get this?" Almost a whisper.

"It's ours," Naryn asserted. "As are the rest."

KaeCee licked his lips, eyes flicking between all the M'hiray. "There's more?"

"Well, well?" Louli interjected. "That what I think it is? What do you think?"

He reached into the crate with care, pulling out a bag. The bag itself rippled with color. Not only color, but numbers. "Watch." When he set it gently on the table, the numbers moved across the bag's surface, coming together in a final, complex pattern. "That's a Triad seal, Louli. Can't be forged. Only the First from a site can apply it."

Do you know what he's talking about? Enris asked her.

No.

Naryn's eyes never left the bag. *I do. Hush.*

"Open it."

There were beads of sweat on his forehead. "Is the room tight?" When Louli didn't answer at once, sharper. "Is it?"

"Will be." She moved one of the hanging carpets, revealing a panel. After pushing a few controls, she let the carpet drop and returned to the circle around the table, staring down at the bag. "We're tight. No one in or out."

Worin leaked *anxiety.* Enris soothed him. Let the Humans believe they'd locked the M'hiray in, Aryl thought, amused.

"I'm going to open this." KaeCee didn't pull out a knife or ask for one. He took the bag by two upper corners and pulled those apart very slowly.

It split neatly down the middle. Not a protection, Aryl realized. The covering had served as identification.

What lay exposed caught the flickering light from the flames on the other tables, caught it and reflected it everywhere.

Aryl drew back, disappointed. It appeared to be a device, hardly larger than the force blade hidden in her pocket, shaped to be held in a hand and pointed. The reflections were from crystals stuck all over it. It looked like the ornaments worn by the Humans in the bar below.

She kept her opinion to herself. The Humans were transfixed by the thing, their mouths slightly open, eyes dilated. They found value in it; that was what mattered.

"Is this the right price?" Naryn asked, her voice low and soft.

"Price?" KaeCee tore his eyes from the object and visibly collected himself. "I admit to some interest. What do you want for it?"

"Wait there, KaeCee!" Louli bristled. "This is my deal. You're here to authenticate the value, not push me gone."

"And where could you go to sell Hoveny artifacts, except to me?"

"Hoveny." The word might have had taste, the way Louli savored it. "I knew you weren't wasting our time, Enris Friend."

She was too confident. Too calm. Something wasn't right. Aryl tensed. *Naryn!*

I know what I'm doing. "What we want is a home for our people."

"I told them about Lynn," Louli said quickly. "Seemed to suit."

"The Towers?" Blue eyebrows rose. "Aiming pretty high."

"We can arrange our own transport. We would want to move as quickly as possible. Tonight, if possible."

KaeCee gestured to the artifact. "For this, I could maybe get the five of you rooms in a Sun Layer resort. Best service in Norval. Say for a week. But a Tower?"

"That's only a sample," Naryn assured him, her hair rising on her shoulders. "The least of what we have to trade. Everything is Triad sealed and authenticated."

His eyes followed her hair. "I'm sure we can do business, Femmine."

Reading Human expressions was not, Aryl would be the first to admit, like reading M'hiray emotion. But there was something ominous in Louli's small, tight smile.

Then, she knew. "What have you done?" she demanded. "While you wasted our time, what have you done?"

The smile widened. "My dancing boys report to me first, Aryl of the Clan. I know you came up from the deep. Likely the Buried Theater. Your people are down there? Well, so are mine. Those are my artifacts now—or they will be very soon."

Gijs and his scouts have been following some intruders. Haxel's matching smile was even colder. "Did you think we wouldn't be watching?"

"What I think is that sample of Clan blood I took means my people can take out yours with no risk at all. Don't worry. It'll be quick. I don't waste time."

BEWARE! Naryn drove the warning through the M'hir. *GO!* Aryl sent into its echo.

Haxel, Enris, and Worin disappeared, leaving them to deal with the Humans.

"Neat trick," KaeCee commented, his voice almost steady. "What was that? Projected illusion? I'd like to see the specs. I could have a buyer."

Dangerous indeed. "It's Clan," Aryl said warningly. She brought out the force blade and thumbed it on as Gurdo had demonstrated.

Louli had been backing away. Now she leaped forward to snatch the glittering artifact from the table. Aryl swept the force blade down as she would a knife . . .

Only to have Louli's arms come apart before the line of force touched them. Not only her arms, but her chest and legs and shoulders!

Every piece snapped neatly away from the others, where the differing fabric met. Once apart, they landed on the floor and sprouted fleshy limbs. They scurried in various directions, ran around legs and circled back to dive under the one table. "What is that—them!?" Naryn demanded with a horror Aryl shared.

"Assembler," the Human informed them. "Did you think she was Human?"

The head had landed on top of the table. Having lost—or absorbed—its face, the thing looked like a large hairless pox but still wore its tall white cap. It pounced on the artifact, stuffed it under its cap, then dropped to the floor and scurried under the table with the rest.

"Get the hat!" KaeCee shouted.

Hat. Not cap. Aryl absorbed the new word as she shut off the force blade and exchanged it for her short knife, being safer under furniture.

She and the Human dove under the table together. KaeCee cried out as what had been a knee sprung up and hit him in the nose, but didn't back away. Aryl squirmed between the table legs, watched for movement in the dim light. Where were the rest?

And the hat?

"There they go!"

He was right. Aryl rushed forward on her elbows, but couldn't stop the next bit—something chest-ish—from jumping through the neat hole cut in the floor. As an escape, she had to admire it.

She glimpsed something white. "Get the hat!"

KaeCee grabbed; Aryl reached. They had it!

The hat came off in their hands, the artifact rolling free on the carpet, while the last piece of Lawren Louli plunged through its hole to safety. To put themselves back together below? Aryl let go of the hat and wiggled forward, cautiously peeking down the hole as she picked up the artifact.

It didn't open to the lower level of *Doc's Dive* but to a curved pipe just wide enough to fit the bits. Clever, Aryl had to admit.

Then KaeCee's hand clamped over her bare wrist. *You are for me. You are MINE!*

She could *hear* him?

MINE!

Waves of *heat* and *need* and *domination*. Something *fumbled* at her mind. Inept, untrained, blind to what it violated. *MINE! You will want ME!*

Repulsed on every level, Aryl freed herself with a quick twist, shields now firmly in place. She hurried out from under the table and to her feet, putting the artifact back on the table. Not that it mattered.

ARYL!? Enris, there at once. *Are you all right? What was that?*

The Human. He has some kind of Power. He touched *me.*

The flood of *fury* that answered made her hands shake. *I'm coming!*

No. Stay. Protect the others. Aryl calmed herself and sent *reassurance* and *determination.*

Naryn and I will handle this.

KaeCee straightened his jacket as he stood, smiling with triumph.

The Human's a fool, she finished, and smiled back.

"You are ours, now," said Aryl di Sarc.

YOU ARE OURS! Naryn's Power struck the Human's mind.

He staggered, smile gone. "So that's your game, is it? Filthy mindcrawlers! If it's a fight you want, that's fine with me. I'll make you beg," with quite inexplicable confidence. Unless the Human couldn't imagine abilities greater than his own.

He'd learn. *Scan him,* Aryl suggested coldly. *All we need is to know who will buy the artifacts, what to expect.* They could leave the body here.

Naryn lifted an eyebrow. *Oh, I think our KaeCee has much more to offer than information.* "Hold him."

The last thing she wanted to do was touch him again, but Aryl didn't hesitate. The Human was pitifully slow. Before he could begin to evade or struggle, she slammed the side of his face against the tabletop, her arm around his sweaty neck and a knee in his spine. It wasn't helping the M'hiray below. It wasn't being with Enris. It did, however, feel remarkably satisfying.

"That will do." Naryn laid her palm along his forehead. *Now, Human. Teach me.*

He began to scream.

Just as well, Aryl thought coldly, the Assembler had such a private space. She kept her shields at their most impenetrable. Even so, she *felt* the Power Naryn drew through his mind, like a knife through flesh.

More than an echo, she *felt* a surge of Power from another source altogether, like a welcome breath of fresh air. *Pride. Relief.* She had to smile. Enris. Whatever he'd done, it would protect the M'hiray from Louli. Her smile faded. Good.

She couldn't leave Naryn now.

The screams were replaced by a soft moan with each inward breath. He had no shields—no shields against M'hiray.

Suddenly, the moans stopped. The body in her hands relaxed. Naryn took away her hand.

Let him go.

Aryl released her grip slowly and stood back, tensed to spring at the Human if he offered any threat.

There was none. His face was reddened on one side. Trails of clear fluid glistened on his cheek and chin, but a peaceful smile played over his mouth. His hands straightened his jacket, then tidied his hair. His eyes were shot through with blood, and absolutely calm. He stood at ease, as if waiting. For what?

She stared at Naryn. *What have you done?*

"It's called 'influence,'" with unutterable *disgust*. At herself, or the Human? Both, Aryl decided, gorge rising in her throat. "KaeCee's an expert. That's what he wanted to do to you. Turn you into—" Naryn shook her head. "—it doesn't matter. The technique only works on Humans, and only those Humans with their M'hirless version of Power. Telepaths. Weak minds, susceptible to suggestion. The effect is permanent."

"Why?"

Naryn sat down and took hold of the artifact, tipping it to send reflections over his face. "KaeCee? What should we do with the Hoveny artifacts?"

The Human answered at once, his tone sure and brisk. "It means a deep cut in price, but I've buyers in mind on Unaligned worlds. No Commonwealth or Trade Pact connections to worry about. We couldn't move them on any Innersystem world, or within any space held by the First. I'll ensure no one can trace the artifacts to you. I regret this will take time to arrange, but I've sufficient creds in my hidden accounts to get the Clan into proper accommodations immediately. And to buy clothes, idents. You'll want to be able to move around Grandie society without undue notice. When the artifacts are sold, I'll deposit the funds in various separate accounts and will recommend suitable individuals to manage each for maximum growth. The Clan won't have to worry about wealth." Finished, he stood, waiting. Peaceful, content.

Better to have slit his throat, Aryl thought, sickened to her core. *Naryn . . .*

Think I enjoyed being in a Human's mind? That I wanted to learn this? Her mindvoice was weary. *That I wanted to do this, even to him?* Aloud, "How many Humans are on this world, Aryl? How many of them could help us? Of those who could, how many would? Council will agree with my actions. We couldn't afford to waste this opportunity. There might not be another."

"There are thirty-one Human telepaths in Norval," KaeCee corrected. "Fourteen of those are under my influence. They could be useful. I'll introduce you."

"See what I mean? I can't imagine a better Human."

"Naryn!"

Naryn tucked the artifact within her robe. "Haxel's sure our people are safe for now. KaeCee, we'll 'port with you to your office in the Sun Layer and you can . . ."

Aryl stopped listening.

Naryn's quick thinking, her sacrifice—for soiling her mind had been that, too—had probably saved the M'hiray.

She closed her eyes.

What Naryn had done—she wished she could believe it would never happen again. But she couldn't.

Aryl *reached,* feeling strangely fragile. *Enris?*

Beloved. With *joy* and *relief.*

Almost—almost enough to ease the turmoil inside. *I felt your Power,* she ventured, sharing *curiosity.* So much safer than anything else.

We locked the door. With *pride.* Then, something *dark* stirred. *Tell me he's dead. That Human.*

Peace, Enris. Naryn's dealt with him. She learned what we need to do. Even better—she tightened her shields—*we know how to influence his mind.*

You mean control. That's what he wanted to do. Make you obey him.

He'll save the M'hiray. He has no choice. Aryl opened her eyes and stared at KaeCee's too-peaceful face. *We've left him none.*

Interlude

THEY'RE IN SIGHT.
   Come back.
   When Veca appeared beside her, Haxel snapped aloud: "How many?"
   The Chosen held up both hands, fingers outstretched. "Syb and I could have handled them." With barely restrained *frustration*.
   Enris shook his head. "Not with knives," he said, remembering Louli's threat. That it involved his blood still made him flinch inwardly, as if he'd betrayed his own. "And not if more keep coming." And they would. He and Haxel had *shared* with the M'hiray what they'd seen above; he'd added what Aryl had shown him of the homes built one upon the other, the rooftops filled with Humans and other beings. No M'hiray doubted there were even more above.
   "He's right." Haxel turned to the waiting Council.
   Enris lost whatever was said, whatever he could see around him, his mind suddenly consumed with *heat* and *need* and something *twisted* and *dark* . . . It was in their Joining. After his Chosen!
   ARYL!?
   The sense of violation was gone as quickly as he'd felt it. *Are you all right? What was that?*

The Human. With *revulsion. He has some kind of Power. He* touched *me.*

Enris could hardly breathe for the rage coursing through him. *I'm coming!*

But even as he formed the locate . . . *No. Stay. Protect the others.* With reassuring calm. *Naryn and I will handle this.* That, not calm at all.

His hands were fists. Enris made himself relax. Protect the others. She was right.

"You paying attention?" Haxel asked. "Council's agreed."

"Move everyone back," he warned. Everyone but those he'd picked for this task: Worin and Fon, Kran and Netta. UnChosen and young. They were nervous, not afraid. *We can do this,* he told them, believing it.

Though he couldn't have explained why.

Once the M'hiray had climbed to the uppermost ledges, Enris and the others positioned themselves on the lowest. "Those first," he said, pointing to the crates of rattlers. An easy start that rid them of a potential threat.

Power surged from all four. Stacks of crates rose in the air. Disturbed, the creatures made their rattling sound. "Don't drop them," Enris advised mildly.

Worin made a face, but concentrated.

Stack by stack, the crates were carefully placed across the opening.

"Now."

He'd *shown* each what to move. Worin and Netta displaced the supports within the opening. Kran and Fon raised a mass of rubble into the air and flung it at the crates. While Enris concentrated, focused . . .

. . . . and *dropped* the wall above.

As the roar subsided, they grinned at one another, faces covered in dust. Cheers broke out from the others. A swell of *pride* and *relief* moved from mind-to-mind. They were safe, Enris thought.

For now.

Haxel jumped down beside him. "Good. The lights still work."

He squinted at her in disbelief. "You let us do this without being sure?"

"Weth was ready," with absolute calm. "We've oillights."

Pebbles tumbled; stone continued to groan into place. He cast an eye over the rest of the wall. Some carvings had lost their faces—if those had been faces. A crack snaked upward from where he'd *tugged* rock out of position. But nothing else appeared ready to fall. Enris ruffled Worin's dusty hair. "Well done. All of you."

Coughing, Fon frowned. "What's to stop the Humans using Power to remove it?"

"They can't." Gur had joined them. "Feel the M'hir, unChosen. Do you sense anyone there but us? Of course not. It is ours alone. As for the Humans? Our most Powerful Adepts have *reached* to their limit. Some open minds, none capable of answering. Humans are lesser beings. The feeble Power of a few is no threat."

Enris? Quiet. Too quiet.

Beloved. Enris didn't hide *joy* or *relief.* The *something* loathsome was gone from their link. It had been like a whiff of rotting food . . .

I felt your Power. Familiar *curiosity.*

We locked the door. Gur claimed Humans were no threat, but he'd *felt* what one had tried to do. *Tell me he's dead. The Human.* To dare touch his Chosen—not only her skin, but her mind. He fought to keep his shields tight.

Peace, Enris. So much for that effort. *Naryn's dealt with the Human. She's learned what we need to do. Even better,* an underlying *unease* contradicted her words, *we know how to influence his mind.*

His blood pounded in his ears. *You mean control. That's* what he wanted to do. *Make you obey him.* What were Humans, to conceive of such a thing? The enormity of that trespass—

"What's wrong?"

He didn't acknowledge Worin's question. Couldn't.

Why isn't he dead? Enris asked with what remained of his control.

He'll save the M'hiray. He has no choice. With a bleakness he'd never *sensed* from her before. *We've left him none.*

Enris shut his mind. Closed his eyes. Wished he didn't understand.

But he did.

This was the price of their future.

Chapter 5

NARYN'S EYES WERE HALF-SHUT, her face beaded with sweat. Her hair, freed of its net—the M'hiray no longer confined their hair—lashed against the mattress. She was conscious. And impatient. "How long will this take?"

Seru didn't laugh, but dimples appeared in her cheeks. "As long as it does." She busied herself rearranging towels.

Aryl perched on the windowsill and poked the *senglass* with a finger. Still hard. "Nippy outside," she commented. The transparent stuff responded to its environment as well as the wishes of those inside. As the day warmed, it would open to let through the breezes and whatever smells or sounds Naryn had decided to enjoy. She wasn't fond of florals.

The warming was controlled, too. As befitted an Innersystem world, Stonerim III had civilized weather, thoroughly planned and implemented. Necessary rain was scheduled during sleep cycles, unless other arrangements had been requested. For a fee—there was always a fee—a rousing thunderstorm could be supplied to order, or an evening kept summer warm and dry for an outdoor party.

"No one else is coming."

Aryl met Seru's troubled look, then hopped off the sill to sit on the end of Naryn's bed. "Who else do you need?" she asked lightly. "You've our Birth Watcher and me. I can call Enris if you like."

"That big oaf?" Naryn almost smiled. "No, thanks." She grimaced as another powerful contraction rippled over her abdomen. The sheets were dark purple na-fiber—nothing but the best for the M'hiray—but she'd tossed off her coverings. "Hurry up, will you?"

Don't you listen, Aryl sent inwardly, her hand on the so-far quiet bulge at her waist. The *presence* within acknowledged this attention with a cheerful *ticklemeticklemeTICKLEME* that she quickly shielded from the other adults, then obliged, fluttering her fingers against a protruding foot. Conversation would come eventually, she supposed, but babies were all about needs and wants.

There should be others here. A birth was attended by the other pregnant Chosen. Should be celebrated by family and friends.

And the father.

Which was the problem. Aryl gazed at Naryn, filled with her own curiosity. No one, not even Naryn, could explain how she'd Commenced and become pregnant without a Joining. At first, they'd assumed she'd somehow survived when her Chosen had failed to make the journey from the Clan Homeworld, or been left behind during the Stratification.

A place and event with names now, the beginnings of M'hiray history, kept with care.

But none of their Healers, not even Sian, with his ability with the mind, could find any trace of a Joining. Worse, they'd found no trace of a mind within the developing child.

No one else was here, because no one, Aryl thought sadly, expected a live birth. The M'hiray respected Naryn too much to be witness to her failure.

Not that Naryn di S'udlaat admitted the possibility.

"Oh," she said suddenly. "Oh. I think something's going on," in a strangely calm voice. "Seru?" That, not so calm.

Seru bent over Naryn, ran fingers lightly over the distended skin.

"OH!"

"We'll help you stand. Aryl?"

They eased Naryn to her feet. Her abdomen flexed in and out, each powerful contraction driving air from her lungs. Her hair lifted in a blinding cloud and Aryl batted it away with her free hand, holding her friend tight with the other.

If her hands were busy . . . *Seru, how are we going to catch—*

Before she could finish, the birth sac slipped free with a rush of clear liquid, landing on the pillows her more experienced cousin had wisely put in place. Easing Naryn into Aryl's arms, Seru went to her knees to pick up the sac in a towel.

Welcome . . . The sending died away. "There you are," her cousin said aloud instead, cradling the sac. She turned her back to them, hair limp to her waist.

"Let me see her." *Aryl, please!*

She slipped an arm under Naryn's shoulder and helped her to where Seru stood before the hammock.

The sac was as black as Seru's hair, flecked with star-like patches of pale, new-grown skin. It steamed in the room air.

It didn't move. It should move.

"Naryn—" Aryl began, her heart thudding in her chest.

"She knew," Naryn said, the strangest look on her face. She reached a trembling hand to the sac, touched it lightly. "She couldn't come with us. All along, she knew but didn't say a word."

"Who knew?"

"This wasn't her time." Naryn staggered, and both Aryl and Seru supported her.

Fingers brushed Aryl's. *Get her back to bed. I'll look after this.*

Wait! She knew what—who—Naryn meant. Didn't she? Someone old but strong, someone . . .

The memory slipped away, no matter how hard Aryl tried to hold it.

"To bed," Seru insisted. "You're getting cold."

Naryn didn't move. "The vessel is empty. Look in the M'hir. See for yourself. Please, Aryl!"

The M'hir? Aryl eased into that *other* place, rested in its steady motion, then tried to *see* what Naryn meant.

Their glows—Naryn, her cousin and her baby, the life within her own body—lit the darkness. The glorious pulse of Power that was her Joining to Enris, his comfort *there* if she needed it. Always.

Nothing more.

But something made her keep *looking*, though the M'hir reacted to the effort and became turbulent and distrustful. *Looking, looking* until . . .

Something *looked* back.

Something *interested*.

A Watcher. Or more than one. No M'hiray was sure of their number, only that they'd brought with them from the Homeworld a presence—or more than one—that existed in the M'hir and nowhere else.

Benign, declared Council. Guardians of the M'hir. They never spoke, only watched. But this . . . she almost grasped *identity*.

Who are you? Aryl demanded.

And was answered by a mindvoice so different and distant, she wasn't sure it was real. *We are you.*

Meaning what? *What do you want?*

What do you want?

Not an echo. Not her imagination. She held on as the M'hir crashed against her, held on and poured Power into her sending. *I want the baby to live! Fill the vessel! Where is it?*

A question so ordinary and impossible to answer, it threw Aryl out of the M'hir.

She stared at the sac. "Make her move."

"Aryl—it's—"

"I'll do it." Naryn grabbed the sac in both hands.

Seru pulled it away from her and put it down again. "Naryn. Come to bed. I'm sorry, but there's nothing more we can do. Aryl. It's time to remove the husk—"

"She still has a chance to live," Aryl said bluntly. "The Watchers have to find her. She has to move."

"What are you—" her cousin stopped, her hair lashing her shoulders. "Stop this, Aryl. You aren't helping."

Cousin, trust me, Aryl sent, *encouragement* and *love* beneath the words. *We have to try.*

For a heartbeat, Seru hesitated, then gave a tiny shrug. "Naryn in bed first," she insisted.

"Aryl?"

"Listen to your Birth Watcher," Aryl told Naryn and helped her lie down. The other was shivering and spent. Seru brought over a soft blanket and set it to warm.

"Stay there," she ordered.

Naryn's eyes filled with tears. "You'll try, Seru? Promise me."

"That's all I can promise."

"It's enough." Naryn closed her eyes.

The sac was hard, hard and cold. Aryl shuddered to imagine her own like this. "A force blade?"

Seru shook her head. "All the technology in the Trade Pact doesn't change what we are. A birth sac opens from within. There's only one choice."

Aryl blinked at her. "What?"

"If the Watchers need to find her," Seru said simply, "take her to them."

Her hand found Aryl's. *If this doesn't work, leave the husk in the M'hir.*

The more Powerful called it *suspension*, to begin a 'port then linger in the M'hir. Those Adepts who studied that *other space* called it a valuable technique; those who wanted to arrive safely called it reckless. For the longer the mind stayed within the M'hir, the less likely that mind would remain whole.

The longer within, the more likely to encounter the unreal presence of a Watcher. Another reason normal M'hiray nipped in and out as quickly as possible.

I'll be careful, Aryl promised her Chosen. *But I have to try.*

I know. A warmth, like his arms around her.

Aryl thought of her favorite place, and concentrated . . .

. . . then *HELD* . . .

. . . and *HELD* . . .

Power crackled around her, disturbing the M'hir. She was used to the effect and ignored it. *Where are you?*

Where are you?

. . . she *HELD* . . .

Power crackled and bled away, or was it self that diminished?

. . . she *HELD* . . . but for how long? *Where are you?*

Here. Here. Here. Here.

She was surrounded. Or was she alone? Aryl fought to keep her wits. *Where are you?*

A Presence. *The vessel awaits.*

The darkness boiled with movement. Something was coming.

Not coming. Being *forced* toward her. Chased. Pursued. Hemmed in despite frantic efforts to flee. Helpless and despairing, it lunged at her!

Aryl flung herself away and . . .

. . . found herself standing on the roof of the Tower, the sun warm on her face. She took a deep breath, savoring the smell of growing things. What had just happened?

Enris appeared beside her and threw his arm around her shoulders. "You did it!"

Aryl looked down at the sac in her hands. It squirmed and flexed, then split open down its middle.

A tiny fist pushed through, then a foot. *HUNGER!!!*

They both winced. "Back to your mother," Aryl told the newest M'hiray.

Their first birth in their new home. Small wonder everyone wanted to celebrate. If there were questions, they'd wait. For now, Aryl thought peacefully, life was good.

"Knew I'd find you here." Enris approached the roof edge cautiously, then sat beside her. "Though why you like doing this, I don't know."

Aryl snuggled against his shoulder. She didn't know either. But it relaxed her to sit here, dangling her feet over nothing—though the Tower had its safeguards, among them automated netting to catch anything or anyone that dropped off its roof or balconies. The view perhaps. "It's lovely up here."

The Towers of Lynn glittered night and day. Each rose almost to cloud height and stood apart. Each was unique in design. All were beautiful, like flowers of crystal and light. Those closest to the M'hiray belonged to methane breathers, and had senglass windows that modified their atmosphere. Though neighbors were always perilous, these were safer than most: unable to leave their homes, unwilling to exert the effort to invite guests. Below was the well-groomed and exclusive expanse of forest, sand, and ocean called the Necridi Coast. It had been a hunting preserve when Humans first colonized Stonerim III, for there'd been an indigenous population. One the Humans had cheerfully absorbed within three generations.

They were good at that, Humans. At changing worlds. At changing those around them. Abruptly chilled, Aryl was glad of her Chosen's big arm around her shoulders. His fingers played with her hair, or her hair played with his fingers. A meaningless distinction, she thought, nest-ling closer.

Then his fingers paused on the side of her neck, his touch lighter, curious. *Anything?*

She tried not to stiffen. *No.* The deep scar looked like a bite, but from no animal they'd been able to find in a database. Similar ones marred her shins, different ones ran up her arms. More than most M'hiray, less than others. Like symbols none of them could remember to read. "Have you heard if Council's come to a decision?" she asked aloud, changing the subject.

"They'll vote for dispersal. I don't think anyone doubts that. We're crowded here. Too vulnerable, all in one place."

"I want to stay here."

"I'm sure there are death-defying heights on other worlds."

Worlds with locates taken from KaeCee or any of the other Human telepaths influenced by M'hiray scouts. That's all they hunted now, Aryl thought grimly. The weak-minded. Occasionally, their Humans hunted for them. It was—more convenient—to nip curiosity using what KaeCee called "traditional" methods. The M'hiray didn't ask details.

Survival, by any name.

The Humans offered *maps*. The M'hiray found them irrelevant. What was distance, when Power was what mattered? What was the point of aligning stars or plot-ting orbits, of landmarks or descriptions when the *real* of a place could be set in a mind, ready for use and infal-lible? As for schedules?

Aryl snorted. The Humans imprisoned themselves in time. The only use M'hiray found for it was to note when interesting events would begin. They'd discovered plays and drama. And music that wasn't played by a 'botband.

"I just don't want to move anymore." Her hair wove

itself over his shoulders and neck. "We've left too much behind already. I'm afraid if we—if I go any further—I won't be the same."

"You'll always be my Chosen," Enris assured her, gathering her into his arms as white birds flew past below. "You'll always be who you are."

Aryl held on with all her strength.

And wished she could believe.

Chapter 6

THE M'HIRAY WOULD DISPERSE. How far was determined by the practicalities of 'porting. No one trusted the starships that plied between worlds, let alone was willing to be confined for days with Humans or Assemblers, though belongings would travel as freight. As for who would go, and where?

Where was determined by the practicalities of wealth. Human worlds—the Inner ones, long-settled—offered technology and luxury suited to M'hiray bodies and acquired tastes. Among those worlds, the most suitable had laws offering protection and privacy to offworlders and their investments, since M'hiray would not mingle with Human.

Seven families were selected, each to establish a House under his or her family name. Caraat, Friesnen, Mendolar, Parth, S'udlaat, Sarc, and Serona. The title of First Chosen would go to the most Powerful female M'hiray of each House. Other families would live with them at first, but ultimately move to their own.

UnChosen would no longer travel alone, even if strong enough to 'port such distances by themselves. Thus candidates seeking Choice in any particular House would seek the approval of Council, who would consult with the First Chosen. There was talk of fostering promising children within other Houses, to prevent any being too isolated, but it was only talk so far. Still, all agreed, whatever could be done to protect the M'hiray, should be done.

It was a start.

"First Chosen," Aryl grumbled. "It's not as if I want to be in charge of anything."

Enris grinned at her. "What, not interested in hosting our Council? They'll still meet here, you realize. And had the good taste to ask me to consider a Council seat, when the next comes open." With distinct *smug*.

He'd make an outstanding Councillor, Aryl thought, carefully keeping her *pride* private. "Since you have to be fed anyway . . ."

"At least you don't have to pack." Seru's eyes were suspiciously bright, and she leaked *unhappiness* through her shields.

Ezgi gave her a quick kiss. "I said I'd pack."

"And we'll visit," Aryl promised.

Sarc had been given the Tower on Stonerim III. Teerac would stay here, too, for now, as would Vendan, Gethen, and five other families. The First Chosen of S'udlaat, Naryn, had elected to remain here with young Lilia until she could be replaced on Council, but Worin would leave with Ruis di Mendolar—until, as all expected but the two youngsters, Council allowed him to offer Choice to Ziba Uruus.

Nothing would be the same.

"It won't be the same." Seru threw herself awkwardly into Aryl's arms. The two managed to hug despite their growing bellies.

The M'hir connects us. It always will. "Besides, I expect you back for my birthing."

"Then be thoughtful and time it for a Council Meeting." They both laughed.

The door chimed and opened. Haxel leaned in. "Enris, you ready?"

He glanced hopefully at Aryl. *Sure you won't come?*

To sort the remainder of the M'hiray's belongings in the Buried Theater?

Quite sure.

The artifacts had been removed a month earlier and moved to safekeeping within the Tower. All but one. Naryn had given Enris the very first. A start to their new history, she'd called it. So long as he kept it out of her sight, Aryl thought. The rest—hard to imagine a use for the tattered things they'd brought with them. Hard to imagine a life where they'd been useful. The hairnet yes, but though she missed wearing it, such wasn't a fashion that suited Norval society. No one wore knives here.

The force blade, however, she refused to leave in a drawer.

Once Seru and Ezgi left, once Enris was gone, Aryl found herself unsettled. She went to the roof and sat in her spot.

Nightfall. The Towers of Lynn outshone the stars, reflected in the white caps that danced over the ocean. Their exterior lights could be turned off at whim, sen-glass set to keep the interior from shining through, but Aryl liked the glitter. Safer, she thought, hugging herself. Always safer to have glows at night.

A thought as useless as the packs beneath Norval. She tried to ignore it. Sometimes it was easy.

Sometimes, like now, everything became *not-real*, from the taste of the air in her mouth to the words in her mind. Everything but having her toes over an edge. Everything but Enris and ... and ... she cradled the swell at her waist.

They'd given their baby a name.

Hadn't they?

Aryl rested her chin on one knee and stared at the methane breathers' Tower.

Were they this confused by life here?

"Other than the somgelt Sian wanted—he says the Humans should be able to culture it—there wasn't much of value. We left the rest."

Value? The gleaming inlaid floor of the Sarc gathering chamber was covered in rags and dirty tools. Aryl sighed as she picked her way around gourds of unrefined lamp oil. "You couldn't have left those, too?" She pointed to the bags of seed. "Stonerim doesn't look kindly on exotics."

Enris laughed. "Husni worried about vermin. I told her we'd store everything properly. But you have to admit the parches were a find."

"So long as we don't have them here." Which they wouldn't. Dann d'sud Friesnen had pounced on the rolled lists of names and ancestors, happy to offer his House as the keeper of M'hiray history. Though how history could come from names for people no one remembered, she didn't understand. All she knew was that their existence reminded her of what they'd lost and endangered what they'd kept.

He held out a pack. "Yours." With a little shake. "Might be something nice inside."

"I have closets of nice things," Aryl reminded him. Naryn enjoyed shopping. Or rather spending, which was the same thing.

"Which you don't wear," he observed. "Maybe you'd prefer what's in here." The suggestion was only half in fun. Enris watched her, waiting for a reaction.

Because he thought her old things might stir memories. Aryl glowered. *We agreed not to try and remember. That our former lives were gone.*

Are they? You cry in your sleep.

"I—" She closed her mouth, taken aback.

"Every night."

"Why don't you stop it? Wake me?"

A gentle smile. "Because I'm asleep, too, Beloved."

Chosen *shared* dreams. Not always, not all, but the emotional load, that passed from mind to mind.

Aryl gestured apology then shook her head. "I won't sleep again."

"I'm no Healer," Enris chuckled. "But I think it'd be easier to find out what's upsetting you."

"I'm not—" she glared, "—upset!"

He slid the bag across the floor to her feet, then sat in the closest chair and stretched out his long legs. Smiling all the while.

Annoying, irritating... She grabbed the bag and dumped its contents on the floor, nudging them apart with the toe of her slipper. Nondescript scraps of fabric, not all of it clean. Had she had no access to a fresher? Boots worn and patched. Because she'd liked them or been forced to live in them? "As I thought. Nothing useful. I—" Aryl stopped.

"What is it?"

Something that didn't belong. She bent to pick it up. "An image disk."

"Ordinary enough." Enris put his hands behind his head.

"Here," Aryl emphasized. "Has anyone else found a Trade Pact device in their gear?"

Oran and Bern appeared near the doorway. The Adept noticed the clutter on the floor. "Redecorating?" Oran asked with a sly smile. "I thought you'd wait till we'd all left."

"Aryl found a Trade Pact image disk in her things— from the Homeworld," Enris offered, being a little too helpful, Aryl thought, closing her hand over the palm-sized device. Her Chosen loved a puzzle.

For no reason she could name, she couldn't share this one. Not yet. "Is everything settled with Yao?"

As she'd hoped, the change of subject made both frown. "No," Oran snapped. "The child's being difficult."

Enris chuckled. "Haven't found her yet, have you?"

Not helping. The Powerful child's ability at 'port and seek was becoming a problem. Though Aryl sym-

pathized. When Council had insisted the unChosen be
tested for Talent, Yao had turned out to be the only potential Healer. Each of the M'hiray's adult Healers had
been considered as her teacher; Council and Yao's parents had picked Oran di Caraat.

No one had asked Yao. Who'd been hiding ever
since.

Aloud, "I'm sure Yao's grateful for the opportunity
you've offered, Oran—"

"You're First Chosen," Bern interrupted. "Can't you
control those in your own House?"

Any desire Aryl had to be conciliatory vanished.
"M'hiray don't control one another, Bern d'sud Caraat,"
she told him, hair billowing over her shoulders.

"Excuse my Chosen," Oran replied smoothly and
Bern subsided, looking sullen. "He doesn't appreciate
the burden of our new responsibilities. As First Chosen
of the House of di Caraat, I'm sure I, too, will have the
occasional—difficulty—to handle."

Smooth, dignified, and with a flick of Power. Perhaps
unintended.

Perhaps not. Aryl let her own swell past her shields,
saw with no satisfaction how the other's mouth tightened in response. Games. Did Oran not see how pointless they were? How destructive they could become?

"Feel free to leave this particular difficulty to the
House of Sarc," she suggested. "I appreciate how much
work you have ahead of you."

The two disappeared without another word.

Enris raised an eyebrow. "Husni's right. 'Porting
could use some manners."

Aryl gazed at the place where they'd been. "I shouldn't
have done that," she sighed. "Bern's . . ."

*He stopped being your heart-kin the moment he let
Oran control him.* Beneath, something *cold.* Enris wasn't
about to forgive Bern.

"She's more Powerful—"

"Since when did that matter between Chosen? Between any of us?"

"Since we came here."

Once said, the words were like the mended clothing spread over the expensive floor. Out of place. Impossible to ignore. Aryl gestured apology and wasn't sure why.

"Is that what we tell our children?" Enris asked, drawing in his feet, his face clouded. "Is that our future? Power to be the measure of a M'hiray's worth. Power to be what decides right from wrong. Will it be our excuse for every mistake?"

Aryl went to sit on the floor beside him. She laid her cheek on his knee, felt his fingers seek comfort in her hair. *Power is all we have. We need it to protect ourselves. We need it to survive among the Humans.* The wealth from the artifacts wouldn't last; already scouts on other worlds sought Humans who could keep wealth flowing to the Clan, more Humans susceptible to their "influence." They had no other choice. *Only Power will keep our children safe.*

Enris pressed his lips to her head. *What if that's why we're here?*

She twisted to meet his somber gaze. "What do you mean?"

"What if our mothers and fathers had planned a different path for our kind? What if we—the M'hiray—were the ones who became 'difficult,' like Yao, and refused to do what we were told?"

"So our families threw us out? Took our memories so we'd never come back?" About to protest, Aryl found the words died in her throat. Being terrible to contemplate didn't make it wrong.

He sighed. "All I know is that believing we left because we were somehow superior is dangerous. It encourages M'hiray like Oran, who already judge others by Power alone. Power shouldn't mean privilege."

"Of course not," Aryl scowled. "Those with more Power have a duty to those with less."

Enris smiled slowly, his eyes growing bright. "Which is why you—" he interrupted himself to give her an enthusiastic kiss, "—will be such a fine First Chosen for the House of Sarc. And mother." With a nerve-tingling surge of *affection* and *heat*.

Pushing all other thoughts aside, she leaned in happily. He laughed and held her away. "Yao?"

She'd had to mention duty.

But first . . . with *desire* blazing across their link, Aryl took his hand and concentrated . . .

. . . after all, being First Chosen of Sarc entitled her to a very large and private bedroom.

Aryl dressed. A loud snore made her smile, a smile so deep and *shared* she watched it curve his sleeping lips. Chosen could do that.

Loath as she was to leave Enris, he'd been right. Yao needed to be found. By her, no one else. On impulse, Aryl slipped the mysterious image disk into a pocket. From the clothes in her pack, she'd always preferred pockets.

She tried again to tug her favorite jacket down over her stomach, then gave up. After the baby was born, it would fit.

No need to play 'port and seek through the Tower and startle those enjoying their evening. She couldn't catch the child that way regardless. There were rooms in the extravagant building even she hadn't seen, whether because of the sheer size of the place or because they were the domain of 'bots. Aryl frowned. Humans appeared to accept the mindless servants. No M'hiray was comfortable in their presence.

The Tower contained three hundred and forty apartments, each large and luxurious, plus nine that were more like buildings within a building. These would be home to the families staying here, with the topmost belonging to Sarc. And its roof, Aryl thought contentedly.

Among her duties as First Chosen, she decided, would be the manners Husni wanted. No surprise 'ports, unless an emergency. Polite farewells before disappearing. Not that children would pay attention, but it would help.

Yao.

Aryl nodded to herself and added a handlight to her pocket. The best place to escape an unwanted future?

In the only past they knew.

The lights no longer worked. Aryl switched on hers before she moved, though there was one glow in the darkness. A small fire burned on the stage. A smaller hand fed it.

Aryl took her time climbing down the ledges between. When she spotted a piece of debris that would burn, she picked it up. She had a small armload by the time she reached the bottom. "May I join you?"

Yao's eyes caught the firelight, reflected red and yellow. "If you want."

Impeccable shields. To Aryl's *inner* sense, the little figure seated across from her was almost invisible. No matter. She made herself comfortable, added a handful to the fire.

Waited.

The flames took her offering; the extra light revealed dusty knees covered with scrapes. The injuries were new since yesterday; the healing process well underway. Power indeed. "Oran's left."

The knees pulled out of the light. "Don't care." Very quiet. Very sure.

Aryl pulled out the image disk. "This was with my

things—from before." She turned it over and over in her hands. It had finger-sized depressions on both sides but poking them accomplished nothing. "I think it's broken."

"You aren't doing it right."

She held it out without a word or smile. A shadow became Yao, who took the device. Careful not to touch skin.

Too young for the caution of an adult; too old to forget it now.

She could have intervened at the start, Aryl realized with sudden guilt. Being First Chosen, it was her responsibility to speak up for those who looked to her.

Yao didn't go back to the other side; she did, however, stay out of reach. "Like this," she announced, holding the device in both small hands. She pressed several places at once.

No wonder it hadn't worked for her, Aryl thought with wry amusement, then stared as four figures took shape above the fire.

"They aren't real," Yao assured her.

Two adult females, two children. Human, if appearance could be trusted. The one adult had long red hair, and held the youngest. A girl. The older child was a boy.

"Why would I have images of strangers in my pack?"

"They aren't strangers," as if she was being silly. "This is his family. Marcus'."

The name from the artifacts. Aryl swallowed, staring at the Humans. "Marcus Bowman."

"That's right!" Yao smiled. "I wanted him for my father because . . . because . . . " Her smile faded. "I don't understand," she said, her voice trembling. "Why do I think my father—my real father—how can I think he didn't love me before?"

Because he hadn't. Aryl knew it, as surely as she knew her own name. Hoyon d'sud Gethen had spurned his own daughter, his only child, until arriving on Stonerim III. Why, she couldn't imagine, feeling sick inside.

"We don't—we don't remember our lives before coming here, Yao. Maybe that's for the best. Your father loves you now. You know that."

"Will he love me tomorrow?"

Children made a game of falling. Dared the worst to happen. Taught themselves to survive. She wasn't as brave as a child anymore, Aryl realized. She didn't dare answer such a question.

Then the image changed. "I didn't do that," Yao said quickly.

A face gazed at them over the sinking fire. "It's all right," Aryl heard herself say. But it wasn't. It wasn't all right. Her breath caught in her throat. Her pulse pounded. She *knew* that face, even battered and bruised.

The lips moved. Yao did something and the quiet voice rose to every ledge in the Buried Theater. The voice that belonged here.

"My name is ... Marcus Bowman. This ... device contains my ... final message for my ... daughter. Karina Bowman ... Norval, Stonerim III ... Anyone who finds ... this. Please take ... it to the nearest ... offworld authority ... Make sure she ... hears this. Please."

The image and voice vanished.

Yao calmly passed the disk back to Aryl, who took it with numb fingers. "Can I come with you? To find Karina?"

"What?" Aryl shuddered back to reality. "No. We're going home, to the Tower. You don't have to go with Oran," she added before the child could 'port away. "But I need you to promise to stay with your mother until I get back."

"From finding Karina." Yao sounded satisfied. "I won't tell anyone."

"I'm not—" Aryl closed her mouth, remembering that tormented face with green-brown eyes.

Apparently she was.

She looked up, into the darkness above Yao's little fire. There were hundreds of millions of Humans living within the layers of Norval.

"How do I find one?" she said out loud.

Even Yao didn't have an answer.

Interlude

"ARYL DI SARC IS NOT in the Tower."

"I know Aryl's not here," Enris glared at the panel. What use was a machine that gave answers he knew? "Where did she go?"

"I am unable to answer that question. Do you wish me to initiate a missing person's report with the constabulary?"

"No," Naryn said firmly. She reached by him to turn off the Tower interface. "Enris. Aryl's shielded herself from any of us. If you won't *send* to her, at least let me contact one of our Humans."

" 'Our Humans?' " he repeated acidly. "When did the mind-wipes become property?"

Naryn's eyes flashed, but she restrained her temper. "The name Yao gave us is the one from the artifacts. If Aryl uses it among Humans who aren't—sensitive—to Clan concerns—she could stir up trouble we can't control or survive. Have you thought of that?"

"Aryl has." With all the *belief* he had in his Chosen. "You know she would never endanger us. She wants to deliver a father's dying message, a message entrusted to her. There's nothing wrong with that."

"A Human's message." Cetto shook his big head. "From the Homeworld. It makes no sense, Enris."

Not for the first time since Yao's return—by herself—Enris was grateful he only had two members of Council under the same roof. "You should trust her," he insisted.

"You want to find her, too," observed Naryn, with a lift of one brow.

"Because I don't trust anyone else." Enris forced his hands to relax. Over the past hours, they'd tended to form fists. "I can't send to her. She's hunting." He had no other way to describe the way his Chosen *felt*, how her mind had focused until all he sensed were movements, the flick of her eyes side to side, the graceful, careful steps she took, her alert patience.

But Cetto nodded as if he knew what Enris meant. "Best not to distract her, then. She'll *reach* you if she needs help."

Aryl, call for help? Enris wanted to laugh. Joined for life and deeply in love, yes, but that didn't make his Chosen any less independent. Her first impulse would be to keep him out of trouble, not bring him into it. Which was why she'd simply 'ported back with Yao, picked up some things, and left again without anyone, including the Tower machines, any wiser.

He'd know if she were hurt or afraid. Which could be too late. Power, courage, and strength meant nothing against the kind of weapons possessed by the Humans and other aliens of this world.

She expected him to trust her and do nothing. Which meant pacing in the Tower, while others expected him to do something.

Aryl di Sarc was the most stubborn, annoying . . .

"We wait," he told Naryn.

And hoped that wasn't a mistake.

Chapter 7

SEEN FROM THE AIR, Norval resembled a mountain, its sides cloaked with green, its peak sparkling
with what might have been snow. None of it real, Aryl
thought as the aircar went around to the shadowed side
and slowed on approach. The city squatted on the ruins
of what had been there before, pressing the past into
the soft marshy land that had once surrounded it. Not
only ruins. On occasion, it had reinvented itself, burying
the streets and architecture of before beneath the latest
craze in materials and style. Or to hide design mistakes
of the past.

Humans hadn't started the process; three other civilizations, of other shape and mind, had built atop one
another over time in this place. As usual, Humanity had
added its own enthusiasm.

Producing this. A city where access to light was determined by wealth, its outer skin garden-bedecked luxury and senglass, topped by towers of privilege. Broad
openings allowed light—and storm runoff—to nourish
the businesses below. Narrow openings and pipes shed
some light—and all refuse—down through subsequent
layers to be used or dealt with by the least wealthy, until
the utter dark of the machine domain.

No wonder starships couldn't land anywhere near

here, Aryl thought wryly. For all its bulk and history, Norval was a fragile beast, ultimately dependent on pillars and stone no one had seen in centuries.

Except Marcus Bowman. She gripped the slippery memory as the automatics brought the aircar in for a landing. He'd rediscovered the Buried Theater. It had been his place, while he'd been on this world.

Making his the memories Naryn had used to bring them here.

"Amni InterWorld Shopping Concourse, Sun Layer. Your one-stop—" Aryl hit the button to silence the machine voice, though tempted to gesture apology afterward. This was how M'hiray entered the Human part of the world. The automated aircars were everywhere here, buzzing around Norval and Stonerim's other cities like the insects called flies over too-ripe fruit left outside. They waited for their next passengers in quiet parking areas; the M'hiray owned several such, careful to remove all monitoring devices.

The shopping concourse was the only address Aryl knew, having used the system only once, with Naryn. She didn't care to be near Humans, in small numbers or large.

She especially didn't care to be near the ones "influenced" by the scouts. The ones who had only been "encouraged" to trust M'hiray were almost worse.

None of them here.

The concourse lay within a bubble of senglass that erupted from Sun Layer, that cover set to exclude most of the outside world. Why, when the outside was a limited commodity, Aryl couldn't guess. But much of what Humans did confounded her.

Not shopping. She could understand the pleasure of walking through colorful, changing displays as a couple or in a family group. Most of those here, however, didn't appear interested in the displays, though a few attracted the most interest. She joined one such cluster around a

storefront, curious, only to find it was display of small
furred animals, tumbling around one another.

Aryl walked away before teeth showed.

She had a good plan, she told herself, eyes flicking
from side to side. There was a restaurant here, with
food she'd enjoyed. More importantly, every table had a
comport. Safely in her pocket, with the image disk, was
the burst Constable Maynard had given her to summon
him.

He would come at once, she'd give him the disk, and
then she'd return home.

What could go wrong?

The first thing that went wrong was the constable's
arrival—or rather lack of it. Two hours later, on her
seventh order of sombay and fifth run to cope with the
result, Aryl had began to wonder if she'd misunderstood.
It had sounded straightforward. Drop the burst into any
comport or reader, he'd know where she was, and he'd
come.

She plucked another feather from the decorative
bowl and began stripping the soft bits from it, adding to
the growing pile.

How long should she wait? she wondered glumly.
What if he'd died? How long did Humans live, anyway?

The staff wouldn't care if she stayed forever. The
M'hiray had been told the importance of generosity.
Aryl was quite sure they'd never been paid so much for
a beverage and her wish for privacy had been taken seri-
ously. No one was seated at the nearby tables. A family
that tried had been forcibly removed.

Feather stripped, she pulled out the disk, careful not
to press any of the depressions. Small. Ordinary. Old-
fashioned, from what she'd seen in the stores that sold
such things. There were signs of wear. Scratches on the

dull gray metal. None deep. It was sturdily built. Made to last.

To carry a message from a dying father.

Why hadn't hers sent a message? Why nothing from those left behind?

Enris wanted to know what she dreamed that made her cry in her sleep. Wanted to help her find out, so she'd stop.

Aryl's finger traced the nicked edges of the disk. Oh, she knew well enough.

She dreamed the end of the world.

Every night.

She dreamed the M'hiray were the last of their kind, survivors of a catastrophe so complete, they couldn't bear to remember it.

Or that they'd caused.

Dreams like that, Aryl thought heavily, didn't stop. She'd try to wake up more often, before she disturbed Enris. The baby would help there.

"I came as soon as I could, Femmine."

Aryl looked up, annoyed to have let herself be startled. Not that it was Maynard's fault. "I kept busy," she told him.

His lips twitched as he noticed the ruined feathers. "May I sit?"

Courtesy. She nodded, grateful for the moment to recover her calm. Too much sombay. A server delicately caught her attention and she nodded again to bring him to the table. "A drink?"

"Water, please."

"For you, Femmine? More sombay?"

Aryl shook her head, queasy at the thought.

"More, ah, feathers?"

"I've had enough for now," she assured him.

Once the server had left an iced pitcher of water and a glass for the constable, Aryl pushed the disk to the middle of the small table. "I need to you deliver this."

Maynard paused, glass halfway to his lips. "You don't waste time, Femmine."

She'd wasted hours, Aryl thought, but kept that to herself. "It belongs to a Human, a young child. All I know is her name and that she lives in this city."

He took a sip, regarded her over the top. He looked almost elegant in the fitted black jacket, symbols in red and gold at cuff and collar. No sign of a weapon, but she doubted he was unarmed. Dressed for the Sun Layer wealthy. Human protocols. "You look different," he commented.

The baby was bigger. Then Aryl realized he meant the Human clothes. "I've been shopping."

"Expensive place, the concourse." With this oblique comment, he put down his glass and stared at her. "I didn't think KaeCee could afford it."

KaeCee? Aryl's confusion must have answered some unasked question, for Maynard colored and leaned back. "My apologies. Let's start again. May I know your name, Femmine?"

"My name."

"You know mine." He had a pleasant smile.

There was no harm in it, Aryl realized. She was a property owner on his world—hers too, now. The First Chosen of Sarc shouldn't hesitate to deal with local authority.

In fact, that was probably her responsibility, too. Enris, she decided, would be laughing at her right now.

"My name is Aryl di Sarc." She tapped the disk. "I need you to find the person this belongs to and make sure she receives it. Please." Her hair slid over her shoulders as if to add its encouragement. She shoved it back.

His eyes dismissed the hair. "So that's not evidence to help me convict KaeCee or any other criminal. You used a burst to call me to run an errand." Maynard stood, his face and manner cold. "Thank you for the water, Femmine Sarc."

This would be, Aryl decided, the second thing to go wrong. "Wait. I can pay—"

"I'm sure you can. But I'm not for sale."

He turned and left, walking with the stiffness of someone truly offended. The servers backed out of his way.

Three. Her plan, she thought bitterly as she hurried after him, was a disaster.

"Will you wait?"

Maynard glared over his shoulder, then stopped. "I can have you arrested for following me."

"No, you can't," Aryl guessed. They were standing at the edge of one of the storefront crowds.

"Wasting my time. I can certainly arrest you for that, if you don't go away. Good evening, Femmine."

"I'm sorry," Aryl said quickly, getting in his way. "Here." She handed him the burst. "I thought this meant you'd help me. I didn't know who else to ask."

He took it between two fingers and rubbed it pensively, then looked her in the eyes. "I'm listening."

"This belonged to a—a friend of mine who died. Not long ago. Offworld. He left it with me. It contains a message for his daughter. But I'm—"

"Not from here," he finished when she hesitated.

"Not from here," Aryl agreed. "I don't know how to begin to find her. I can't trust—" she stopped before saying "anyone." "There are reasons I can't attract attention to her. But she should have this. A daughter should hear what her father wanted to say."

Maynard shook his head. It wasn't at her, since he said, "Let's walk."

Once they were away from the crowd, he began asking quiet questions. "Don't say her name. Not here. She's Human? Local?"

"Yes. Human children stay with their mothers, don't they?"

That drew a considering look. "Usually. Do you have her name? Don't say it."

"Yes."

They walked in silence. As he seemed deep in thought, Aryl held back her own questions. Finally he spoke again, so quietly she had to step close to hear him. "If you don't want to attract attention, you can't leave with me."

"Why?"

Almost a smile. "There are two kinds of people on Stonerim III, Aryl. Grandies and Commons. Grandies pay exorbitant taxes so the law will ignore them, as long as they keep their noses clean dirtside. Commons? Well, they pay as little as they can to have help when they need it."

"I need your help," Aryl pointed out, sure of that, if not taxes.

A real smile. "I get that. But to those looking at us, you're a Grandie. It's one thing for me to meet you on your terms, but you'd never get into my vehicle or go with me anywhere. I want you to go out the doors we'll pass soon, take the lower path until you come to a small garden, and wait there for me. Will you do that?"

Aryl nodded. Caution was never a bad strategy.

"If you see anyone who makes you nervous, come back here. We'll find another way."

"I have a force blade," she assured him. "If anyone makes me nervous."

"Please don't tell me things like that."

"Whatever you say, Constable." Aryl hid her own smile.

They came to the doors. Without a backward look, she went through them into the warm evening air.

No one made her nervous. No one else was outside. Aryl supposed it was the rain.

Well-behaved rain. She lifted her face to the steady drizzle, enjoying how it collected on her cheekbones then ran down her neck. The plants lining the well-lit lower path enjoyed it, too, their leaves dancing in the drops. Aryl drew the air through her nostrils, promising herself she'd go to the base of the Tower every night, to smell this, wondering why she hadn't before.

No puddles threatened her delicate shoes. The path was made of a material that whisked away moisture. The buildings to either side, even the light poles, refused to get wet.

Too tidy. Too polite. She stuck out her tongue.

The small garden where she was to wait was easy to find. The path widened to go around an island of yellow -and-white flowers. Their striped faces were upturned to the rain, too. Aryl stepped closer, noticing that the water dripping from the petals and leaves fell into a clear pipe. She followed it to where it plunged into the ground.

How many Grandies had seen where the water went? Aryl gazed at the towers that grew like a forest high above, thinking of the maze of giant pipes far below. Of the Commons who'd been stealing fuel and died for it. If not for the artifacts, which would the M'hiray be?

She came to attention as a shadow stopped overhead, taking away the rain, then waited as the black aircar moved ahead, then slowly descended to almost touch the path. A door in its side opened, but no light welcomed her.

Aryl drew the force blade and switched it on. The line of energy turned the rain to steam.

The aircar jigged up and down, as if impatient.

The constable.

Embarrassed, she put away the weapon and climbed in, feeling her way to a bench. Once the door closed, the lights came on.

Maynard set the machine in motion, then came back to sit across from her. "We can't be overheard in here."

Haxel and others who routinely left the Tower used

scramblers and other tricks they'd learned from the Clan's Humans, careful to leave normal traces but not reveal too much. Anyone who could afford it did the same. She should have. Aryl winced at the lecture she'd doubtless receive—and deserve—on her return. She gestured gratitude, then thought "Human" and added "Thank you."

"Wait till we see if I actually can help," he advised. "The names?"

"Karina Bowman is the daughter. The mother's name is Kelly Bowman. The father's—he was—" For some reason, Aryl found herself unable to say it. She pulled out the image disk and handed it to Maynard, folding her hands on her lap. "It's in there."

He touched the insignia on his jacket. "Look up 'Karina and Kelly Bowman.' Norval city limits to start. All occurrences." He lifted his fingers away. "That'll start the data flow. Now." Like Yao, the constable had no problem operating the disk.

She watched him, not the images; saw how he gazed without expression at the image of the four, how, when Marcus' face appeared, muscles along his jaw clenched. Maynard played the message through once, then again. Again.

Aryl closed her eyes.

"He was *tortured*."

She opened them, saw his anger and didn't understand. "Injured—"

"You call that 'injured'? Ossirus save me from fools!" His anger was at her now. "I know torture when I see it. That was deliberate harm, Aryl di Sarc, by someone who wanted answers, information, something from this Bowman. Who? Where did this happen? When?"

Tears filled her eyes. Marcus had been tortured? "I don't know," she fumbled. "Offworld. I—I found the disk in my things when we unpacked. I don't know how it got there, only that I—I must have promised him. To give it to Karina. Why else would I have it?"

His eyes were cold. "Why, indeed?"

Aryl stiffened. "Will you help me or not?"

Without answering, Maynard took the disk and went to his seat at the front of the aircar.

Aryl stayed where she was, looking down at her hands, and did her best to keep her thoughts—and her feelings about them—from Enris.

Torture.

Did that terrible word describe what Naryn had done to KaeCee? What M'hiray scouts did to any Human vulnerable to Power?

If so, they were no better than those who'd tormented Marcus Bowman. He hadn't deserved to be treated like that.

He'd only tried to help them. To help their ... it faded ...

No, she wouldn't lose the memory. She wouldn't!

... help their world. Marcus Bowman had been a friend, not only to her, but to the M'hiray. A Human friend, of his own will.

Had he died for it?

Aryl waited, lost in her own concerns. She didn't know how long it was before the constable swiveled his seat to look at her again. "You say he was your friend."

"Yes. Have you found something?"

"A puzzle. I hate puzzles," Maynard added almost lightly. "In my line of work, they mean elements who prefer to hide certain truths. Elements who will be distinctly unhappy if I happen to find them."

Aryl didn't bother working this out. "Did you find Karina?"

"I found Marcus Bowman."

She blinked.

"In the records. What's left of them. He's listed as having died offworld—but not where or how. His work appears in the indices of various academic publications, where he's described as a prominent xenoarchaeologist and Triad Analyst—but the First won't comment on whether or not a Marcus Bowman did research for them. According to a source, any and all original materials attributed to a Marcus Bowman have been sealed and removed from public access.

"The one item that does keep surfacing? Marcus Bowman was an expert on the Hoveny Concentrix. Does that mean anything to you?"

KaeCee said the artifacts were Hoveny. Marcus Bowman had put his name on them as proof. "A past civilization," Aryl said. "One that ruled this section of space a long time ago."

"Hoveny relics are rare. Incredibly valuable," the constable informed her, leaning his arm on the back of his chair. His eye glinted. "Our mutual friend KaeCee would be interested, but the oddest thing? There hasn't been so much as a whiff of anything untoward about his activities in weeks. Since you've arrived, in fact. Have you been a good influence?"

She tried not to flinch. Maynard was on the hunt; she knew the signs. She'd been wrong to come, Aryl realized, her mouth dry. Wrong not to see the dangers in names and data. Haxel would want this Human "handled."

Not going to happen, Aryl told herself fiercely. "Did you find Karina Bowman?"

"She's dropped off."

She'd never understand the Human fondness for meaningless expressions. "Off what?"

Maynard regarded her. "The First may not acknowledge Marcus Bowman, but they legally claimed everything he owned. Home. Credit deposits. Savings. We've no current location or work address for anyone in his family. My guess is those who got wind of the claim took what they could and ran offworld. It happens." With a shrug. "Puts them out of my jurisdiction."

Offworld. It meant away from here. But where?

Like most M'hiray, Aryl wasn't quite convinced the locates for the seven Houses were on other planets entirely and struggled with the scope of the newly formed and growing Trade Pact. Worlds. Solar Systems. Quadrants. Galaxy. Words. That's all they were. Offworld said it all.

"They're gone?"

He brandished the disk in one hand. "Which leaves this. Whatever Bowman put in here, it's encrypted. Secret," at her questioning look. "You'd need his code to access it. Might be for privacy. But secrets raise another possibility. Not a pleasant one."

"Nothing about this is," she retorted. "What possibility?"

"That Bowman never intended this for his daughter. The First's claim went through about the time you arrived. Maybe he knew she'd be gone. Maybe he expected someone else to obtain it from you, someone with the code."

Aryl relaxed and smiled. "If there's one thing I'm sure of, it's that this is for the baby."

"Baby?" His gaze sharpened. "What baby?"

"Karina."

Maynard activated the image disk again. "The little girl here?"

"Of course."

"You don't know—I see." He turned off the image. "This vid was made fourteen standard years ago."

No. That was Marcus' family. He'd shown her. Talked of them. They'd been alone together, both lonely ... Family was everything. To him as well.

Aryl surged to her feet. "I don't believe it!"

The constable didn't move. "City records state Kelly Bowman dissolved their partnership shortly after this was taken, keeping the son, Howard. The daughter became the sister's ward, Cindy Bowman, and both were last known to reside in the Bowman home in Norval. Karina Bowman isn't a baby anymore."

"Why would he show me this?" Aryl sank back down. "Why this and not the truth?"

"It wasn't a lie," Maynard said quietly. "At a guess,

Bowman was far from home. Living like that—you take your best memories with you, not your failures. Do you understand?"

"Lie" she understood. Now. Another meaning revealed. To say what wasn't true, to do it on purpose. She didn't like the words the constable taught her. She didn't like them at all.

"If Marcus didn't lie to me," Aryl replied with a scowl, "he lied to himself." To pick and choose parts of a life to remember, parts to forget? If that was what the M'hiray had done, they'd lied to themselves, too. She should go home. There was no point to this. To any of it.

The past was broken.

"Listen to me, Aryl di Sarc." Maynard came and sat across from her, the disk held flat between his palms. "I said this was a puzzle. It's not an ordinary one. Parts of your friend's life are being hidden by those in power. There's a stench to what's being left in the open. If Hoveny relics show up anywhere, right after a Triad Analyst is declared dead and his belongings confiscated? The snoops will be all over it. Bowman will be accused and convicted by opinion. His reputation won't be worth a pox's piss."

"There's nothing I can do about that." Besides believe him. Besides believe it was all their doing, that by selling the artifacts the M'hiray had done exactly what this Human predicted: plant suspicion on Marcus.

Who'd known this would happen.

The look in his eyes from the vid. Why hadn't she seen it?

Marcus Bowman had known what giving the M'hiray the artifacts, what sending both to Stonerim III would mean. The destruction of his reputation. The cost to his family.

He'd traded it all for them.

"There's nothing I can do,' Aryl repeated, hair sliding limp over her cheeks. "It's too late."

"Might be." Maynard pressed the disk into her hands.

"Might not. Keep this," he said gruffly. "I'll see what I can do. No promises, mind you. It could take a while—a long while. I can't make this a public search. Not and avoid—certain elements." His sudden smile was predatory. "But if I find her, you'll know."

"Then what?"

"Then, Aryl, you give Marcus Bowman's daughter the truth. Some of it, which is more than she has now."

Her hair slipped down her arms to cover their hands. Aryl gazed at the constable and for a instant saw another face, with wise green-brown eyes and a smile that quirked at the corner.

"You have a daughter."

He half smiled. "Three."

If she'd met Maynard first that night . . . if the M'hiray had found a better kind of Human in Norval, one to trust instead of use . . . so much would be different.

As well wish for a world of their own.

"I'll be waiting, Constable," she said solemnly. "As long as it takes."

Chapter 8

FIRST TEERAC, THEN VENDAN moved, establishing their place away from Sarc. Aryl missed them all, something she kept to herself. She seemed the only one who wanted the M'hiray to stay together; happiest when they gathered again, quiet for days when they left.

Enris believed it was the baby. "Who should," Aryl whispered to the considerable bulk that preceded her, "be out by now." She wasn't, according to Seru and Sian, late. As her cousin had given birth two weeks ago, and Sian's Chosen had never had a child, she didn't think much of their opinions. "Late you are."

Notlisteningnotlistening.

Opinions, her baby did have. And a will as strong as her Chosen's. "You'd be happier out." To prove it, Aryl walked through the door to the upper balcony to greet the morning.

The gardeners had finished only days ago. Other M'hiray, especially Naryn, had thought this the strangest notion she'd had yet. Being First Chosen, Aryl thought smugly, she didn't have to think much of those opinions either.

The balcony stretched out from the Tower, curved back, and formed a gentle ramp as it wrapped completely around the Sarc holding. She could walk to the roof from here.

Not quickly. The gardeners had followed her instructions with Human enthusiasm, accomplishing more than she'd imagined. Where other balconies had transparent floors or rich surfaces of tile and wood, that of Sarc was soft turf. Vines climbed the Tower walls. Sections of the senglass were programmed to allow their flowering tips to pass through, so at night, it was hard to tell where the garden ended and their home began.

As she did every morning now, Aryl plucked a wide, sturdy leaf, sniffed its pungent fragrance, then absently folded it once, then again. Once more, she decided. She went to the railing and tossed it gently into the wind. The folded leaf flew straight for a few seconds and she began to smile, then it tumbled and spiraled straight down. "Not right," she murmured.

Taller plants made islands of shade and foliage. Nothing appeared groomed or tame, though of course it all was. But when she stood here during the nightly rain, in the midst of growing things, Aryl could almost touch . . .

"Thought I'd find you here." Enris wandered in, ducked a low-hanging branch, and flung himself down on a sunny spot of turf. "How's our bundle?"

She smiled and brought over a stool, having discovered their "bundle" resented the amount of bending required to lie on the ground. Her bare toes caressed the turf. "Not as impatient as I am."

"Did you hear Council asked Lymin and Suen to consider our daughter for their son's Choice?" He rolled over on his back and grinned at her. "Suen said to remind them in fourteen years or so. Not that he has anything against ties with the Sarcs."

Aryl laughed. "As if Council can dictate Choice." *Warmth* slipped between their minds, as soothing as the sun on her back.

You two dressed?

Enris snorted.

We're fit for company, Aryl replied, smiling as Naryn materialized. "Glad you've decided to—"

"I'm not here to visit." Naryn's red hair writhed over her shoulders, dipped across one eye. "There's a Human asking for you in the Tower antechamber. She won't give a name."

Uninvited visitors didn't reach the Towers of Lynn. There were abundant—and costly—measures to ensure the privacy of those who lived here. Enris sat up. "How did she get this far?"

"She was brought in an undeclared vehicle. It had the right codes. Cader took a look. He says," Naryn's lip curled with distaste, "it was one of the stealth pursuits used by Norval's constabulary. How your nephew would know this is something you should investigate, First Chosen."

Maynard.

Aryl rose to her feet, heart pounding. "Have her brought—have her brought here."

Who is it?

"Here?" Naryn's eyebrow lifted.

"Here."

To Enris. *I know who I hope it is.*

How long did it take to come up the lift? Enris had gone down to greet their guest—greet and assess any risk she posed. Time enough for Aryl to stand in the shade of a willow, move back into the sun, shift to be next to a small fountain, only to wind up on the stool again when her ankles protested.

All this time, there'd been no word from the constable. Aryl had known not to seek it, had done her best, after confiding in Enris, to put the affairs of Marcus Bowman from her mind and concentrate on her people.

Even when rumors had indeed spread into the news, linking Bowman's name to more words she didn't like:

collusion, treachery, greed. Not that there was proof.
But proof didn't seem necessary. The mysterious death
of several researchers. The confiscated goods of one. A
now-sealed world. More than enough to condemn the
innocent.

Wrong.

Aryl smoothed the blue silk that covered their bundle
with one hand. The other held the image disk.

We're here.

She looked up eagerly.

Careful. From his mind; nothing but welcome showed
on his face as Enris d'sud Sarc graciously bowed the first
non-M'hiray to set foot in the House of Sarc through
the door.

Warned, Aryl stayed where she was, and schooled the
smile from her face.

Young, this Human, and not. Her eyes were old. They
didn't acknowledge the luxury of a Lynn Tower, or the
magnificent view that encompassed the horizon. They
locked on her and waited with a hard patience.

What had Maynard told her was waiting, Aryl wondered desperately, that she looked so angry?

"I'll wait up top," Enris said easily, and strode up the
ramp. He saw no threat, then. The caution hadn't been
for her sake, but for the Human's. Aryl waited until his
footsteps faded.

"You're Karina Bowman."

"You want to run my code, too?"

Aryl ignored what she didn't understand. "Please,
have a seat." There were more stools.

"I won't be here that long."

"For the sake of my neck," Aryl suggested gently.
"You're tall." Like her mother. With the same red hair,
though Karina's scalp was shaved with the exception of
a single long strand that fell behind her left ear. Beads
were tied through its length.

Aryl's hair lifted in protest, and she pushed it back.

"Quite the trick." With all the disdain of someone

who couldn't afford new clothes, let alone the kind of ornamentation Grandies preferred.

"Trust me, it gets annoying," she replied calmly.

Something in her tone eased the defensive stance. The Human grabbed one of the stools and moved it, then sat.

Graceful. Lean. Worn. That was it. Worn.

A sudden tilt of the head—curiosity. The movement was achingly familiar. Aryl blinked before tears filled her eyes. "I have something of yours, Karina."

"Kari. I go by Kari."

"And I by Aryl." This old-child made her feel like Husni. "It's a message from your father." She held out the disk.

The laugh was harsh and bitter. "What is it? An apology? A 'sorry I abandoned you as a baby' or 'sorry I made sure to ruin your life'?"

"I don't know."

"Then what do you know?" The Human sprang to her feet again with such violence Aryl had to fight not to react. "Are you the ones he stole for? Did he pay for all this?"

"Yes." It felt as though she'd plunged a knife into her own heart.

Karina hadn't expected an answer—or that answer. For the first time, there was something vulnerable on her face. Then it was gone again. "So what now? Are you going to give me creds?"

" 'Creds?' "

"Set me up or shut me up."

"The House of Sarc will always include you and yours," Aryl said. And it would. She would see to it that this debt was never forgotten. The child had no conception of the resources that had been waiting for her arrival. Funds, in the right amount and no more, from sources above suspicion. Human sources. A suitable home. An education. The protection of the M'hiray, that always. "But that isn't why you're here."

She pressed her fingers to both surfaces of the disk as Yao had shown her. First the image of the family, then ...

His face gazed at them, bruised and worn.

"My name is ... Marcus Bowman. This ... device contains my ... final message for my ... daughter. Karina Bowman ... Norval, Stonerim III ... Anyone who finds ... this. Please take ... it to the nearest ... offworld authority ... Make sure she ... hears this. Please."

Karina didn't move. Didn't seem to breathe.

"The message for you is encrypted. No one else has heard it." Aryl rose and put the image disk in Karina's unresisting hand. "I trust Marcus to have made it possible for you to access it. I'll be waiting, inside, when you're done. Take your time."

A hand, broken-nailed and callused, fastened on her wrist.

Worry/hope/grief.

Aryl strengthened her shields, unsurprised. "What is it?"

Karina stared at the disk. "Why are you doing this?"

"Because your father was my friend," Aryl told her. "His loss was the hardest of them all."

And then, as if a wind had blown through her mind and taken with it all the mist and confusion,

"I could never forget him."

Interlude

ARYL FOUND ENRIS, sitting on the roof's edge, dangling his bare feet over the air. "I thought you didn't like it up here." She used his shoulder to ease down beside him.

"I'm getting used to it."

She leaned against his comforting bulk. *I remember now. Not all of it. Not most. But Marcus. I remember Marcus.*

And felt light inside, for the first time.

"I'll want you to show me," he said, putting his arm around her. "But first, I have something to tell you. I've thought of a name for our daughter."

Aryl smiled to herself. "Not 'Bundle'?"

"What do you think of Taisal? It's your mother's name."

"I know." They'd all looked at the parches, hunting connections to the past.

As Karina did now, Aryl realized, listening to her father's voice.

Unlike Marcus, the name brought no resonance of meaning or emotion. Still . . . she hesitated.

Enris stopped smiling. "We don't have to—"

Aryl put her fingers over his lips. *Taisal she'll be. Thank you.*

Then, as if she'd been waiting, Taisal di Sarc chose that moment to announce she was ready to be born.

NOWNOWNOW!!

Epilogue

THE WATCHERS WERE A PALPABLE, disconcerting *presence*. Others, more tangible and equally impatient, at least waited outside the door. Mirim di Sarc pressed her sweat-soaked face into her pillow, wishing she could hide from both.

Not that they cared about her. They awaited the one she carried. Her grandmother Naryn hadn't approved Council's candidate for her Choice; was this why? Impossible to ask the dead. Impossible to defy the living. Mirim moved fretfully, glad of the unfashionable net that bound her hair, the one trace of *before* she could claim as her own. Before. Before. Before.

Her hands sought her swollen abdomen, felt the band of muscle grown tight and strong, the slight movement beneath. *Peace,* she sent, in no hurry to give her daughter to them.

For Mirim could taste *change*. That was her Talent, her only strength of worth.

Change would begin with this birth, more profound and far-reaching than anything a M'hiray could imagine. *I warned them.*

The impatient fools told her they knew better. That what she sensed was Power. Power they'd control.

She knew better.

Sira di Sarc would change everything.

The M'hiray—
Clan of the Trade Pact

FIRST HOUSES OF THE CLAN
Caraat
Friesen
Mendolar
Parth
S'udlaat
Sarc
Serona

Non-M'hiray of Note

Brocheuse (Dancer, *Doc's Dive*, Human)
Cindy Bowman (Sister of Marcus, Human)
Gene Maynard (Norval Constabulary, Human)
Gurdo Wymratoo'kk (Bartender, *Doc's Dive*, Carasian)
Howard Bowman (Brother of Karina, Human)
KaeCee Britain (Antiquities Dealer, Human)
Karina Bowman (Sister of Howard, Human)
Kelly Bowman (Mother of Karina and Howard, Human)
Lawren Louli (Owner, *Doc's Dive*, Assembler)
Marcus Bowman (Triad First, Analyst, Father of Howard and Karina, Human)
Yirs (Server, *Doc's Dive*, Undetermined)

Author's Note

Rift in the Sky concludes the story of Aryl di Sarc and her Om'ray. It begins that of the M'hiray, the Clan, forced to live within the alien conglomeration known as the Trade Pact. The next installment of *The Clan Chronicles* concerns Aryl's great-granddaughter, Sira di Sarc. (The Trade Pact trilogy: *A Thousand Words for Stranger, Ties of Power,* and *To Trade the Stars.*)

But all good stories have an end. This one comes in the *Reunification* trilogy, where Sira and the M'hiray rediscover their past and claim a heritage no one could have foreseen.

Except me, of course. That's my job and I love it.

I hope you enjoy the first six books of *The Clan Chronicles*. Once you have, I hope you paid attention and have questions.

Because I promise . . .

You ain't seen nothing yet.

Julie Czerneda

Julie E. Czerneda
Stratification

In this earlier time of Czerneda's Trade Pact universe, the Clan has not yet learned how to travel between worlds. Instead, they are a people divided into small tribes, scattered over a fraction of their world, prevented from advancing by two other powerful races. But aliens have begun to explore the Clan's home planet, upsetting the delicate balance between the three intelligent races...

Now available in mass market paperback:

REAP THE WILD WIND
978-0-7564-0487-1

RIDERS ON THE STORM
978-0-7564-0561-8

RIFT IN THE SKY
978-0-7564-0609-7

"A creative voice and a distinctive vision. A writer to watch." —C.J. Cherryh

To Order Call: 1-800-788-6262
www.dawbooks.com

DAW 80

Julie E. Czerneda
Species Imperative

"This novel bears the hallmarks of Czerneda's earlier books: strong, complex, and appealing characters and a thoughtful, intricate plot. Czerneda creates an original and terrific alien species, and Brymn—large, blue, and given to wearing sequined eyeliner—is no exception. and the plot is packed with vivid images and events. Czerneda is a masterful storyteller and one of the best of the recent voices in science fiction." —*Voya*

SURVIVAL
978-0-7564-0261-1

MIGRATION
978-0-7564-0346-1

REGENERATION
978-0-7564-0411-6

*"A creative voice and a distinctive vision.
A writer to watch."* —*C.J. Cherryh*

DAW 158

Julie E. Czerneda

THE TRADE PACT UNIVERSE

"Space adventure mixes with romance...a heck of a
lot of fun." —*Locus*

Sira holds the answer to the survival of her species, the Clan, within the multi-species Trade
Pact. But it will take a Human's courage to
show her the way.

A THOUSAND WORDS FOR STRANGER
0- 88677-769-0
TIES OF POWER
0-88677-850-6
TO TRADE THE STARS
0-7564-0075-9

To Order Call: 1-800-788-6262
www.dawbooks.com

LOGO

Julie E. Czerneda
Web Shifters

"A great adventure following an engaging character across a divertingly varied series of worlds."—*Locus*

Esen is a shapeshifter, one of the last of an ancient race. Only one Human knows her true nature—but those who suspect are determined to destroy her!

BEHOLDER'S EYE
0-88677-818-2

CHANGING VISION
0-88677-815-8

HIDDEN IN SIGHT
0-7564-0139-9

Also by Julie E. Czerneda:
IN THE COMPANY OF OTHERS
0-88677-999-7
"An exhilarating science fiction thriller"
—*Romantic Times*

To Order Call: 1-800-788-6262
www.dawbooks.com